Charles King

Two Years Ago

Vol. 2

Charles Kingsley

Two Years Ago
Vol. 2

ISBN/EAN: 9783348007634

Printed in Europe, USA, Canada, Australia, Japan

Cover: Foto ©Andreas Hilbeck / pixelio.de

More available books at **www.hansebooks.com**

THE BIDEFORD EDITION

NOVELS, POEMS & LETTERS
OF CHARLES KINGSLEY

TWO
YEARS AGO

VOLUME II

BY CHARLES KINGSLEY

ILLUSTRATED

NEW YORK AND LONDON
THE CO-OPERATIVE
PUBLICATION SOCIETY

CONTENTS

VOLUME II

TWO YEARS AGO

———•———

CHAPTER XV

THE CRUISE OF THE "WATERWITCH"

THE middle of August is come at last; and with it the solemn day on which Frederick Viscount Scoutbush may be expected to revisit the home of his ancestors. Elsley has gradually made up his mind to the inevitable, with a stately sulkiness: and comforts himself, as the time draws near, with the thought that, after all, his brother-in-law is not a very formidable personage.

But to the population of Aberalva in general, the coming event is one of awful jubilation. The shipping is all decked with flags; all the Sunday clothes have been looked out, and many a yard of new ribbon and pound of bad powder bought; there have been arrangements for a procession, which could not be got up; for a speech which nobody would undertake to pronounce; and, lastly, for a dinner, about which last there was no hanging back. Yea, also, they have hired from Carcarrow Churchtown, sackbut, psaltery, dulcimer, and all kinds of music; for Frank has put down the old choir band at Aberalva — another of his mistakes — and there is but one fiddle and a clarionet now left in the town. So the said town waits all the day on tiptoe, ready to worship, till out of the soft brown haze the stately "Waterwitch" comes sliding in, like a white ghost, to fold her wings in Aberalva bay.

And at that sight the town is all astir. Fishermen shake themselves up out of their mid-day snooze, to admire the beauty, as she slips on and on through water smooth as glass, her hull hidden by the vast curve of the balloon-jib, and her broad wings boomed out alow and aloft, till it seems marvellous how that vast screen does not topple headlong, instead of floating (as it seems) self-supporting above its image in the mirror. Women hurry to put on their best bonnets; the sexton toddles up with the church key in his hand, and the ringers at his heels; the coastguard lieutenant bustles down to the Manby's mortar, which he has hauled out in readiness on the pebbles. Old Willis hoists a flag before his house, and half a dozen merchant skippers do the same. Bang goes the harmless mortar, burning the British nation's powder without leave or license; and all the rocks and woods catch up the echo, and kick it from cliff to cliff, playing at football with it till its breath is beaten out; a rolling fire of old muskets and bird-pieces crackles along the shore, and in five minutes a poor lad has blown a ramrod through his hand. Never mind, lords do not visit Penalva every day. Out burst the bells above with merry peal; Lord Scoutbush and the "Waterwitch" are duly "rung in" to the home of his lordship's ancestors; and he is received, as he scrambles up the pier steps from his boat, by the curate, the churchwardens, the lieutenant, and old Tardrew, backed by half a dozen ancient sons of Anak,

lineal descendants of the free fishermen to whom,
six hundred years before, St. Just of Penalva did
grant privileges hard to spell, and harder to understand, on the condition of receiving, whensoever
he should land at the quay head, three brass
farthings from the 'free fishermen of Aberalva.'

Scoutbush shakes hands with curate, lieutenant,
Tardrew, churchwar lens; and then come forward
the three farthings, in an ancient leather purse

"Hope your lordship will do us the honor to
shake hands with us too; we are your lordship's
free fishermen, as we have been your forefathers',"
says a magnificent old man, gracefully acknowl-
edging the feudal tie, while he claims the exemption.

Little Scoutbush, who is the kindest-hearted of
men, clasps the great brown fist in his little white
one, and shakes hands heartily with every one of
them, saying, "If your forefathers were as much
taller than mine, as you are than me, gentlemen,
I should n't wonder if they took their own freedom,
without asking his leave for it!"

A lord who begins his progress with a jest!
That is the sort of aristocrat to rule in Aberalva!
And all agree that evening, at the Mariners' Rest,
that his lordship is as nice a young gentleman as
ever trod deal board, and deserves such a yacht as
he's got, and long may he sail her!

How easy it is to buy the love of men! Gold
will not do it: but there is a little angel, may be,
in the corner of every man's eye, who is worth
more than gold, and can do it free of all charges:
unless a man drives him out, and "hates his
brother; and so walks in darkness; not knowing
whither he goeth," but running full butt against

men's prejudices, and treading on their corns, till they knock him down in despair — and all just because he will not open his eyes, and use the light which comes by common human good-nature !

Presently Tom hurries up, having been originally one of the deputation, but kept by the necessity of binding up the three fingers which the ramrod had spared to poor Jem Burman's hand. He bows, and the lieutenant — who (Frank being a little shy) acts as her Majesty's representative — introduces him as "deputy medical man to our district of the union, sir — Mr. Thurnall."

"Dr. Heale was to have been here, by the by. Where is Dr. Heale?" says some one.

"Very sorry, my lord; I can answer for him — professional calls, I don't doubt — nobody more devoted to your lordship."

One need not inquire where Dr. Heale was: but if elderly men will drink much brandy-and-water in hot summer days, after a heavy early dinner, then will those men be too late for deputations and for more important employments.

"Never mind the doctor, daresay he 's asleep after dinner: do him good!" says the viscount, hitting the mark with a random shot; and thereby raising his repute for sagacity immensely with his audience, who laughed outright.

"Ah! Is it so, then? But — Mr. Thurnall, I think, you said? — I am glad to make your acquaintance, sir. I have heard your name often: you are my friend Mellot's old friend, are you not?"

"I am a very old friend of Claude Mellot's."

"Well, and there he is on board, and will be delighted to do the honors of my yacht to you whenever you like to visit her. You and I must know each other better, sir."

Tom bows low — his lordship does him too much honor: the cunning fellow knows that his fortune is made in Aberalva, if he chooses to work it out: but he humbly slips into the rear, for Frank has to be supported, not being over popular; and the lieutenant may "turn crusty," unless he has his lordship to himself before the gaze of assembled Aberalva.

Scoutbush progresses up the street, bowing right and left, and stopped half a dozen times by red-cloaked old women, who curtsey under his nose, and will needs inform him how they knew his grandfather, or nursed his uncle, or how his "dear mother, God rest her soul, gave me this very cloak as I have on," and so forth; still Scoutbush comes to the conclusion that they are a very loving and lovable set of people — as indeed they are — and his heart smites him somewhat for not having seen more of them in past years.

No sooner is Thurnall released than he is off to the yacht as fast as oars can take him, and in Claude's arms.

"Now!" (after all salutations and inquiries have been gone through) "let me introduce you to Major Campbell." And Tom was presented to a tall and thin personage, who sat at the cabin table, bending over a microscope.

"Excuse my rising," said he, holding out a left hand, for the right was busy. "A single jar will give me ten minutes' work to do again. I am delighted to meet you: Mellot has often spoken to me of you as a man who has seen more, and faced death more carelessly, than most men."

"Mellot flatters, sir. Whatsoever I have done, I have given up being careless about death; for I have some one beside myself to live for."

"Married at last? has Diogenes found his Aspasia?" cried Claude.

Tom did not laugh.

"Since my brothers died, Claude, the old gentleman has only me to look to. You seem to be a naturalist, sir."

"A dabbler," said the major, with eye and hand still busy.

"I ought not to begin our acquaintance by doubting your word: but these things are no dabbler's work;" and Tom pointed to some exquisite photographs of minute corallines, evidently taken under the microscope.

· "They are Mellot's."

"Mellot turned man of science? Impossible!"

"No; only photographer. I am tired of painting nature clumsily, and then seeing a sun-picture outdo all my efforts — so I am turned photographer, and have made a vow against painting for three years and a day."

"Why, the photographs only give you light and shade."

"They will give you color, too, before seven years are over — and that is more than I can do, or any one else. No; I yield to the new dynasty. The artist's occupation is gone henceforth, and the painter's studio, like 'all charms, must fly, at the mere touch of cold philosophy.' So Major Campbell prepares the charming little cockyoly birds, and I call in the sun to immortalize them."

"And perfectly you are succeeding! They are quite new to me, recollect. When I left Melbourne, the art had hardly risen there above guinea portraits of bearded desperadoes, a nugget in one hand and a £50 note in the other: but this is new, and what a forward step for science!"

"You are a naturalist, then?" said Campbel, looking up with interest.

"All my profession are, more or less," said Tom, carelessly; "and I have been lucky enough here to fall on untrodden ground, and have hunted up a few sea-monsters this summer."

"Really? You can tell me where to search then, and where to dredge, I hope. I have set my heart on a fortnight's work here, and have been dreaming at night, like a child before a twelfth-night party, of all sorts of impossible hydras, gorgons and chimeras dire, fished up from your western deeps."

"I have none of them; but I can give you Turbinolia Milletiana and Zoanthus Couchii. I have a party of the last gentlemen alive on shore."

The major's face worked with almost childish delight.

"But I shall be robbing you."

"They cost me nothing, my dear sir. I did very well, moreover, without them, for five-and-thirty years; and I may do equally well for five-and-thirty more."

"I ought to be able to say the same, surely," answered the major, composing his face again, and rising carefully. "I have to thank you, exceedingly, my dear sir, for your prompt generosity: but it is better discipline for a man, in many ways, to find things for himself than to have them put into his hands. So, with a thousand thanks, you shall let me see if I can dredge a Turbinolia for myself."

This was spoken with so sweet and polished a modulation, and yet so sadly and severely withal, that Tom looked at the speaker with interest.

He was a very tall and powerful man, and would have been a very handsome man, both in face and figure, but for the high cheekbone, long neck, and narrow shoulders, so often seen north of Tweed. His brow was very high and full; his eyes — grave, but very gentle, with large drooping eyelids — were buried under shaggy gray eyebrows. His mouth was gentle as his eyes; but compressed, perhaps by the habit of command, perhaps by secret sorrow; for of that, too, as well as of intellect and magnanimity, Thurnall thought he could discern the traces. His face was bronzed by long exposure to the sun; his close-cut curls, which had once been auburn, were fast turning white, though his features looked those of a man under five-and-forty; his cheeks were as smooth shaven as his chin. A right, self-possessed, valiant soldier he looked; one who could be very loving to little innocents, and very terrible to full-grown knaves.

"You are practising at self-denial, as usual," said Claude.

"Because I may, at any moment, have to exercise it in earnest. Mr. Thurnall, can you tell me the name of this little glass arrow, which I just found shooting about in the sweeping net?"

Tom did know the wonderful little link between the fish and the insect; and the two chatted over its strange form till the boat returned to take them ashore.

"Do you make any stay here?"

"I propose to spend a fortnight here in my favorite pursuit. I must draw on your kindness and knowledge of the place to point me out lodgings.'

Lodgings, as it befell, were to be found, and good ones, close to the beach, and away from the noise of the harbor on Mrs. Harvey's first floor; for the local preacher, who generally occupied them, was away.

"But Major Campbell might dislike the noise of the school?"

"The school? What better music for a lonely old bachelor than children's voices?"

So, by sunset the major was fairly established over Mrs. Harvey's shop. It was not the place which Tom would have chosen; he was afraid of "running over" poor Grace, if he came in and out as often as he could have wished. Nevertheless, he accepted the major's invitation to visit him that very evening.

"I cannot ask you to dinner yet, sir; for my *ménage* will be hardly settled: but a cup of coffee, and an exceedingly good cigar, I think my establishment may furnish you by seven o'clock tonight; — if you think them worth walking down for."

Tom, of course, said something civil, and made his appearance in due time. He found the coffee ready, and the cigars also; but the major was busy, in his shirt sleeves, unpacking and arranging jars, nets, microscopes, and what not of scientific lumber; and Tom proffered his help.

"I am ashamed to make use of you the first moment that you become my guest."

"I shall enjoy the mere handling of your

tackle," said Tom; and began breaking the tenth commandment over almost every article he touched; for everything was first-rate of its kind.

"You seem to have devoted money, as well as thought, plentifully to the pursuit."

"I have little else to which to devote either; and more of both than is, perhaps, safe for me."

"I should hardly complain of a superfluity of thought, if superfluity of money was the condition of it."

"Pray understand me. I am no Dives; but I have learned to want so little, that I hardly know how to spend the little which I have."

"I should hardly have called that an unsafe state."

"The penniless fakir who lives on chance handfuls of rice has his dangers, as well as the rich Parsee who has his ventures out from Madagascar to Canton. Yes, I have often envied the schemer, the man of business, almost the man of pleasure; their many wants at least absorb them in outward objects, instead of leaving them too easily satisfied, to sink in upon themselves, and waste away in useless dreams."

"You found out the best cure for that malady when you took up the microscope and the collecting-box."

"So I fancied once. I took up natural history in India years ago to drive away thought, as other men might take to opium, or to brandy-pawnee, but, like them, it has become a passion now and a tyranny: and I go on hunting, discovering, wondering, craving for more knowledge; and — *cui bono ?* I sometimes ask ——"

"Why, this at least, sir; that, without such men as

you, who work for mere love, science would be now fifty years behind her present standing-point; and we doctors should not know a thousand important facts which you have been kind enough to tell us, while we have not time to find them out for ourselves."

" *Sic vos non vobis* —— "

"Yes, you have the work, and we have the pay which is a very fair division of labor, considering the world we live in.'

"And have you been skilful enough to make science pay you here, in such an out-of-the-way little world as that of Aberalva must be?"

"She is a good stalking-horse anywhere;" and Tom detailed, with plenty of humor, the effect of his microscope and his lecture on the drops of water. But his wit seemed so much lost on Campbell, that he at last stopped almost short, not quite sure that he had not taken a liberty.

"No; go on, I beg you; and do not fancy that I am not interested and amused too, because my laughing muscles are a little stiff from want of use. Perhaps, too, I am apt to take things too much *au grand sérieux :* but I could not help thinking, while you were speaking, how sad it was that people were utterly ignorant of matters so vitally necessary to health."

"And I, perhaps, ought not to jest over the subject: but, indeed, with cholera staring us in the face here, I must indulge in some emotion; and as it is unprofessional to weep, I must laugh as long as I dare."

The major dropped his coffee-cup upon the floor, and looked at Thurnall with so horrified a gaze, that Tom could hardly believe him to be the same man. Then recollecting himself, he darted down upon the remains of his cup; and looking up again: "A thousand pardons; but — did I hear you aright? cholera staring us in the face?"

"How can it be otherwise? It is drawing steadily on from the eastward week by week; and, in the present state of the town, nothing but some miraculous caprice of Dame Fortune's can deliver us."

"Don't talk of fortune, sir! at such a moment. Talk of God!" said the major, rising from his chair, and pacing the room. "It is too horrible! Intolerable! When do you expect it here?"

"Within the month, perhaps, hardly before. I should have warned you of the danger, I assure you, had I not understood from you that you were only going to stay a fortnight."

The major made an impatient gesture.

"Do you fancy that I am afraid for myself? No; but the thought of its coming to — to the poor people in the town, you know. It is too dreadful. I have seen it in India — among my own men — among the natives. Good heavens, I never shall forget — and to meet the fiend again here, of all places in the world! I fancied it so clean and healthy, swept by fresh sea-breezes."

"And by nothing else. A half-hour's walk round would convince you, sir; I only wish that you could persuade his lordship to accompany you."

"Scoutbush! Of course he will, — he shall, — he must. Good heavens! whose concern is it more than his? You think, then, that there is a chance of staving it off — by cleansing, I mean?"

"If we have heavy rains during the next week

or two, yes. If this drought last, better leave ill alone; we shall only provoke the devil by stirring him up."

"You speak confidently," said the major, gradually regaining his own self-possession, as he saw Tom so self-possessed. "Have you — allow me to ask so important a question — have you seen much of cholera? "

"I have worked through three. At Paris, at St. Petersburg, and in the West Indies; and I have been thinking up my old experience for the last six weeks, foreseeing what would come."

"I am satisfied, sir; perhaps I ought to ask your pardon for the question."

"Not at all. How can you trust a man, unless you know him? "

"And you expect it within the month? You shall go with me to Lord Scoutbush to-morrow, and — and now we will talk of something more pleasant." And he began again upon the zoöphyses.

Tom, as they chatted on, could not help wondering at the major's unexpected passion; and could not help remarking, also, that in spite of his desire to be agreeable, and to interest his guest in his scientific discoveries, he was yet distraught, and full of other thoughts. What could be the meaning of it? Was it mere excess of human sympathy? The countenance hardly betokened that; but still, who can trust altogether the expression of a weather-hardened visage of forty-five? So the doctor set it down to tenderness of heart, till a fresh vista opened on him.

Major Campbell, he soon found, was as fond of insects as of sea-monsters; and he began inquiring about the woods, the heaths, the climate, which seemed to the doctor, for a long time, to mean nothing more than the question which he put plainly, "Where have I a chance of rare insects?" But he seemed, after a while, to be trying to learn the geography of the parish in detail, and especially of the ground round Vavasour's house. "However, it's no business of mine," thought Thurnall, and told him all he wanted, till:

"Then the house lies quite in the bottom of the glen? Is there a good fall to the stream, for a stream I suppose there is?"

Thurnall shook his head. "Cold boggy stewponds in the garden, such as our ancestors loved, damming up the stream. They must needs have fish in Lent, we know; and paid the penalty of it by ague and fever."

"Stewponds damming up the stream? Scoutbush ought to drain them instantly!" said the major, half to himself. "But still the house lies high, with regard to the town, I mean. No chance of malaria coming up?"

"Upon my word, sir, as a professional man, that is a thing that I dare not say. The chances are not great; the house is two hundred yards from the nearest cottage; but if there be an east wind —— "

"I cannot bear this any longer. It is perfect madness!"

"I trust, sir, that you do not think that I have neglected the matter. I have pointed it all out, I assure you, to Mr. Vavasour."

"And it is not altered?"

"I believe it is to be altered — that is — the truth is, sir, that Mr. Vavasour shrinks so much from the very notion of cholera, that—— "

"That he does not like to do anything which may look like believing in its possibility?"

"He says," quoth Tom, parrying the question, but in a somewhat dry tone, "that he is afraid of alarming Mrs. Vavasour and the servants."

The major said something under his breath, which Tom did not catch, and then, in an appeased tone of voice:

"Well, that is at least a fault on the right side. Mrs. Vavasour's brother, as owner of the place, is of course the proper person to make the house fit for habitation." And he relapsed into silence, while Thurnall, who suspected more than met the ear, rose to depart.

"Are you going? It is not late — not ten o'clock yet."

"A medical man, who may be called up at any moment, must make sure of his ' beauty sleep.' "

"I will walk with you, and smoke my last cigar."

So they went out, and up to Heale's. Tom went in, but he observed that his companion, after standing awhile in the street irresolutely, went on up the hill, and, as far as he could see, turned up the lane to Vavasour's.

"A mystery here," thought he, as he put matters to rights in the surgery ere going upstairs. "A mystery which I may as well fathom. It may be of use to poor Tom, as most other mysteries are. That is, though, if I can do it honorably; for the man is a gallant gentleman. I like him, and I am inclined to trust him. Whatsoever his secret is, I don't think that it is one which he need be ashamed of. Still, ' there 's a deal of human natur' in man,' and there may be in him; and what matter if there is?"

Half an hour afterwards the major returned, took the candle from Grace, who was sitting up for him, and went upstairs with a gentle " good-night," but without looking at her.

He sat down at the open window, and looked out leaning on the sill.

"Well, I was too late; I daresay there was some purpose in it. When shall I learn to believe that God takes better care of His own than I can do? I was faithless and impatient to-night. I am afraid I betrayed myself before that man. He looks like one, certainly, who could be trusted with a secret; yet I had rather that he had not mine. It is my own fault, like everything else! Foolish old fellow that you are, fretting and fussing to the end! 'Is not that scene a message from above, saying, 'Be still, and know that I am God'?"

And the major looked out upon the summer sea, lit by a million globes of living fire, and then upon the waves which broke in flame upon the beach, and then up to the spangled stars above.

"What do I know of these, with all my knowing? Not even a twentieth part of those medusæ, or one in each thousand of those sparks among the foam. Perhaps I need not know. And yet why was the thirst awakened in me, save to be satisfied at last? Perhaps to become more intense with every fresh delicious draught of knowledge. . . . Death, beautiful, wise, kind death; when will you come and tell me what I want to know? I courted you once and many a time, brave old Death, only to give rest to the weary. That was a coward's wish, and so you would not come. I ran you close in Afghanistan, old Death, and at Sobraon, too, I was not far behind you; and I thought I had you safe among that jungle grass at Aliwal; but you slipped through my hand; I was not worthy of you.   And now I will not hunt you any more, old Death; do you bide your time, and I mine; though who knows if I may not meet you here?   Only when you come, give me not rest, but work.   Give work to the idle, freedom to the chained, sight to the blind!   Tell me a little about finer things than zoöphytes — perhaps about the zoöphytes as well — and you shall still be brave old Death, my good camp-comrade now for many a year."

Was Major Campbell mad?   That depends upon the way in which the reader may choose to define the adjective.

.   .   .   .

Meanwhile Scoutbush had walked into Penalva Court — where an affecting scene of reconciliation took place?

Not in the least.   Scoutbush kissed Lucia, shook hands with Elsley, hugged the children, and then settled himself in an armchair, and talked about the weather, exactly as if he had been running in and out of the house every week for the last three years, and so the matter was done; and for the first time a *partie carrée* was assembled in the dining-room.

The evening passed off at first as uncomfortably as it could, where three out of the four were well-bred people.   Elsley was, of course, shy before Lord Scoutbush, and Scoutbush was equally shy before Elsley, though as civil as possible to him; for the little fellow stood in extreme awe of Elsley's talents, and was afraid of opening his lips before a poet.   Lucia was nervous for both their sakes, as well she might be; and Valentia had to make all the talking, and succeeded capitally in drawing out both her brother and her brother-in-law, till both of them found the other, on the whole, more like other people than he had expected. The next morning's breakfast, therefore, was easy and gracious enough; and when it was over, and Lucia fled to household matters:

" You smoke, Vavasour? " asked Scoutbush.

Vavasour did not smoke.

" Really? I thought poets always smoked. You will not forbid my having a cigar in your garden, nevertheless, I suppose? Do walk round with me, too, and show me the place, unless you are going to be busy."

Oh no; Elsley was at Lord Scoutbush's service, of course, and had really nothing to do. So out they went.

"Charming old pigeon-hole it is," said its owner. " I have not seen it since I went into the Guards. Campbell says it's a shame of me, and so it is one, I suppose; but how beautiful you have made the garden look ! "

"Lucia is very fond of gardening," said Elsley, who was very fond of it also, and had great taste therein; but he was afraid to confess any such tastes before a man who, he thought, would not understand him.

" And that fine old wood — full of cocks it used to be — I hope you worked it well last year."

Elsley did not shoot; but he had heard there was plenty of game there.

" Plenty of cocks," said his guest, correcting him; " but for game, the less we say about that the better. I really wonder you do not shoot; it fills up time so in the winter."

"There is really no winter to fill up here, thanks to this delicious climate; and I have my books."

"Ah! I wish I had. I wish heartily," said he, in a confidential tone. "you, or Campbell, or some of your clever men, would sell me a little of their book-learning; as Valentia says to me, 'brains are so common in the world, I wonder how none fell to your share.'"

"I do not think that they are an article which is for sale, if Solomon is to be believed."

"And if they were, I couldn't afford to buy, with this Irish Encumbered Estates' Bill. But now, this is one thing I wanted to say. Is everything here just as you would wish? Of course no one could wish a better tenant; but any repairs, you know, or improvements which I ought to do, of course? Only tell me what you think should be done; for, of course, you know more about these things than I do — can't know less."

"Nothing, I assure you, Lord Scoutbush. I have always left those matters to Mr. Tardrew."

"Ah, my dear fellow, you shouldn't do that. He is such a screw, as all honest stewards are. Screws me, I know, and I dare say has screwed you too."

"Never, I assure you. I never gave him the opportunity, and he has been most civil."

"Well, in future, just order him to do what you like, and just as if you were landlord, in fact; and if the old man haggles, write to me, and I'll blow him up. Delighted to have a man of taste like you here, who can improve the place for me."

"I assure you, Lord Scoutbush, I need nothing, nor does the place. I am a man of very few wants."

"I wish I were," sighed Scoutbush, pulling out another of Hudson's highest-priced cigars.

"And I am bound to say" — and here Elsley choked a little; but the viscount's frankness and humility had softened him, and he determined to be very magnanimous — "I am bound in honor, after owing to your kindness such an exquisite retreat — all that either I or Lucia could have fancied for ourselves, and more — not to trouble you by asking for little matters which we really do not need."

And so Elsley, instead of simply asking to have the house-drains set right, which Lord Scoutbush would have had done upon the spot, chose to be lofty-minded, at the risk of killing his wife and children.

"My dear fellow, you really must not 'lord' me any more; I hate it. I must be plain Scout-bush here among my own people, just as I am in the Guards' mess-room. And as for owing me any, — really, it is we that are in your debt, — to see my sister so happy, and such beautiful children, and so well too — and altogether — and Valentia so delighted with your poems — and, and altogether —— " and there Lord Scoutbush stopped, having hoisted, as he considered, the flag of peace once and for all, and very glad that the thing was over.

Elsley was going to say something in return; but his guest turned the conversation as fast as he could. "And now, I know you want to be busy, though you are too civil to confess it; and I must be with that old fool Tardrew at ten, to settle accounts; he'll scold me if I do not — the precise old pedant — just as if I was his own child. Good-bye."

"Where are you going, Frederick?" called Lucia, from the window; she had been watching the interview anxiously enough, and could see that it had ended well.

"To old Stot-and-kye at the farm; do you want anything?"

"No; only I thought you might be going to the yacht; and Valentia would have walked down with you.   She wants to find Major Campbell."

"I want to scold Major Campbell," said Valentia, tripping out on the lawn in her walking dress. "Why has he not been here an hour ago? I will undertake to say that he was up at four this morning."

"He waits to be invited, I suppose," said Scoutbush.

"I suppose I must do it," said Elsley to himself, sighing.

"Just like his primness," said Valentia.   "I shall go down and bring him up myself this minute, and Mr. Vavasour shall come with me. Of course you will! You do not know what a delightful person he is, when once you can break the ice."

Elsley, like most vain men, was of a jealous temper; and Valentia's eagerness to see Major Campbell jarred on him. He wanted to keep the exquisite creature to himself, and Headley was quite enough of an intruder already. Besides, the accounts of the newcomer, his learning, his military prowess, the reverence with which all, even Scoutbush, evidently regarded him, made him prepared to dislike the major; and all the more, now he heard there was an ice-crust to crack. Impulsive men like Elsley, especially

when their self-respect and certainty of their
own position is not very strong, have instinc-
tively a defiant fear of the strong, calm, self-con-
tained man, especially if he has seen the world;
and Elsley set down Major Campbell as a proud,
sarcastic fellow, before whom he must be at the
pains of being continually on his guard. He
wished him a hundred miles away. However,
there was no refusing Valentia anything; so he
got his hat, but with so bad a grace, that Valentia
saw his chagrin, and from mere naughtiness of
heart amused herself with it by talking all the
way of nothing but Major Campbell.

"And Lucia," she said at last, "will be so glad
to see him again. We knew him so well, you
know, in Eaton Square years ago."

"Really," said Elsley, wincing, "I never met
him there." He recollected that Lucia had expressed more pleasure at Major Campbell's
coming than even at that of her brother: and
a dark, undefined phantom entered his heart,
which, though he would have been too proud
to confess it to himself, was none other than
jealousy.

"Oh — did you not? No; it was the year before we first knew you. And we used to laugh at
him together, behind his back, and christened him
the wild Indian, because he was so gauche and
shy. He was a major in the Indian army then:
but a few months afterwards he sold out and went
into the line — no one could tell why, for he threw
away very brilliant prospects, they say, and might
have been a general by now, instead of a mere
major still. But he is so improved since then; he
is like an elder brother to Scoutbush; guides him

in everything. I call him the blind man, and the major his dog!"

"So much the worse," thought Elsley, who disliked the notion of Campbell's having power over a man to whom he was indebted for his house-room; but by this time they were at Mrs. Harvey's door.

Mrs. Harvey opened it, curtseying to the very ground; and Valentia ran upstairs, and knocked at the sitting-room door herself.

"Come in," shouted a pre-occupied voice inside.

"Is that a proper way in which to address a lady, sir?" answered she, putting in her beautiful head.

Major Campbell was sitting, Elsley could see, in his shirt sleeves, cigar in mouth, bent over his microscope; but instead of the unexpected prim voice, he heard a very gay and arch one answer, "Is that a proper way in which to come peeping into an old bachelor's sanctuary, ma'am? Go away this moment, till I make myself fit to be seen."

Valentia shut the door again, laughing.

"You seem very intimate with Major Campbell," said Elsley.

"Intimate? I look on him as my father almost. Now, may we come in?" said she, knocking again in pretty petulance. "I want to introduce Mr. Vavasour."

"I shall be only too happy," said the major, opening his door (this time with his coat on); "there are few persons in the world whom I have more wished to know than Mr. Vavasour." And he held out his hand, and quite led Elsley in. He spoke in a tone of grave interest, looking intently at Elsley as he spoke. Valentia remarked the interest — Elsley only the compliment.

" It is a great kindness of you to call on me so
soon," said he. " I met Mrs. Vavasour several
times in years past; and though I saw very little of
her, I saw enough to long much for the acquaintance of the man who has been worthy to become
her husband."

Elsley blushed, for his conscience smote him a
little at that word " worthy," and muttered some
common-place civility in return. Valentia saw it,
and attributing it to his usual awkwardness, drew
off the conversation to herself.

" Really, Major Campbell! You bring in Mr.
Vavasour, and let me walk behind as I can; and
then let me sit three whole minutes in your house
without deigning to speak to me ! "

" Ah ! my dear Queen Whims ! " answered he,
returning suddenly to his gay tone; " and how
have you been misbehaving yourself since we met
last ? "

" I have not been misbehaving myself at all,
mon cher Saint Père, as Mr. Vavasour will answer
for me, during the most delightful fortnight I ever
spent ! "

" Delightful indeed ! " said Elsley, as he was
bound to say; but he said it with an earnestness
which made the major fix his eyes on him.
" Why should he not find any and every fortnight
as delightful as his last ? " said he to himself; but
now Valentia began bantering him about his
books and his animals; wanting to look through
his microscope, pulling off her hat for the purpose,
laughing when her curls blinded her, letting them
blind her in order to toss them back in the prettiest
way, jesting at him about " his old fogies " at the
Linnæan Society; clapping her hands in ecstasy

when he answered that they were not old fogies at all, but the most charming set of men in England, and that (with no offence to the name of Scout-bush) he was prouder of being an F.L.S., than if he were a peer of the realm — and so forth; all which harmless pleasantry made Elsley cross, and more cross — first, because he did not mix in it; next, because he could not mix in it if he tried. He liked to be always in the seventh heaven; and if other people were anywhere else, he thought them bores.

At last: " Now, if you will be good for five minutes," said the major, " I will show you something really beautiful."

" I can see that," answered she, with the most charming impudence, " in another glass besides your magnifying one."

" Be it so: but look here, and see what an exquisite world there is, of which you never dream; and which behaves a great deal better in its station than the world of which you do dream ! "

When Campbell spoke in that way, Valentia was good at once; and as she went immediately to the microscope, she whispered, " Don't be angry with me, *mon Saint Père*."

" Don't be naughty, then, *ma chère enfant*," whispered he; for he saw something about Elsley's face which gave him a painful suspicion.

She looked long, and then lifted up her head suddenly — " Do come and look, Mr. Vavasour, at this exquisite little glass fairy, like — I cannot tell what like, but a pure spirit hovering in some nun's dream ! Come ! "

Elsley came, and looked; and when he looked he started, for it was the very same zoöphyte which

Thurnall had shown him on a certain memorable day.

"Where did you find the fairy, *mon Saint Père?*"

"I had no such good fortune. Mr. Thurnall, the doctor, gave it me."

"Thurnall?" said she, while Elsley kept still looking, to hide cheeks which were growing very red. "He is such a clever man, they say. Where did you meet him? I have often thought of asking Mr. Vavasour to invite him up for an evening with his microscope. He seems so superior to the people round him. It would be a charity, really, Mr. Vavasour."

Vavasour kept his eyes fixed on the zoöphyte, and said:

"I shall be only too delighted, if you wish it."

"You will wish it yourself a second time," chimed in Campbell, "if you try it once. Perhaps you know nothing of him but professionally. Unfortunately for professional men, that too often happens."

"Know anything of him — I? I assure you not, save that he attends Mrs. Vavasour and the children," said Vavasour, looking up at last: but with an expression of anger which astonished both Valentia and Campbell.

Campbell thought that he was too proud to allow rank as a gentleman to a country doctor; and despised him from that moment, though, as it happened, unjustly. But he answered quietly:

"I assure you, that whatever some country practitioners may be, the average of them, as far as I have seen, are cleverer men, and even of higher tone than their neighbors; and Thurnall is beyond the average: he is a man of the world — even too much of one — and a man of science; and I fairly confess that, what with his wit, his *savoir vivre*, and his genial good temper, I have quite fallen in love with him in a single evening; we began last night on the microscope, and ended on all heaven and earth."

"How I should like to make a third!"

"My dear Queen Whims would hear a good deal of sober sense, then; at least on one side: but I shall not ask her, for Mr. Thurnall and I have our deep secrets together."

So spoke the major, in the simple wish to exalt Tom in a quarter where he hoped to get him practice; and his "secret" was a mere jest, unnecessary, perhaps, as he thought afterwards, to pass off Tom's want of orthodoxy.

"I was a babbler then," said he to himself the next moment; "how much better to have simply held my tongue!"

"Ah, yes; I know men have their secrets, as well as women," said Valentia, for the mere love of saying something: but as she looked at Vavasour, she saw an expression in his face which she had never seen before. What was it? All that one can picture for oneself branded into the countenance of a man unable to repress the least emotion, who had worked himself into the belief that Thurnall had betrayed his secret.

"My dear Mr. Vavasour," cried Campbell, of course unable to guess the truth, and supposing vaguely that he was "ill;" "I am sure that — that the sun has overpowered you" (the only possible thing he could think of). "Lie down on the sofa a minute" (Vavasour was actually reeling with rage and terror), "and I will run up to Thurnall's for salvolatile."

Elsley, who thought him the most consummate of hypocrites, cast on him a look which he intended to have been withering, and rushed out of the room, leaving the two staring at each other.

Valentia was half inclined to laugh, knowing Elsley's petulance and vanity: but the impossibility of guessing a cause kept her quiet.

Major Campbell stood for full five minutes; not as one astounded, but as one in deep and anxious thought.

"What can be the matter, *mon Saint Père?*" asked she at last, to break the silence.

"That there are more whims in the world than yours, dear Queen Whims; and I fear darker ones. Let us walk up together after this man. I have offended him."

"Nonsense! I dare say he wanted to get home to write poetry, as you did not praise what he had written. I know his vanity and flightiness."

"You do?" asked he, quickly, in a painful tone. "However, I have offended him, I can see; and deeply. I must go up, and make things right, for the sake of—for everybody's sake."

"Then do not ask me anything. Lucia loves him intensely, and let that be enough for us."

The major saw the truth of the last sentence no more than Valentia herself did; for Valentia would have been glad enough to pour out to him, with every exaggeration, her sister's woes and wrongs, real and fancied, had not the sense of her own folly with Vavasour kept her silent and conscience-stricken.

Valentia remarked the major's pained look as
they walked up the street.

"You dear conscientious *Saint Père*, why will
you fret yourself about such a foolish matter? He
will have forgotten it all in an hour; I know him
well enough."

Major Campbell was not the sort of person to
admire Elsley the more for throwing away capriciously such deep passion as he had seen him
show, any more than for showing the same.

"He must be of a very volatile temperament."

"Oh, all geniuses are."

"I have no respect for genius, Miss St. Just; I
do not even acknowledge its existence when there
is no strength and steadiness of character. If any
one pretends to be more than a man, he must
begin by proving himself a man at all. Genius?
Give me common sense and common decency!
Does he give Mrs. Vavasour, pray, the benefit of
any of these pretty flights of genius?"

Valentia was frightened. She had never heard
her *Saint Père* speak so severely and sarcastically;
and she feared that if he knew the truth, he would
be terribly angry. She had never seen him angry;
but she knew well enough that that passion, when
it rose in him in a righteous cause, would be very
awful to see; and she was one of those women who
always grow angry when they are frightened. So
she was angry at his calling her Miss St. Just; she
was angry because she chose to think he was talking at her; though she reasonably might have
guessed it, seeing that he had scolded her a hundred times for want of steadiness of character.
She was more angry than all, because she knew
that her own vanity had caused — at least disa-

greement — between Lucia and Elsley. All which (combined with her natural wish not to confess an unpleasant truth about her sister) justified her, of course, in answering:

" Miss St. Just does not intrude into the secrets of her sister's married life ; and if she did, she would not repeat them."

Major Campbell sighed, and walked on a few moments in silence, then:

" Pardon, Miss St. Just; I asked a rude question, and I am sorry for it."

" Pardon you, my dear *Saint Père ?*" cried she, almost catching at his hand. " Never! I must either believe you infallible, or hate you eternally. It is I that was naughty; I always am; but you will forgive Queen Whims?"

" Who could help it?" said the major, in a sad, sweet tone. " But here is the postman. May I open my letters?"

" You may do as you like, now you have forgiven me. Why, what is it, *mon Saint Père ?*"

A sudden shock of horror had passed over the major's face, as he read his letter: but it had soon subsided into stately calm.

" A gallant officer, whom we and all the world knew well, is dead of cholera at his post, where a man should die. . . . And, my dear Miss St. Just, we are going to the Crimea."

" We ? — you ? "

" Yes. The expedition will really sail, I find."

" But not you ? "

" I shall offer my services. My leave of absence will, in any case, end on the first of September: and even if it did not, my health is quite enough restored to enable me to walk up to a cannon's mouth."

"Ah, *mon Saint Père*, what words are these?"

"The words of an old soldier, Queen Whims, who has been so long at his trade that he has got to take a strange pleasure in it."

"In killing?"

"No; only in the chance of ——. But I will not cast an unnecessary shadow over your bright soul. There will be shadows enough over it soon, without my help."

"What do you mean?"

"That you, and thousands more as delicate, if not as fair as you, will see, ere long, what the realities of human life are; and in a way of which you have never dreamed."

And he murmured, half to himself, the words of the prophet, — "' Thou saidst, I shall sit as a lady for ever: but these two things shall come upon thee in one day, widowhood and the loss of children. They shall even come upon thee.' No! not in their fulness! There are noble elements underneath the crust, which will come out all the purer from the fire; and we shall have heroes and heroines rising up among us as of old, sincere and earnest, ready to face their work, and to do it, and to call all things by their right names once more; and Queen Whims herself will become what Queen Whims might be!"

Valentia was awed, as well she might have been; for there was a very deep sadness about Campbell's voice.

"You think there will be def —— disasters?" said she at last.

"How can I tell? That we are what we always were, I doubt not. Scoutbush will fight as merrily as I. But we owe the penalty of many sins, and we shall pay it."

It would be as unfair, perhaps, as easy, to make Major Campbell a prophet after the fact, by attributing to him any distinct expectation of those mistakes which have been but too notorious since. Much of the sadness in his tone may have been due to his habitual melancholy; his strong belief that the world was deeply diseased, and that some terrible purgation would surely come, when it was needed. But it is difficult, again, to conceive that those errors were altogether unforeseen by many an officer of Campbell's experience and thoughtfulness.

" We will talk no more of it just now." And they walked up to Penalva Court, seriously enough.

" Well, Scoutbush, any letters from town?" said the major.

" Yes."

" You have heard what has happened at D—— Barracks?"

" Yes."

" You had better take care, then, that the like of it does not happen here."

" Here?"

" Yes. I 'll tell you all presently. Have you heard from headquarters?"

" Yes; all right," said Scoutbush, who did not like to let out the truth before Valentia.

Campbell saw it, and signed to him to speak out.

" All right?" asked Valentia. " Then you are not going?"

" Ay, but I am! Orders to join my regiment by the first of October, and to be shot as soon afterwards as is fitting for the honor of my country. So, Miss Val, you must be quick in making good friends with the heir-at-law; or else you won't get your bills paid any more."

"Oh, dear, dear!" And Valentia began to cry bitterly. It was her first real sorrow.

Strangely enough, Major Campbell, instead of trying to comfort her, took Scoutbush out with him, and left her alone with her tears. He could not rest till he had opened the whole cholera question.

Scoutbush was honestly shocked. Who would have dreamed it? No one had ever told him that the cholera had really been there before. What could he do? Send for Thurnall?

Tom was sent for; and Scoutbush found, to his horror, that what little he could have ever done ought to have been done three months ago, with Lord Minchampstead's improvements at Pentremochyn.

The little man walked up and down, and wrung his hands. He cursed Tardrew for not telling him the truth; he cursed himself for letting the cottages go out of his power; he cursed A, B, and C, for taking the said cottages off his hands; he cursed up, he cursed down, he cursed all around, things which ought to have been cursed, and things which really ought not — for half of the worse sanatory sinners, in this blessed age of ignorance, yclept of progress and science (how our grandchildren will laugh at the epithets!), are utterly unconscious and guiltless ones.

But cursing leaves him, as it leaves other men, very much where he had started.

To do him justice, he was in one thing a true nobleman, for he was above all pride; as are most men of rank, who know what their own rank means.

It is only the upstart, unaccustomed to his new eminence, who stands on his dignity, and " asserts his power."

So Scoutbush begged humbly of Thurnall only to tell him what he could do.

" You might use your moral influence, my lord."

" Moral influence?" in a tone which implied naïvely enough, " I 'd better get a little morals myself before I talk of using the same."

" Your position in the parish ——"

" My good sir ! " quoth Scoutbush in his shrewd way; " do you not know yourself what these fine fellows who were ready yesterday to kiss the dust off my feet would say, if I asked leave to touch a single hair of their rights? ' Tell you what, my lord; we pays you your rent, and you takes it. You mind your business, and we 'll mind ourn.' You forget that times are changed since my seventeenth progenitor was lord of life and limb over man and maid in Aberalva."

" And since your seventeenth progenitor took the trouble to live at Penalva Court," said Campbell, " instead of throwing away what little moral influence he had by going into the Guards, and spending his time between Rotten Row and Cowes."

" Hardly fair, Major Campbell! " quoth Tom; " you forget that in the old times, if the Lord of Aberalva was responsible for his people, he had also by law the power of making them obey him."

" The long and the short of it is, then," said Scoutbush, a little tartly, " that I can do nothing."

" You can put to rights the cottages which are still in your hands, my lord. For the rest, my only remaining hope lies in the last person whom one would usually depute on such an errand."

" Who is that ? "

" The schoolmistress."

" The who ? " asked Scoutbush.

" The schoolmistress; at whose house Major Campbell lodges."

And Tom told them, succinctly, enough to justify his strange assertion.

" If you doubt me, my lord, I advise you to ask Mr. Headley. He is no friend of hers; being a high churchman, while she is a little inclined to be schismatic; but an enemy's opinion will be all the more honest."

" She must be a wonderful woman," said Scoutbush; " I should like to see her."

" And I too," said Campbell. " I passed a lovely girl on the stairs last night, and thought no more of it. Lovely girls are common enough in West-country ports."

" We 'll go and see her," quoth his lordship.

Meanwhile Aberalva pier was astonished by a strange phenomenon. A boat from the yacht landed at the pier-head not only Claude Mellot, whose beard was an object of wonder to the fishermen, but a tall three-legged box and a little black tent; which, being set upon the pier, became the scene of various mysterious operations, carried on by Claude and a sailor lad.

" I say ! " quoth one of the fishing elders, after long suspicious silence; " I say, lads, this won't do. We can't have no outlandish foreigners taking observations here ! "

And then dropped out one wild suspicion after another.

"Maybe he's surveying for a railroad!"

"Maybe he's from the Trinity House, going to make a new harbor; or maybe a lighthouse. And then we'd better not meddle wi' him."

"I'll tell you what he be. He's that here government chap as the doctor said he'd bring down to set our drains right."

"If he goes meddling with our drains, and knocking of our backyards about, he'll find himself over quay before he's done."

"Steady! steady! He come with my loord, mind."

"He might 'a' taken in his loordship, and be a Roossian spy to the bottom of him after all. They mak' munselves up into all manner of disguisements, specially beards. I've seed the Roossians with their beards many a time."

"Maybe 't is witchcraft. Look to mun, putting mun's head under that black bag now! He'm after no good, I'll warrant. If they be n't works of darkness, what be?"

"Leastwise he'm no right to go spying here on our quay, and never ax with your leave, or by your leave. I'll just goo mak' mun out."

And Claude, who had just retreated into his tent, had the pleasure of finding the curtain suddenly withdrawn, and as a flood of light rushed in, spoiling his daguerreotype plate, hearing a voice as of a sleepy bear:

"Ax your pardon, sir; but what be you arter here?"

"Murder! shut the screen!" But it was too late; and Claude came out, while the eldest-born of Anak stood sternly inquiring:

"I say, what be you arter here, mak' so boold?"

"Taking sun-pictures, my good sir; and you have spoilt one for me."

"Sun-picturs, saith a?" in a very incredulous tone.

"Daguerreotypes of the place for Lord Scoutbush."

"Oh! if it's his lordship's wish, of course! Only things is very well as they are, and needs no mending, thank God. Only, ax pardon, sir. You see, we don't generally allow no interfering on our pier without lave, sir; the pier being ourn, we pays for the repairing. So if his lordship intends making of alterations, he'd better to have spoken to us first."

"Alterations?" said Claude, laughing; "the place is far too pretty to need any improvement."

"Glad you think so, sir! But whatever be you arter here?"

"Taking views! I'm a painter, an artist! I'll take your portrait, if you like!" said Claude, laughing more and more.

"Bless my heart, what vules we be! 'T is a painter gentleman, lads!" roared he.

"What on earth did you take me for? A Russian spy?"

The elder shook his head, grinned solemnly, and peace was concluded. "We'm old-fashioned folks here, you see, sir; and don't like no new-fangled meddlecomes. You'll excuse us; you'm very welcome to do what you like, and glad to see you here." And the old fellow made a stately bow, and moved away.

"No, no! you must stay and have your portrait taken; you'll make a fine picture."

"Hum; might ha', they used to say, thirty

years agone; I'm over old now. Still, my old woman might like it. Make so bold, sir, but what's your charge?"

"I charge nothing. Five minutes' talk with an honest man will pay me."

"Hum: if you'd 'a' let me pay you, sir, well and good; but I maunt take up your time for nought; that's not fair."

However, Claude prevailed, and in ten minutes he had all the sailors on the quay round him; and one after another came forward blushing and grinning to be "taken off." Soon the children gathered round, and when Valentia and Major Campbell came on the pier, they found Claude in the midst of a ring of little dark-haired angels; while a dozen honest fellows grinned when their own visages appeared, and chaffed each other about the sweethearts who were to keep them while they were out at sea. And in the midst little Claude laughed and joked, and told good stories, and gave himself up, the simple, the sunny-hearted fellow, to the pleasures of pleasing, till he earned from one and all the character of "the pleasantest-spokenest gentleman that was ever into the town."

"Here's her ladyship! make room for her ladyship!" But Claude held up a warning hand. He had just arranged a masterpiece — half a dozen of the prettiest children, sitting beneath a broken boat, on spars, sails, blocks, lobster-pots, and what not, arranged in picturesque confusion; while the black-bearded sea-kings round were promising them rock and bulls-eyes, if they would only sit still like "gude maids."

But at Valentia's coming the children all looked

round, and jumped up and curtsied, and then were afraid to sit down again.

"You have spoilt my group, Miss St. Just, and you must mend it!"

Valentia caught the humor, regrouped them all forthwith; and then placed herself in front of them by Claude's side.

"Now, be good children! Look straight at me, and listen!" And lifting up her finger, she began to sing the first song of which she could think, "The Landing of the Pilgrim Fathers."

She had no need to bid the children look at her and listen; for not only they, but every face upon the pier was fixed upon her; breathless, spell-bound, at once by her magnificent beauty and her magnificent voice, as up rose, leaping into the clear summer air, and rolling away over the still blue sea, that glorious melody which has now become the national anthem to the nobler half of the New World. Honor to woman, and honor to old England, that from Felicia Hemans came the song which will last, perhaps, when modern Europe shall have shared the fate of ancient Rome and Greece!

Valentia's singing was the reflex of her own character; and therefore, perhaps, all the more fitted to the song, the place, and the audience. It was no modest cooing voice, tender, suggestive, trembling with suppressed emotion, such as, even though narrow in compass, and dull in quality, will touch the deepest fibres of the heart, and, as delicate scents will sometimes do, wake up long-forgotten dreams, which seem memories of some antenatal life.

It was clear, rich, massive, of extraordinary

compass, and yet full of all the graceful ease, the
audacious frolic, of perfect physical health, and
strength, and beauty; had there been a trace
of effort in it, it might have been accused of
"bravura": but there was no need of effort where
nature had bestowed already an all but perfect
organ, and all that was left for science was to
teach not power, but control. Above all, it was
a voice which you trusted; after the first three
notes you felt that that perfect ear, that perfect
throat, could never, even by the thousandth part
of a note, fall short of melody; and you gave your
soul up to it, and cast yourself upon it, to bear
you up and away, like a fairy steed, whither it
would, down into the abysses of sadness, and up
to the highest heaven of joy; as did those wild
and rough, and yet tender-hearted and imaginative
men that day, while every face spoke new delight,
and hung upon those glorious notes —

"As one who drinks from a charmed cup
　Of sparkling, and foaming, and murmuring wine " —

and not one of them, had he had the gift of words,
but might have said with the poet:

"I have no life, Constantia, now but thee,
　While, like the world-surrounding air, thy song
Flows on, and fills all things with melody.
　Now is thy voice tempest swift and strong,
On which, like one in a trance upborne,
　Secure o'er rocks and waves I sweep,
Rejoicing like a cloud of morn.
　Now 't is the breath of summer night,
Which, when the starry waters sleep
　Round western isles, with incense-blossoms bright,
　Lingering, suspends my soul in its voluptuous flight."

At last it ceased: and all men drew their breaths once more; while a low murmur of admiration ran through the crowd, too well-bred to applaud openly, as they longed to do.

"Did you ever hear the like of that, Gentleman Jan?"

"Or see? I used to say no one could hold a candle to our Grace, but she — she looked like a born queen all the time!"

"Well, she belongs to us, too, so we've a right to be proud of her. Why, here's our Grace all the while!"

True enough; Grace has been standing among the crowd all the while, rapt, like them, her eyes fixed on Valentia, and full, too, of tears. They had been called up first by the melody itself, and then, by a chain of thought peculiar to Grace, by the faces round her.

"Ah! if Grace had been here!" cried one, "we'd have had her dra'ed off in the midst of the children."

"Ah! that would ha' been as nat'ral as life!"

"Silence, you!" says Gentleman Jan, who generally feels a mission to teach the rest of the quay good manners. "'Tis the gentleman's pleasure to settle who he'll dra' off, and not wer'n."

To which abnormal possessive pronoun Claude rejoined:

"Not a bit! whatever you like. I could not have a better figure for the center. I'll begin again."

"Oh, do come and sit among the children, Grace!" says Valentia.

"No, thank your ladyship."

Valentia began urging her; and many a voice round, old as well as young, backed the entreaty.

" Excuse me, my lady," and she slipped into the crowd; but as she went she spoke low, but clear enough to be heard by all: " No: it will be time enough to flatter me, and ask for my picture, when you do what I tell you — what God tells you ! "

" What 's that, then, Grace dear? "

" You know ! I 've asked you to save your own lives from cholera, and you have not the common sense to do it. Let me go home and pray for you ! "

There was an awkward silence among the men, till some fellow said:

" She 'm gone mad after that doctor, I think, with his muck-hunting notions."

And Grace went home, to await the hour of afternoon school.

" What a face ! " said Mellot.

" Is it not? Come and see her in her school, when the children go in at two o'clock. Ah! there are Scoutbush and *Saint Père.*"

" We are going to the school, my lord. Don't you think that, as patron of things in general here, it would look well if you walked in, and signified your full approbation of what you know nothing about? "

" So much so, that I was just on my way there with Campbell. But I must just speak to that lime-burning fellow. He wants a new lease of the kiln, and I suppose he must have it. At least, here he comes, running at me open-mouthed, and as dry as his own waistband. It makes one thirsty to look at him. I 'll catch you up in five minutes ! "

So the three went off to the school.

Grace was telling, in her own sweet way, that charming story of the Three Trouts, which, by the by, has been lately pirated (as many things are) by a religious author, whose book differs sufficiently from the liberal and wholesome morality of the true author of the tale.

"What a beautiful story, Grace!" said Valentia. "You will surpass Ians Andersen some day."

Grace blushed, and was silent a moment.

"It is not my own, my lady."

"Not your own I should have thought that no one but you and Andersen could have made such an ending to it."

Grace gave her one of those beseeching, half-reproachful looks, with which she always answered praise; and then — "Would you like to hear the children repeat a hymn, my lady?"

"No. I want to know where that story came from."

Grace blushed, and stammered.

"I know where," said Campbell. "You need not be ashamed of having read the book, Miss Harvey. I doubt not that you took all the good from it, and none of the harm, if harm there be."

Grace looked at him; at once surprised and relieved.

"It was a foolish romance-book, sir, as you seem to know. It was the only one which I ever read, except Hans Andersen's — which are not romances, after all. But the beginning was so full of God's truth, sir, — romance though it was, — and gave me such precious new light about educating children, that I was led on unawares. I hope I was not wrong."

"This schoolroom proves that you were not,"

said Campbell. "'To the pure, all things are pure.'"

"What is this mysterious book? I must know!" said Valentia.

"A very noble romance, which I made Mellot read once, containing the ideal education of an English nobleman in the middle of the last century."

"'The Fool of Quality'?" said Mellot. "Of course! I thought I had heard the story before. What a well-written book it is, too, in spite of all extravagance and prolixity. And how wonderfully ahead of his generation the man who wrote it, in politics as well as in religion?"

"I must read it," said Valentia. "You must lend it me, *Saint Père*."

"Not yet, I think."

"Why?" whispered she, pouting. "I suppose I am not as pure as Grace Harvey?"

"She has the children to educate, who are in daily contact with coarse sins, of which you know nothing — of which she cannot help knowing. It was written in an age when the morals of our class (more shame to us) were on the same level with the morals of her clas now. Let it alone. I often have fancied I should edit a corrected edition of it. When I do, you shall read that."

"Now, Miss Harvey," said Mellot, who had never taken his eyes off her face, "I want to turn schoolmaster, and give your children a drawing lesson. Get your slates, all of you!"

And taking possession of the blackboard and a piece of chalk, Claude began sketching them imps and angels, dogs and horses, till the school rang with shrieks of delight.

"Now," said he, wiping the board, "I'll draw something, and you shall copy it."

And without taking off his hand, he drew a single line; and a profile head sprang up, as if by magic, under his firm, unerring touch.

"Somebody!" "A lady!" "No, 't aint; 't is schoolmistress!"

"You can't copy that; I'll draw you another face." And he sketched a full face on the board.

"That's my lady." "No, it's schoolmistress again!" "No, it's not!"

"Not quite sure, my dears?" said Claude, half to himself. "Then here!" and wiping the board once more, he drew a three-quarters face, which elicited a shout of approbation.

"That's schoolmistress, her very self!"

"Then you cannot do anything better than try and draw it. I'll show you how." And going over the lines again, one by one, the crafty Claude pretended to be giving a drawing lesson, while he was really studying every feature of his model.

"If you please, my lady," whispered Grace to Valentia; "I wish the gentleman would not."

"Why not?"

"O madam, I do not judge any one else; but why should this poor perishing flesh be put into a picture? We wear it but for a little while, and are blessed when we are rid of its burden. Why wish to keep a copy of what we long to be delivered from?"

"It will please the children, Grace," said Valentia, puzzled. "See how they are all trying to copy it, from love of you."

"Who am I? I want them to do things from love of God. No, madam, I was pained (and no offence to you) when I was asked to have my likeness taken on the quay. There's no sin in it, of course; but let those who are going away to sea, and have friends at home, have their pictures taken; not one who wishes to leave behind her no likeness of her own, only Christ's likeness in these children; and to paint Him to other people, not to be painted herself. Do ask him to rub it out, my lady!"

"Why, Grace, we were all just wishing to have a likeness of you. Every one has their picture taken for a remembrance."

"The saints and martyrs never had theirs, as far as I ever heard, and yet they are not forgotten yet. I know it is the way of great people like you. I saw your picture once, in a book Miss Heale had; and did not wonder, when I saw it, that people wished to remember such a face as yours; and since I have seen you, I wonder still less."

"My picture? where?"

"In a book; 'The Book of Beauty,' I believe they called it."

"My dear Grace," said Valentia, laughing and blushing, "if you ever looked in your glass, you must know that you are quite as worthy of a place in 'The Book of Beauty' as I am."

Grace shook her head with a serious smile. "Every one in their place, madam. I cannot help knowing that God has given me a gift, but why, I cannot tell. Certainly not for the same purpose as He gave it to you for— a simple country girl like me. If He have any use for it, He will use it, as He does all His creatures, without my help. At all events it will not last long; a few years more, perhaps a few months, and it will be food for

worms; and then people will care as little about
my looks as I care now. I wish, my lady, you
would stop the gentleman ! "

"Mr. Mellot, draw the children something simpler, please; a dog or a cat."   And she gave
Claude a look which he obeyed.

Valentia felt in a more solemn mood than usua
as she walked home that day.

"Well," said Claude, "I have here every line
and shade, and she cannot escape me. I'll go on
board and paint her right off from memory, while
it is fresh. Why, here come Scoutbush and the
major."

"Miss Harvey," said Scoutbush, trying, as he
said to Campbell, "to look as grand as a sheep-
dog among a pack of fox-hounds, and very thankful all the while he had no tail to be bitten off " —
"Miss Harvey, I — we — have heard a great deal
in praise of your school, and so I thought I should
like to come and see it."

"Would your lordship like to examine the children?" says Grace, curtseying to the ground.

" No — thanks — that is — I have no doubt you
teach them all that's right, and we are exceedingly
gratified with the way in which you conduct the
school. I say, Val," cried Scoutbush, who could
support the part of patron no longer, " what pretty
little ducks they are, I wish I had a dozen of them !
Come you here ! " and down he sat on a bench,
and gathered a group round him.

" Now, are you all good children? I'm sure
you look so ! " said he, looking round into the
bright pure faces, fresh from heaven, and feeling
himself the nearer heaven as he did so. " Ah ! I
see Mr. Mellot's been drawing you pictures. He's

a clever man, a wonderful man, is n't he? I can't
draw you pictures, nor tell you stories, like your
schoolmistress. What shall I do?"

"Sing to them, Fred!" said Valentia.

And he began warbling a funny song, with a
child on each knee, and his arms round three or
four more, while the little faces looked up into his,
half awe-struck at the presence of a live lord, half
longing to laugh, but not sure whether it would be
right.

Valentia and Campbell stood close together,
exchanging looks.

"Dear fellow!" whispered she, "so simple and
good when he is himself! And he must go to
that dreadful war!"

"Never mind. Perhaps by this very act he is
earning permission to come back again, a wiser
and a more useful man."

"How then?"

"Is he not making friends with angels who
always behold our Father's face? At least he is
showing capabilities of good, which God gave; and
which therefore God will never waste."

"Now, shall I sing you another song?"

"Oh yes, please!" rose from a dozen little
mouths.

"You must not be troublesome to his lordship,"
says Grace.

"Oh no, I like it. I'll sing them one more
song, and then—I want to speak to you, Miss
Harvey."

Grace curtsied, blushed, and shook all over.
What could Lord Scoutbush want to say to
her?

That indeed was not very easy to discover at

first; for Scoutbush felt so strongly the oddity of taking a pretty young woman into his counsel on a question of sanitary reform, that he felt mightily inclined to laugh, and began beating about the bush in a sufficiently confused fashion.

"Well, Miss Harvey, I am exceedingly pleased with — with what I have seen of the school — that is, what my sister tells, and the clergyman ——"

"The clergyman?" thought Grace, surprised, as she well might be, at what was entirely an impromptu invention of his lordship's.

"And — and — there is ten pounds towards the school, and — and, I will give an annual subscription the same amount."

"Mr. Headley receives the subscriptions, my lord," said Grace, drawing back from the proffered note.

"Of course," quoth Scoutbush, trusting again to an impromptu; "but this is for yourself — a small mark of our sense of your — your usefulness."

If any one has expected that Grace is about to conduct herself, during this interview, in any wise like a prophetess, tragedy queen, or other exalted personage; to stand upon her native independence, and scorning the bounty of an aristocrat, to read the said aristocrat a lecture on his duties and responsibilities, as landlord of Aberalva town; then will that person be altogether disappointed. It would have looked very well, doubtless; but it would have been equally untrue to Grace's womanhood, and to her notions of Christianity. Whether all men were or were not equal in the sight of Heaven, was a notion which had never crossed her mind. She knew that they would all be equal in heaven, and that was enough for her. Meanwhile, she found

"Well, and I shall, at all events, go off and give them my mind on the matter; though I suppose" (with a glance at Grace) "I can't expect to be heard where Miss Harvey has not been."

"O my lord," cried Grace, "if you would but speak ——" And there she stopped; for was it her place to tell him his duty? No doubt he had wiser people than her to counsel him.

But the moment the party left the school, Grace dropped into her chair; her head fell on the table, and she burst into an agony of weeping, which brought the whole school round her.

"O my darlings! my darlings!" cried she at last, looking up, and clasping them to her by twos and threes; "is there no way of saving you? No way? Then we must make the more haste to be good, and be all ready when Jesus comes to take us." And shaking off her passion with one strong effort, she began teaching those children as she had never taught them before, with a voice, a look, as of Stephen himself when he saw the heavens opened.

For that burst of weeping was the one single overflow of long pent passion, disappointment, and shame.

She had tried, indeed. Ever since Tom's conversation and Frank's sermon had poured in a flood of new light on the meaning of epidemics, and bodily misery, and death itself, she had been working as only she could work; exhorting, explaining, coaxing, warning, entreating with tears, offering to perform with her own hands the most sickening offices; to become, if no one else would, the common scavenger of the town. There was no depth to which, in her noble enthusiasm, she

would not have gone down. And behold, it had
been utterly in vain! Ah! the bitter disappointment of finding her influence fail her utterly, the
first time that it was required for a great practical
work! They would let her talk to them about
their souls, then! They would even amend a few
sins here and there, of which they had been all
along as well aware as she. But to be convinced
of a new sin; to have their laziness, pride, cove -
ousness, touched; that, she found, was what they
would not bear; and where she had expected, if
not thanks, at least a fair hearing, she had been met
with peevishness, ridicule, even anger and insult.

Her mother had turned against her. " Why
would she go getting a bad name from every one,
and driving away customers?" The preachers,
who were (as is too common in West-country
villages) narrow, ignorant, and somewhat un-
scrupulous men, turned against her. They had
considered the cholera, if it was to come, as so
much spiritual capital for themselves; an occasion
which they could " improve " into a sensation,
perhaps a " revival ;" and to explain it upon
mere physical causes was to rob them of their
harvest. Coarse viragos went even further still,
and dared to ask her " whether it was the curate
or the doctor she was setting her cap at; for she
never had anything in her mouth now but what
they had said." And those words went through
her heart like a sword. Was she disinterested?
Was not love for Thurnall, the wish to please him,
mingling with all her earnestness? And again,
was not self-love mingling with it? and mingling,
too, with the disappointment, even indignation,
which she felt at having failed? Ah — what

hitherto hidden spots of self-conceit, vanity, pharisaic pride, that bitter trial laid bare, or seemed to lay, till she learned to thank her unseen Guide even for it!

Perhaps she had more reason to be thankful for her humiliation than she could suspect, with her narrow knowledge of the world. Perhaps that sudden downfall of her fancied queenship was needed, to shut her out, once and for all, from that downward path of spiritual intoxication, followed by spiritual knavery, which, as has been hinted, was but too easy for her.

But meanwhile the whole thing was but a fresh misery. To bear the burden of Cassandra day and night, seeing in fancy — which yet was truth — the black shadow of death hanging over that doomed place; to dream of whom it might sweep off — perhaps, worst of all, her mother, unconfessed and impenitent!

Too dreadful! And dreadful, too, the private troubles which were thickening fast; and which seemed, instead of drawing her mother to her side, to estrange her more and more, for some mysterious reason. Her mother was heavily in debt. This ten pounds of Lord Scoutbush's would certainly clear off the miller's bill. Her scanty quarter's salary, which was just due, would clear off a little more. But there was a long-standing account of the wholesale grocer's for five-and-twenty pounds, for which Mrs. Harvey had given a two months' bill. That bill would become due early in September; and how to meet it, neither mother nor daughter knew; it lay like a black plague-spot on the future, only surpassed in horror by the cholera itself.

It might have been three or four days after, that Claude, lounging after breakfast on deck, was hailed from a dingy, which contained Captain Willis and Gentleman Jan.

"Might we take the liberty of coming aboard to speak with your honor?"

"By all means!" and up the side they came; their faces evidently big with some great purpose, and each desirous th it the other should begin.

"You speak, cap ain," says Jan, "you'm oldest;" and then he began himself. "If you please, sir, we'm come on a sort of deputation — Why don't you tell the gentleman, captain?"

Willis seemed either doubtful of the success of his deputation or not over desirous thereof; for, after trying to put John Beer forward as spokesman, he began:

"I'm sorry to trouble you, sir, but these young men will have it so — and no shame to them — on a matter which I think will come to nothing. But the truth is, they have heard that you are a great painter, and they have taken it into their heads to ask you to paint a picture for them."

"Not to ask you a favor, sir, mind!" interrupted Jan; "we'd scorn to be so forward; we'll subscribe and pay for it, in course, any price in reason. There's forty and more promised already."

"You must tell me, first, what the picture is to be about," said Claude, puzzled and amused.

"Why didn't you tell the gentleman, captain?"

"Because I think it is no use; and I told them all so from the first. The truth is, sir, they want a picture of my — of our schoolmistress, to hang up in the school or somewhere ——"

"That's it, dra'ed out all natural, in paints, and

her bonnet, and her shawl, and all, just like life;
we was a going to ax you to do one of they garry-
types; but she would have'n noo price; besides
tan't cheerful looking they sort, with your leave;
too much blackamoor wise, you see, and over thick
about the nozzes, most times, to my liking; so we'll
pay you and welcome, all you ask."

"Too much blackamoor wise, indeed!" said
Claude, amused. "And how much do you think
I should ask?"

No answer.

"We'll settle that presently. Come down into
the cabin with me."

"Why, sir, we could n't make so bold. His
lordship ——"

"Oh, his lordship's on shore, and I am skipper
for the time; and if not, he'd be delighted to see
two good seamen here. So come along."

And down they went.

"Bowie, bring these gentlemen some sherry!"
cried Claude, turning over his portfolio. "Now
then, my worthy friends, is that the sort of thing
you want?"

And he spread on the table a water-color
sketch of Grace.

The two worthies gazed in silent delight, and
then looked at each other, and then at Claude, and
then at the picture.

"Why, sir," said Willis; "I could n't have believed it! You've got the very smile of her, and
the sadness of her too, as if you'd known her a
hundred year!"

"'T is beautiful!" sighed Jan, half to himself.
Poor fellow, he had cherished, perhaps, hopes of
winning Grace after all.

" Well, will that suit you? "

" Why, sir, make so bold — but what we thought on was to have her drawn from head to foot, and a child standing by her like, holding to her hand, for a token as she was schoolmistress; and the pier behind, may be, to signify as she was our maid, and belonged to A' eralva "

" A capital thought! Upon my word, you're men of taste here in the West; but what do you think I should charge for such a picture as that?'

" Name your price, sir," said Jan, who was in high good humor a Claude's approbation.

" Two hundred guineas? "

Jan gave a long whistle.

" I told you so, Captain Beer," said Willis, " or ever we got into the boat."

" Now," said Claude, laughing, " I 've two prices, one 's two hundred, and the other is just nothing; and if you won't agree to the one, you must take the other."

" But we wants to pay, we 'd take it an honor to pay, if we could afford it."

" Then wait till next Christmas."

" Christmas? "

" My good friend, pictures are not painted in a day. Next Christmas, if I live, I 'll send you what you shall not be ashamed of, or she either, and do you club your money and put it into a handsome gold frame."

" But, sir," said Willis, " this will give you a sight of trouble, and all for our fancy."

" I like it, and I like you! You 're fine fellows, who know a noble creature when God sends her to you; and I should be ashamed to ask a farthing of your money. There, no more words! "

"Well, you are a gentleman, sir!" said Gentleman Jan.

"And so are you," said Claude. "Now I'll show you some more sketches."

"I should like to know, sir," asked W.llis, " how you got at that likeness. She would not hear of the thing, and that's why I had no liking to come troubling you about nothing."

Claude told them, and Jan laughed heartily, while Willis said:

"Do you know, sir, that's a relief to my mind. There is no sin in being drawn, of course; but I did n't like to think my maid had changed her mind, when once she'd made it up."

So the deputation retired in high glee, after Willis had entreated Claude and Beer to keep the thing a secret from Grace.

It befell that Claude, knowing no reason why he should not tell Frank Headley, told him the whole story, as a proof of the chivalry of his parishioners, in which he would take delight.

Frank smiled, but said little; his opinion of Grace was altering fast. A circumstance which occurred a few days after altered it still more.

Scoutbush had gone forth, as he threatened, and exploded in every direction, with such effect as was to be supposed. Everybody promised his lordship to do everything. But when his lordship's back was turned, everybody did just nothing. They knew very well that he could not make them do anything; and what was more, in some of the very worst cases, the evil was past remedy now, and better left alone. For the drought went on pitiless. A copper sun, a sea of glass, a brown easterly blight, day after day, while Thurnall looked grimly aloft and mystified the sailors with:

"Fine weather for the 'Flying Dutchman' this!"

"Coffins sail fastest in a calm."

"You'd best al out to the quay-head, and whistle for a wind it would be an ill one that would blow nobody good just now!"

But the wind came not, nor the rain; and the cholera crept neare and nearer: while the hearts of all in Aberalva were hardened, and out of very spite against the ag tators, they did less than they would have done otherwise. Even the inhabitants of the half a dozen cottages which Scoutbush, finding that they were in his own hands, whitewashed by main force, filled the town with lamentations over his lordship's tyranny. True—their pigsties were either under their front windows, or within two feet of the wall: but to pull down a poor man's pigstye!—they might ever so well be Rooshian slaves!—and all the town was on their side; for pigs were the normal inhabitants of Aberalva backyards.

Tardrew's wrath, of course, knew no bounds; and meeting Thurnall standing at Willis's door, with Frank and Mellot, he fell upon him open-mouthed.

"Well, sir! I've a crow to pick with you."

"Pick away!" quoth Tom.

"What business have you meddling between his lordship and me?"

"That is my concern," quoth Tom, who evidently was not disinclined to quarrel. "I'm not here to give an account to you of what I choose to do."

"I'll tell you what, sir; ever since you've been in this parish you've been meddling, you and Mr.

Headley too, — I 'll say it to your faces, — I 'll
speak the truth to any man, gentle or simple;
and that ain't enough for you, but you must come
over that poor half-crazed girl, to set her plaguing
honest people, with telling 'em they 'll all be dead
in a month, till nobody can eat their suppers in
peace: and that again ain't enough for you, but
you must go to my lord with your——"

"Hold hard!" quoth Tom. "Don't start two
hares at once. Let's hear that about Miss Harvey
again!"

"Miss Harvey? Why, you should know better
than I."

"Let's hear what you know."

"Why, ever since that night Trebooze caught
you and her together——"

"Stop!" said Tom, "that's a lie!"

"Everybody says so."

"Then everybody lies, that's all; and you may
say I said so, and take care you don't say it again
yourself. But what ever since that night?"

"Why, I suppose you come over the poor thing
somehow, as you seem minded to do over every
one as you can. But she's been running up and
down the town ever since, preaching to 'em about
windilation, and drains, and smells, and cholera,
and it's being a judgment of the Lord against dirt,
till she's frightened all the women so, that many's
the man as has had to forbid her his house. But
you know that as well as I."

"I never heard a word of it before; but now I
have, I 'll give you my opinion on it. That she is
a noble, sensible girl, and that you are all a set of
fools who are not worthy of her; and that the
greatest fool of the whole is you, Mr. Tardrew.

And when the cholera comes, it will serve you exactly right if you are the first man carried off by it. Now, sir, you have given me your mind, and I have given you mine, and I do not wish to hear anything more of you. Good-morning!"

"You hold your head mighty high, to be sure, since you 've had the run of his lordship's yacht."

"If you are impertinent, sir, you will repent it. I shall take care to inform his lordship of this conversation."

"My dear Thurnall," said Headley, as Tardrew withdrew, muttering curses, "the old fellow is certainly right on one point."

"What then?"

"That you have wonderfully changed your tone. Who was to eat any amount of dirt, if he could but save his influence thereby?"

"I have altered my plans. I sha'n't stay here long; I shall just see this cholera over, and then vanish."

"No?"

"Yes. I cannot sit here quietly, listening to the war-news. It makes me mad to be up and doing. I must eastward-ho, and see if trumps will not turn up for me at last. Why, I know the whole country, half a dozen of the languages — oh, if I could get some secret-service work! Go I must! At worst I can turn my hand to doctoring Bashi-bazouks."

"My dear Tom, when will you settle down like other men?" cries Claude.

"I would now, if there was an opening at Whitbury, and low as life would be, I 'd face it for my father's sake. But here I cannot stay."

Both Claude and Headley saw that Tom had

reasons which he did not choose to reveal. However, Claude was taken into his confidence that very afternoon.

"I shall make a fool of myself with that schoolmistress. I have been near enough to it a dozen times already; and this magnificent conduct of hers about the cholera has given the finishing stroke to my brains. If I stay on here, I shall marry her: I know I shall! and I won't! I'd go to-morrow, if it were not that I'm bound, for my own credit, to see the cholera safe into the town and out again."

Tom did not hint a word of the lost money, or of the month's delay which Grace had asked of him. The month was drawing fast to a close now, however: but no sign of the belt. Still, Tom had honor enough in him to be silent on the point, even to Claude.

"By the by, have you heard from the wanderers this week?"

"I heard from Sabina this morning. Marie is very poorly, I fear. They have been at Kissingen, bathing; and are going to Bertrich: somebody has recommended the baths there."

"Bertrich! Where's Bertrich?"

"The most delicious little nest of a place, half way up the Moselle, among the volcano craters."

"Don't know it. Have they found that Yankee?"

"No."

"Why, I thought Sabina had a whole detective force of pets and *protégés*, from Boulogne to Rome."

"Well, she has at least heard of him at Baden; and then again at Stuttgart: but he has escaped them as yet."

" And poor Marie is breaking her heart all the while? I'll tell you what, Claude, it will be well for him if he escapes me as well as them."

"What do you mean?"

" I certainly sha'n't go to the East without shaking hands once more with Marie and Sabina; and if in so doing I pass that fellow, it's a pity if I don't have a snap shot at him."

"Tom! Tom! I had hoped your duelling days were over."

"They will be over, when one can get the law to punish such puppies; but not till then. Hang the fellow! What business had he with her at all, if he did n't intend to marry her?"

" I tell you, as I told you before, it is she who will not marry him."

"And yet she's breaking her heart for him. I can see it all plain enough, Claude. She has found him out only too late. I know him — luxurious, selfish, *blasé*; would give a thousand dollars to-morrow, I believe, like the old Roman, for a new pleasure: and then amuses himself with her till he breaks her heart! Of course she won't marry him: because she knows that if he found out her quadroon blood — ah, that's it! I'll lay my life he has found it out already, and that is why he has bolted!"

Claude had no answer to give. That talk at the Exhibition made it only too probable.

"You think so yourself, I see! Very well. You know that whatever I have been to others, that girl has nothing against me."

"Nothing against you? Why, she owes you honor, life, everything."

" Never mind that. Only when I take a fancy

to begin, I'll carry it through. I took to that girl,
for poor Wyse's sake; and I'll behave by her to
the last as he would wish; and he who insults her,
insults me. I won't go out of my way to find
Stangrave: but if I do, I'll have it out!"

"Then you will certainly fight. My dearest
Tom, do look into your own heart, and see
whether you have not a grain or two of spite
against him left. I assure you you judge him
too harshly."

"Hum — that must take its chance. At least, if
we fight, we fight fairly and equally. He is a brave
man — I will do him that justice — and a cool one;
and used to be a sweet shot. So he has just as
good a chance of shooting me, if I am in the
wrong, as I have of shooting him, if he is."

"But your father?"

"I know. That is very disagreeable; and all
the more so because I am going to insure my
life — a pretty premium they will make me pay!
— and if I'm killed in a duel, it will be forfeited.
However, the only answer to that is, that either I
sha'n't fight, or if I do, I sha'n't be killed. You
know, I don't believe in being killed, Claude."

"Tom! Tom! The same as ever!" said Claude,
sadly.

"Well, old man, and what else would you have
me? Nobody could ever alter me, you know;
and why should I alter myself? Here I am, after
all, alive and jolly; and there is old daddy, as
comfortable as he ever can be on earth; and so
it will be to the end of the chapter. There! let's
talk of something else."

CHAPTER XVI

COME AT LAST

NOW, as if in all things Tom Thurnall and John Briggs were fated to take opposite sides, Campbell lost ground with Elsley as fast as he gained it with Thurnall. Elsley had never forgiven himself for his passion that first morning. He had shown Campbell his weak side, and feared and disliked him accordingly. Besides, what might not Thurnall have told Campbell about him? And what use might not the major make of his secret? Besides, Elsley's dread and suspicion increased rapidly when he discovered that Campbell was one of those men who live on terms of peculiar intimacy with many women; whether for his own good or not, still for the good of the women concerned. For only by honest purity, and moral courage superior to that of the many, is that dangerous post earned; and women will listen to the man who will tell them the truth, however sternly; and will bow, as before a guardian angel, to the strong insight of him whom they have once learned to trust. But it is a dangerous office, after all, for layman as well as for priest, that of father-confessor. The experience of centuries has shown that they must needs exist, wherever fathers neglect their daughters, husbands their wives; wherever the average of the women cannot respect the

average of the men. But the experience of centuries should likewise have taught men, that the
said father-confessors are no objects of envy; that
their temptations to become spiritual coxcombs
(the worst species of all coxcombs), 'f not intrigu-
ers, bullies, and worse, are so extreme, that the soul
which is proo? against them must be either very
great or very small indeed. Whether Campbell
was altogether proof will be seen hereafter. But
one day Elsley found out that such was Campbell's
influence, and did not love him the more for the
discovery.

They were walking round the garden after dinner; Scoutbush was licking his foolish lips over
some common-place tale of scandal.

" I tell you, my dear fellow, she 's booked; and
Mellot knows it as well as I. He saw her that
night at Lady A —— 's."

"We saw the third act of the comi-tragedy.
The fourth is playing out now. We shall see the
fifth before the winter."

" *Non sine sanguine!*" said the major.

" Serve the wretched stick right, at least," said
Scoutbush.   " What right had he to marry such a
pretty woman? "

" What right had they to marry her up to him? "
said Claude. " I don't blame poor January. I
suppose none of us, gentlemen, would have refused
such a pretty toy, if we could have afforded it as
he could."

" Whom do you blame then? " asked Elsley.

" Fathers and mothers who prate hypocritically
about keeping their daughters' minds pure; and
then abuse a girl's ignorance, in order to sell her
to ruin. Let them keep her mind pure, in Heaven's

name; but let them consider themselves all the more bound in honor to use on her behalf the experience in which she must not share."

"Well," drawled Scoutbush, "I don't complain of her bolting; she s a very sweet creature, and always was; but, as Longreach says, — and a very witty fellow he is, though you laugh at him, — 'If she 'd kept to us, I s ould n't have minded; but as guardsmen, we must throw her over. It 's an insult to the whole Guards my dear fellow, after refusing two of us, to marry an attorney, and after all to bolt with a plunger.' "

What bolting with a plunger might signify, Elsley knew not; but ere he could ask, the major rejoined, in an abstracted voice:

"God help us all! And this is the girl I recollect, two years ago, singing there in Cavendish Square, as innocent as a nestling thrush!"

"Poor child!" said Mellot, "sold at first — perhaps sold again now. The plunger has bills out, and she has ready money. I know her settlements."

"She sha'n't do it," said the major, quietly; "I 'll write to her to-night."

Elsey looked at him keenly. "You think then, sir, that you can, by simply writing, stop this intrigue?"

The major did not answer. He was deep in thought.

"I should n't wonder if he did," said Scoutbush; "two to one on his balking the plunger!"

"She is at Lord ——'s now, at those silly private theatricals. Is he there?"

"No," said Mellot; "he tried hard for an invitation — stooped to work me and Sabina. I believe she told him that she would sooner see him in the morgue than help him; and he is gone to the moors now, I believe."

"There is time then: I will write to her to-night;" and Campbell took up his hat and went home to do it.

"Ah," said Scoutbush, taking his cigar medita-tively from his mouth, "I wonder how he does it! It's a gift, I always say, a wonderful gift! Before he has been a week in a house, he'll have the confidence of every woman in it — and 'gad, he does it by saying the rudest things! — and the confidence of all the youngsters the week after."

"A somewhat dangerous gift," said Elsley, drily.

"Ah, yes; he might play tricks if he chose: but there's the wonder, that he don't. I'd answer for him with my own sister. I do every day of my life — for I believe he knows how many pins she puts into her dress — and yet there he is. As I said once in the mess-room — there was a young-ster there who took on himself to be witty, and talked about the still sow supping the milk — the snob! You recollect him, Mellot? the attorney's son from Brompton, who sold out — we shaved his mustachios, put a bear in his bed, and sent him home to his ma. And he said that Major Camp-bell might be very pious, and all that: but he'd warrant — they were the fellow's own words — that he took his lark on the sly, like other men — the snob! so I told him, I was no better than the rest, and no more I am; but if any man dared to say that the major was not as honest as his own sister, I was his man at fifteen paces. And so I am, Claude!"

All which did not increase Elsley's love to the

major, conscious as he was that Lucia's confidence was a thing which he had not wholly; and which it would be very dangerous to him for any other man to have at all.

Into the drawing-room they went. Frank Healley had been asked up to tea; and he stood at the piano, listening to Valentia's singing.

As they came in, the maid came in also. "Mr. Thurnall wished to speak to Major Campbell."

Campbell went out, and returned in two minutes somewhat hurriedly.

"Mr. Thurnall wishes Lord Scoutbush to be informed at once, and I think it is better that you should all know it — that — it is a painful surprise: but there is a man ill in the street, whose symptoms he does not like, he says."

"Cholera?" said Elsley.

"Call him in," said Scoutbush.

"He had rather not come in, he says."

"What! is it infectious?"

"Certainly not, if it be cholera, but —— "

"He don't wish to frighten people, quite right" (with a half glance at Elsley); "but is it cholera, honestly?"

"I fear so."

"O my children!" said poor Mrs. Vavasour.

"Will five pounds help the poor fellow?" said Scoutbush.

"How far off is it?" asked Elsley.

"Unpleasantly near. I was going to advise you to move at once."

"You hear what they are saying?" asked Valentia of Frank.

"Yes, I hear it," said Frank, in a quiet meaning tone.

Valentia thought that he was half pleased with the news. Then she thought him afraid; for he did not stir.

" You will go instantly, of course? "

" Of course I shall. Good-bye! Do not be afraid. It is not infectious."

" Afraid? And a soldier's sister? " said Valentia, with a toss of her beautiful head, by way of giving force to her somewhat weak logic.

Frank left the room instantly, and met Thurnall in the passage.

" Well, Headley, it 's here before we sent for it, as bad luck usually is."

" I know. Let me go! Where is it? Whose house? " asked Frank, in an excited tone.

" Humph! " said Thurnall, looking intently at him, " that is just what I shall not tell you."

" Not tell me."

" No, you are too pale, Headley. Go back and get two or three glasses of wine, and then we will talk of it."

" What do you mean? I must go instantly! It is my duty — my parishioner! "

" Look here, Headley! Are you and I to work together in this business, or are we not? "

" Why not, in Heaven's name? "

" Then I want you, not for cure, but for prevention. You can do them no good when they have once got it. You may prevent dozens from having it in the next four-and-twenty hours, if you will be guided by me."

" But my business is with their souls, Thurnall."

" Exactly; to give them the consolations of religion, as they call it. You will give them to the people who have not taken it. You may

bring them safe through it by simply keeping up
their spirits; while if you waste your time on
poor dying wretches - —— "

"Thurnall, you must not talk so! I will do all
you ask: but my place is at the death-bed, as well
as elsewhere. These perishing souls are in my
care."

"And how do you know, pray, that they are perishing?" answered Tom, with something very like
a sneer. "And if they were, do you honestly believe that any talk of yours can change in five
minutes a character which has been forming for
years, or prevent a man's going where he ought to
go, — which, I suppose, is the place to which he
deserves to go?"

"I do," said Frank, firmly.

"Well. It is a charitable and hopeful creed.
My great dread was, lest you should kill the poor
wretches before their time, by adding to the fear
of cholera the fear of hell. I caught the Methodist
parson at that work an hour ago, took him by the
shoulders and shot him out into the street. But,
my dear Headley " (and Tom lowered his voice to
a whisper), " wherever poor Tom Beer deserved to
go to, he is gone to it already. He has been dead
this twenty minutes."

"Tom Beer dead? One of the finest fellows in
the town! And I never sent for?"

"Don't speak so loud, or they will hear you. I
had no time to send for you; and if I had, I
should not have sent, for he was past attending
to you from the first. He brought it with him, I
suppose, from C——. Had had warnings for a
week, and neglected them. Now listen to me:
that man was but two hours ill; as sharp a case as

I ever saw, even in the West Indies. You must summon up all your good sense, and play the man for a fortnight; for it 's coming on the poor souls like hell!" said Tom between his teeth, and stamped his foot upon the ground. Frank had never seen him show so much feeling; he fancied he could see tears glistening in his eyes.

"I will, so help me God!" said Frank.

Tom held out his hand, and grasped Frank's.

"I know you will. You're all right at heart. Only mind three things: don't frighten them; don't tire yourself; don't go about on an empty stomach; and then we can face the worst like men. And now go in, and say nothing to these people. If they take a panic, we shall have some of them down to-night as sure as fate. Go in, keep quiet, persuade them to bolt anywhere on earth by daylight to-morrow. Then go home, eat a good supper, and come across to me; and if I 'm out, I 'll leave word where."

Frank went back again; he found Campbell, who had had his cue from Tom, urging immediate removal as strongly as he could, without declaring the extent of the danger. Valentia was for sending instantly for a fly to the nearest town, and going to stay at a watering-place some forty miles off. Elsley was willing enough at heart, but hesitated; he knew not, at the moment, poor fellow, where to find the money. His wife knew that she could borrow of Valentia; but she, too, was against the place. The cholera would be in the air for miles round. The journey in the hot sun would make the children sick and ill; and watering-place lodgings were such horrid holes, never ventilated, and full of smells — people caught fevers at them so often. Valentia was inclined to treat this as " mother's nonsense ; " but Major Campbell said gravely that Mrs. Vavasour was perfectly right as to fact, and her arguments full of sound reason ; whereon Valentia said that " of course if Lucia thought it, Major Campbell would prove it; and there was no arguing with such Solons as he ——— "

Which Elsley heard, and ground his teeth. Whereon little Scoutbush cried joyfully :

" I have it; why not go by sea? Take the yacht, and go ! Where? Of course, I have it again. 'Pon my word I 'm growing clever, Valentia, in spite of all your prophecies. Go up the Welsh coast. Nothing so healthy and airy as a sea voyage : sea as smooth as a mill-pond, too, and likely to be. And then land, if you like, at Port Madoc, as I meant to do; and there are my rooms at Beddgelert lying empty. Engaged them a week ago, thinking I should be there by now ; so you may as well keep them aired for me. Come, Valentia, pack up your millinery ! Lucia, get the cradles ready, and we 'll have them all on board by twelve. Capital plan, Vavasour, is n't it? and, by Jove, what stunning poetry you will write there under Snowdon ! "

" But will you not want your rooms yourself, Lord Scoutbush? " said Elsley.

" My dear fellow, never mind me. I shall go across the country, I think, see an old friend, and get some otter-hunting. Don't think of me till you 're there, and then send the yacht back for me. She must be doing something, you know ; and the men are only getting drunk every day here. Come — no arguing about it, or I shall turn you all out of doors into the lane, eh? "

And the little fellow laughed so good-naturedly,
that Elsley could not help liking him: and feeling
that he would be both a fool, and cruel to his
family, if he refused so good an offer, he gave in to
the scheme, and went out to arrange matters:
while Scoutbush went out into the hall with
Campbell, and scrambled into his pea-jacket, to go
off to the yacht that moment.

"You 'll see to them, there 's a good fellow," as
they lighted their cigars at the door. "That
Vavasour is greener than grass, you know, *tant pis*
for my poor sister."

"I am not going."

"Not going?"

"Certainly not; so my rooms will be at their
service; and you had much better escort them
yourself. It will be much less disagreeable for
Vavasour, who knows nothing of commanding
sailors," or himself, thought the major, "than finding himself master of your yacht in his absence,
and you will get your fishing as you intended."

"But why are you going to stay?"

"Oh, I have not half done with the sea-beasts
here. I found two new ones yesterday."

"Quaint old beetle-hunter you are, for a man
who has fought in half a dozen battles!" and
Scoutbush walked on silently for five minutes.

Suddenly he broke out:

"I cannot! By George, I cannot; and what 's
more, I won't!"

"What?"

"Run away. It will look so — so cowardly, and
there 's the truth of it, before those fine fellows
down there: and just as I am come among them,
too! The commander-in-chief to turn tail at the first

shot! Though I can't be of any use, I know, and I should have liked a fortnight's fishing so," said he, in a dolorous voice, " before going to be eaten up with flies at Varna — for this Crimean expedition is all moonshine."

"Don't be too sure of that," said Campbell. "We shall go; and some of us who go will never come back, Freddy. I know those Russians better than many, and I have been talking them over lately with Thurnall, who has been in their service."

" Has he been at Sevastopol?"

" No. Almost the only place on earth where he has not been: but from all he says, and from all I know, we are undervaluing our foes, as usual, and shall smart for it!"

"We'll lick them, never fear!"

"Yes; but not at the first round. Scoutbush, your life has been child's play as yet. You are going now to see life in earnest, — the sort of life which average people have been living, in every age and country, since Adam's fall; a life of sorrow and danger, tears and blood, mistake, confusion, and perplexity; and you will find it a very new sensation; and, at first, a very ugly one. All the more reason for doing what good deeds you can before you go; for you may have no time left to do any on the other side of the sea."

Scoutbush was silent awhile.

"Well; I'm afraid of nothing, I hope: only I wish one could meet this cholera face to face, as one will those Russians, with a good sword in one's hand, and a good horse between one's knees; and have a chance of giving him what he brings, instead of being kicked off by the cowardly Rockite, no one knows how; and not even from behind a turf dyke, but out of the very clouds."

"So we all say, in every battle, Scoutbush. Who ever sees the man who sent the bullet through him? And yet we fight on. Do you not think the greatest terror, the only real terror, in any battle, is the chance shots which come from no one knows where, and hit no man can guess whom? If you go to the Crimea, as you will, you will feel what I felt at the Cape, and Cabul, and the Punjab, twenty times — the fear of dying like a dog, one knew not how."

"And yet I'll fight, Campbell!"

"Of course you will, and take your chance. Do so now!"

"By Jove, Campbell — I always say it — you're the most sensible man I ever met; and, by Jove, the doctor comes the next. My sister shall have the yacht, and I'll go up to Penalva."

"You will do two good deeds at once, then," said the major. "You will do what is right, and you will give heart to many a poor wretch here. Believe me, Scoutbush, you will never repent of this."

"By Jove, it always does one good to hear you talk in that way, Campbell! One feels — I don't know — so much of a man when one is with you; not that I sha'n't take uncommonly good care of myself, old fellow; that is but fair: but as for running away, as I said, why — why — why, I can't, and so I won't."

"By the by," said the major, "there is one thing which I have forgotten, and which they will never recollect. Is the yacht victualled — with fresh meat and green stuff, I mean?"

" Whew — w ——"

" I will go back, borrow a lantern, and forage in the garden, like an old campaigner. I have cut a salad with my sword before now."

"And made it in your helmet, with macassar sauce?" And the two went their ways.

Meanwhile, before they had left the room, a notable conversation had been going on between Valentia and Headley.

Headley had re-entered the room so much paler than he went out, that everybody noticed his altered looks. Valentia chose to attribute them to fear.

"So! Are you returned from the sick man already, Mr. Headley?" asked she, in a marked tone.

"I have been forbidden by the doctor to go near him at present, Miss St. Just," said he, quietly, but in a sort of under voice, which hinted that he wished her to ask no more questions. A shade passed over her forehead, and she began chatting rather noisily to the rest of the party, till Elsley, her brother, and Campbell went out.

Valentia looked up at him, expecting him to go too. Mrs. Vavasour began bustling about the room, collecting little valuables, and looking over her shoulders at the now unwelcome guest. But Frank leant back in a cosy arm-chair, and did not stir. His hands were clasped on his knees; he seemed lost in thought; very pale: but there was a firm set look about his lips which attracted Valentia's attention. Once he looked up in Valentia's face, and saw that she was looking at him. A flush came over his cheeks for a moment, and then he seemed as impassive as ever. What could he want there? How very gauche and rude of him; so unlike him, too! And she said, civilly enough, to him, " I fear, Mr. Headley, we must begin packing up now."

" I fear you must, indeed," answered he, as if starting from a dream. He spoke in a tone, and with a look, which made both the women start; for what they meant it was impossible to doubt.

" I fear you must. I have foreseen it a long time; and so, I fear " (and he rose from his seat), " must I, unless I mean to be very rude. You will at least take away with you the knowledge that you have given to one person's existence, at least for a few weeks, pleasure more intense than he thought earth could hold."

" I trust that pretty compliment was meant for me," said Lucia, half playful, half reproving.

" I am sure that it ought not to have been meant for me," said Valentia, more downright than her sister. Both could see for whom it was meant, by the look of passionate worship which Frank fixed on a face which, after all, seemed made to be worshipped.

" I trust that neither of you," answered he, quietly, " think me impertinent enough to pretend to make love, as it is called, to Miss St. Just. I know who she is, and who I am. Gentleman as I am, and the descendant of gentlemen " (and Frank looked a little proud, as he spoke, and very handsome), " I see clearly enough the great gulf fixed between us; and I like it; for it enables me to say truth which I otherwise dare not have spoken; as a brother might say it to a sister, or a subject to a queen. Either analogy will do equally well, and equally ill."

Frank, without the least intending it, had taken up the very strongest military position. Let a man once make a woman understand, or fancy, that he knows that he is nothing to her; and confess boldly that there is a great gulf fixed between them, which he has no mind to bridge over: and then there is little that he may not see or do, for good or for evil.

And therefore it was that Lucia answered gently, "I am sure you are not well, Mr. Headley. The excitement of the night has been too much for you."

"Do I look excited, my dear madam?" he answered quietly; "I assure you that I am as calm as a man must be who believes that he has but a few days to live, and trusts, too, that when he dies, he will be infinitely happier than he has ever been on earth, and lay down an office which he has never discharged otherwise than ill; which has been to him a constant source of shame and sorrow."

"Do not speak so!" said Valentia, with her Irish impetuous generosity; "you are unjust to yourself. We have watched you, felt for you, honored you, even when we differed from you." — What more she would have said, I know not, but at that moment Elsley's peevish voice was heard calling over the stairs, "Lucia! Lucia!"

"Oh dear! He will wake the children!" cried Lucia, looking at her sister, as much as to say, "how can I leave you?"

"Run, run, my dear creature!" said Valentia, with a self-confident smile: and the two were left alone.

The moment that Mrs. Vavasour quitted the room there vanished from Frank's face that intense

look of admiration which had made even Valentia
uneasy. He dropped his eyes, and his voice faltered as he spoke again. He acknowledged the
change in their position, and Valentia saw that
he did so, and liked him the better for it.

, "I shall not repeat, Miss St. Just, now that we
are alone, what I said just now of the pleasure
which I have had during the last month. I am
not poetical, or given to string metaphors together; and I could only go over the same dull
words once more. But I could ask, if I were not
asking too much, leave to prolong at least a shadow
of that pleasure to the last moment. That I shall
die shortly, and of this cholera, is with me a fixed
idea, which nothing can remove. No, madam —·
it is useless to combat it! But had I anything, by
which to the last moment I could bring back to
my fancy what has been its sunlight for so long;
even if it were a scrap of the hem of your garment,
aye, a grain of dust off your feet — God forgive
me! He and His mercy ought to be enough to
keep me up: but one's weakness may be excused
for clinging to such slight floating straws of
comfort."

Valentia paused, startled, and yet affected. How
she had played with this deep pure heart! And
yet, was it pure? Did he wish, by exciting her
pity, to trick her into giving him what he might
choose to consider a token of affection?

And she answered coldly enough:

"I should be sorry, after what you have just
said, to chance hurting you by refusing. I put
it to your own good feeling — have you not asked
somewhat too much?"

"Certainly too much, madam, in any common

case," said he, quite unmoved. "Certainly too much, if I asked you for it, as I do not, as the token of an affection which I know well you do not, cannot feel. But — take my words as they stand — were you to — it would be returned if I die, in a few weeks and returned still sooner if I live. And, madam " said he, lowering his voice, "I vow to you, before Him who sees us both, that, as far as I am concerned, no human being shall ever know of the fact."

Frank had at last touched the wrong chord.

"What, Mr. Headley? Can you think that I am to have secrets in common with you, or with any other man? No, sir! If I granted your request, I should avow it as openly as I shall refuse it."

And she turned sharply toward the door.

Frank Headley was naturally a shy man: but extreme need sometimes bestows on shyness a miraculous readiness — (else why, in the long run, do the shy men win the best wives? which is a fact, and may be proved by statistics, at least as well as anything else can) so he quietly stepped to Valentia's side, and said in a low voice:

"You cannot avow the refusal half as proudly as I shall avow the request, if you will but wait till your sister's return. Both are unnecessary, I think: but it will only be an honor to me to confess that, poor curate as I am —— "

"Hush!" and Valentia walked quietly up to the table, and began turning over the leaves of a book, to gain time for her softened heart and puzzled brain.

In five minutes Frank was beside her again. The book was Tennyson's "Princess." She had wandered — who can tell why? — to that last exquisite scene, which all know; and as Valentia read, Frank quietly laid a finger on the book, and arrested her eyes at last —

> " If you be, what I think you, some sweet dream,
>
> .   .   .   .
>
> Stoop down, and seem to kiss me ere I die!"

Valentia shut the book up hurriedly and angrily. A moment after she had made up her mind what to do, and with the slightest gesture in the world, motioned Frank proudly and coldly to follow her back into the window. Had she been a country girl, she would have avoided the ugly matter; but she was a woman of the world enough to see that she must, for her own sake and his, talk it out reasonably.

"What do you mean, Mr. Headley? I must ask! You told me just now that you had no intention of making love to me."

"I told you the truth," said he, in his quiet impassive voice. "I fixed on these lines as a *pis aller;* and they have done all, and more than I wished, by bringing you back here for at least a moment."

"And do you suppose — you speak like a rational man, therefore I must treat you as one — that I can grant your request?"

"Why not? It is an uncommon one. If I have guessed your character aright, you are able to do uncommon things. Had I thought you enslaved by etiquette, and by the fear of a world which you can make bow at your feet if you will, I should not have asked you. But" — and here his voice took a tone of deepest earnestness — "grant it —

only grant it, and you shall never repent it. Never, never, never will I cast one shadow over a light which has been so glorious, so life-giving; which I watched with delight, and yet lose without regret. Go your way, and God be with you! I go mine; grant me but a fortnight's happiness, and then let what will come!"

He had conquered. The quiet earnestness of the voice, the child-like simplicity of the manner, of which every word conveyed the most delicate flattery — yet, she could see, without intending to flatter, without an afterthought — all these had won the impulsive Irish nature. For all the dukes and marquises in Belgravia she would not have done it; for they would have meant more than they said, even when they spoke more clumsily: but for the plain country curate she hesitated, and asked herself, "What shall I give him?"

The rose from her bosom? No. That was too significant at once, and too common-place; besides, it might wither, and he find an excuse for not restoring it. It must be something valuable, stately, formal, which he must needs return. And she drew off a diamond hoop, and put it quietly into his hand.

"You promise to return it?"

"I promised long ago."

He took it, and lifted it — she thought that he was going to press it to his lips. Instead, he put it to his forehead, bowing forward, and moved it slightly. She saw that he made with it the sign of the Cross.

"I thank you," he said, with a look of quiet gratitude. "I expected as much, when you came to understand my request. Again, thank you!"

and he drew back humbly, and left her there
alone; while her heart smote her bitterly for all
the foolish encouragement which she had given
to one so tender, and humble, and delicate and
true.

And so did Frank Headley get what he wanted;
by that plain earnest simplicity which has more
power (let worldlings pride themselves as they
will on their knowledge of women) than all the
cunning wiles of the most experienced rake; and
only by aping which, after all, can the rake conquer. It was a strange thing for Valentia to do, no
doubt; but the strange things which are done in
the world (which are some millions daily) are just
what keep the world alive.

CHAPTER XVII

BAALZEBUB'S BANQUET

THE next day there were three cholera cases; the day after there were thirteen.

He had come at last, Baalzebub, god of flies, and of what flies are bred from; to visit his self-blinded worshippers, and bestow on them his own Cross of the Legion of Dishonor. He had come suddenly, capriciously, sportively, as he sometimes comes; as he had come to Newcastle the summer before, while yet the rest of England was untouched. He had wandered all but harmless about the West-country that summer; as if his maw had been full glutted five years before, when he sat for many a week upon the Dartmoor hills, amid the dull brown haze, and sunburnt bents, and dried-up water-courses of white dusty granite, looking far and wide over the plague-struck land, and listening to the dead-bell booming all day long in Tavistock churchyard. But he was come at last, with appetite more fierce than ever, and had darted aside to seize on Aberalva, and not to let it go till he had sucked his fill.

And all men moved about the streets slowly, fearfully; conscious of some awful unseen presence, which might spring on them from round every corner; some dreadful inevitable spell, which lay upon them like a nightmare weight; and walked to and fro warily, looking anxiously into

each other's faces, not to ask, "How are you?"
but "How am I?" "Do I look as if——?" and
glanced up ever and anon restlessly, as if they
expected to see, like the Greeks, in their tainted
camp by Troy, the pitiless Sun-god shooting his
keen arrows down on beast and man.

All night long the curdled cloud lay low upon
the hills, wrapping in its hot blanket the sweltering
breathless town; and rolled off sullenly when the
sun rose high, to let him pour down his glare, and
quicken into evil life all evil things. For Baalzebub is a sunny fiend; and loves not storm and
tempest, thunder, and lashing rains; but the broad
bright sun, and broad blue sky, under which he
can take his pastime merrily, and laugh at all the
shame and agony below; and, as he did at his
great banquet in New Orleans once, madden all
hearts the more by the contrast between the pure
heaven above and the foul hell below.

And up and down the town the foul fiend
sported, now here, now there; snapping daintily at
unexpected victims, as if to make confusion worse
confounded; to belie Thurnall's theories and prog-
nostics, and harden the hearts of fools by fresh
excuses for believing that he had nothing to do
with drains and water; that he was "only"—such
an only!—"the Visitation of God."

He has taken old Beer's second son; and now
he clutches at the old man himself; then across
the street to Gentleman Jan, his eldest; but he is
driven out from both houses by chloride of lime
and peat dust, and the colony of the Beers has
peace awhile.

Alas! there are victims enough and to spare
beside them, too ready for the sacrifice, and up

the main street he goes unabashed, springing in
at one door and at another, on either side of the
street, but fondest of the western side, where the
hill slopes steeply down to the house-backs.

He fleshes his teeth on every kind of prey.
The drunken cobbler dies, of course; but spotless
cleanliness and sobriety does not save the mother
of seven children, who has been soaking her brick
floor daily with water from a poisoned well, defiling
where she meant to clean. Youth does not save
the buxom lass, who has been filling herself, as girls
will do, with unripe fruit; nor innocence the two
fair children who were sailing their feather-boats
yesterday in the quay-pools, as they have sailed
them for three years past, and found no hurt;
piety does not save the bedridden old dame,
bedridden in the lean-to garret, who moans, "It
is the Lord!" and dies. It is "the Lord" to her,
though Baalzebub himself be the angel of release.

And yet all the while sots and fools escape
where wise men fall; weakly women, living amid
all wretchedness, nurse, unharmed, strong men
who have breathed fresh air all day. Of one
word of Scripture at least Baalzebub is mindful;
for "one is taken and another left."

Still, there is a method in his seeming madness.
His eye falls on a blind alley, running back from
the main street, backed at the upper end by a
high wall of rock. There is a Godsend for him —
a devil's-send, rather, to speak plain truth; and
in he dashes; and never leaves that court, let
brave Tom wrestle with him as he may, till he
has taken one from every house.

That court belonged to Treluddra, the old fish-
jowder. He must do something. Thurnall attacks

him; Major Campbell, Headley; the neighbors
join in the cry; for there is no mistaking cause
and effect there, and no one bears a great love
to him; besides, terrified and conscience-stricken
men are glad of a scapegoat; and some of those
who were his stoutest backers in the vestry are
now, in their terror, the loudest against him,
ready to impute the whole cholera to him. Indeed, old Beer is ready to declare that it was
Treluddra's fish-heaps which poisoned him and
his; so, all but mobbed, the old sinner goes up
— to set the houses to rights? No; to curse
the whole lot for a set of pigs, and order them
to clean the place out themselves, or he will turn
them into the street. He is one of those base
natures, whom fact only lashes·into greater fury
— a Pharaoh whose heart the Lord himself can
only harden; such men there are, and women,
too, grown gray in lies, to reap at last the fruit
of lies. But he carries back with him to his fish-
heaps a little invisible somewhat which he did not
bring; and ere nightfall he is dead hideously, he,
his wife, his son; and now the Beers are down
again, and the whole neighborhood of Treluddra's
house is wild with disgusting agony.

Now the fiend is hovering round the fish-curing
houses; but turns back, disgusted with the pure
scent of the tanyard, where not hides, but nets
are barked; skips on board of a brig in the quay-
pool; and a poor collier's 'prentice dies, and goes
to his own place. What harm has he done? Is it
his sin that, ill-fed and well-beaten daily, he has
been left to sleep on board, just opposite the
sewer's mouth, in a berth some four feet long by
two feet high and broad?

Or is it that poor girl's sin who was just now in Heale's shop, talking to Miss Heale safe and sound, that she is carried back into it, in half an hour's time, fainting, shrieking? One must draw a veil over the too hideous details.

No, not her fault; but there, at least, the curse has not come without a cause. For she is Tardrew's daughter.

But whither have we got? How long has the cholera been in Aberalva? Five days, five minutes, or five years? How many suns have risen and set since Frank Headley put into his bosom Valentia's pledge?

It would be hard for him to tell, and hard for many more; for all the days have passed as in a fever dream. To cowards the time has seemed endless; and every moment, ere their term shall come, an age of terror, of self-reproach, of superstitious prayers and cries, which are not repentance. And to some cowards, too, the days have seemed but as a moment; for they have been drunk day and night.

Strange and hideous, yet true.

It has now become a mere common-place, the strange power which great crises, pestilences, famines, revolutions, invasions, have to call out in their highest power, for evil and for good alike, the passions and virtues of man; how, during their stay, the most desperate recklessness, the most ferocious crime, side by side with the most heroic and unexpected virtue, are followed generally by a collapse and a moral death, alike of virtue and of vice. We should explain this nowadays, and not ill, by saying that these crises put the human mind into a state of exaltation; but the truest explanation, after all, lies in the old

Bible belief, that in these times there goes abroad the unquenchable fire of God, literally kindling up all men's hearts to the highest activity, and showing, by the light of their own strange deeds, the inmost recesses of their spirits, till those spirits burn down again, self-consumed, while the chaff and stubble are left as ashes, not valueless, after all, as manure for some future crop; and the pure gold, if gold there be, alone remains behind.

Even so it was in Aberalva during that fearful week. The drunkards drank more; the swearers swore more than ever; the unjust shopkeeper clutched more greedily than ever at the last few scraps of mean gain which remained for him this side the grave; the selfish wrapped themselves up more brutally than ever in selfishness; the shameless women mingled desperate debauchery with fits of frantic superstition; and all base souls cried out together, "Let us eat and drink, for to-morrow we die!"

But many a brave man and many a weary woman possessed their souls in patience, and worked on, and found that as their day their strength should be. And to them the days seemed short indeed; for there was too much to be done in them for any note of time.

Headley and Campbell, Grace and old Willis, and last, but not least, Tom Thurnall, these and three or four brave women, organized themselves into a right gallant and well-disciplined band, and commenced at once a visitation from house to house, saving thereby, doubtless, many a life; but ere eight-and-forty hours were passed, the house visitation languished. It was as much as they could do to attend to the acute cases.

And little Scoutbush? He could not nurse, nor doctor; but wha: he could, he did. He bought, and fetched all 'hat money could procure. He galloped over to the justices, and obtained such summary powers as he could; and then, like a true Irishman, ex eeded them recklessly, breaking into premises right and left, in an utterly burglarious fashion; he organized his fatigue-party, as he called them, of scavengers, and paid the cowardly clods five shilling: a day each to work at removing all removable nuisances; he walked up and down the streets for hours, giving the sailors cigars from his own case, just to show them that he was not afraid, and therefore they need not be: and if it was somewhat his fault that the horse was stolen, he at least did his best after the event to shut the stable-door. The five real workers toiled on, meanwhile, in perfect harmony and implicit obedience to the all-knowing Tom, but with the most different inward feelings. Four of them seemed to forget death and danger; but each remembered them in his own fashion.

Major Campbell longed to die, and courted death. Frank believed that he should die, and was ready for death. Grace longed to die, but knew that she should not die till she had found Tom's belt, and was content to wait. Willis was of opinion that an " old man must die some day, and somehow, — as good one way as another;" and all his concern was to run about after his maid, seeing that she did not tire herself, and obeying all her orders with sailor-like precision and cleverness.

And Tom? He just thought nothing about death and danger at all. Always smiling, always cheerful, always busy, yet never in a hurry, he went up and down, seemingly ubiquitous. Sleep he got when he could, and food as often as he could; into the sea he leapt, morning and night, and came out fresher every time; the only person in the town who seemed to grow healthier, and actually happier, as the work went on.

"You really must be careful of yourself," said Campbell at last. "You carry no charmed life."

"My dear sir, I am the most cautious and selfish man in the town. I am living by rule; I have got — and what greater pleasure? — a good stand-up fight with an old enemy; and be sure I shall keep myself in condition for it. I have written off for help to the Board of Health, and I shall not be shoved against the ropes till the government man comes down."

"And then?"

"I shall go to bed and sleep for a month. Never mind me; but mind yourself: and mind that curate; he's a noble brick — if all parsons in England were like him, I'd — What's here now?"

Miss Heale came shrieking down the street.

"O Mr. Thurnall! Miss Tardrew! Miss Tardrew!"

"Screaming will only make you ill, too, miss. Where is Miss Tardrew?"

"In the surgery, — and my mother!"

"I expected this," said Tom. "The old man will go next."

He went into the surgery. The poor girl was in collapse already. Mrs. Heale was lying on the sofa, stricken. The old man hanging over her, brandy bottle in hand.

"Put away that trash!" cried Tom; "you've had too much already."

"O Mr. Thurnall, she's dying, and I shall die too!"

"You! you were all right this morning."

"But I shall die; I know I shall, and go to hell!"

"You'll go where you ought: and if you give way to this miserable cowardice, you'll go soon enough. Walk out, sir! Make yourself of some use, and forget your fear! Leave Mrs. Heale to me."

The wretched old man obeyed him, utterly cowed, and went out; but not to be of use: he had been hopelessly boozy from the first — half to fortify his body against infection, half to fortify his heart against conscience. Tom had never reproached him for his share in the public folly. Indeed, Tom had never reproached a single soul. Poor wretches who had insulted him had sent for him with abject shrieks. "O doctor, doctor, save me! Oh, forgive me! oh, if I'd minded what you said! Oh, don't think of what I said!" And Tom had answered cheerfully, "Tut-tut; never mind what might have been; let's feel your pulse."

But though Tom did not reproach Heale, Heale reproached himself. He had just conscience enough left to feel the whole weight of his abused responsibility, exaggerated and defiled by superstitious horror; and maudlin tipsy, he wandered about the street, moaning that he had murdered his wife, and all the town, and asking pardon of every one he met; till seeing one of the meeting-houses open, he staggered in, in the vain hope of comfort which he knew he did not deserve.

In half an hour Tom was down the street again to Headley's. "Where is Miss Harvey?"

"At the Beers'."

"She must go up to Heale's instantly. The mother will die. Those cases of panic seldom recover. And Miss Heale may very likely follow her. She has shrieked and sobbed herself into it, poor fool! and Grace must go to her at once; she may bring her to common sense and courage, and that is the only chance."

Grace went, and literally talked and prayed Miss Heale into life again.

"You are an angel," said Tom to her that very evening, when he found the girl past danger.

"Mr. Thurnall!" said Grace, in a tone of sad and most meaning reproof.

"But you are! And these owls are not worthy of you."

"This is no time for such language, sir! After all, what am I doing more than you?" And Grace went upstairs again, with a cold hard countenance which belied utterly the heart within.

That was the critical night of all. The disease seemed to have done its worst in the likeliest spots: but cases of panic increased all the afternoon; and the gross number was greater than ever.

Tom did not delay inquiring into the cause; and he discovered it. Headley, coming out the next morning, after two hours' fitful sleep, met him at the gate; his usual business-like trot was exchanged for a fierce and hurried stamp. When he saw Frank, he stopped short, and burst out into a story which was hardly intelligible, so interlarded was it with oaths.

"For Heaven's sake! Thurnall, calm yourself, and do not swear so frightfully; it is so unlike you! What can have upset you thus?"

"Why should I not curse and swear in the street," gasped he, ' while every fellow who calls himself a preacher is allowed to do it in the pulpit with impunity! Fin · him five shillings for every curse, as you might if people had courage and common sense, and then complain of me! I am a fool, I know, though. But I cannot stand it ' To have all my work undone by a brutal ignorant fanatic! It is too much! Here, if you will believe it, are those preaching fellows getting up a revival, or some such invention, just to make money out of the cholera! They have got down a great gun from the county town. Twice a-day they are preaching at them, telling them that it is all God's wrath against their sins; that it is impious to interfere, and that I am fighting against God, and the end of the world is coming, and they and the devil only know what. If I meet one of them, I'll wring his neck, and be hanged for it! O you parsons! you parsons!" and Tom ground his teeth with rage.

"Is it possible? How did you find this out?"

"Mrs. Heale had been in, listening to their howling, just before she was taken. Heale went in when I turned him out of doors: came home raving mad, and is all but blue now. Three cases of women have I had this morning, all frightened into cholera, by their own confession, by last night's tomfoolery. Came home howling, fainted, and were taken before morning. One is dead, the other two will die. You must stop it, or I shall have half a dozen more to-night! Go into the meeting, and curse the cur to his face!"

"I cannot," cried Frank, with a gesture of despair, "I cannot!"

"Ah, your cloth forbids you, I suppose, to enter the non-conformist opposition shop."

"You are unjust, Thurnall! What are such rules at a moment like this? I'd break them, and the bishop would hold me guiltless. But I cannot speak to these people. I have no eloquence — no readiness — they do not trust me — would not believe me — God help me!" and Frank covered his face with his hands, and burst into tears.

"Not that, for Heaven's sake!" said Tom, "or we shall have you blue next, my good fellow. I'd go myself, but they'd not hear me, for certain; I am no Christian, I suppose; at least, I can't talk their slang — but I know who can! We'll send Campbell!"

Frank hailed the suggestion with rapture, and away they went; but they had an hour's good search from sufferer to sufferer before they found the major.

He heard them quietly. A severe gloom settled over his face. "I will go," said he.

At six o'clock that evening the meeting-house was filled with terrified women, and half-curious, half-sneering men; and among them the tall figure of Major Campbell, in his undress uniform (which he had put on, wisely, to give a certain dignity to his mission), stalked in, and took his seat in the back benches.

The sermon was what he expected. There is no need to transcribe it. Such discourses may be heard often enough in churches as well as chapels.

The preacher's object seemed to be — for some
purpose or other which we have no right to judge
— to excite in his hearers the utmost intensity of
selfish fear, by language which certainly, as Tom
had said, came under the law against profane curs
ing and swearing. He described the next world
in language which seemed a strange jumble of
Virgil's Æneid, the Koran, the dreams of those
rabbis who crucified our Lord, and of those medi
æval inquisitors who tried to convert sinners (and
on their own ground, neither illogically nor over-
harshly) by making his world for a few hours as
like as possible to what, so they held, God was
going to make the world to come for ever.

At last he stopped suddenly, when he saw that
the animal excitement was at the very highest, and
called on all who felt " convinced " to come forward and confess their sins.

In another minute there would have been (as
there have been ere now) four or five young girls
raving and tossing upon the floor, in mad terror
and excitement; or, possibly, half the congregation might have rushed out (as a congregation has
rushed out ere now) headed by the preacher himself, and ran headlong down to the quay pool, with
shrieks and shouts, declaring that they had cast the
devil out of Betsy Pennington, and were hunting
him into the sea; but Campbell saw that the madness must be stopped at once, and rising, he
thundered, in a voice which brought all to their
senses in a moment:

" Stop ! I, too, have a sermon to preach to
you; I trust I am a Christian man, and that not of
last year's making, or the year before. Follow me
outside, if you be rational beings, and let me tell

you the truth — God's truth! Men!" he said,
with an emphasis on the word, "you, at least, will
give me a fair hearing, and you too, modest married women! Leave that fellow with the shameless hussies who like to go into fits at his feet."

The appeal was not in vain. The soberer
majority followed him out; the insane minority
soon followed, in the mere hope of fresh excitement; while the preacher was fain to come also, to
guard his flock from the wolf. Campbell sprang
upon a large block of stone, and taking off his cap,
opened his mouth, and spake unto them.

Readers will doubtless desire to hear what Major
Campbell said: but they will be disappointed; and
perhaps it is better for them that they should be.
Let each of them, if they think it worth while,
write for themselves a discourse fitting for a Christian man, who loved and honored his Bible too
much to find in a few scattered texts, all misinter-
preted, and some mistranslated, excuses for deny-
ing fact, reason, common justice, the voice of God
in his own moral sense, and the whole remainder
of the Bible from beginning to end.

Whatsoever words he spoke they came home
to those wild hearts with power. And when he
paused, and looked intently into the faces of his
auditory, to see what effect he was producing, a
murmur of assent and admiration rose from the
crowd, which had now swelled to half the population of the town. And no wonder; no wonder
that, as the men were enchained by the matter, so
were the women by the manner. The grand head,
like a gray granite peak against the clear blue sky;
the tall figure, with all its martial stateliness and

ease; the gesture of his long arm, so graceful, and yet so self-restrained the tones of his voice, which poured from beneath that proud moustache, now tender as a girl's, now ringing like a trumpet over roof and sea. The e were old men there, old beyond the years of man, who said they had neve seen nor heard the l ke: but it must be like what their fathers had told them of, when John Wesley, on the cliffs of St. Ives, out-thundered the thunde of the gale. To Grace he seemed one of the old Scotch Covenanters of whom she had read, risen from the dead to preach there from his rock beneath the great temple of God's air, a wider and a juster creed than theirs. Frank drew Thurnall's arm through his, and whispered, " I shall thank you for this to my dying day: " but Thurnall held down his head. He seemed deeply moved. At last, half to himself:

"Humph! I believe that between this man and that girl you will make a Christian even of me some day! "

But the lull was only for a moment. For Major Campbell, looking round, discerned among the crowd the preacher, whispering and scowling amid a knot of women; and a sudden fit of righteous wrath came over him.

"Stand out there, sir, you preacher, and look me in the face, if you can! " thundered he. "We are here on common ground as free men, beneath God's heaven and God's eye. Stand out, sir! and answer me if you can; or be for ever silent! "

Half in unconscious obedience to the soldier-like word of command, half in jealous rage, the preacher stepped forward, gasping for breath:

"Don't listen to him! He is a messenger of

Satan sent to damn you — a lying prophet! Let the Lord judge between me and him! Stop your ears — a messenger of Satan — a Jesuit in disguise!"

"You lie, and you know that you lie!" answered Campbell, twirling slowly his long moustache, as he always did when choking down indignation. "But you have called on the Lord to judge; so do I. Listen to me, sir! Dare you, in the presence of God, answer for the words which you have spoken this day?"

A strange smile came over the preacher's face.

"I read my title clear, sir, to mansions in the skies. Well for you if you could do the same."

Was it only the setting sun, or was it some inner light from the depths of that great spirit, which shone out in all his countenance, and filled his eyes with awful inspiration, as he spoke, in a voice calm and sweet, sad and regretful, and yet terrible from the slow distinctness of every vowel and consonant?

"Mansions in the skies? You need not wait till then, sir, for the presence of God. Now, here, you and I are before God's judgment-seat. Now, here, I call on you to answer to Him for the innocent lives which you have endangered and destroyed, for the innocent souls to whom you have slandered their heavenly Father by your devil's doctrines this day! You have said it. Let the Lord judge between you and me. He knows best how to make His judgment manifest."

He bowed his head awhile, as if overcome by the awful words which he had uttered, almost in spite of himself, and then stepped slowly down from the stone, and passed through the crowd, which rever-

ently made way for him; while many voices cried,
" Thank you, sir! Thank you!" and old Captain
Willis, stepping forward, held out his hand to him,
a quiet pride in his gray eye.

"You will not refuse an old fighting man's
thanks, sir! This has been like Elijah's day with
Baal's priests on Carmel."

Campbell shook his hand in silence: but turned
suddenly, for another and a coarser voice caught
his ear. It was Jones, the lieutenant's.

" And now, my lads, take the Methodist parson,
neck and heels, and heave him into the quay pool,
to think over his summons!"

Campbell went back instantly. "No, my dear
sir, let me entreat you for my sake. What has
passed has been too terrible to me already; if it
has done any good, do not let us break it by
spoiling the law."

" I believe you 're right, sir: but my blood is up,
and no wonder. Why, where is the preacher?"

He had stood quite still for several minutes
after Campbell's adjuration. He had, often, perhaps, himself hurled forth such words in the excitement of preaching; but never before had he heard
them pronounced in spirit and in truth. And as
he stood, Thurnall, who had his doctor's eye on
him, saw him turn paler and more pale. Suddenly
he clenched his teeth, and stooped slightly for-
wards for a moment, drawing his breath. Thurnall walked quickly and steadily up to him.

Gentleman Jan and two other riotous fellows had
already laid hold of him, more with the intention
of frightening, than of really ducking him.

" Don't! don't! cried he, looking round with
eyes wild — but not with terror.

"Hands off, my good lads," said Tom, quietly. "This is my business now, not yours, I can tell you."

And passing the preacher's arm through his own, with a serious face, Tom led him off into the house at the back of the chapel.

In two hours more he was blue; in four he was a corpse. The judgment, as usual, had needed no miracle to enforce it.

Tom went to Campbell that night, and apprised him of the fact. "Those words of yours went through him, sir, like a Minie bullet. I was afraid of what would happen when I heard them."

"So was I, the moment after they were spoken. But, sir, I felt a power upon me — you may think it a fancy — that there was no resisting."

"I dare impute no fancies, when I hear such truth and reason as you spoke upon that stone, sir?"

"Then-you do not blame me?" asked Campbell, with a subdued, almost deprecatory voice, such as Thurnall had never heard in him before.

"The man deserved to die, and he died, sir. It is well that there are some means left on earth of punishing offenders whom the law cannot touch."

"It is an awful responsibility."

"Not more awful than killing a man in battle, which we both have done, sir, and yet have felt no sting of conscience."

"An awful responsibility still. Yet what else is life made up of, from morn to night, but of deeds which may earn heaven or hell? . . . Well, as he did to others, so was it done to him. God forgive him! At least, our cause will be soon tried and judged: there is little fear of my not meeting him again — soon enough." And Campbell, with a sad smile, lay back in his chair and was silent.

"My dear sir," said Tom, " allow me to remind you, after this excitement comes a collapse; and that is not to be trifled with just now. Medicne I dare not give you. Food I must."

Campbell shook his head.

" You must go now, my dear fellow. It is now half-past ten, and I will be at Pennington's at one o'clock, to see how he goes on; so you need not go there. And, meanwhile, I must take a little medicine."

" Major, you are not going to doctor yourself?" cried Tom.

" There is a certain medicine called prayer, Mr. Thurnall — an old specific for the heartache, as you will find one day — which I have been neglecting much of late, and which I must return to in earnest before midnight. Good-bye, God bless and keep you!" And the major retired to his bedroom, and did not stir off his knees for two full hours. After which he went to Pennington's, and thence somewhere else; and Tom met him at four o'clock that morning musing amid unspeakable horrors, quiet, genial, almost cheerful.

"You are a man," said Tom to himself; "and I fancy at times something more than a man; more than me at least."

Tom was right in his fear that after excitement would come collapse; but wrong as to the person to whom it would come. When he arrived at the surgery door, Headley stood waiting for him.

"Anything fresh? Have you seen the Heales?"

"I have been praying with them. Don't be

frightened. I am not likely to forget the lesson of this afternoon."

"Then go to bed. It is full twelve o'clock."

"Not yet, I fear. I want you to see old Willis. All is not right."

"Ah! I thought the poor dear old man would kill himself. He has been working too hard, and presuming on his sailor's power of tumbling in and taking a dog's nap whenever he chose."

"I have warned him again and again: but he was working so magnificently, that one had hardly heart to stop him. And beside, nothing would part him from his maid."

"I don't wonder at that," quoth Tom to himself. "Is she with him?"

"No: he found himself ill; slipped home on some pretence; and will not hear of our telling her."

"Noble old fellow! Caring for every one but himself to the last." And they went in.

It was one of those rare cases, fatal, yet merciful withal, in which the poison seems to seize the very center of the life, and to preclude the chance of lingering torture, by one deadening blow.

The old man lay paralyzed, cold, pulseless, but quite collected and cheerful. Tom looked, inquired, shook his head, and called for a hot bath of salt and water.

"Warmth we must have, somehow. Anything to keep the fire alight."

"Why so, sir?" asked the old man. "The fire's been flickering down this many a year. Why not let it go out quietly, at threescore years and ten? You're sure my maid don't know?"

They put him into his bath, and he revived a little.

"No; I am not going to get well; so don't you waste your time on me, sirs! I'm taken while doing my duty, as I hoped to be. And I've lived to see my maid do hers, as I knew she would, when the Lord called on her. I have — but don't tell her, she's well employed, and has sorrows enough already, some that you 'll know of some day — - "

"You must not talk," quoth Tom, who guessed his meaning, and wished to avoid the subject.

"Yes, but I must, sir. I've no time to lose. If you'd but go and see after those poor Heales, and come again. I'd like to have one word with Mr. Headley; and my time runs short."

"A hundred, if you will," said Frank.

"And now, sir," when they were alone, "only one thing, if you'll excuse an old sailor," and Willis tried vainly to make his usual salutation; but the cramped hand refused to obey — "and a dying one too."

"What is it?"

"Only don't be hard on the people, sir; the people here. They're good-hearted souls, with all their sins, if you'll only take them as you find them, and consider that they've had no chance."

"Willis, Willis, don't talk of that! I shall be a wiser man henceforth, I trust. At least I shall not trouble Aberalva long."

"O sir, don't talk so; and you just getting a hold of them!"

"I?"

"Yes, you, sir. They've found you out at last, thank God. I always knew what you were, and said it. They've found you out in the last week: and there's not a man in the town but what would die for you, I believe."

This announcement staggered Frank. Some men it would have only hardened in their pedantry, and have emboldened them to say: "Ah! then these men see that a High Churchman can work like any one else, when there is a practical sacrifice to be made. Now I have a standing ground which no one can dispute, from which to go on and enforce my idea of what he ought to be."

But, rightly or wrongly, no such thought crossed Frank's mind. He was just as good a churchman as ever — why not? Just as fond of his own ideal of what a parish and a church service ought to be — why not? But the only thought which did rise in his mind was one of utter self-abasement.

"Oh, how blind I have been! How I have wasted my time in laying down the law to these people; fancying myself infallible, as if God were not as near to them as He is to me — certainly nearer than to any book on my shelves — offending their little prejudices, little superstitions, in my own cruel self-conceit and self-will! And now, the first time that I forget my own rules; the first time that I forget almost that I am a priest, even a Christian at all! that moment they acknowledge me as a priest, as a Christian. The moment I meet them upon the commonest human ground, helping them as one heathen would help another, simply because he was his own flesh and blood, that moment they soften to me, and show me how much I might have done with them twelve months ago, had I had but common sense!"

He knelt down and prayed by the old man, for him and for himself.

"Would it be troubling you, sir?" said the old

man at last. "But I'd like to take the sacrament before I go."

"Of course. Whom shall I ask in?"

The old man paused awhile.

"I fear it's selfish: but it seems to me — I would not ask it, but that I know I'm going. I should like to take it with my maid, once more before I die."

"I'll go for he," said Frank, "the moment Thurnall comes back to watch you."

"What need to go yourself, sir? Old Sarah will go, and willing."

Thurnall came in at that moment.

"I am going to fetch Miss Harvey. Where is she, captain?"

"At Janey Headon's, along with her two poor children."

"Stay," said Tom, "that's a bad quarter, just at the fish-house back. Have some brandy before you start?"

"No! no Dutch courage!" and Frank was gone. He had a word to say to Grace Harvey, and it must be said at once.

He turned down the silent street, and turned up over stone stairs, through quaint stone galleries and balconies such as are often huddled together on the cliff sides in fishing towns; into a stifling cottage, the door of which had been set wide open, in the vain hope of fresh air. A woman met him, and clasped both his hands, with tears of joy.

"They're mending, sir! They're mending, else I'd have sent to tell you. I never looked for you so late."

There was a gentle voice in the next room. It was Grace's.

"Ah, she's praying by them now. She'm giving

them all their medicines all along! Whatever I should have done without her! — and in and out all day long, too; till one fancies at whiles the Lord must have changed her into five or six at once, to be everywhere to the same minute."

Frank went in, and listened to her prayer. Her face was as pale and calm as the pale, calm faces of the two worn-out babes, whose heads lay on the pillow close to hers: but her eyes were lit up with an intense glory, which seemed to fill the room with love and light.

Frank listened: but would not break the spell.

At last she rose, looked round and blushed.

"I beg your pardon, sir, for taking the liberty. If I had known that you were about, I would have sent: but hearing that you were gone home, I thought you would not be offended, if I gave thanks for them myself. They are my own, sir, as it were ——"

"O Miss Harvey, do not talk so! While you can pray as you were praying then, he who would silence you might be silencing unawares the Lord himself!"

She made no answer, though the change in Frank's tone moved her; and when he told her his errand, that thought also passed from her mind.

At last, "Happy, happy man!" she said calmly, and putting on her bonnet, followed Frank out of the house.

"Miss Harvey," said Frank, as they hurried up the street, "I must say one word to you, before we take that sacrament together."

"Sir?"

"It is well to confess all sins before the Eucharist, and I will confess mine. I have been unjust to you. I know that you hate to be praised; so I will not tell you what has altered my opinion. But Heaven forbid that I should ever do so base a thing as to take the school away from one who is far more fit to rule in it than ever I shall be!"

Grace burst into tears.

"Thank God! And I thank you, sir! Oh, there's never a storm but what some gleam breaks through it! And now, sir, I would not have told you it before, lest you should fancy that I changed for the sake of gain — though, perhaps, that is pride, as too much else has been. But you will never hear of me inside either of those chapels again."

"What has altered your opinion of them, then?"

"It would take long to tell, sir: but what happened this morning filled the cup. I begin to think, sir, that their God and mine are not the same. Though why should I judge them, who worshipped that other God myself till no such long time since; and never knew, poor fool, that the Lord's name was Love?"

"I have found that out, too, in these last days. More shame to me than to you that I did not know it before."

"Well for us both that we do know it now, sir. For if we believed Him now, sir, to be aught but perfect love, how could we look round here to-night, and not go mad?"

"Amen!" said Frank.

And now had the pestilence, of all things on earth, revealed to those two noble souls that God is Love?

Let the reader, if he have supplied Campbell's sermon, answer the question for himself.

They went in, and upstairs to Willis.

Grace bent over the old man tenderly, but with no sign of sorrow. Dry-eyed, she kissed the old man's forehead; arranged his bed-clothes, woman-like, before she knelt down; and then the three received the sacrament together.

"Don't turn me out," whispered Tom. "It's no concern of mine, of course: but you are all good creatures, and somehow, I should like to be with you."

So Tom stayed; and what thoughts passed through his heart are no concerns of ours.

Frank put the cup to the old man's lips; the lips closed, sipped — then opened . . . the jaw had fallen.

"Gone," said Grace, quietly.

Frank paused, awe-struck.

"Go on, sir," said she, in a low voice. "He hears it all more clearly than he ever did before." And by the dead man's side, Frank finished the Communion Service.

Grace rose when it was over, kissed the calm forehead, and went out without a word.

"Tom," said Frank, in a whisper, "come into the next room with me."

Tom hardly heard the tone in which the words were spoken, or he would perhaps have answered otherwise than he did.

"My father takes the Communion," said he, half to himself. "At least, it is a beautiful old ——"

Howsoever the sentence would have been finished, Tom stopped short:

"Hey? — What does that mean?"

"At last?" gasped Frank, gently enough. "Excuse me!" He was bowed almost double, crushing Thurnall's arm in the fierce grip of pain.

"Pish! — Hang it! — Impossible — There, you are all right now!"

"For the time. I can understand many things now. Curious sensation it is, though. Can you conceive a sword put in on one side of the waist, just above the hip-bone, and drawn through, handle and all, till t passes out at the opposite point?"

"I have felt it twice; and therefore you will be pleased to hold your tongue and go to bed. Have you had any warnings?"

"Yes — no — that is — this morning; but I forgot. Never mind! What matter a hundred years hence? There it is again! God help me!"

"Humph!" growled Thurnall to himself. "I'd sooner have lost a dozen of these herring-hogs, whom nobody misses, and who are well out of their life-scrape; but the parson, just as he was making a man!"

There is no use in complaints. In half an hour Frank is screaming like a woman, though he has bitten his tongue half through to stop his screams.

CHAPTER XVIII

THE BLACK HOUND

PAH! Let us escape anywhere for a breath of fresh air, for even the scent of a clean turf. We have been watching saints and martyrs — perhaps not long enough for the good of our souls, but surely too long for the comfort of our bodies. Let us away up the valley, where we shall find, if not indeed a fresh healthful breeze (for the drought lasts on), at least a cool refreshing down-draught from Carcarrow Moor before the sun gets up. It is just half-past four o'clock, on a glorious August morning. We shall have three hours at least before the heavens become one great Dutch-oven again.

We shall have good company, too, in our walk; for here comes Campbell fresh from his morning's swim, swinging up the silent street toward Frank Headley's lodging.

He stops, and tosses a pebble against the window-pane. In a minute or two Thurnall opens the street door and slips out to him.

"Ah, major! Overslept myself at last; that sofa is wonderfully comfortable. No time to go down and bathe. I'll get my header somewhere up the stream."

"How is he?"

"He? sleeping like a babe, and getting well as fast as his soul will allow his body. He has something on his mind. Nothing to be ashamed of, though, I will warrant; for a purer, nobler fellow I never met."

" When can we move him? "

" Oh, to-morrow if he will agree. You may all depart and leave me and the government n an to make out the returns of killed and wound·d. We shall have no more cholera. Eight days without a new case   We shall do now. I'm glad you are coming up with us."

" I will just see ·he hounds throw off, and then go back and get Headley's breakfast."

" No, no! you must n't, sir; you want a day's play."

" Not half as much as you. And I am in no hunting mood just now. Do you take your fill of the woods and the streams, and let me see our patient. I suppose you will be back by noon? "

" Certainly." And the two swing up the street, and out of the town, along the vale toward Trebooze.

For Trebooze, of Trebooze, has invited them, and Lord Scoutbush, and certain others, to come out otter-hunting; and otter-hunting they will go.

Trebooze has been sorely exercised, during the last fortnight, between fear of the cholera and desire of calling upon Lord Scoutbush — " as I ought to do, of course, as one of the gentry round; he 's a Whig, of course, and no more to me than anybody else; but one don't like to let politics interfere; " by which Trebooze glosses over to himself and friends the deep flunkeydom with which he lusteth after a live lord's acquaintance, and one especially in whom he hopes to find even such a one as himself. . . . " Good fellow, I hear he is, too — good sportsman, smokes like a chimney," and so forth.

So at last, when the cholera has all but disappeared, he comes down to Penalva, and introduces himself, half swaggering, half servile; begins by a string of apologies for not having called before — "Mrs. Trebooze so afraid of infection, you see, my lord," — which is a lie: then blunders out a few fulsome compliments to Scoutbush's courage in staying; then takes heart at a little joke of Scoutbush's, and tries the free and easy style; fingers his lordship's high-priced Hudsons, and gives a broad hint that he would like to smoke one on the spot; which hint is not taken, any more than the bet of a "pony" which he offers five minutes afterwards, that he will jump his Irish mare in and out of Aberalva pound; is utterly "thrown on his haunches" (as he informed his friend Mr. Creed afterwards) by Scoutbush's praise of Tom Thurnall, as an "invaluable man, a treasure in such an out-of-the-way place, and really better company than ninety-nine men out of a hundred;" recovers himself again when Scoutbush asks after his otter-hounds, of which he has heard much praise from Tardrew; and launches out once more into sporting conversation of that graceful and lofty stamp which may be perused and perpended in the pages of "Handley Cross," and Mr. Sponge's "Sporting Tour," books painfully true to that uglier and baser side of sporting life which their clever author has chosen so wilfully to portray.

So, at least, said Scoutbush to himself, when his visitor had departed.

"He's just like a page out of Sponge's 'Tour,' though he's not half as good a fellow as Sponge himself; for Sponge knew he was a snob, and lived up to his calling honestly: but this fellow wants all the while to play at being a gentleman; and — Ugh! how the fellow smelt of brandy, and worse! His hand, too, shook as if he had the palsy, and he chattered and fidgetted like a man with St. Vitus' dance."

"Did he, my lord?" quoth Tom Thurnall, when he heard the same, in a very meaning tone.

And Trebooze, "or his part, could n't make out that lord — uncommonly agreeable, and easy and all that: but shoves a fellow off, and sets him down somehow, and in such a . . . civil way, that you don't know where to have him."

However, Trebooze departed in high spirits; for Lord Scoutbush has deigned to say that he will be delighted to see the otter-hounds work any morning that Trebooze likes, and anyhow — no time too early for him. "He will bring his friend Major Campbell?"

"By all means."

"Expect two or three sporting gentlemen from the neighborhood, too. Regular good ones, my lord — though they are county bucks — very much honored to make your lordship's acquaintance."

Scoutbush expresses himself equally honored by making their acquaintance, in a tone of bland simplicity, which utterly puzzles Trebooze, who goes a step further.

"Your lordship 'll honor us by taking pot luck afterwards. Can't show you French cookery, you know, and your souffleys and glacys, and all that. Honest saddle o' mutton, and the grounds of old port. My father laid it down, and I take it up, eh?" And Trebooze gave a wink and a nudge of his elbow, meaning to be witty.

His lordship was exceedingly sorry; it was the

most unfortunate accident: but he had the most particular engagement that very afternoon, and must return early from the otter-hunt, and probably sail the next day for Wales. " But," says the little man, who knows all about Trebooze's household, " I shall not fail to do myself the honor of calling on Mrs. Trebooze, and expressing my regret," etc.

So to the otter-hunt is Scoutbush gone, and Campbell and Thurnall after him; for Trebooze has said to himself, " Must ask that blackguard of a doctor — hang him! I wish he were an otter himself; but if he 's so thick with his lordship, it won't do to quarrel." For, indeed, Thurnall might tell tales. So Trebooze swallows his spite and shame, — as do many folk who call themselves his betters, when they have to deal with a great man's hanger-on, — and sends down a note to Tom:

" Mr. Trebooze requests the pleasure of Mr. Thurnall's company with his hounds at . . ."

And Tom accepts — why not? and chats with Campbell, as they go, on many things; and among other things on this:

" By the by," said he, " I got an hour's shore-work yesterday afternoon, and refreshing enough it was. And I got a prize, too. The sucking barnacle which you asked for: I was certain I should get one or two, if I could have a look at the pools this week. Jolly little dog! he was paddling and spinning about last night, and enjoying himself, ' ere age with creeping ' — what is it? — ' hath clawed him in his clutch.' That fellow's destiny is not a hopeful analogy for you, sir, who believe that we shall rise after we die into some higher and freer state."

" Why not? "

" Why, which is better off, the free swimming larva, or the perfec cirrhipod, rooted for ever motionless to the ro k? "

" Which is better off, the roving young fellow who is sowing his w d oats, or the man who has settled down, and become a respectable landowner with a good house ver his head? "

" And begun to p opagate his species? Well you have me there, ir, as far as this life is concerned; but you wil confess that the barnacle's history proves that all crawling grubs don't turn into butterflies."

" I dare say the barnacle turns into what is best for him; at all events, what he deserves. That rule of yours will apply to him, to whomsoever it will not."

" And so does penance for the sins of his youth, as some of us are to do in the next world? "

" Perhaps yes; perhaps no; perhaps neither."

" Do you speak of us or the barnacle? "

" Of both."

" I am glad of that; for on the popular notion of our being punished a million years hence for what we did when we were lads, I never could see anything but a misery and injustice in our having come into the world at all."

" I can," said the major, quietly.

" Of course I meant nothing rude; but I had to buy my experience, and paid for it dearly enough in folly."

" So had I to buy mine."

" Then why be punished over and above? Why have to pay for the folly, which was itself only the necessary price of experience? "

"For being, perhaps, so foolish as not to use the experience after it has cost you so dear."

"And will punishment cure me of the foolishness?"

"That depends on yourself. If it does, it must needs be so much the better for you. But perhaps you will not be punished, but forgiven."

"Let off? That would be a very bad thing for me, unless I become a very different man from what I have been as yet. I am always right glad now to get a fall whenever I make a stumble. I should have gone to sleep in my tracks long ago else, as one used to do in the backwoods on a long elk hunt."

"Perhaps you may become a very different man."

"I should be sorry for that, even if it were possible."

"Why? Do you consider yourself perfect?"

"No. . . . But somehow, Thomas Thurnall is an old friend of mine, the first I ever had; and I should be sorry to lose his company."

"I don't think you need fear doing so. You have seen an insect go through strange metamorphoses, and yet remain the same individual; why should not you and I do so likewise?"

"Well?"

"Well — there are some points about you, I suppose, which you would not be sorry to have altered?"

"A few," quoth Tom, laughing. "I do not consider myself quite perfect yet."

"What if those points were not really any part of your character, but mere excrescences of disease; or if that be too degrading a notion, mere scars of old wounds, and of the wear and tear of life; and what if, in some future life, all those disappeared, and the true Mr. Thomas Thurnall, pure and simple, were alone left?"

"It is a very hopeful notion. Only, my dear sir, one is quite self-conceited enough in this imperfect state. What intolerable coxcombs we should all be if we were perfect, and could sit admiring ourselves for ever and ever!"

"But what if that self-conceit and self-dependence were the very root of all the disease, the cause of all the scars, the very thing which will have to be got rid of, before our true character and true manhood can be developed?"

"Yes, I understand. Faith and humility. . . . You will forgive me, Major Campbell. I shall learn to respect those virtues when good people have defined them a little more exactly, and can show me somewhat more clearly in what faith differs from superstition, and humility from hypocrisy."

"I do not think any man will ever define them for you. But you may go through a course of experiences, more severe, probably, than pleasant, which may enable you at last to define them for yourself."

"Have you defined them?" asked Tom, bluntly, glancing round at his companion.

"Faith?—Yes, I trust. Humility?—No, I fear."

"I should like to hear your definition of the former, at least."

"Did I not say that you must discover it for yourself?"

"Yes. Well. When the lesson comes, if it does come, I suppose it will come in some learn-

able shape; and till then, I must shift for myself—
and if self-dependence be a punishable sin, I shall,
at all events, have plenty of company whithersoever I go.   There is Lord Scoutbush and
Trebooze!"

Why did not Campbell speak his mind more
clearly to Thurnall?

Because he knew that with such men words are
of little avail. The disease was entrenched too
strongly in the very center of the man's being.   It
seemed at moments as if all his strange adventures
and hair-breadth escapes had been sent to do him
harm and not good; to pamper and harden his
self-confidence, not to crush it.   Therefore Campbell seldom argued with him; but he prayed for
him often; for he had begun, as all did who saw
much of Tom Thurnall, to admire and respect him,
in spite of all his faults.

And now, turning through a woodland path,
they descend toward the river, till they can hear
voices below them; Scoutbush laughing quietly,
Trebooze laying down the law at the top of his
voice.

" How noisy the fellow is, and how he is hopping
about!" says Campbell.

" No wonder; he has been soaking, I hear, for
the last fortnight, with some worthy compeers, by
way of keeping off cholera. I must have my eye
on him to-day."

Scrambling down through the brushwood, they
found themselves in such a scene as Creswick alone
knows how to paint; though one element of beauty,
which Creswick uses full well, was wanting; and
the whole place was seen, not by slant sunrays
gleaming through the boughs, and dappling all

the pebbles with a lacework of leaf shadows, but in the uniform and sober gray of dawn.

A broad bed of shingle, looking just now more like an ill-made turnpike road than the bed of Alva stream; above it, a long shallow pool, which showed every stone through the transparent water; on the right, a craggy bank, bedded with deep wood sedge and orange-tipped king ferns, clustering beneath sallow and maple bushes already tinged with gold; on the left, a long bar of gravel, covered with giant "butterbur" leaves; in and out of which the hounds are brushing — beautiful black-and-tan dogs, of which poor Trebooze may be pardonably proud; while round the burleaf-bed dances a rough white Irish terrier, seeming, by his frantic self-importance, to consider himself the master of the hounds.

Scoutbush is standing with Trebooze beyond the bar, upon a little lawn set thick with alders. Trebooze is fussing and fidgetting about, wiping his forehead perpetually; telling everybody to get out of the way, and not to interfere; then catching hold of Scoutbush's button to chatter in his face; then starting aside to put some part of his dress to rights. His usual lazy drawl is exchanged for foolish excitement. Two or three more gentlemen, tired of Trebooze's absurdities, are scrambling over the rocks above in search of spraints. Old Tardrew waddles stooping along the line where grass and shingle meet, his bull-dog visage bent to his very knees.

"Tardrew out hunting?" says Campbell. "Why, it is but a week since his daughter was buried!"

"And why not? I like him better for it. Would he bring her back again by throwing away a good day's sport?   Better turn out, as he has done, and forget his feelings, if he has any."

"He has feelings enough, don't doubt.   But you are right.   There is something very characteristic in the way in which the English countryman never shows grief, never lets it interfere with business, even with pleasure."

"Hillo!   Mr. Trebooze!" says the old fellow looking up.   "Here it is!"

"Spraint? Spraint? Spraint? Where? Eh—what?" cries Trebooze.

"No; but what's as good: here on this alder stump, not an hour old.   I thought they beauties' starns were n't flemishing for nowt."

"Here! here! here! here! Musical, Musical! Sweetlips!   Get out of the way!" and Trebooze runs down.

Musical examines, throws her nose into the air, and answers by the rich bell-like note of the true otter-hound; and all the woodlands ring as the pack dashes down the shingle to her call.

"Over!" shouts Tom.   "Here's the fresh spraint our side!"

Through the water splash squire, viscount, steward, and hounds, to the horror of a shoal of par, the only visible tenants of a pool which, after a shower of rain, would be alive with trout.   Where those trout are in the meanwhile is a mystery yet unsolved.

Over dances the little terrier, yapping furiously, and expending his superfluous energy by snapping right and left at the par.

"Hark to Musical! hark to Sweetlips!   Down the stream?   No!   the old girl has it; right up the bank!"

"How do, doctor? How do, Major Campbell?
Forward! Forward! Forward!" shouts Trebooze,
glad to escape a longer parley, as with his spear
in his left hand, he clutches at the overhanging
boughs with his right, and swings himself up, with
Peter, the huntsman, after him. Tom follows him;
and why?

Because he does not like his looks. That bull-
eye is red, and almost bursting; his cheeks are
flushed, his lips blue, his hand shakes; and
Tom's quick eye has already remarked, from a
distance, over and above his new fussiness, a sudden shudder, a quick, half frightened glance behind him; and perceived, too, that the moment
Musical gave tongue, he put the spirit-flask to his
mouth.

Away go the hounds at score through tangled
cover, their merry peal ringing from brake and
briar, clashing against the rocks, moaning musi-
cally away through distant glens aloft.

Scoutbush and Tardrew "take down" the river-
bed, followed by Campbell. It is in his way
home; and though the major has stuck many a
pig, shot many a gaur, rhinoceros, and elephant,
he disdains not, like a true sportsman, the less
dangerous but more scientific excitement of an
otter-hunt.

"Hark to the merry merry Christchurch bells!
She's up by this time; that don't sound like a
drag now!" cries Tom, bursting desperately, with
elbow-guarded visage, through the tangled scrub.
"What's the matter, Trebooze? No, thanks!
'Modest quenchers' won't improve the wind just
now."

For Trebooze has halted, panting and bathed in

perspiration; has been at the brandy flask again; and now offers Tom a " quencher," as he calls it.

" As you like," says Trebooze, sulkily, having meant it as a token of reconciliation, and pushes on.

They are now upon a little open meadow, girdled by green walls of wood; and along the river-bank the hounds are fairly racing. Tom and Peter hold on; Trebooze slackens.

" Your master don't look right this morning, Peter."

Peter lifts his hand to his mouth, to signify the habit of drinking; and then shakes it in a melancholy fashion, to signify that the sad habit has reached a lamentable and desperate point.

Tom looks back. Trebooze has pulled up, and is walking, wiping still at his face. The hounds have overrun the scent, and are back again, flemishing about the plashed fence on the river brink.

" Over! over! over!" shouts Peter, tumbling over the fence into the stream, and staggering across.

Trebooze comes up to it, tries to scramble over, mutters something, and sits down astride of a bough.

" You are not well, squire?"

" Well as ever I was in my life. Only a little sick — have been several times lately; could n't sleep either — have n't slept an hour this week. Don't know what it is."

" What ducks of hounds these are!" says Tom, trying, for ulterior purposes, to ingratiate himself. " How they are working there all by themselves, like so many human beings. Perfect! ——— "

" Yes — don't want us — may as well sit here

a minute. Awfully hot, eh? What a splendid creature that Miss St. Just is! I say, Peter!"

"Yes, sir," shouts Peter, from the other side.

"Those hounds a n't right!" with an oath.

"Not right, sir?'

"Did n't I tell you?— five couple and a half-— no, five couple — no, six. Hang it! I can't see, I can't think! How many hounds did I tell you to bring out?"

"Five couple, sir.'

"Then . . . why did you bring out that other?"

"Which other?" shouts Peter, while Thurnall eyes Trebooze keenly.

"Why, that! He's none o' mine! Nasty black cur, how did he get here?"

"Where? There's never no cur here!"

"You lie, you oaf — no — why — doctor — How many hounds are there here?"

"I can't see," says Tom, "among those bushes."

"Can't see, eh? Why don't those brutes hit it off?" says Trebooze, drawling, as if he had forgotten the matter, and lounging over the fence, drops into the stream, followed by Tom, and wades across.

The hounds are all round him, and he is couraging them on, fussing again more than ever; but without success.

"Gone to hole somewhere here," says Peter.

". . .!" cries Trebooze, looking round, with a sudden shudder, and face of terror. "There's that black brute again! there, behind me! Hang it, he'll bite me next!" and he caught up his leg, and struck behind him with his spear.

There was no dog there.

Peter was about to speak, but Tom silenced him by a look, and shouted:

" Here we are! Gone to holt in this alder root."

" Now, then, little Carlingford! Out of the way, puppies!" cries Trebooze, righted again for the moment by the excitement, and thrusting the hounds right and left, he stoops down to put in the little terrier.

Suddenly he springs up, with something like a scream, and then bursts out on Peter with a volley of oaths.

" Did n't I tell you to drive that cur away?"

" Which cur, sir?" cries Peter, trembling, and utterly confounded.

" That cur! . . . Can't I believe my own eyes? Will you tell me that the beggar did n't bolt between my legs this moment, and went into the hole before the terrier?"

Neither answered. Peter from utter astonishment; Tom because he saw what was the matter.

" Don't stoop, squire. You 'll make the blood fly to your head. Let me ——"

But Trebooze thrust him back with curses.

" I 'll have the brute out, and send the spear through him!" and flinging himself on his knees again, Trebooze began tearing madly at the roots and stones, shouting to the half-buried terrier to tear the intruder.

Peter looked at Tom, and then wrung his hands in despair.

" Dirty work — beastly work!" muttered Trebooze. " Nothing but slugs and evats! Toads, too, — hang the toads! What a plague brings all this vermin? Curse it!" shrieked he, springing back, " there 's an adder! and he 's gone up my sleeve! Help me! doctor! Thurnall! or I 'm a dead man!"

Tom caught the arm, thrust his hand up the sleeve, and seemed to snatch out the snake, and hurl it back into the river.

"All right now! — a near chance, though!"

Peter stood open mouthed.

"I never saw no snake!" cried he.

Tom caught him a buffet which sent him reeling "Look after your hounds, you blind ass! How are you now, Trebooze? And he caught the squire round the waist, for he was reeling.

"The world! The world upside down! rocking and swinging! Who's put me feet upwards, like a fly on a ceiling? I'm falling, falling off, into the clouds — into hell-fire — hold me! Toads and adders! and wasps — to go to holt in a wasp's nest! Drive 'em away, — get me a green bough! I shall be stung to death!"

And tearing off a green bough, the wretched man rushed into the river, beating wildly right and left at his fancied tormentors.

"What is it?" cry Campbell and Scoutbush, who have run up breathless.

"Delirium tremens. Campbell, get home as fast as you can, and send me up a bottle of morphine. Peter, take the hounds home. I must go after him."

"I'll go home with Campbell, and send the bottle up by a man and horse," cries Scoutbush; and away the two trot at a gallant pace, for a cross-country run home.

"Mr. Tardrew, come with me, there's a good man! I shall want help."

Tardrew made no reply, but dashed through the river at his heels.

Trebooze had already climbed the plashed

fence, and was running wildly across the meadow. Tom dragged Tardrew up it after him.

"Thank 'ee, sir," but nothing more. The two had not met since the cholera.

Trebooze fell, and lay rolling, trying in vain to shield his face from the phantom wasps.

They lifted him up, and spoke gently to him.

"Better get home to Mrs. Trebooze, sir," said Tardrew, with as much tenderness as his gruff voice could convey.

"Yes, home! home to Molly! My Molly's always kind. She won't let me be eaten up alive. Molly, Molly!"

And shrieking for his wife, the wretched man started to run again.

"Molly, I'm in hell! Only help me! you're always right! only forgive me! and I'll never, never again —— "

And then came out hideous confessions; then fresh hideous delusions.

. . . .

Three weary up-hill miles lay between them and the house; but home they got at last.

Trebooze dashed at the house, tore it open; slammed and bolted it behind him, to shut out the pursuing fiends.

"Quick, round by the back-door!" said Tom, who had not opposed him for fear of making him furious, but dreaded some tragedy if he were left alone.

But his fear was needless. Trebooze looked into the breakfast-room. It was empty; she was not out of bed yet. He rushed upstairs into her bedroom, shrieking her name; she leaped up to meet him; and the poor wretch buried his head in that faithful bosom, screaming to her to save him from he knew not what.

She put her arms round him, soothed him, wept over him sacred tears. "My William! my own William! Yes, I will take care of you! Nothing shall hurt you, — my own, own!"

Vain, drunken, brutal, unfaithful. Yes: but her husband still.

There was a knock at the door.

"Who is that?" she cried, with her usual fierceness, terrified for his character, not terrified for herself.

"Mr. Thurnall, madam. Have you any laudanum in the house?"

"Yes, here! Oh, come in! Thank God you are come! What is to be done?"

Tom looked for the laudanum bottle, and poured out a heavy dose.

"Make him take that, madam, and put him to bed. I will wait downstairs awhile!"

"Thurnall, Thurnall!" calls Trebooze: "don't leave me, old fellow! you are a good fellow. I say, forgive and forget. Don't leave me! Only don't leave me, for the room is as full of devils as —— "

.   .   .   .

An hour after, Tom and Tardrew were walking home together.

"He is quite quiet now, and fast asleep."

"Will he mend, sir?" asks Tardrew.

"Of course he will: and perhaps in more ways than one. Best thing that could have happened — will bring him to his senses, and he'll start fresh."

"We'll hope so, — he's been mad, I think, ever since he heard of that cholera."

"So have others: but not with brandy," thought Tom: but he said nothing.

"I say, sir," quoth Tardrew, after a while, "how's Parson Headley?"

"Getting well, I'm happy to say."

"Glad to hear it, sir. He's a good man, after all; though we did have our differences. But he's a good man, and worked like one."

"He did."

Silence again.

"Never heard such beautiful prayers in all my life, as he made over my poor maid."

"I don't doubt it," said Tom. "He understands his business at heart, though he may have his fancies."

"And so do some others," said Tardrew, in a gruff tone, as if half to himself, "who have no fancies. . . . Tell you what it is, sir: you was right this time; and that's plain truth. I'm sorry to hear talk of your going."

"My good sir," quoth Tom, "I shall be very sorry to go. I have found place and people here as pleasant as man could wish: but go I must."

"Glad you're satisfied, sir; wish you was going to stay," says Tardrew. "Seen Miss Harvey this last day or two, sir?"

"Yes. You know she's to keep her school?"

"I know it. Nursed my girl like an angel."

"Like what she is," said Tom.

"You said one true word once: that she was too good for us."

"For this world," said Tom; and fell into a great musing.

By those curt and surly utterances did Tardrew, in true British bull-dog fashion, express a repentance too deep for words; too deep for all confessionals, penances, and emotions or acts of contrition; the repentance not of the excitable and theatric southern, unstable as water, even in his most violent remorse : but of the still, deep-hearted northern, whose pride breaks slowly and silently. but breaks once for all; who tells to God what he will never tell to man ; and having told it, is a new creature from that day forth for ever.

CHAPTER XIX

BEDDGELERT

THE pleasant summer voyage is over. The "Waterwitch" is lounging off Port Madoc, waiting for her crew. The said crew are busy on shore drinking the ladies' healths, with a couple of sovereigns which Valentia has given them, in her sister's name and her own. The ladies, under the care of Elsley, and the far more practical care of Mr. Bowie, are rattling along among children, maids, and boxes, over the sandy flats of the Traeth Mawr, beside the long reaches of the lazy stream, with the blue surges of the hills in front, and the silver sea behind. Soon they begin to pass wooded knolls, islets of rock in the alluvial plain. The higher peaks of Snowdon sink down behind the lower spurs in front; the plain narrows; closes in, walled round with woodlands clinging to the steep hillsides; and, at last, they enter the narrow gorge of Pont-Aberglaslyn — pretty enough, no doubt, but much over-praised; for there are in Devon alone a dozen passes far grander, both for form and size.

Soon they emerge again on flat meadows, mountain-cradled; and the grave of the mythic greyhound, and the fair old church, shrouded in tall trees; and last, but not least, at the famous Leek Hotel, where ruleth Mrs. Lewis, great and wise, over the four months' Babylon of guides, cars, chambermaids, tourists, artists, and reading-parties, camp-stools, telescopes, poetry-books, blue uglies, red petticoats, and parasols of every hue.

There they settle down in the best rooms in the house, and all goes as merrily as it can, while the horrors which they have left behind them hang, like a black background, to all their thoughts. However, both Scoutbush and Campbell send as cheerful reports as they honestly can; and gradually the exceeding beauty of the scenery, and the amusing bustle of the village, make them forget, perhaps, a good deal which they ought to have remembered.

As for poor Lucia, no one will complain of her for being happy; for feeling that she has got a holiday, the first for now four years, and trying to enjoy it to the utmost. She has no household cares. Mr. Bowie manages everything, and does so, in order to keep up the honor of the family, on a somewhat magnificent scale. The children, in that bracing air, are better than she has ever seen them. She has Valentia all to herself; and Elsley, in spite of the dark fancies over which he has been brooding, is better behaved, on the whole, than usual.

He has escaped — so he considers — escaped from Campbell, above all from Thurnall. From himself, indeed, he has not escaped; but the company of self is, on the whole, more pleasant to him than otherwise just now. For though he may turn up his nose at tourists and reading-parties, and long for contemplative solitude, yet there is a certain pleasure to some people, and often strongest in those who pretend most shyness, in the " *digito monstrari, et dicier, hic est:*" in taking for granted that everybody has read his poems; that everybody is saying in their hearts, " There goes Mr. Vavasour, the distinguished poet. I wonder what he is writing now! I wonder where he has been to-day, and what he has been thinking of."

So Elsley went up Hebog, and looked over the glorious vista of the vale, over the twin lakes, and the rich sheets of woodland, with Aran and Moel Meirch guarding them right and left, and the gray-stone glaciers of the Glyder walling up the valley miles above. And they went up Snowdon, too, and saw little beside fifty fog-blinded tourists, five-and-twenty dripping ponies, and five hundred empty porter bottles; wherefrom they returned, as do many, disgusted, and with great colds in their heads. But most they loved to scramble up the crags of Dinas Emrys, and muse over the ruins of the old tower, " where Merlin taught Vortigern the courses of the stars; " till the stars set and rose as they had done for Merlin and his pupil, behind the four great peaks of Aran, Siabod, Cnicht, and Hebog, which point to the four quarters of the heavens: or to lie by the side of the boggy spring, which once was the magic well of the magic castle, till they saw in fancy the white dragon and the red rise from its depths once more, and fight high in the air the battle which foretold the fall of the Cymry before the Sassenach invader.

One thing, indeed, troubled Elsley, — that Claude was his only companion; for Valentia avoided carefully any more *tête-à-tête* walks with him. She had found out her mistake, and devoted herself now to Lucia. She had a fair excuse enough, for Lucia was not just then in a state for rambles and scrambles; and of that Elsley certainly had no right to complain; so that he was forced to leave them both at home, with as good grace as he could muster, and to wander by himself, scribbling his fancies, while they lounged and worked in the pleasant garden of the hotel, with Bowie fetching and carrying for them all day long, and intimating pretty roundly to Miss Clara his " opeeenion," that he " was very proud and thankful of the office: but he did think that he had to do a great many things for Mrs. Vavasour every day which would come with a much better grace from Mr. Vavasour himself; and that, when he married, he should not leave his wife to be nursed by other men."

Which last words were spoken with an ulterior object, well understood by the hearer; for between Clara and Bowie there was one of those patient and honorable attachments so common between worthy servants. They had both " kept company," though only by letter, for the most part, for now five years; they had both saved a fair sum of money; and Clara might have married Bowie when she chose, had she not thought it her duty to take care of her mistress; while Bowie considered himself equally indispensable to the welfare of that " puir feckless laddie," his master.

So they waited patiently, amusing the time by little squabbles of jealousy, real or pretended; and Bowie was faithful, though Clara was past thirty now, and losing her good looks.

" So ye 'll see your lassie, Mr. Bowie ! " said Sergeant MacArthur, his intimate, when he started for Aberalva that summer. " I 'm thinking ye 'd better put her out of her pain soon. Five years is ower lang courting, and she's na pullet by now, saving your pardon."

"Hoooo——," says Bowie; "leave the green gooseberries to the lads, and gi' me the ripe fruit, sergeant."

However, he found love-making in his own fashion so pleasant that, not content with carrying Mrs. Vavasour's babies about all day long, he had several times to be gently turned out of the nursery, where he wanted to assist in washing and dressing them, on the ground that an old soldier could turn his hand to anything.

So slipped away a fortnight and more, during which Valentia was the cynosure of all eyes, and knew it also: for Claude Mellot, half to amuse her, and half to tease Elsley, made her laugh many a time by retailing little sayings and doings in her praise and dispraise, picked up from rich Manchester gentlemen, who would fain have married her without a penny, and from strong-minded Manchester ladies, who envied her beauty a little, and set her down, of course, as an empty-minded worldling, and a proud aristocrat. The majority of the reading-parties, meanwhile, thought a great deal more about Valentia than about their books. The Oxford men, it seemed, though of the same mind as the Cambridge men in considering her the model of all perfection, were divided as to their method of testifying the same. Two or three of them, who were given to that simpering and flirting tone with young ladies to which Oxford would-be-fine gentlemen are so pitiably prone, hung about the inn-door to ogle her; contrived always to be walking in the garden when she was there, dressed out as if for High Street at four o'clock on a May

afternoon; tormented Claude by fruitless attempts
to get from him an introduction, which he had
neither the right nor the mind to give; and at last
(so Bowie told Claude one night, and Claude told
the whole party next morning) tried to bribe and
flatter Valentia's maid into giving them a bit of
ribbon, or a cast-off glove, which had belonged to
the idol. Whereon that maiden, in virtuous indignation, told Mr. Bowie, and complained moreover
(as maids are bound to do to valets for whom they
have a *penchant*) of their having dared to compliment her on her own good looks: by which act
succeeded, of course, in making Mr. Bowie understand that other people still thought her pretty, if
he did not; and also in arousing in him that
jealousy which is often the best helpmate of sweet
love. So Mr. Bowie went forth in his might that
very evening, and finding two of the Oxford men,
informed them in plain Scotch, that, " Gin he
caught them, or any ither such skellums, philan-
dering after his leddies, or his leddies' maids, he'd
jist knock their empty pows togither." To which
there was no reply but silence; for Mr. Bowie stood
six feet four without his shoes, and had but the
week before performed, for the edification of the
Cambridge men, who held him in high honor, a
few old Guards' feats; such as cutting in two at one
sword-blow a suspended shoulder of mutton, lifting
a long table by his teeth, squeezing a quart pewter
pot flat between his fingers, and other little recrea-
tions of those who are " born unto Rapha."

But the Cantabs, and a couple of gallant Oxford
boating men who had fraternized with them, testi-
fied their admiration in their simple honest way,
by putting down their pipes whenever they saw

Valentia coming, and just lifting their hats when they met her close. It was taking a liberty, no doubt. "But I tell you, Mellot," said Wynd, as brave and pure-minded a fellow as ever pulled in the University eight, "the Arabs, when they see such a creature, say, 'Praise Allah for beautiful women,' and quite right; they may remind some fellows of worse things, but they always remind me of heaven and the angels; and my hat goes off to her by instinct, just as it does when I go into a church."

That was all; simple chivalrous admiration, and delight in her loveliness, as in that of a lake, or a mountain sunset; but nothing more. The good fellows had no time, indeed, to fancy themselves in love with her, or her with them, for every day was too short for them; what with reading all the morning, and starting out in the afternoon in strange garments (which became shabbier and more ragged very rapidly as the weeks slipped on) upon all manner of desperate errands; walking unheard-of distances, and losing their way upon the mountains; scrambling cliffs, and now and then falling down them; camping all night by unpronounceable lakes, in the hope of catching mythical trout; trying in all ways how hungry, thirsty, dirty, and tired a man could make himself, and how far he could go without breaking his neck, any approach to which catastrophe was hailed (as were all other mishaps) as "all in the day's work," and "the finest fun in the world," by that unconquerable English "lebensglückseligkeit," which is a perpetual wonder to our sober German cousins. Ah, glorious twenty-one, with your inexhaustible powers of doing and enjoying, eating and hungering, sleeping and sitting up, reading and playing! Happy are those who still possess you, and can take their fill of your golden cup, steadied, but not saddened, by the remembrance, that for all things a good and loving God will bring them into judgment. Happier still those who (like a few) retain in body and soul he health and buoyancy of twenty-one on to the very verge of forty, and seeming to grow younger-hearted as they grow older-headed, can cast off care and work at a moment's warning, laugh and frolic now as they did twenty years ago, and say with Wordsworth —

> " So was it when my life began . . .
> So be it when I shall grow old,
> Or let me die !"

Unfortunately, as will appear hereafter, Elsley's especial *bêtes noirs* were this very Wynd and his inseparable companion, Naylor, who happened to be not only the best men of the set, but Mellot's especial friends. Both were Rugby men, now reading for their degree. Wynd was a Shropshire squire's son, a lissom fair-haired man, the handiest of boxers, rowers, riders, shots, fishermen, with a noisy superabundance of animal spirits, which maddened Elsley. Yet Wynd had sentiment in his way, though he took good care never to show it Elsley; could repeat Tennyson from end to end; spouted the "Mort d'Arthur" up hill and down dale, and chanted rapturously, " Come into the garden, Maud ! " while he expressed his opinion of Maud's lover in terms more forcible than delicate. Naylor, fidus Achates, was a Gloucestershire parson's son, a huge heavy-looking man, with a thick curling lip and a sleepy eye; but he had brains enough to become a first-rate classic; and in that same sleepy eye and heavy lip lay an infinity of quiet humor; racy old country stories, quaint scraps of out-of-the-way learning, jovial old ballads, which he sang with the mellowest of voices, and a slang vocabulary, which made him the dread of all bargees from Newnham pool to Upware. Him also Elsley hated, because Naylor looked always as if he was laughing at him, which indeed he was.

And the worst was, that Elsley had always to face them both at once. If Wynd vaulted over a gate into his very face, with a "How d'ye do, Mr. Vavasour? Had any verses this morning?" in the same tone as if he had asked, "Had any sport?" Naylor's round face was sure to look over the stone-wall, pipe in mouth, with a "Don't disturb the gentleman, Tom; don't you see he's a composing of his rhymes?" in a strong provincial dialect put on for the nonce. In fact, the two young rogues, having no respect whatsoever for genius, perhaps because they had each of them a little genius of their own, made a butt of the poet, as soon as they found out that he was afraid of them.

But worse *bêtes noirs* than either Wynd or Naylor were on their way to fill up the cup of Elsley's discomfort. And at last, without a note of warning, appeared in Beddgelert a phenomenon which rejoiced some hearts, but perturbed also the spirits not only of the Oxford "philanderers," but those of Elsley Vavasour, and, what is more, of Valentia herself.

She was sitting one evening at the window with Lucia, looking out into the village and the pleasure-grounds before the hotel. They were both laughing and chatting over the groups of tourists in their pretty Irish way, just as they had done when they were girls; for Lucia's heart was expanding under the quiet beauty of the place, the freedom from household care, and what was more, from money anxieties; for Valentia had slipped into her hand a cheque for fifty pounds from Scoutbush, and assured her that he would be quite angry if she spoke of paying the rent of the rooms; Elsley was mooning down the river by himself; Claude was entertaining his Cambridge acquaintances, as he did every night, with his endless fun and sentiment. Gradually the tourists slipped in one by one, as the last rays of the sun faded off the peaks of Aran, and the mist settled down upon the dark valley beneath, and darkness fell upon that rock-girdled paradise; when up to the door below there drove a car, at sight whereof out rushed, not waiters only and landlady, but Mr. Bowie himself, who helped out a very short figure in a pea-jacket and a shining boating hat, and then a very tall one in a wild shooting-coat and a military cap.

"My brother and *mon Saint Père !* Lucia! too delightful! This is why they did not write." And Valentia sprang up, and was going to run downstairs to them, when she paused at Lucia's call.

"Who have they with them? Val, — come and look! who can it be?"

Campbell and Bowie were helping out carefully a tall man, covered up in many wrappers. It was too dark to see the face; but a fancy crossed Valentia's mind which made her look grave, in spite of her pleasure.

He was evidently weak, as from recent illness; for his two supporters led him up the steps, and Scoutbush seemed full of directions and inquiries, and fussed about with the landlady, till she was tired of curtseying to " my lord."

A minute afterwards Bowie threw open the door grandly. " My lord, my ladies! " and in trotted Scoutbush, and began kissing them fiercely, and then dancing about.

" O my dears! Here at last — out of that horrid city of the plague! Such sights as I have seen —— " and then he paused. " Do you know, Val and Lucia, I'm glad I've seen it; I don't know, but I feel as if I should be a better man all my life; and those poor people, how well they did behave! And the major, he's an angel! And so's that brick of a doctor, and the mad schoolmistress, and the curate. Everybody, I think, but me. Hang it, Val! but your words sha'n't come true! I will be of some use yet before I die! But I've —— " and Valentia went up to him and kissed him, while he ran on, and Lucia said :

" You have been of use already, dear Fred. You have sent me and the dear children to this sweet place, where we have been safer and happier than —— " (she checked herself) ; " and your generous present too. I feel quite a girl again, thanks to you. Val and I have done nothing but laugh all day long; " and she began kissing him too.

> " How happy could I be with either,
> Were t' other dear charmer away!"

broke out Scoutbush. " What a pity it is now, that I should have two such sweet creatures making love to me, and can't marry either of them? Why did ye go and be my father's daughters, mavourneen? I'd have made a peeress of the one of ye, if ye'd had the sense to be anybody else's sisters"

At which they all laughed, and laughed, and chattered broad Irish together as they used to do for fun in old Kilnbaggan Castle, before Lucia was a weary wife, and Valentia a worldly fine lady, and Scoutbush a rackety guardsman, breaking half of the ten commandments every week, rather from ignorance than vice

"Well, I'm glad ye're pleased with me, asthore," said he at last to Lucia; "but I've done another good little deed, I flatter myself; for I've brought away the poor spalpeen of a priest, and have got him safe in the house."

Valentia stopped short in her fun.

"Why, what have ye to say against that, Miss Val?"

"Why, won't he be a little in the way?" said Valentia, not knowing what to say.

"Faith, he needn't trouble you; and I shall take very good care — I wonder when the supper is coming — that neither he nor any one else troubles me. But really," said he, in his natural voice, and with some feeling, "I was ashamed to go away and leave him there. He would have died if we had. He worked day and night. Talk of saints and martyrs! Campbell himself said he was an idler by the side of him."

"Oh! I hope Major Campbell has not over-exerted himself!"

"He? nothing hurts him. He's as hard as his own sword. But the poor curate worked on till he got the cholera himself. He always expected it, longed for it; Campbell said — wanted to die. Some love affair, I suppose, poor fellow! and a terrible bout he had for eight-and-forty hours. Thurnall thought him gone again and again; but he pulled the poor fellow through, after all; and we got some one (that is, Campbell did) to take his duty; and brought him away, after a good deal of persuasion; for he would not move as long as there was a fresh case in the town; that is why we never wrote. We did not know till the last hour when we should start; and we expected to be with you in two days, and give you a pleasant surprise. He was half dead when we got him on board; but the week's sea-air helped him through; so I must not grumble at these northerly breezes. ' It's an ill wind that blows nobody good,' they say!'"

Valentia heard all this as in a dream, and watched her chattering brother with a stupefied air. She comprehended all now; and bitterly she blamed herself. He had really loved her, then: set himself manfully to die at his post, that he might forget her in a better world. How shamefully she had trifled with that noble heart! How should she ever meet — how have courage to look him in the face? And not love, or anything like love, but sacred pity and self-abasement filled her heart, as his fair, delicate face rose up before her, all wan and shrunken, with sad upbraiding eyes; and round it such a halo, pure and pale, as crowns, in some old German picture, a martyr's head.

"He has had the cholera! he has been actually dying?" asked she at last, with that strange wish to hear over again bad news, which one knows too well already.

"Of course he has. Why, you are not going away, Valentia? You need not be afraid of infection. Campbell, and Thurnall, too, says that's all nonsense; and they must know, having seen it so often. Here comes Bowie at last with supper!"

"Has Mr. Headley had anything to eat?" asked Valentia, who longed to run away to her own room, but dared not.

"He is eating now like any ged, ma'am; and Major Campbell's making him eat too."

"He must be very ill," thought she, "for *mon Saint Père* never to have come near us yet:" and then she thought with terror that her *Saint Père* might have guessed the truth, and be angry with her. And yet she trusted in Frank's secrecy. He would not betray her.

Take care, Valentia. When a woman has to trust a man not to betray her, and does trust him, she may soon find it not only easy, but necessary, to do more than trust him.

However, in five minutes Campbell came in. Valentia saw at once that there was no change in his feelings to her: but he could talk of nothing but Headley, his self-devotion, courage, angelic gentleness, and humility; and every word of his praise was a fresh arrow in Valentia's conscience; at last:

"One knows well enough what is the matter," said he, almost bitterly; "what is the matter, I sometimes think, with half the noblest men in the world, and nine-tenths of the noblest women; and with many a one, too, God help them! who is none of the noblest, and therefore does not know how to take the bitter cup, as he knows —— "

"What does the philosopher mean now?" asked

Scoutbush, looking up from the cold lamb. Valentia knew but too well what he meant.

"He has a history, my dear lord."

"A history? What! is he writing a book?"

Campbell laughed a quiet under-laugh, half sad, half humorous.

"I am very tired," said Valentia; "I really think I shall go to bed."

She went to her room, but to bed she did not go; she sat down and cried till she could cry no more, and lay awake the greater part of the night, tossing miserably. She would have done better if she had prayed; but prayer, about such a matter, was what Valentia knew nothing of. She was regular enough at church, of course, and said her prayers and confessed her sins in a general way, and prayed about her "soul," as she had been taught to do, — unless she was too tired: but to pray really, about a real sorrow, a real sin like this, was a thought which never entered her mind; and if it had, she would have driven it away again: just because the anxiety was so real, practical, human, it was a matter which had nothing to do with religion; which it seemed impertinent — almost wrong to lay before the throne of God.

So she came downstairs next morning, pale, restless, unrefreshed in body or mind; and her peace of mind was not improved by seeing, seated at the breakfast-table, Frank Headley, whom Lucia and Scoutbush were stuffing with all manner of good things.

She blushed scarlet — do what she would she could not help it — when he rose and bowed to her. Half-choked, she came forward and offered her hand. She was "so shocked to hear that he had been so dangerously ill,—no one had even told them of it,—it had come upon them so suddenly;" and so forth.

She spoke kindly, but avoided the least tone of tenderness; for she felt that if she gave way, she might be only too tender; and to re-awaken hope in his heart would be only cruelty. And, therefore, and for other reasons also, she did not look him in the face as she spoke.

He answered so cheerfully that she was half disappointed, in spite of her remorse, at his not being as miserable as she had expected. Still, if he had overcome the passion, it was so much better for him. But yet Valentia hardly wished that he should have overcome it, so self-contradictory is woman's heart; and her pity had sunk to half-ebb, and her self-complacency was rising with a flowing tide, as he chatted on quietly, but genially, about the voyage, and the scenery, and Snowdon, which he had never seen, and which he would ascend that very day.

"You will do nothing of the kind, Mr. Headley!" cried Lucia. "Is he not mad, Major Campbell, quite mad?"

"I know I am mad, my dear Mrs. Vavasour; I have been so a long time: but Snowdon ponies are in their sober senses—and I shall take one of them."

"Fulfil the old pun? Begin beside yourself, and end beside your horse! I am sure he is not strong enough to sit over those rocks. No, you shall stay at home comfortably here: Valentia and I will take care of you."

"And *mon Saint Père* too. I have a thousand things to say to him."

"And so has he to Queen Whims."

So Scoutbush sent Bowie for "John Jones Clerk," the fisherman (may his days be as many as his salmon and as good as his flies!) and the four stayed at home, and talked over the Aberalva tragedies, till, as it befell, both Lucia and Campbell left the room awhile.

Immediately Frank rose, and walking across to Valentia, laid the fatal ring on the arm of her chair, and returned to his seat without a word.

"You are very ——. I hope that it ——," stammered Valentia.

"You hope that it was a comfort to me? It was; and I shall be always grateful to you for it."

Valentia heard an emphasis on the "was." It checked the impulse (foolish enough) which rose in her, to bid him keep the ring.

So, prim and dignified, she slipped it into its place on her finger, and went on with her work; merely saying:

"I need not say that I am happy that anything which I could do should have been of use to you in such a fearful time."

"It was a fearful time! but for myself, I cannot be too glad of it. God grant that it may have been as useful to others as to me! It cured me of a great folly. Now I look back, I am astonished at my own absurdity, rudeness, presumption. You must let me say it! I do not know how to thank you enough. I cannot trust myself with the fit words, they would be so strong! but I owe this confession to you, and to your exceeding goodness and kindness, when you would have been justified in treating me as a madman. I was mad, I believe: but I am in my right mind now, I assure you," said he, gaily. "Had I not been, I need hardly say you would not have seen me here. What a prospect this is!" And he rose and looked out of the window.

Valentia had heard all this with downcast eyes and unmoved face. Was she pleased at it? Not in the least, the naughty child that she was; and more, she grew quite angry with herself, ashamed of herself, for having thought and felt so much about him the night before. "How silly of me! He is very well, and does not care for me. And who is he, pray, that I should even look at him?"

And, as if in order to put her words into practice, she looked at him there and then. He was gazing out of the window, leaning gracefully and yet feebly against the shutter with the full glory of the forenoon sun upon his sharp-cut profile and rich chestnut locks; and after all, having looked at him once, she could not help looking at him again. He was certainly a most gentleman-like man, elegant from head to foot; there was not an ungraceful line about him, to his very boots, and the white nails of his slender fingers; even the defects of his figure — the too great length of the neck and slope of the shoulders — increased his likeness to those saintly pictures with which he had been mixed up in her mind the night before. He was at one extreme pole of the different types of manhood, and that burly doctor who had saved his life at the other: but her *Saint Père* alone perfectly combined the two. There was nobody like him, after all. Perhaps her wisest plan, as Headley had forgotten his fancy, was to confess all to the *Saint Père* (as she usually did her little sins), and get some sort of absolution from him.

However, she must say something in answer:

"Yes, it is a very lovely view: but really I must say one more word about this matter. I have to thank you, you know, for the good faith which you have kept with me."

He looked round, seemingly amused. "*Cela va sans dire !*" and he bowed; "pray do not say any more about the matter;" and he looked at her with such humble and thankful eyes, that Valentia was sorry not to hear more from him than:

"Pray tell me — for of course you know — the name of this exquisite valley up which I am looking."

"Gwynnant. You must go up it when you are well enough, and see the lakes; they are the only ones in Snowdon from the banks of which the primæval forest has not disappeared."

"Indeed? I must make shift to go there this very afternoon, for — do not laugh at me — but I never saw a lake in my life."

"Never saw a lake?"

"No. I am a true Lowlander: born and bred among bleak Norfolk sands and fens — so much the worse for this chest of mine; and this is my first sight of mountains. It is all like a dream to me, and a dream which I never expected to be realized."

"Ah, you should see our Irish lakes and mountains — you should see Killarney !"

"I am content with these; I suppose it is as wrong to break the tenth commandment about scenery, as about anything else."

"Ah, but it seems so hard that you, who I am sure would appreciate fine scenery, should have been debarred from it, while hundreds of stupid people run over the Alps and Italy every summer, and come home, as far as I can see, rather more stupid than they went; having made confusion worse confounded by filling their poor brains with hard names out of Murray."

"Not quite so hard as that thousands, every day, who would enjoy a neat dinner, should have nothing but dry bread, and not enough of that. I fancy sometimes, that in some mysterious way, that want will be made up to them in the next life; and so with all the beautiful things which travelled people talk of — I comfort myself with the fancy that I see as much as is good for me here, and that if I make good use of that, I shall see the Alps and the Andes in the world to come, or something much more worth seeing. Tell me now, how far may that range of crags be from us? I am sure that I could walk there after luncheon, this mountain air is strengthening me so."

"Walk thither? I assure you they are at least four miles off."

"Four? And I thought them one! So clear and sharp as they stand out against the sky, one fancies that one could almost stretch out a hand and touch those knolls and slabs of rock, as distinct as in a photograph; and yet so soft and rich withal, dappled with pearly-gray stone and purple heath. Ah! So it must be, I suppose. The first time that one sees a glorious thing, one's heart is lifted up towards it in love and awe, till it seems near to one — ground on which one may freely tread, because one appreciates and admires; and so one forgets the distance between its grandeur and one's own littleness."

The allusion was palpable: but did he intend it?

Surely not, after what he had just said. And yet there was a sadness in the tone which made Valentia fancy that some feeling for her might still linger; but he evidently had been speaking to himself, forgetful, for the moment, of her presence; for he turned to her with a start and a blush — "But now — I have been troubling you too long with this stupid *tête-à-tête* sentimentality of mine. I will make my bow, and find the major. I am afraid, if it be possible for him to forget any one, he has forgotten me in some new moss or other."

He went out, and to Valentia's chagrin she saw him no more that day. He spent the forenoon in the garden, and the afternoon in lying down, and at night complained of fatigue, and stayed in his own room the whole evening, while Campbell read him to sleep. Next morning, however, he made his appearance at breakfast, well and cheerful.

"I must play at sick man no more, or I shall rob you, I see, of Major Campbell's company; and I owe you all far too much already."

"Unless you are better than you were last night, you must play at sick man," said the major. "I cannot conceive what exhausted you so; unless you ladies are better nurses, I must let no one come near him but myself. If you had been scolding him the whole morning, instead of praising him as he deserves, he could not have been more tired last night."

"Pray do not!" cried Frank, evidently much pained: "I had such a delightful morning, and every one is so kind — you only make me wretched, when I feel all the trouble I am giving."

"My dear fellow," said Scoutbush, *en grand*

sérieux, " after all that you have done for our people at Aberalva, I should be very much shocked if any of my family thought any service shown to you a trouble."

"Pray do not speak so," said Frank, "I am fallen among angels when I least expected."

"Scoutbush as an angel!" shouted Lucia, clapping her hands. "Elsley, don't you see the wings sprouting already, under his shooting-jacket?"

"They are my braces, I suppose, of course." said Scoutbush, who never understood a joke about himself, though he liked one about other people; while Elsley, who hated all jokes, made no answer — at least none worth recording. In fact, as the reader may have discovered, Elsley, save *tête-à-tête* with some one who took his fancy, was somewhat of a silent and morose animal, and, as little Scoutbush confided to Mellot, there was no getting a rise out of him. All which Lucia saw as keenly as any one, and tried to pass off by chatting nervously and fussily for him, as well as for herself; whereby she only made him the more cross, for he could not the least understand her argument — "Why, my dear, if you don't talk to people, I must!"

"But why should people be talked to?"

"Because they like it, and expect it!"

"The more foolish they. Much better to hold their tongues and think."

"Or read your poetry, I suppose," and then would begin a squabble.

Meanwhile there was one, at least, of the party, who was watching Lucia with most deep and painful interest. Lord Scoutbush was too busy with his own comforts, especially with his fishing, to think much of this moroseness of Elsley's. " If he suited Lucia, very well. His taste and hers differed : but it was her concern, not his " — was a very easy way of freeing himself from all anxiety on the matter : but not so with Major Campbell. He saw all this ; and knew enough of human nature to suspect that the self-seeking which showed as moroseness in company, might show as downright bad temper in private. Longing to know more of Elsley, if possible, to guide and help him, he tried to be intimate with him, as he had tried at Aberalva ; paid him court, asked his opinion, talked to him on all subjects which he thought would interest him. His conclusion was more favorable to Elsley's head than to his heart. He saw that Elsley was vain, and liked his attentions ; and that lowered him in his eyes : but he saw too that Elsley shrank from him ; at first he thought it pride, but he soon found that it was fear ; and that lowered him still more in his eyes.

Perhaps Campbell was too hard on the poet : but his own purity itself told against Elsley. "Who am I, that any one should be afraid of me, unless they have done something wrong?" So, with his dark suspicions roused, he watched intently every word and every tone of Elsley's to his wife ; and here he came to a more unpleasant conclusion still. He saw that they were, sometimes at least, not happy together ; and from this he took for granted, too hastily, that they were never happy together ; that Lucia was an utterly ill-used person ; that Elsley was a bad fellow, who ill-treated her : and a black and awful indignation against the man grew up within him ; all the more fierce because it seemed utterly righteous, and because, too, it had, under heavy penalties, to be utterly concealed beneath a courteous and genial manner: till many a t me he felt inclined to knock Elsley down for little roughnesses to her, which were really the fruit of mere *gaucherie ;* and then accused himself for a hypocri e, because he was keeping up the courtesies of life with such a man. For Campbell, like most n en of his temperament, was over-stern, and someti nes a little cruel and unjust, in demanding of othe s the same lofty code which he had laid down for himself, and in demanding it, too, of some more than of others, by a very questionable exercise of private judgment. On the whole, he was right, no doubt, in being as indulgent as he dared to the publicans and sinners like Scoutbush ; and in being as severe as he dared on all Pharisees, and pretentious persons whatsoever: but he was too much inclined to draw between the two classes one of those strong lines of demarcation which exist only in the fancies of the human brain; for sins, like all diseased matters, are complicated and confused matters; many a seeming Pharisee is at heart a self-condemned publican, and ought to be comforted, and not cursed; while many a publican is, in the midst of all his foul sins, a thorough exclusive and self-complacent Pharisee, and needs not the right hand of mercy, but the strong arm of punishment.

Campbell, like other men, had his faults: and his were those of a man wrapped up in a pure and stately, but an austere and lonely creed, disgusted with the world in all its forms, and looking down upon men in general nearly as much as Thurnall did. So he set down Elsley for a bad man, to whom he was forced by hard circumstances to behave as if he were a good one.

The only way, therefore, in which he could vent his feeling, was by showing to Lucia that studied attention which sympathy and chivalry demand of a man toward an injured woman. Not that he dared, or wished, to conduct himself with her as he did with Valentia, even had she not been a married woman; he did not know her as intimately as he did her sister: but still he had a right to behave as the most intimate friend of her family, and he asserted that right; and all the more determinedly because Elsley seemed now and then not to like it. "I will teach him how to behave to a charming woman," said he to himself; and perhaps he had been wiser if he had not said it: but every man has his weak point, and chivalry was Major Campbell's.

"What do you think of that poet, Mellot?" said he once, on returning from a picnic, during which Elsley had never noticed his wife; and at last, finding Valentia engaged with Headley, had actually gone off, *pour pis aller*, to watch Lord Scoutbush fishing.

"Oh, clever enough, and to spare; and as well read a man as I know. One of the *Sturm-und-Drang* party, of course; the express locomotive school, scream-and-go-ahead: and thinks me, with my classicism, a benighted pagan. Still, every man has a right to his opinion. Live and let live."

"I don't care about his taste," said the major, impatiently. "What sort of man is he? — man, Claude?"

"Ahem, humph! '*Irritabile genus poetarum.*' But one is so accustomed to that among literary men, one never expects them to be like anybody else, and so takes their whims and oddities for granted."

" And their sins, too, eh?"

"Sins? I know of none on his part."

" Don't you call temper a sin?"

" No; I call it a determination of blood to the
head, or of animal spirts to the wrong place, or—
my dear major, I am no moralist. I take people,
you know, as I find them. But he is a bore; and
I should not wonder if that sweet little woman had
found it out ere now."

Campbell ground something between his teeth.
He fancied himself full of righteous wrath: he was
really in a very unchristian temper. Be it so:
perhaps there were excuses for him (as there are
for many men), of which we know nothing.

Elsley, meanwhile, watched Campbell with fast
lowering brow. Losing a woman's affections? He
who does so deserves his fate. Had he been in
the habit of paying proper attention to Lucia, he
would have liked Campbell all the more for his
conduct. There are few greater pleasures to a
man who is what he should be to his wife, than to
see other men admiring what he admires, and trying to rival him where he knows that he can have
no rival. Let them worship as much as they will.
Let her make herself as charming to them as she
can. What matter? He smiles at them in his
heart; for has he not, over and above all the
pretty things which he can say and do ten times as
well as they, a talisman—a dozen talismans which
are beyond their reach?—in the strength of which
he will go home and laugh over with her, amid
sacred caresses, all which makes mean men mad?
But Elsley, alas for him, had neglected Lucia himself, and therefore dreaded comparison with any
other man; and the suspicions which had taken

root in him at Aberalva grew into ugly shape and strength. However, he was silent, and contented himself with coldness and all but rudeness.

There were excuses for him. In the first place, it would have been an ugly thing to take notice of any man's attentions to a wife; it could not be done but upon the strongest grounds, and done in a way which would make a complete rupture necessary, so breaking up the party in a sufficiently unpleasant way. Besides, to move in the matter at all would be to implicate Lucia; for of whatsoever kind Campbell's attentions were, she evidently liked them; and a quarrel with her on that score was more than Elsley dared face. He was not a man of strong moral courage; he hated a scene of any kind; and he was afraid of being worsted in any really serious quarrel, not merely by Campbell, but by Lucia. It may seem strange that he should be afraid of her, though not so that he should be afraid of Campbell. But the truth is, that the man who bullies his wife very often does so — as Elsley had done more than once — simply to prove to himself his own strength, and hide his fear of her. He knew well that woman's tongue, when once the " fair beast " is brought to bay, is a weapon far too trenchant to be faced by any shield but that of a very clear conscience toward her; which was more than Elsley had.

Besides — and it is an honor to Elsley Vavasour, amid all his weakness, that he had justice and chivalry enough left to know what nine men out of ten ignore — behind all, let the worst come to the worst, lay one just and terrible rejoinder, which he, though he had been no worse than the average of men, could only answer by silent shame:

"At least, sir, I was pure when I came to you! You best know whether you were so likewise."

And yet even that, so all-forgiving is woman, might have been faced by some means; but the miserable complication about the false name still remained. Elsley believed that he was in his wife's power; that she could, if she chose, turn upon him, and proclaim him to the world as a scoundrel and an impostor. And, as it is of the nature of man to hate those whom he fears, Elsley began to have dark and ugly feelings toward Lucia. Instead of throwing them away, as a strong man would have done, he pampered them almost without meaning to do so. For he let them run riot through his too vivid imagination, in the form of possible speeches, possible scenes, till he had looked and looked through a hundred thoughts which no man has a right to entertain for a moment. True; he had entertained them with horror; but he ought not to have entertained them at all; he ought to have kicked them contemptuously out and back to the devil, from whence they came. It may be, again, that this is impossible to man; that prayer is the only refuge against that Walpurgis-dance of the witches and the fiends, which will, at hapless moments, whirl unbidden through a mortal brain; but Elsley did not pray.

So, leaving these fancies in his head too long, he soon became accustomed to them; and accustomed, too, to the Nemesis which they bring with them, of chronic moodiness and concealed rage. Day by day he was lashing himself up into fresh fury, and yet day by day he was becoming more careful to conceal that fury. He had many reasons: moral cowardice, which made him shrink from the tremendous consequences of an explosion — equally tremendous, were he right or wrong. Then the secret hope, perhaps the secret consciousness, that he was wrong, and was only saying to God, like the self-deceiving prophet, "I do well to be angry;" then the honest fear of going too far; of being surprised at last into some hideous and irreparable speech or deed, which he might find out too late was utterly unjust; then at moments (for even that would cross him) the devilish notion that, by concealment, he might lure Lucia on to give him a safe ground for attack. All these, and more, tormented him for a wretched fortnight, during which he became, at such an expense of self-control as he had not exercised for years, courteous to Campbell, more than courteous to Lucia; hiding under a smiling face wrath which increased with the pressure brought to bear upon it.

Campbell and Lucia, Mellot, Valentia, and Frank, utterly deceived, went on more merrily than ever, little dreaming that they walked and talked daily with a man who was fast becoming glad to flee to the pit of hell, but for the fear that "God would be there also."

They, meanwhile, chatted on, enjoying, as human souls are allowed to do at rare and precious moments, the mere sensation of being; of which they would talk at times in a way which led them down into deep matters; for instance :

" How pleasant to sit here for ever ! " said Claude, one afternoon, in the inn garden at Beddgelert, "and say, not with Descartes, ' I think, therefore I exist; ' but simply, ' I enjoy, therefore I exist.'

I almost think those Emersonians are right at times when they crave the 'life of plants, and stones, and rain.' Stangrave said to me once, tha his ideal of perfect bliss was that of an oyster in the Indian seas, drinking the warm salt wate motionless, and troubling himself about nothing while nothing troubled itself about him."

"Till a diver came and tore him up for the sake of his pearls!" said Valentia.

"He did not intend to contain any pearls. A pearl, you know, is a disease of the oyster, the product of some irritation. He wished to be the oyster pure and simple, a part of nature."

"And to be of no use?" asked Frank.

"Of none whatsoever. Nature had made him what he was, and all besides was her business, and not his. I don't deny that I laughed at him, and made him wroth by telling him that his doctrine was 'the apotheosis of loafing.' But my heart went with him, and the jolly oyster too. It is very beautiful after all, that careless nymph and shepherd life of the old Greeks, and that Marquesas romance of Herman Melville's — to enjoy the simple fact of living, like a Neapolitan lazzaroni, or a fly upon a wall."

"But the old Greek heroes fought and labored to till the land, and rid it of giants and monsters," said Frank. "And as for the Marquesas, Mr. Melville found out, did he not — as you did once — that they were only petting and fattening him for the purpose of eating him? There is a dark side to that pretty picture, Mr. Mellot."

"*Tant pis pour eux!* But that is an unnecessary appendage to the idea, surely. It must be possible to realize such a simple, rich, healthy life, without wickedness, if not without human sorrow. It is no dream, and no one shall rob me of it. I have seen fragments of it scattered up and down the world; and I believe they will all meet in Paradise — where and when I care not; but they will meet. I was very happy in the South Sea Islands, after that, when nobody meant to eat me; and I am very happy here, and do not intend to be eaten, unless it will be any pleasure to Miss St. Just. No; let man enjoy himself when he can, and take his fill of those flaming red geraniums, and glossy rhododendrons, and feathered crown ferns, and the gold green lace of those acacias tossing and whispering overhead, and the purple mountains sleeping there aloft, and the murmur of the brook over the stones: and drink in scents with every breath — what was his nose made for, save to smell? I used to torment myself once by asking them all what they meant. Now, I am content to have done with symbolisms, and say, 'What you all mean, I care not, all I know is, that I can draw pleasure from the mere sight of you, as, perhaps, you do from the mere sight of me; so let us sit together, nature and I, and stare into each other's eyes like two young lovers, careless of the morrow and its griefs.' I will not even take the trouble to paint her. Why make ugly copies of perfect pictures? Let those who wish to see her take a railway ticket, and save us academicians colors and canvas. *Quant à moi*, the public must go to the mountains, as Mahomet had to do; for the mountains shall not come to the public."

"One of your wilful paradoxes, Mr. Mellot; why, you are photographing them all day long."

"Not quite all day long, madam. And after all, *il faut vivre:* I want a few luxuries; I have no capacity for keeping a shop; photographing pays better than painting, considering the time it takes and it is only nature reproducing herself, no caricaturing her. But if any one will ensure me a poor two thousand a year, I will promise to photograph no more but vanish to Sicily or Calabria, and sit with Sabina in an orchard all my days, twining rose garlands for her pretty head like Theocritus and his friends, while the 'pears drop on our shoulders, and the apples by our side.'"

"What do you think of all this?" asked Valentia of Frank.

"That I am too like the Emersonian oyster here, very happy, and very useless; and, therefore, very anxious to be gone."

"Surely you have earned the right to be idle awhile?"

"No one has a right to be idle."

"Oh!" groaned Claude; "where did you find that eleventh commandment?"

"I have done with all eleventh commandments; for I find it quite hard work enough to keep the ancient ten. But I find it, Mellot, in the deepest abyss of all; in the very depth from which the commandments sprang. But we will not talk about it here."

"Why not?" asked Valentia, looking up. "Are we so very naughty as to be unworthy to listen?"

"And are these mountains," asked Claude, "so ugly and ill-made that they are an unfit pulpit for a sermon? No; tell me what you mean. After all, I am half in jest."

"Do not courtesy, pity, chivalry, generosity,

self-sacrifice — in short, being of use — do not our hearts tell us that they are the most beautiful, noble, lovely things in the world?"

"I suppose it is so," said Valentia.

"Why does one admire a soldier? Not for his epaulettes and red coat, but because one knows that, coxcomb though he be at home here, there is the power in him of that same self-sacrifice; that, when he is called, he will go and die, that he may be of use to his country. And yet — it may seem invidious to say so just now — but there are other sorts of self-sacrifice, less showy, but even more beautiful."

"O Mr. Headley, what can a man do more than die for his countrymen?"

"Live for them. It is a longer work, and therefore a more difficult and a nobler one."

Frank spoke in a somewhat sad and abstracted tone.

"But tell me," she said, "what all this has to do with — with the deep matter of which you spoke?"

"Simply that it is the law of all earth, and heaven, and Him who made them. That God is perfectly powerful, because He is perfectly and infinitely of use; and perfectly good, because He delights utterly and always in being of use; and that, therefore, we can become like God — as the very heathens felt that we can, and ought to become — only in proportion as we become of use. I did not see it once. I tried to be good, not knowing what good meant. I tried to be good, because I thought it would pay me in the world to come. But, at last, I saw that all life, all devotion, all piety, were only worth anything, only Divine,

and God-like, and God-beloved, as they were
means to that one end — to be of use."

"It is a noble thought, Headley," said Claude,
but Valentia was silent.

"It is a noble thought, Mellot, and all thoughts
become clear in the light of it; even that most
difficult thought of all, which so often torments
good people, when they feel, 'I ought to love
God, and yet I do not love Him.' Easy to love
Him, if one can once think of Him as the concen-
tration, the ideal perfection of all which is most
noble, admirable, lovely in human character! And
easy to work, too, when one once feels that one is
working for such a Being, and with such a Being
as that! The whole world round us, and the
future of the world, too, seem full of light, even
down to its murkiest and foulest depths, when we
can but remember that great idea, — an infinitely
useful God over all, who is trying to make each of
us useful in his place. If that be not the beatific
vision of which old mystics spoke so rapturously,
one glimpse of which was perfect bliss, I at least
know none nobler, desire none more blessed.
Pray forgive me, Miss St. Just! I ought not to
intrude thus!"

"Go on!" said Valentia.

"I — I really have no more to say. I have said
too much. I do not know how I have been betrayed so far," stammered Frank, who had the just
dislike of his school of anything like display on
such solemn matters.

"Can you tell us too much truth? Mr. Headley is right, Mr. Mellot, and you are wrong."

"It will not be the first time, Miss St. Just. But
what I spoke in jest, he has answered in earnest"

"He was quite right. We are none of us half earnest enough. There is Lucia with the children." And she rose and walked across the garden.

"You have moved the fair trifler somewhat," said Claude.

"God grant it! but I cannot think what made me."

"Why think? You spoke out nobly, and I shall not forget your sermon."

"I was not preaching at you, most affectionate and kindly of men."

"And laziest of men, likewise. What can I do now, at this moment, to be of use to any one? Set me my task."

But Frank was following with his eyes Valentia, as she went hurriedly across to Lucia. He saw her take two of the children at once off her sister's hands, and carry them away down a walk. A few minutes afterwards he could hear her romping with them; but he could not have guessed, from the silver din of those merry voices, that Valentia's heart was heavy within her.

For her conscience was really smitten. Of what use was she in the world? Major Campbell had talked to her often about her duties to this person and to that, of this same necessity of being useful; but she had escaped from the thought, as we have seen her, in laughing at poor little Scoutbush on the very same score. But why had not Major Campbell's sermons touched her heart as this one had? Who can tell? Who is there among us to whom an oft-heard truth has not become a tiresome and superfluous common-place, till one day it has flashed before us utterly new, indubitable,

not to be disobeyed, written in letters of fire across
the whole vault of heaven! All one can say is,
that her time was not come. Besides, she looked
on Major Campbell as a being utterly superior to
herself; and that very superiority, while it allowed
her to be as familiar wi h him as she chose, excused
her in her own eyes fr)m opening to him her real
heart. She could safe ly jest with him, let him pet
her, play at being his daughter, while she felt that
between him and her lay a gulf as wide as between
earth and heaven: and that very notion comforted
her in her naughtiness. for in that case, of course,
his code of morals was not meant for her; and
while she took his warnings (as many of them at
least as she chose), she thought herself by no
means bound to follow his examples. She all but
worshipped him as her guardian angel: but she
was not meant for an angel herself; so she could
indulge freely in those little escapades and frivoli-
ties for which she was born, and then, whenever
frightened, run for shelter under his wings. But
to hear the same, and even loftier words, from the
lips of the curate, whom she had made her toy,
almost her butt, was to have them brought down
unexpectedly and painfully to her own level. If
this was his ideal, why ought it not to be hers?
Was she not his equal, perhaps his superior? And
so her very pride humbled her, as she said to herself, "Then I ought to be useful. I can be: I will
be!"

"Lucia," asked she, that very afternoon, "will
you let me take the children off your hands while
Clara is busy in the morning?"

"O you dear good creature! but it would be
such a *gêne!* They are really stupid, I am afraid,

sometimes, or else I am. They make me so miserably cross at times."

" I will take them. It would be a relief to you, would it not? "

" My dear! " said poor Lucia, with a doleful smile, which seemed to Valentia's self-accusing heart to say, " Have you only now discovered that fact? "

From that day Valentia courted Headley's company more and more. To fall in love with him was of course absurd; and he had cured himself of his passing fancy for her. There could be no harm, then, in her making the most of conversation so different from what she heard in the world, and which in her heart of hearts she liked so much better. For it was with Valentia as with all women; in this common fault of frivolity, as in most others, the men rather than they are to blame. Valentia had cultivated in herself those qualities which she saw admired by the men whom she met, and some one of whom, of course, she meant to marry; and as their female ideal was a butterfly ideal, a butterfly she became. But beneath all lay, deep and strong, the woman's love of nobleness and wisdom, the woman's longing to learn and to be led, which has shown itself in every age in so many a fantastic and even ugly shape, and which is their real excuse for the flirting with " geniuses," casting themselves at the feet of directors; which had tempted her to coquette with Elsley, and was now bringing her into " undesirable " intimacy with the poor curate.

She had heard that day, with some sorrow, his announcement that he wished to be gone; but as he did not refer to it again, she left the thought alone, and all but forgot it. The subject, however, was renewed about a week afterwards. "When you return to Aberalva," she had said, in reference to some commission.

"I shall never return to Aberalva."

"Not return?"

"No; I have already resigned the curacy. I believe your uncle has appointed to it the man whom Campbell found for me: and an excellent man, I hear, he is. At least he will do better there than I."

"But what could have induced you? How sorry all the people will be."

"I am not sure of that," said he, with a smile. "I did what I could at last to win back at least their respect, and to leave at least not hatred behind me: but I am unfit for them. I did not understand them. I meant — no matter what I meant; but I failed. God forgive me! I shall now go somewhere where I shall have simpler work to do; where I shall at least have a chance of practising the lesson which I learnt there. I learnt it all, strange to say, from the two people in the parish from whom I expected to learn least."

"Whom do you mean?"

"The doctor and the schoolmistress."

"Why from them less than from any in the parish? She so good, and he so clever?"

"That I shall never tell to any one now. Suffice it that I was mistaken."

Valentia could obtain no further answer; and so the days ran on, every one becoming more and more intimate, till a certain afternoon, on which they were all to go and picnic, under Claude's pilotage, above the lake of Gwynnant. Scoutbush was to have been with them; but a heavy day's rain in the meanwhile swelled the streams into fishing order; so the little man ordered a car, and started at three in the morning for Bettws with Mr. Bowie, who, however loth to give up the arrangements of plates and the extraction of champagne corks, considered his presence by the river-side a natural necessity.

" My dear Miss Clara, ye see, there 'll be no-body to see that his lordship pits on dry stock-ings; and he 's always getting over the tops of his water-boots, being young and daft, as we 've all been, and no offence to you; and to tell you truth, I can stand all temptations — in moderation, that is, — save an' except the chance o' cleiking a fish."

CHAPTER XX

THE spot which Claude had chosen for the picnic was on one of the lower spurs of that great mountain of The Maiden's Peak, which bounds the vale of Gwynnant to the south. Above, a wilderness of gnarled volcanic dykes and purple heather ledges; below, broken into glens, in which still linger pale green ash-woods, relics of that great primeval forest in which, in Bess's days, great Leicester used to rouse the hart with hound and horn.

Among these Claude had found a little lawn, guarded by great rocks, out of every cranny of which the ashes grew as freely as on flat ground. Their feet were bedded deep in sweet fern and wild raspberries, and golden-rod, and purple scabious, and tall blue campanulas. Above them, and before them, and below them, the ashes shook their green filigree in the bright sunshine; and through them glimpses were seen of the purple cliffs above, and, right in front, of the great cataract of Nant Gwynnant, a long snow-white line zigzagging down coal-black cliffs for many a hundred feet, and above it, depth beyond depth of purple shadow away into the very heart of Snowdon, up the long valley of Cwm-dyli, to the great amphitheatre of Clogwyn-y-Garnedd; while over all the cone of Snowdon rose, in perfect symmetry, between his attendant peaks of Lliwedd and Crib Coch.

There they sat, and laughed, and talked, the pleasant summer afternoon, in their pleasant summer bower; and never regretted the silence of the birds, so sweetly did Valentia's song go up in many a rich sad Irish melody; while the lowing of the milch kine, and the wild cooing of the herd-boys, came softly up from the vale below, "and all the air was filled with pleasant noise of waters."

Then Claude must needs photograph them all, as they sat, and group them first according to his fancy; and among his fancies was one, that Valentia should sit as queen, with Headley and the major at her feet. And Headley lounged there, and looked into the grass, and thought it well for him could he lie there for ever.

Then Claude must photograph the mountain itself; and all began to talk of it.

"See the breadth of light and shadow," said Claude; "how the purple depth of the great lap of the mountain is thrown back by the sheet of green light on Lliwedd, and the red glory on the cliffs of Crib Coch, till you seem to look away into the bosom of the hill, mile after mile."

"And so you do," said Headley. "I have learnt to distinguish mountain distances since I have been here. That peak is four miles from us now; and yet the shadowed cliffs at its foot seem double that distance."

"And look, look," said Valentia, "at the long line of glory with which the western sun is gilding the edge of the left hand slope, bringing it nearer and nearer to us every moment, against the deep blue sky!"

"But what a form! Perfect lightness, perfect symmetry!" said Claude. "Curve sweeping over curve, peak towering over peak, to the highest point, and then sinking down again as gracefully as they rose. One can hardly help fancying that the mountain moves; hat those dancing lines are not instinct with life."

"At least," said He dley, "that the mountain is a leaping wave, frozen just ere it fell."

"Perfect," said Va entia. "That is the very expression! So conc se, and yet so complete."

And Headley, poor fool, felt as happy as if he had found a gold mine

"To me," said Elsley, "the fancy rises of some great Eastern monarch sitting in royal state; with ample shoulders sloping right and left, he lays his purple-mantled arms upon the heads of two of those Titan guards who stand on either side his foot-stool."

"While from beneath his throne," said Headley, "as Eastern poets would say, flow everlasting streams, life-giving, to fertilize broad lands below."

"I did not know that you, too, were a poet," said Valentia.

"Nor I, madam. But if such scenes as these, and in such company, cannot inspire the fancy of even a poor country curate to something of exaltation, he must be dull indeed."

"Why not put some of these thoughts into poetry?"

"What use?" answered he, in so low, sad, and meaning a tone, meant only for her ear, that Valentia looked down at him: but he was gazing intently upon the glorious scene. Was he hinting at the vanity and vexation of poor Elsley's versifying? Or did he mean that he had now no purpose in life — no prize for which it was worth while to win honor?

She did not answer him: but he answered himself — perhaps to explain away his own speech:

"No, madam! God has written the poetry already; and there it is before me. My business is not to re-write it clumsily, but to read it humbly, and give Him thanks for it."

More and more had Valentia been attracted by Headley during the last few weeks. Accustomed to men who tried to make the greatest possible show of what small wits they possessed, she was surprised to find one who seemed to think it a duty to keep his knowledge and taste in the background. She gave him credit for more talent than appeared; for more, perhaps, than he really had. She was piqued, too, at his very modesty and self-restraint. Why did not he, like the rest who dangled about her, spread out his peacock's train for her eyes, and try to show his worship of her by setting himself off in his brightest colors? and yet this modesty awed her into respect of him; for she could not forget that, whether he had sentiment much or little, sentiment was not the staple of his manhood: she could not forget his cholera work; and she knew that, under that delicate and bashful outside, lay virtue and heroism, enough and to spare.

"But, if you put these thoughts into words, you would teach others to read that poetry."

"My business is to teach people to do right; and if I cannot, to pray God to find some one who can."

"Right, Headley!" said Major Campbell, laying his hand on the curate's shoulder. "God dwells no more in books written with pens than in temples made with hands; and the sacrifice which pleases Him is not verse, but righteousness. Do you recollect, Queen Whims, what I wrote once in your album?

> "'Be good, sweet maid, and let who will be clever,
>   Do noble things, not dream them, all day long,
>   So making life, death and that vast forever,
>   One grand, sweet song.'"

"But, you naughty, hypocritical *Saint Père*, you write poetry yourself, and beautifully."

"Yes, as I smoke my cigar, to comfort my poor rheumatic old soul. But if I lived only to write poetry, I should think myself as wise as if I lived only to smoke tobacco."

Valentia's eyes could not help glancing at Elsley, who had wandered away to the neighboring brook, and was gazing with all his eyes upon a ferny rock, having left Lucia to help Claude with his photographing.

Frank saw her look, and read its meaning; and answered her thoughts, perhaps too hastily.

"And what a really well-read and agreeable man he is, all the while! What a mine of quaint learning, and beautiful old legend! If he would but bring it into the common stock for every one's amusement, instead of hoarding it up for himself!"

"Why, what else does he do but bring it into the common stock, when he publishes a book which every one can read?" said Valentia, half out of the spirit of contradiction.

"And few understand," said Headley, quietly.

"You are very unjust; he is a very discerning and agreeable person, and I shall go and talk to him." And away went Valentia to Elsley, somewhat cross. Woman-like, she allowed, for the sake of her sister's honor, no one but herself to depreciate Vavasour, and chose to think it impertinent on Headley's part.

Headley began quietly talking to Major Campbell about botany, while Valentia, a little ashamed of herself all the while, took her revenge on Elsley by scolding him for his unsocial ways, in the very terms which Headley had been using.

At last Claude, having finished his photographing, departed downward to get some new view from the road below, and Lucia returned to the rest of the party. Valentia joined them at once, bringing up Elsley, who was not in the best of humors after her diatribes; and the whole party wandered about the woodland, and scrambled down beside the torrent beds.

At last they came to a point where they could descend no farther; for the stream, falling over a cliff, had worn itself a narrow chasm in the rock, and thundered down it into a deep narrow pool.

Lucia, who was basking in the sunshine and the flowers as simply as a child, would needs peep over the brink, and made Elsley hold her while she looked down. A quiet happiness, as of old recollections, came into her eyes, as she watched the sparkling and foaming water —

> " And beauty, born of murmuring sound,
>   Did pass into her face."

Campbell started. The Lucia of seven years ago seemed to bloom out again in that pale face and wrinkled forehead; and a smile came over his face, too, as he looked.

"Just like the dear old waterfall at Kilanbaggan. You recollect it, Major Campbell?"

Elsley always disliked recollections of Kilanbaggan; recollections of her life before he knew her; recollections of pleasures in which he had not shared; especially recollections of her old acquaintance with the major.

"I do not, I am ashamed to say," replied the major.

"Why, you were there a whole summer. Ah! I suppose you thought about nothing but your salmon fishing. If Elsley had been there he would not have forgotten a rock or a pool. Would you, Elsley?"

"Really, in spite of all salmon, I have not forgotten a rock or a pool about the place which I ever saw: but at the waterfall I never was."

"So he has not forgotten? What cause had he to remember so carefully?" thought Elsley.

"O Elsley, look! What is that exquisite flower, like a ball of gold, hanging just over the water?"

If Elsley had not had the evil spirit haunting about him, he would have joined in Lucia's admiration of the beautiful creature, as it dropped into the foam from its narrow ledge, with its fan of palmate leaves bright green against the black mosses of the rock, and its golden petals glowing like a tiny sun in the darkness of the chasm: as it was, he answered:

"Only a buttercup."

"I am sure it's not a buttercup! It is three times as large, and a so much paler yellow! Is it a buttercup, now, Major Campbell?"

Campbell looked down.

"Very nearly one, after all: but its real name is the globe flower. It is common enough here in spring; you may see the leaves in every pasture. But I suppose this plant, hidden from the light, has kept its flowers till the autumn."

"And till I came to see it, darling that it is! I should like to reward it by wearing it home."

"I dare say it would be very proud of the honor; especially if Mr. Vavasour would embalm it in verse, after it had done service to you."

"It is doing good enough service where it is," said Elsley. "Why pluck out the very eye of that perfect picture?"

"Strange," said Lucia, "that such a beautiful thing should be born there all alone upon these rocks, with no one to look at it."

"It enjoys itself sufficiently without us, no doubt," said Elsley.

"Yes; but I want to enjoy it. Oh, if you could but get it for me!"

Elsley looked down. There was fifteen feet of somewhat slippery rock; then a ragged ledge a foot broad, in a crack of which the flower grew; then the dark boiling pool. Elsley shrugged his shoulders, and said, smiling, as if it were a fine thing to say, "Really, my dear, all men are not knight errants enough to endanger their necks for a bit of weed; and I cannot say that such rough *tours de force* are at all to my fancy."

Lucia turned away: but she was vexed. Campbell could see that a strange fancy for the plant had seized her. As she walked from the spot, he could hear her talking about its beauty to Valentia.

Campbell's blood boiled. To be asked by that woman — by any woman — to get her that flower and to be afraid! It was bad enough to be ill tempered; but to be a coward, and to be proud thereof! He yielded to a temptation, which he had much better have left alone, seeing that Lucia had not asked him; swung himself easily enough down the ledge; got the flower, and put it, quietly bowing, into Mrs. Vavasour's hand.

He was frightened when he had done it; for he saw, to his surprise, that she was frightened. She took the flower, smiling thanks, and expressing a little common-place horror and astonishment at his having gone down such a dangerous cliff: but she took it to Elsley, drew his arm through hers, and seemed determined to make as much of him as possible for the rest of the afternoon. "The fellow was jealous, then, in addition to his other sins!" And Campbell, who felt that he had put himself unnecessarily forward between husband and wife, grew more and more angry; and somehow, unlike his usual wont, refused to confess himself in the wrong, because he was in the wrong. Certainly it was not pleasant for poor Elsley; and so Lucia felt, and bore with him when he refused to be comforted, and rendered blessing for railing when he said more than one angry word; but she had been accustomed to angry words by this time.

All might have passed off, but for that careless Valentia, who had not seen the details of what had passed; and so advised herself to ask where Lucia got that beautiful plant.

"Major Campbell picked it up for her from the cliff," said Elsley, drily.

"Ah! at the risk of his neck, I don't doubt. He is the most matchless *cavaliere servente.*"

"I shall leave Mrs. Vavasour to his care, then — that is, for the present," said Elsley, drawing his arm from Lucia's.

"I assure you," answered she, roused in her turn by his determined bad temper, "I am not the least afraid of being left in the charge of so old a friend."

Elsley made no answer, but sprang down through the thickets, calling loudly to Claude Mellot.

It was very naughty of Lucia, no doubt: but even a worm will turn; and there are times when people who have not courage to hold their peace must say something or other; and do not always, in the hurry, get out what they ought, but only what they have time to think of. And she forgot what she had said the next minute, in Major Campbell's question:

"Am I, then, so old a friend, Mrs. Vavasour?"

"Of course; who older?"

Campbell was silent a moment. If he was inclined to choke, at least Lucia did not see it.

"I trust I have not offended your — Mr. Vavasour?"

"Oh!" she said, with a forced gaiety, "only one of his poetic fancies. He wanted so much to see Mr. Mellot photograph the waterfall. I hope he will be in time to find him."

"I am a plain soldier, Mrs. Vavasour, and I only ask because I do not understand. What are poetic fancies?"

Lucia looked up in his face puzzled, and saw there an expression so grave, pitying, tender, that her heart leaped up toward him, and then sank back again.

"Why do you ask? Why need you know? You are no poet."

"And for that very cause I ask you."

"Oh, but," said she, guessing at what was in his mind, and trying, woman-like, to play purposely at cross purposes, and to defend her husband at all risks   "he has an extraordinary poetic faculty, all the world agrees to that, Major Campbell."

"What matter?" said he. Lucia would have been very angry, and perhaps ought to have been so; for what business of Campbell's was it whether her husband were kind to her or not) — but there was a deep sadness, almost despair, in the tone, which disarmed her.

"O Major Campbell, is it not a glorious thing to be a poet?   And is it not a glorious thing to be a poet's wife? Oh, for the sake of that — if I could but see him honored, appreciated, famous, as he will be some day! Though I think " (and she spoke with all a woman's pride) "he is somewhat famous now, is he not? "

"Famous? Yes," answered Campbell, with an abstracted voice, and then rejoined quickly, " If you could but see that, what then? "

"Why then," said she, with a half smile (for she had nearly entrapped herself into an admission of what she was determined to conceal), " why then, I should be still more what I am now, his devoted little wife, who cares for nobody and nothing but putting his study to rights, and bringing up his children."

" Happy children ! " said he, after a pause, and

half to himself, " who have such a mother to bring
them up."

" Do you really think so?   But flattery used not
to be one of your sins.   Ah, I wish you could give
me some advice about how I am to teach them."

" So it is she who has the work of education,
not he ! " thought Campbell to himself, and then
answered gaily :

" My dear madam, what can a confirmed old
bachelor like me know about children ? "

" Oh, don't you know " (and she gave one of her
pretty Irish laughs) " that it is the old maids who
always write the children's books, for the benefit
of us poor ignorant married women?   But " (and
she spoke earnestly again) " we all know how wise
and good you are.   I did not know it in old times.
I am afraid I used to torment you when I was
young and foolish."

" Where on earth can Mellot and Mr. Vavasour
be ? " asked Campbell.

" Oh, never mind; Mr. Mellot has gone wandering down the glen with his apparatus, and my
Elsley has gone wandering after him, and will find
him in due time, with his head in a black bag, and
a great bull just going to charge him from behind,
like that hapless man in ' Punch.'   I always tell
Mr. Mellot that will be his end."

Campbell was deeply shocked to hear the light
tone in which she talked of the passionate temper
of a man whom she so surely loved.   How many
outbursts of it there must have been; how many
paroxysms of astonishment, shame, grief — perhaps, alas ! counterbursts of anger — ere that
heart could have become thus proof against the
ever-lowering thunderstorm !

"Well," he said, " all we can do is to walk down to the car, and let them follow; and, meanwhile, I will give you my wise opinion about this education question, whereof I know nothing."

" It will be all o acular to me, for I know nothing either;" and she put her arm through his, and walked on.

" Did you hurt yourself then? I am sure you are in pain."

" I? Never less free from it, with many thanks to you. What made you think so?"

" I heard you breathe so hard, and quite stamp your feet, I thought. I suppose it was fancy."

It was not fancy, nevertheless. Major Campbell was stamping down something, and succeeded, too, in crushing it.

They walked on toward the car, Valentia and Headley following them; ere they arrived at the place where they were to meet it, it was quite dark; but what was more important, the car was not there.

"The stupid man must have mistaken his orders, and gone home."

" Or let the horse go home of itself, while he was asleep inside. He was more than half tipsy when we started."

So spoke the major, divining the exact truth. There was nothing to be done but to walk the four miles home, and let the two truants follow as they could.

" We shall have plenty of time for our educational lecture," said Lucia.

" Plenty of time to waste, then, my dear lady."

" Oh, I never talk with you five minutes — I do not know why — without feeling wiser and happier. I envy Valentia for having seen so much of you of late."

Little thought poor Lucia, as she spoke those innocent words, that within four yards of her, crouched behind the wall, his face and every limb writhing with mingled curiosity and rage, was none other but her husband.

He had given place to the devil: and the devil (for the "superstitious" and "old world" notion which attributes such frenzies to the devil has not yet been superseded by a better one) had entered into him, and concentrated all the evil habits and passions which he had indulged for years into one flaming hell within him.

Miserable man! His torments were sevenfold: and if he had sinned, he was at least punished. Not merely by all which a husband has a right to feel in such a case, or fancies that he has a right; not merely by tortured vanity and self-conceit, by the agony of seeing any man preferred to him, which to a man of Elsley's character was of itself unbearable — not merely by the loss of trust in one whom he had once trusted utterly — but, over and above all, and worst of all, by the feeling of shame, self-reproach, self-hatred, which haunts a jealous man, and which ought to haunt him; for few men lose the love of women who have once loved them, save by their own folly or baseness — by the recollection that he had traded on her trust; that he had drugged his own conscience with the fancy that she must love him always, let him do what he would; and had neglected and insulted her affection, because he fancied, in his conceit, that it was inalienable. And with the loss of self-respect, came recklessness of it, and drove him on, as it has jealous men in all ages, to meannesses unspeakable, which have made them for centuries, poor wretches, the butts of worthless play-wrights, and the scorn of their fellow-men.

Elsley had wandered, he hardly knew how or whither, for his calling to Mellot was the merest blind, — stumbling over rocks, bruising himself against tree-trunks, to this wall. He knew they must pass it. He waited for them, and had his reward. Blind with rage, he hardly waited for the sound of their footsteps to die away before he had sprung into the road, and hurried up in the opposite direction, — anywhere, everywhere, — to escape from them, and from self. Whipt by the furies, he fled along the road and up the vale, he cared not whither.

And what were Headley and Valentia, who of necessity had paired off together, doing all the while?

They walked on silently side by side for ten minutes; then Frank said:

"I have been impertinent, Miss St. Just, and I beg your pardon."

"No, you have not," said she, quite hastily. "You were right, too right, — has it not been proved within the last five minutes? My poor sister! What can be done to mend Mr. Vavasour's temper? I wish you could talk to him, Mr. Headley."

"He is beyond my art. His age, and his talents, and his — his consciousness of them," said Frank, using the mildest term he could find, " would prevent so insignificant a person as me having any influence. But what I cannot do, God's grace may."

"Can it change a man's character, Mr. Headley?

It may make good men better — but can it cure temper?"

"Major Campbell must have told you that it can do anything."

"Ah, yes: with men as wise, and strong, and noble as he is; but with such a weak, vain man ——"

"Miss St. Just, I know one who is neither wise, nor strong, nor noble, but as weak and vain as any man; in whom God has conquered — as He may conquer yet in Mr. Vavasour — all which makes man cling to life."

"What, all?" asked she, suspecting, and not wrongly, that he spoke of himself.

"All, I suppose, which it is good for them to have crushed. There are feelings which last on, in spite of all struggles to quench them — I suppose, because they ought to last; because, while they torture, they still ennoble. Death will quench them: or if not, satisfy them: or if not, set them at rest somehow."

"Death?" answered she, in a startled tone.

"Yes. Our friend, Major Campbell's friend, death. We have been seeing a good deal of him together lately, and have come to the conclusion that he is the most useful, pleasant, and instructive of all friends."

"O Mr. Headley, do not speak so! Are you in earnest?"

"So much in earnest, that I have resolved to go out as an army chaplain, to see in the war somewhat more of my new friend."

"Impossible! Mr. Headley; it will kill you! All that horrible fever and cholera!"

"And what possible harm can it do me, if it does kill me, Miss St. Just!"

"Mr. Headley, this is madness! I — we cannot allow you to throw away your life thus — so young, and — and such prospects before you! And there is nothing that my brother would not do for you, were it only for your heroism at Aberalva. There is not one of the family who does not love and respect you, and long to see all the world appreciating you as we do; and your poor mother ——"

"I have told my mother all, Miss St. Just. And she has said, Go; it is your only hope. She has other sons to comfort her. Let us say no more of it. Had I thought that you would have disapproved of it, I would never have mentioned the thing."

"Disapprove of — your going to die? You shall not! And for me, too: for I guess all — all is my fault!"

"All is mine," said he, quietly: "who was fool enough to fancy that I could forget you — conquer my love for you;" and at these words his whole voice and manner changed in an instant into wildest passion. "I must speak — now and never more — I love you still, fool that I am! Would God I had never seen you! No, not that. Thank God for that to the last: but would God I had died of that cholera! that I had never come here, conceited fool that I was, fancying that it was possible, after having once —— No! Let me go, go anywhere, where I may burden you no more with my absurd dreams! You, who have had the same thing said to you, and in finer words, a hundred times, by men who would not deign to speak to me!" and covering his face in his hands, he strode on, as if to escape.

"I never had the same thing said to me!"

"Never? How often have fine gentlemen, noblemen, sworn that they were dying for you?"

"They never have said to me what you have done."

"No — I am clumsy, I suppose ——"

"Mr. Headley, indeed you are unjust to yourself — unjust to me!"

"I — to you? Never! I know you better than you know yourself — see in you what no one else sees. Oh, what fools they are who say that love is blind! Blind? He sees souls with God's own light; not as they have become: but as they ought to become — can become — are already in the sight of Him who made them!"

"And what might I become?" asked she, half-frightened by the new earnestness of his utterance.

"How can I tell? Something infinitely too high for me, at least, who even now am not worthy to kiss the dust off your feet."

"Oh, do not speak so: little do you know ——! No, Mr. Headley, it is you who are too good for me; too noble, single-eyed, self-sacrificing, to endure my vanity and meanness for a day."

"Madam, do not speak thus! Give me no word which my folly can distort into a ray of hope, unless you wish to drive me mad. No! it is impossible; and, were it possible, what but ruin to my soul? I should live for you, and not for my work. I should become a schemer, ambitious, intriguing, in the vain hope of proving myself to the world worthy of you. No; let it be. 'Let the dead bury their dead, and follow thou me.'"

She made no answer — what answer was there to make? And he strode on by her side in silence for full ten minutes. At last she was forced to speak.

"Mr. Headley, recollect that this conversation has gone too far for us to avoid coming to some definite understanding ——"

"Then it shall, Miss St. Just. Then it shall, once and for all: formally and deliberately, it shall end now. Suppose — I only say suppose — that I could, without failing in my own honor, my duty to my calling, make myself such a name among good men, that, poor parson though I be, your family need be ashamed of nothing about me, save my poverty. Tell me, now and for ever, could it be possible ——"

He stopped. She walked on, silent, in her turn.

"Say no, as a matter of course, and end it!" said he, bitterly. She drew a long breath as if heaving off a weight.

"I cannot — dare not say it."

"It? Which of the two? yes, or no?"

She was silent.

He stopped, and spoke calmly and slowly. "Say that again, and tell me that I am not dreaming. You? the admired! the worshipped! the luxurious! — and no blame to you that you are what you were born — could you endure a little parsonage, the teaching village school-children, tending dirty old women, and petty cares the whole year round?"

"Mr. Headley," answered she, slowly and calmly, in her turn, "I could endure a cottage — a prison, I fancy, at moments — to escape from this world of which I am tired, which will soon be tired of me; from women who envy me, impute to me ambitions as base as their own; from men who admire — not me, for they do not know me, and never will — but what in me — I hate them ! — will give them pleasure. I hate it all, despise it all; despise myself for it all every morning when I wake ! What does it do for me, but rouse in me the very parts of my own character which are most despicable, most tormenting? If it goes on, I feel I could become as frivolous, as mean, ay, as wicked as the worst. You do not know — you do not know ——. I have envied the nuns their convents. I have envied Selkirk his desert island. I envy now the milkmaids there below: anything to escape and be in earnest, anything for some one to teach me to be of use ! Yes, this cholera — and this war — though only, only its coming shadow has passed over me — and your words too " — cried she, and stopped and hesitated, as if afraid to tell too much — " they have wakened me — to a new life — at least to the dream of a new life ! "

" Have you not Major Campbell?" said Headley, with a terrible effort of will.

" Yes — but has he taught me? He is dear, and good, and wise; but he is too wise, too great for me. He plays with me as a lion might with a mouse; he is like a grand angel far above in another planet, who can pity and advise, but who cannot — What am I saying? " and she covered her face with her hand.

She dropped her glove as she did so. Headley picked it up and gave it to her: as he did so their hands met; and their hands did not part again.

" You know that I love you, Valentia St. Just."

" Too well! too well! "

" But you know, too, that you do not love me."

" Who told you so? What do you know? What

do I know? Only that I long for some one to make me — to make me as good as you are!" And she burst into tears.

"Valentia, will you trust me?"

"Yes!" cried she, looking up at him suddenly: "if you will not go to the war."

"No — no — no! Would you have me turn traitor and coward to God; and now, of all moments in my life?"

"Noble creature!" said she; "you will make me love you whether I wish or not."

What was it, after all, by which Frank Headley won Valentia's love? I cannot tell. Can you tell, sir, how you won the love of your wife? As little as you can tell of that still greater miracle — how you have kept her love since she found out what manner of man you were.

So they paced homeward, hand in hand, beside the shining ripples, along the Dinas shore. The birches breathed fragrance on them; the night-hawk churred softly round their path; the stately mountains smiled above them in the moonlight, and seemed to keep watch and ward over their love, and to shut out the noisy world, and the harsh babble and vain fashions of the town. The summer lightning flickered to the westward; but round them the rich soft night seemed full of love, — as full of love as their own hearts were, and like them, brooding silently upon its joy. At last the walk was over; the kind moon sank low behind the hills; and the darkness hid their blushes as they paced into the sleeping village, and their hands parted unwillingly at last.

When they came into the hall through the group of lounging gownsmen and tourists, they found

Bowie arguing with Mrs. Lewis, in his dogmatic Scotch way:

"So ye see, madam, there's no use defending the drunken loon any more at all; and here will my leddies have just walked their bonny legs off, all through that carnal sin of drunkenness, which is the curse of your Welsh populaaation."

"And not quite unknown north of Tweed either, Bowie," said Valentia, laughing. "There now, say no more about it. We have had a delightful walk, and nobody is the least tired. Don't say any more, Mrs. Lewis: but tell them to get us some supper. Bowie, so my lord has come in?"

"This half-hour good!"

"Has he had any sport?"

"Sport! ay, troth! Five fish in the day. That's a river indeed at Bettws! Not a pawky wee burn, like this Aberglaslyn thing."

"Only five fish?" said Valentia, in a frightened tone.

"Fish, my leddy, not trouts, I said. I thought ye knew better than that by this time."

"Oh, salmon?" cried Valentia, relieved. "Delightful. I'll go to him this moment."

And upstairs to Scoutbush's rooms she went.

He was sitting in dressing-gown and slippers, sipping his claret, and fondling his fly-book (the only one he ever studied *con amore*) with a most complacent face. She came in and stood demurely before him, holding her broad hat in both hands before her knees, like a schoolgirl, her face half-hidden in the black curls. Scoutbush looked up and smiled affectionately, as he caught the light of her eyes, and the arch play of her lips.

"Ah! there you are, at a pretty time of night!

How beautiful you look, Val! I wish my wife may be half as pretty!"

Valentia made him a prim courtesy.

"I am delighted to hear of my lord's good sport. He will choose to be in a good humor, I suppose."

"Good humor? *ça va sans dire!* Three stone of fish in three hours!'

"Then his little sister is going to do a very foolish thing, and wants his leave to do it; which if he will grant, she will let him do as many foolish things as he likes without scolding him, as long as they both shall live."

"Do it then, I beg. What is it? Do you want to go up Snowdon with Headley to-morrow, to see the sun rise? You'll kill yourself!"

"No," said Valentia, very quietly; "I only want to marry him."

"Marry him!" cried Scoutbush, starting up.

"Don't try to look majestic, my dear little brother, for you are really not tall enough; as it is, you have only hooked all your flies into your dressing-gown."

Scoutbush dashed himself down into his chair again.

"I'll be shot if you shall!"

"You may be shot just as surely, whether I do or not," said she, softly; and she knelt down before him, and put her arms round him, and laid her head upon his lap. "There, you can't run away now; so you must hear me quietly. And you know it may not be often that we shall be together again thus; and O Scoutbush! brother! if anything was to happen to you — I only say if — in this horrid war, you would not like to think that you had refused the last thing your little Val asked for, and that she was miserable and lonely at home."

"I'll be shot if you shall!" was all the poor viscount could get out.

"Yes, miserable and lonely; you gone away, and *mon Saint Père* too; and Lucia, she has her children — and I am so wild and weak — I must have some one to guide me and protect me — indeed I must!"

"Why, that was what I always said! That was why I wanted you so to marry this season! Why did not you take Chalkclere, or half a dozen good matches who were dying for you, and not this confounded black parson, of all birds in the air?"

"I did not take Lord Chalkclere for the very reason that I do take Mr. Headley. I want a husband who will guide me, not one whom I must guide."

"Guide?" said Scoutbush, bitterly, with one of those little sparks of practical shrewdness which sometimes fell from him. "Ay, I see how it is! These intriguing rascals of parsons — they begin as father confessors, like so many popish priests; and one fine morning they blossom out into lovers, and so they get all the pretty women, and all the good fortunes — the sneaking, ambitious, low-bred —— "

"He is neither! You are unjust, Scoutbush!" cried Valentia, looking up. "He is the very soul of honor. He might be rich now, and have had a fine living, if he had not been too conscientious to let his uncle buy him one; and that offended his uncle, and he would allow him nothing. And as for being low-bred, he is a gentleman, as you know;

and if his uncle be in business, his mother is a lady, and he will be well enough off one day."

"You seem to know a great deal about his affairs."

"He told me all, months ago — before there was any dream of this. And, my dear," she went on, relapsing into her usual arch tone, "there is no fear but his uncle will be glad enough to patronize him again, when he finds that he has married a viscount's sister."

Scoutbush laughed "You scheming little Irish rogue! But I won't I've said it, and I won't. It's enough to have one sister married to a poor poet, without having another married to a poor parson. Oh! what have I done that I should be bothered in this way? Isn't it bad enough to be a landlord, and to have an estate, and be responsible for a lot of people that will die of the cholera, and have to vote in the House about a lot of things I don't understand, nor anybody else, I believe, but that, over and above, I must be the head of the family, and answerable to all the world for whom my mad sisters marry? I won't, I say!"

"Then I shall just go and marry without your leave! I'm of age, you know, and my fortune's my own; and then we shall come in as the runaway couples do in a play, while you sit there in your dressing-gown as the stern father — won't you borrow a white wig for the occasion, my lord? — and we shall fall down on our knees so," — and she put herself in the prettiest attitude in the world, — "and beg your blessing — please forgive us this time, and we'll never do so any more! And then you will turn your face away, like the baron in the ballad —

"'And brushed away the springing tear
He proudly strove to hide,'

etcetera, etcetera. Finish the scene for yourself,
with a 'Bless ye, my children; bless ye!'"

"Go along, and marry the cat if you like! You
are mad; and I am mad; and all the world's mad,
I think."

"There," she said, "I knew that he would be a
good boy at last!" And she sprang up, threw her
arms round his neck, and, to his great astonishment,
burst into the most violent fit of crying.

"Good gracious, Valentia! do be reasonable!
You'll go into a fit, or somebody will hear you!
You know how I hate a scene. Do be good, there's
a darling! Why did n't you tell me at first how
much you wished for it, and I would have said yes
in a moment."

"Because I did n't know myself," cried she, passionately. "There, I will be good, and love you
better than all the world, except one. And if you
let these horrid Russians hurt you, I will hate
you as long as I live, and be miserable all my life
afterwards."

"Why, Valentia, do you know, that sounds very
like a bull?"

"Am I not a wild Irish girl?" said she, and
hurried out, leaving Scoutbush to return to his
flies.

She bounded into Lucia's room, there to pour
out a bursting heart — and stopped short.

Lucia was sitting on the bed, her shawl and bonnet tossed upon the floor, her head sunk on her
bosom, her arms sunk by her side.

"Lucia, what is it? Speak to me, Lucia!"

She pointed faintly to a letter on the floor. Valentia caught it up: Lucia made a gesture as if to stop her.

"No, you must not read it. Too dreadful!"

But Valentia read it; while Lucia covered her face in her hands, and uttered a long, low, shuddering moan of bitter agony.

Valentia read, with flashing eyes and bursting brow. It was a hideous letter. The words of a man trying to supply the place of strength by virulence. A hideous letter, unfit to be written here.

"Valentia! Valentia! It is false — a mistake; he is dreaming. You know it is false! You will not leave me too?"

Valentia dashed it on the ground, clasped her sister in her arms, and covered her head with kisses.

"My Lucia! My own sweet good sister! Base, cowardly," sobbed she, in her rage; while Lucia's agony began to find a vent in words, and she moaned on:

"What have I done? All that flower, that horrid flower; but who would have dreamed — and Major Campbell, too, of all men upon earth? Valentia, it is some horrid delusion of the devil. Why, he was there all the while, and you too. Could he think that I should before his very face? What must he fancy me? Oh, it is a delusion of the devil, and nothing else!"

"He is a wretch! I will take that letter to my brother; he shall right you!"

"Ah no! no! never! Let me tear it to atoms — hide it! It is all a mistake! He did not mean it! He will recollect himself to-morrow and come back."

"Let him come back if he dare!" cried Valentia, in a tone which said, "I could kill him with my own hands!"

"Oh, he will come back! He cannot have the heart to leave his poor little Lucia. O cruel, cowardly, not to have said one word — not one word to explain all; but it was all my fault, my wicked, odious temper; and after I had seen how vexed he was, too! O Elsley, Elsley, come back, only come back, and I will beg your pardon on my knees! anything! Scold me, beat me, if you will! I deserve it all! Only come back, and let me see your face, and hear your voice, instead of leaving me here all alone, and the poor children too! Oh, what shall I say to them to-morrow, when they wake and find no father?"

Valentia's indignation had no words. She could only sit on the bed, with Lucia in her arms, looking defiance at all the world above that fair head which one moment dropped on her bosom, and the next gazed up into her face in pitiful childlike pleading.

"Oh, if I but knew where he was gone! If I could but find him! One word — one word would set all right! It always did, Valentia, always! He was so kind, so dear in a moment, when I put away my naughty, naughty temper, and smiled in his face like a good wife. Wicked creature that I was! and this is my punishment. O Elsley, one word, one word! I must find him if I went barefoot over the mountains. I must go, I must ——"

And she tried to rise; but Valentia held her down, while she entreated piteously :

"I will go, and see about finding him!" she said at last, as her only resource. "Promise me to be quiet here, and I will."

"Quiet? Yes, quiet here!" and she threw herself upon her face on the floor.

She looked up eagerly. "You will not tell Scoutbush?"

"Why not?"

"He is so — so hasty. He will kill him! Valentia, he will kill him! Promise me not to tell him, or I shall go mad!" And she sat up again, pressing her hands upon her head, and rocking from side to side.

"O Valentia, if I cared only scream! but keeping it in kills me. It is like a sword through my brain now!"

"Let me call Clara."

"No, no! not Clara. Do not tell her. I will be quiet; indeed I will; only come back soon, soon, for I am all alone, alone!" And she threw herself down again upon her face.

Valentia went out. Certain as she was of her sister's innocence, there was one terrible question in her heart which must be answered, or her belief in all truth, goodness, religion, would reel and rock to its very foundations. And till she had an answer to that, she could not sit still by Lucia.

She walked hurriedly, with compressed lips, but quivering limbs, downstairs, and into the sitting-room. Scoutbush was gone to bed. Campbell and Mellot sat chatting still.

"Where is my brother?"

"Gone to bed, as some one else ought to be; for it is past twelve. Is Vavasour come in yet?"

"No."

"Very odd," said Claude; "I never saw him after I left you."

"He said certainly that he was going to find you," said Campbell.

"There is no need for speculating," said Valentia, quietly; "my sister has a note from Mr. Vavasour at Pen-y-gwryd."

"Pen-y-gwryd?" cried both men at once.

"Yes. Major Campbell, I wish to show it to you."

Valentia's tone and manner was significant enough to make Claude Mellot bid them both good-night.

When he had shut the door behind him, Valentia put the letter into the major's hand.

He was too much absorbed in it to look up at her; but if he had done so, he would have been startled by the fearful capacity of passion which changed, for the moment, that gay Queen Whims into a terrible Roxana, as she stood, leaning against the mantelpiece, but drawn up to her full height, her lips tight shut, eyes which gazed through and through him in awful scrutiny, holding her very breath, while a nervous clutching of the little hand said, "If you have tampered with my sister's heart, better for you that you were dead!"

He read it through, once, twice, with livid face; then dashed it on the floor.

"Fool! — cur! — liar! — she is as pure as God's sunlight."

"You need not tell me that," said Valentia, through her closed teeth.

"Fool! — fool! — " And then, in a moment, his voice changed from indignation to the bitterest self-reproach. "And fool I; thrice fool! Who am I, to rail on him? O God! what have I done?" And he covered his face with his hands.

"What have you done?" literally shrieked Valentia.

"Nothing that you or man can blame, Miss St. Just! Can you dream that, sinful as I am, I could ever harbor a thought toward her of which I should be ashamed before the angels of God?"

He looked up as he spoke, with an utter humility and an intense honesty which unnerved her at once.

"O my *Saint Père!*" and she held out both her hands. "Forgive me, if — only for a moment ——"

"I am not your *Saint Père*, nor any one's! I am a poor, weak, conceited, miserable man, who by his accursed impertinence has broken the heart of the being whom he loves best on earth."

Valentia started : but ere she could ask for an explanation, he rejoined wildly :

"How is she? Tell me only that, this once! Has it killed her? Does she hate him?"

"Adores him more than ever. O Major Campbell! it is too piteous, too piteous."

He covered his face with his hands, shuddering. "Thank God! yes, thank God! So it should be. Let her love him to the last, and win her martyr's crown! Now, Valentia St. Just, sit down, if but for five minutes; and listen, once for all, to the last words, perhaps, you will ever hear me speak; unless she wants you? ——"

"No, no! Tell me all, *Saint Père!*" said Valentia, "for I am walking in a dream — a double dream!" as the new thought of Headley, and that walk, came over her. "Tell me all at once, while I have wits left to comprehend."

"Miss St. Just," said he, in a clear calm voice,

"It is fit, for her honor and for mine, that you should know all. The first day that I ever saw your sister, I loved her; as a man loves who can never cease to love, or love a second time. I was a raw, awkward Scotchman then, and she used to laugh at me. Why not? I kept my secret, and determined to become a man at whom no one would wish to laugh. I was in the Company's service then. You recollect her jesting once about the Indian army, and my commanding black people, and saying that the Line only was fit for — some girl's jest?"

"No; I recollect nothing of it."

"I never forgot it. I threw up all my prospects, and went into the Line. Whether I won honor there or not, I need not tell you. I came back to England years after, not unworthy, as I fancied, to look your sister in the face as an equal. I found her married."

He paused a little, and then went on, in a quiet business-like tone.

"Good. Her choice was sure to be a worthy one, and that was enough for me. You need not doubt that I kept my secret then more sacredly than ever. I returned to India, and tried to die. I dared not kill myself, for I was a soldier and a Christian, and belonged to God and my Queen. The Sikhs would not kill me, do what I would to help them. Then I threw myself into science, that I might stifle passion; and I stifled it. I fancied myself cured, and I was cured; and I returned to England again. I loved your brother for her sake; I loved you at first for her sake, then for your own. But I presumed upon my cure; I accepted your brother's invitation; I caught at

the opportunity of seeing her again — happy — as
I fancied; and of proving to myself my own
soundness. I considered myself a sort of Mel-
chisedek, neither young nor old, without passions,
without purpose on earth — a fakir who had
license to do and to dare what others might not.
But I kept my secret proudly inviolate. I do not
believe at this momen she dreams that — do you?"

"She does not."

"Thank God! I was a most conceited fool,
puffed up with spiritual pride, tempting God need-
lessly. I went, I saw her. Heaven is my witness
that, as far as passion goes, my heart is as pure as
yours: but I found that I still cared more for her
than for any being on earth: and I found too the
sort of man upon whom — God forgive me! I
must not talk of that — I despised him, hated him,
pretended to teach him his duty, by behaving better
to her than he did — the spiritual coxcomb that I
was! ' What business had I with it? Why not
have left all to God and her good sense? The
devil tempted me to-day, in the shape of an angel
of courtesy and chivalry; and here the end is
come. I must find that man, Miss St. Just, if I
travel the world in search of him. I must ask his
pardon frankly, humbly, for my impertinence.
Perhaps so I may bring him back to her, and not
die with a curse on my head for having parted
those whom God has joined. And then to the old
fighting-trade once more — the only one, I believe,
I really understand; and see whether a Russian
bullet will not fly straighter than a clumsy Sikh's."

Valentia listened, awe-stricken; and all the more
so because this was spoken in a calm, half-abstracted
voice, without a note of feeling, save where he

alluded to his own mistakes. When it was over, she rose without a word, and took both his hands in her own, sobbing bitterly.

"You forgive me, then, all the misery which I have caused?"

"Do not talk so! Only forgive me having fancied for one moment that you were anything but what you are, an angel out of heaven."

Campbell hung down his head.

"Angel, truly! Azrael, the angel of death, then. Go to her now — go, and leave a humble penitent man alone with God."

"O my *Saint Père!*" cried she, bursting into tears. "This is too wretched — all a horrid dream — and when, too — when I had been counting on telling you something so different! — I cannot now, I have not the heart."

"What, more misery?"

"Oh no! no! no! You will know all to-morrow. Ask Scoutbush."

"I shall be gone in search of that man long before Scoutbush is awake."

"Impossible! you do not know whither he is gone."

"If I employ every detective in Bow Street, I will find him."

"Wait, only wait, till the post comes in to-morrow. He will surely write, if not to her, — wretch that he is! — at least to some of us."

"If he be alive. No. I must go up to Pen-y-gwryd, where he was last seen, and find out what I can."

"They will all be in bed at this hour of the night; and if — if anything has happened, it will be over by now," added she, with a shudder.

"God forgive me! It will indeed: but he may write — perhaps to me. He is no coward, I believe: and he may send me a challenge. Yes, I will wait for the post."

"Shall you accept it if he does?"

Major Campbell smiled sadly.

"No, Miss St. Just you may set your mind at rest upon that point. I have done quite enough harm already to your family. Now, good-bye! I will wait for the post to-morrow: do you go to your sister."

Valentia went, utterly bewildered. She had forgotten Frank, but Frank had not forgotten her. He had hurried to his room; lay till morning, sleepless with delight, and pouring out his pure spirit in thanks for this great and unexpected blessing. A new life had begun for him, even in the jaws of death. He would still go to the East. It seemed easy to him to go there in search of a grave; how much more now, when he felt so full of magic life, that fever, cholera, the chances of war, could not harm him! After this proof of God's love, how could he doubt, how fear?

Little he thought that, three doors off from him, Valentia was sitting up the whole night through, vainly trying to quiet Lucia, who refused to undress, and paced up and down her room, hour after hour, in wild misery, which I have no skill to detail.

CHAPTER XXI

NATURE'S MELODRAMA

WHAT, then, had become of Elsley? And whence had he written the fatal letter? He had hurried up the high road for half an hour and more, till the valley on the left sloped upward more rapidly, in dark dreary bogs, the moonlight shining on their runnels; while the mountain on his right sloped downwards more rapidly in dark dreary down, strewn with rocks which stood out black against the sky. He was nearing the head of the watershed; soon he saw slate roofs glittering in the moonlight, and found himself at the little inn of Pen-y-gwryd, at the meeting of the three great valleys, the central heart of the mountains.

And a genial, jovial little heart it is, and an honest, kindly little heart too, with warm life-blood within. So it looked that night, with every window red with comfortable light, and a long stream of glare pouring across the road from the open door, gilding the fir-tree tops in front: but its geniality only made him shudder. He had been there more than once, and knew the place and the people; and knew, too, that of all people in the world, they were the least like him. He hurried past the doorway, and caught one glimpse of the bright kitchen. A sudden thought struck him. He would go in and write his letter there. But not yet — he could not go in yet; for through

the open door came some sweet Welsh air, so
sweet, that even he paused to listen. Men were
singing in three parts, in that rich metallic temper
of voice, and that perfect time and tune, which
is the one gift still left to that strange Cymry race,
worn out with the long burden of so many thousand years. He knew the air; it was " The rising
of the Lark." Heavens! what a bitter contrast
to his own thoughts! But he stood rooted, as if
spell-bound, to hear it to the end. The lark's
upward flight was over; and Elsley heard him
come quivering down from heaven's gate, fluttering, sinking, trilling self-complacently, springing
aloft in one bar, only to sink lower in the next,
and call more softly to his brooding mate below;
till, worn out with his ecstasy, he murmured one
last sigh of joy, and sank into the nest. The
picture flashed through Elsley's brain as swiftly as
the notes did through his ears. He breathed more
freely when it vanished with the sounds. He strode
hastily in, and down the little passage to the kitchen.

It was a low room, ceiled with dark beams,
from which hung bacon and fishing-rods, harness
and drying stockings, and all the miscellanea
of a fishing inn kept by a farmer, and beneath
it the usual happy, hearty, honest group. There
was Harry Owen, bland and stalwart, his baby
in his arms, smiling upon the world in general;
old Mrs. Pritchard, bending over the fire, putting
the last touch to one of those miraculous soufflets,
compact of clouds and nectar, which transport
alike palate and fancy, at the first mouthful,
from Snowden to Belgrave Square. A sturdy
fair-haired Saxon Gourbannelig sat with his back
to the door, and two of the beautiful children on

his knee, their long locks flowing over the elbows
of his shooting-jacket, as, with both arms round
them, he made Punch for them with his handkerchief and his fingers, and chattered to them in
English, while they chattered in Welsh. By him
sat another Englishman, to whom the three tuneful
Snowdon guides, their music-score upon their knees,
sat listening approvingly, as he rolled out, with
voice as of a jolly blackbird, or jollier monk of old,
the good old Wessex song —

> " My dog he has his master's nose,
>   To smell a knave through silken hose;
>   If friends or honest men go by,
>   Welcome, quoth my dog and I !

> " Of foreign tongues let scholars brag,
>   With fifteen names for a pudding-bag:
>   Two tongues I know ne'er told a lie;
>   And their wearers be, my dog and I !"

"That ought to be Harry's song, and the
colly's too, eh?" said he, pointing to the dear
old dog, who sat with his head on Owen's knee —
"eh, my men? Here's a health to the honest
man and his dog!"

And all laughed and drank; while Elsley's dark
face looked in at the doorway, and half turned to
escape. Handsome lady-like Mrs. Owen, bustling
out of the kitchen with a supper-tray, ran full
against him, and uttered a Welsh scream.

"Show me a room, and bring me a pen and
paper," said he; and then started in his turn, as
all had started at him; for the two Englishmen
looked round, and, behold, to his disgust, the
singer was none other than Naylor; the actor of
Punch was Wynd.

To have found his *bêtes noires* even here, and at such a moment! And what was worse, to hear Mrs. Owen say, "W: have no room, sir, unless these gentlemen —— "

"Of course," said Wynd, jumping up, a child under each arm. " Mr. Vavasour! we shall be most happy to have your company, — for a week if you will ! "

" Ten minutes' solit·ide is all I ask, sir, if I am not intruding too far.'

" Two hours, if you like. We 'll stay here. Mrs. Owen, — the thicker the merrier." But Elsley had vanished into a chamber bestrewn with plaids, pipes, hobnail boots, fishing tackle, mathematical books, scraps of ore, and the wild confusion of a gownsman's den.

"The party is taken ill with a poem," said Wynd.

Naylor stuck out his heavy under-lip, and glanced sidelong at his friend.

"With something worse, Ned. That man's eye and voice had something uncanny in them. Mellot said he would go crazed some day; and be hanged if I don't think he is so now."

Another five minutes, and Elsley rang the bell violently for hot brandy-and-water.

Mrs. Owen came back looking a little startled, a letter in her hand.

" The gentleman had drunk the liquor off at one draught, and ran out of the house like a wild man. Harry Owen must go down to Beddgelert instantly with the letter: and there was five shillings to pay for all."

Harry Owen rises, like a strong and patient beast of burden, ready for any amount of walking, at any hour in the twenty-four. He has been up Snowdon once to-day already. He is going up again at twelve to-night, with a German who wants to see the sun rise; he deputes that office to John Roberts, and strides out.

"Which way did the gentleman go, Mrs. Owen?" asks Naylor.

" Capel Curig road."

Naylor whispers to Wynd, who sets the two little girls on the table, and hurries out with him. They look up the road, and see no one; run a couple of hundred yards, where they catch a sight of the next turn, clear in the moonlight. There is no one on the road.

"Run to the bridge, Wynd," whispers Naylor. "He may have thrown himself over."

"Tally ho!" whispers Wynd in return, laying his hand on Naylor's arm, and pointing to the left of the road.

A hundred yards from them, over the boggy upland, among scattered boulders, a dark figure is moving. Now he stops short, gesticulating; turns right and left irresolutely. At last he hurries on and upward; he is running, springing from stone to stone.

" There is but one thing, Wynd. After him, or he'll drown himself in Llyn Cwm Fynnon."

" No, he's striking to the right. Can he be going up the Glyder?"

" We'll see that in five minutes. All in the day's work, my boy! I could go up Mont Blanc with such a dinner in me."

The two gallant men run in, struggle into their wet boots again, and provisioned with meat and bread, whiskey, tobacco, and plaids, are away upon

Elsley's tracks, having left Mrs. Owen disconsolate by their announcement, that a sudden fancy to sleep on the Glyder has seized them. Nothing more will they tell her, or any one, being gentlemen, however much slang they may talk in private.

Elsley left the door of Pen-y-gwryd, careless whither he went, if he went only far enough.

In front of him rose the Glyder Vawr, its head shrouded in soft mist, through which the moonlight gleamed upon the checquered quarries of that enormous desolation, the dead bones of the eldest-born of time. A wild longing seized him; he would escape up thither; up into those clouds, up anywhere to be alone — alone with his miserable self. That was dreadful enough: but less dreadful than having a companion — ay, even a stone by him — which could remind him of the scene which he had left; even remind him that there was another human being on earth beside himself. Yes — to put that cliff between him and all the world! Away he plunged from the high road, splashing over boggy uplands, scrambling among scattered boulders, across a stormy torrent bed, and then across another and another: — when would he reach that dark marbled wall, which rose into the infinite blank, looking within a stone-throw of him, and yet no nearer after he had walked a mile?

He reached it at last, and rushed up the talus of boulders, springing from stone to stone; till his breath failed him, and he was forced to settle into a less frantic pace. But upward he would go, and upward he went, with a strength which he never had felt before. Strong? How should he not be strong, while every vein felt filled with molten lead; while some unseen power seemed not so much to attract him upwards, as to drive him by magical repulsion from all that he had left below?

So upward and upward ever, driven on by the terrible gadfly, like Io of old he went; stumbling upwards along torrent beds of slippery slate, writhing himself upward through crannies where the waterfall plashed cold upon his chest and face, yet could not cool the inward fire; climbing, hand and knee, up cliffs of sharp-edged rock; striding over downs where huge rocks lay crouched in the grass, like fossil monsters of some ancient world, and seemed to stare at him with still and angry brows. Upward still, to black terraces of lava, standing out hard and black against the gray cloud, gleaming, like iron in the moonlight, stair above stair, like those over which Vathek and the princess climbed up to the halls of Eblis. Over their crumbling steps, up through their cracks and crannies, out upon a dreary slope of broken stones, and then — before he dives upward into the cloud ten yards above his head — one breathless look back upon the world.

The horizontal curtain of mist; gauzy below, fringed with white tufts and streamers, deepening above into the blackness of utter night. Below it a long gulf of soft yellow haze, in which, as in a bath of gold, lie delicate bars of far-off western cloud; and the faint glimmer of the western sea, above long knotted spurs of hill, in deepest shades, like a bunch of purple grapes flecked here and there from behind with gleams of golden light; and beneath them again, the dark woods sleeping

over Gwynnant, and their dark double sleeping in
the bright lake below.

On the right han1 Snowdon rises. Vast sheets
of utter blackness - - vast sheets of shining light.
He can see every c ag which juts from the gre n
walls of Galt-y-Wemalt; and far past it into the
Great Valley of Cwm Dyli; and then the red
peak, now as black as night, shuts out the word
with its huge mist-topped cone. But on the left
hand all is deepest shade. From the highest saw-
edges where Moel Meirch cuts the golden sky,
down to the very de ths of the abyss, all is lustrous
darkness, sooty, and yet golden still. Let the
darkness lie upon it for ever! Hidden be those
woods where she stood an hour ago! Hidden that
road down which, even now, they may be pacing
home together! — Curse the thought! He covers
his face in his hands and shudders in every limb.

He lifts his hands from his eyes at last: — what
has befallen?

Before the golden haze a white veil is falling
fast. Sea, mountain, lake, are vanishing, fading
as in a dream. Soon he can see nothing but the
twinkle of a light in Pen-y-gwryd, a thousand feet
below; happy children are nestling there in innocent sleep. Jovial voices are chatting round the
fire. What has he to do with youth, and health,
and joy? Lower, lower, ye clouds! Shut out
that insolent and intruding spark, till nothing be
seen but the silver sheet of Cwm Fynnon, and, the
silver zig-zag lines which wander into it among
black morass, while down the mountain side go,
softly sliding, troops of white mist-angels. Softly
they slide, swift and yet motionless, as if by some
inner will, which needs no force of limbs; gliding

gently round the crags, diving gently off into the abyss, their long white robes trailing about their feet in upward-floating folds. "Let us go hence," they seem to whisper to the God-forsaken, as legends say they whispered when they left their doomed shrine in old Jerusalem. Let the white fringe fall between him and the last of that fair troop; let the gray curtain follow, the black pall above descend; till he is alone in darkness that may be felt, and in the shadow of death.

Now he is safe at last; hidden from all living things — hidden, it may be, from God; for at least God is hidden from him. He has desired to be alone: and he is alone; the center of the universe, if universe there be. All created things, suns and planets, seem to revolve round him, and he a point of darkness, not of light. He seems to float self-poised in the center of the boundless nothing, upon an ell-broad slab of stone — and yet not even on that: for the very ground on which he stands he does not feel. He does not feel the mist which wets his cheek, the blood which throbs within his veins. He only is; and there is none besides.

Horrible thought! Permitted but to few, and to them — thank God! — but rarely. For two minutes of that absolute self-isolation would bring madness; if, indeed, it be not the very essence of madness itself.

There he stood; he knew not how long; without motion, without thought, without even rage or hate, now — in one blank paralysis of his whole nature; conscious only of self, and of a dull, inward fire, as if his soul were a dark vault, lighted with lurid smoke.

    .   .   .   .   .   .

What was that? He started: shuddered — as well he might. Had he seen heaven opened? or another place? So momentary was the vision, that he scarce knew what he saw —

There it was again! Lasting but for a moment: but long enough to le' him see the whole western heaven transfigured it to one sheet of pale blue gauze, and before it Snowdon towering black as ink, with every saw and crest cut out, hard and terrible, against the lightning-glare: and then the blank of darkness.

Again! The awful black giant, towering high in air, before the gates of that blue abyss of flame: but a black crown of cloud has settled upon his head; and out of it the lightning sparks leap to and fro, ringing his brows with a coronet of fire.

Another moment, and the roar of that great battle between earth and heaven crashed full on Elsley's ears.

He heard it leap from Snowdon, sharp and rattling, across the gulf toward him, till it crashed full upon the Glyder overhead, and rolled and flapped from crag to crag, and died away along the dreary downs. No! There it boomed out again, thundering full against Siabod on the left; and Siabod tossed it on to Moel Meirch, who answered from all her clefts and peaks with a long confused battle-growl, and then tossed it across to Aran; and Aran, with one dull, bluff report from her flat cliff, to nearer Lliwedd; till, worn out with the long buffetings of that giant ring, it sank and died on Gwynnant far below — but ere it died, another and another thunder-crash burst, sharper and nearer every time, to hurry round the hills after the one which roared before it.

Another minute, and the blue glare filled the sky once more: but no black Titan towered before it now.   The storm had leapt Llanberris pass, and all around Elsley was one howling chaos of cloud, and rain, and blinding flame.   He turned and fled again.

By the sensation of his feet, he knew that he was going uphill; and if he but went upward, he cared not whither he went.   The rain gushed through, where the lightning pierced the cloud, in drops like musket balls.   He was drenched to the skin in a moment; dazzled and giddy from the flashes; stunned by the everlasting roar, peal over-rushing peal, echo out-shooting echo, till rocks and air quivered alike beneath the continuous battle-cannonade.   "What matter?   What fitter guide for such a path as mine than the blue lightning flashes?"

Poor wretch!   He had gone out of his way for many a year, to give himself up, a willing captive, to the melodramatic view of nature, and had let sights and sounds, not principles and duties, mould his feelings for him: and now, in his utter need and utter weakness, he had met her in a mood which was too awful for such as he was to resist. The Nemesis had come; and swept away helplessly, without faith and hope, by those outward impressions of things on which he had feasted his soul so long, he was the puppet of his own eyes and ears; the slave of glare and noise.

Breathless, but still untired, he toiled up a steep incline, where he could feel beneath him neither moss nor herb.   Now and then his feet brushed through a soft tuft of parsley fern: but soon even that sign of vegetation ceased; his feet only rasped over rough bare rock, and he was alone in a desert of stone.

What was that sudden apparition above him, seen for a moment dim and gigantic through the mist, hid the next in darkness? The next flash showed him a line of obelisks, like giants crouching side by side, staring down on him from the clouds. Another five minutes he was at their feet, and past them; to see above them again another line of awful watchers through the storms and rains of many a thousand years, waiting, grim and silent, like those doomed senators in the Capitol of Rome, till their own turn should come, and the last lightning stroke hurl them too down, to lie for ever by their fallen brothers, whose mighty bones bestrewed the screes below.

He groped his way between them; saw some fifty yards beyond a higher peak; gained it by fierce struggles and many falls; saw another beyond that; and, rushing down and up two slopes of moss, reached a region where the upright lavaledges had been split asunder into chasms, crushed together again into caves, toppled over each other, hurled up into spires, in such chaotic confusion that progress seemed impossible.

A flash of lightning revealed a lofty cairn above his head. There was yet, then, a higher point! He would reach it, if he broke every limb in the attempt! and madly he hurried on, feeling his way from ledge to ledge, squeezing himself through crannies, crawling on hands and knees along the sharp chines of the rocks, till he reached the foot of the cairn; climbed it, and threw himself at full length on the summit of the Glyder Vawr.

An awful place it always is; and Elsley saw it at

an awful time, as the glare unveiled below him a
sea of rock-waves, all sharp on edge, pointing toward him on every side: or rather one wave-crest
of a sea; for twenty yards beyond, all sloped away
into the abysmal dark.

Terrible were those rocks below; and ten times
more terrible as seen through the lurid glow of his
distempered brain. All the weird peaks and slabs
seemed pointing up at him: sharp-toothed jaws
gaped upward — tongues hissed upward — arms
pointed upward — hounds leaped upward — mon-
strous snake-heads peered upward out of cracks
and caves. Did he not see them move, writhe? or
was it the ever-shifting light of the flashes? Did
he not hear them howl, yell at him? or was it but
the wind, tortured in their labyrinthine caverns?

The next moment, and all was dark again: but
the images which had been called up remained,
and fastened on his brain, and grew there; and
when, in the light of the next flash, the scene
returned, he could see the red lips of the phantom
hounds, the bright eyes of the phantom snakes;
the tongues wagged in mockery; the hands brand-
ished great stones to hurl at him; the moun-
tain-top was instinct with fiendish life — a very
Blocksberg of all hideous shapes and sins.

And yet he did not shrink. Horrible it was; he
was going mad before it. And yet he took a
strange and fierce delight in making it more horrible; in maddening himself yet more and more; in
clothing those fantastic stones with every fancy
which could inspire another man with dread. But
he had no dread. Perfect rage, like perfect love,
casts out fear. He rejoiced in his own misery, in
his own danger. His life hung on a thread; any

Instant might hurl him from that cairn, a blackened corpse.

What better end? Let it come! He was Prometheus on the peak of Caucasus, hurling defiance at the unjust Jove! His hopes, his love, his very honor — curse it! — ruined! Let the lightning stroke come! He were a coward to shrink from it. Let him face the worst, unprotected, bare-headed, naked, and do battle, himself, and nothing but himself, against the universe! And, as men at such moments will do, in the mad desire to free the self-tortured spirit from some unseen and choking bond, he began wildly tearing off his clothes.

But merciful nature brought relief, and stopped him in his mad efforts, or he had been a frozen corpse long ere the dawn. His hands, stiff with cold, refused to obey him: as he delayed he was saved. After the paroxysm came the collapse; he sank upon the top of the cairn half senseless. He felt himself falling over its edge; and the animal instinct of self-preservation, unconsciously to him, made him slide down gently, till he sank into a crack between two rocks, sheltered somewhat, as it befell happily, from the lashing of the rain.

Another minute, and he slept a dreamless sleep.

But there are two men upon that mountain, whom neither rock nor rain, storm nor thunder, have conquered, because they are simply brave honest men; and who are, perhaps, far more "poetic" characters at this moment than Elsley Vavasour, or any dozen of mere verse-writers, because they are hazarding their lives on an errand of mercy; and all the while have so little notion that they are hazarding their lives, or doing anything dangerous or heroic, that, instead of being touched for a moment by nature's melodrama, they are jesting at each other's troubles, greeting each interval of darkness with mock shouts of misery and despair, likening the crags to various fogies of their acquaintance, male and female, and only pulling the cutty pipes out of their mouths to chant snatches of jovial songs. They are Wynd and Naylor, the two Cambridge boating-men, in bedrabbled flannel trousers, and shooting-jackets pocketful of water; who are both fully agreed that hunting a mad poet over the mountains in a thunderstorm is, on the whole, " the jolliest lark they ever had in their lives."

"He must have gone up here somewhere. I saw the poor beggar against the sky as plain as I see you — which I don't —— " for darkness cut the speech short.

"Where be you, William? says the keeper."

" Here I be, sir, says the beater, with my 'ecls above my 'ed."

"Wery well, William; when you get your 'ed above your 'eels, gae on."

" But I'm stuck fast between two stones! Hang the stones!" And Naylor bursts into an old seventeenth century ditty, of the days of "three-man glees."

> "'They stoans, they stoans, they stoans, they stoans —
> They stoans that built George Riddler's oven,
> O they was fetched from Blackeney quarr';
> And George he was a jolly old man,
> And his head did grow above his har'.

> "'One thing in George Riddler I must commend,
> And I hold it for a valiant thing;
> With any three brothers in Gloucestershire
> He swore that his three sons should sing.

"'There was Dick the tribble, and Tom the mane,
    Let every man sing in his own place;
    And William he was the eldest brother,
    And therefore he should sing the base ——'

I'm down again!   This is my thirteenth fall."

"So am I!   I shall just lie and light a pipe."

"Come on, now, and look round the lee side of this crag.   We shall find him bundled up under the lee of one of the n."

"He don't know lee from windward, I dare say."

"He'll soon find out the difference by his skin; if it's half as wet, at least, as mine is."

"I'll tell you what, Naylor, if the poor fellow has crossed the ridge, and tried to go down on the Twll du, he's a dead man by this time."

"He'll have funked it, when he comes to the edge, and sees nothing but mist below.   But if he has wandered on to the cliffs above Trifaen, he's a dead man, then, at all events.   Get out of the way of that flash!   A close shave that!   I believe my whiskers are singed."

"'Pon my honor, Wynd, we ought to be saying our prayers rather than joking in this way."

"We may do both, and be none the worse.   As for coming to grief, old boy, we're on a good errand, I suppose, and the devil himself can't harm us.   Still, shame to him who's ashamed of saying his prayers, as Arnold used to say."

And all the while, these two brave lads have been thrusting their lanthorn into every crack and cranny, and beating round every crag carefully and cunningly, till long past two in the morning.

"Here's the ordnance cairn at last; and — here am I astride of a carving knife, I think!

Come and help me off, or I shall be split to the chin!"

"I'm coming! What's this soft under my feet? Who-o-o-oop! Run him to earth at last!"

And diving down into a crack, Wynd drags out by the collar the unconscious Elsley.

"What a swab! Like a piece of wet blotting-paper. Lucky he's not made of salt."

"He's dead!" says Naylor.

"Not a bit. I can feel his heart. There's life in the old dog yet."

And they begin, under the lee of a rock, chafing him, wrapping him in their plaids, and pouring whiskey down his throat.

It was some time before Vavasour recovered his consciousness. The first use which he made of it was to bid his preservers leave him; querulously at first; and then fiercely, when he found out who they were.

"Leave me, I say! Cannot I be alone if I choose? What right have you to dog me in this way?"

"My dear sir, we have as much right here as any one else; and if we find a man dying here of cold and fatigue ——"

"What business of yours, if I choose to die?"

"There is no harm in your dying, sir," says Naylor. "The harm is in our letting you die; I assure you it is entirely to satisfy our own consciences we are troubling you thus;" and he begins pressing him to take food.

"No, sir; nothing from you! You have shown me impertinence enough in the last few weeks, without pressing on me benefits for which I do not wish. Let me go! If you will not leave me, I shall leave you!"

And he tried to rise; but, stiffened with cold, sank back again upon the rock.

In vain they tried to reason with him; begged his pardon for all past jests: he made effort after effort to get up; and at last, his limbs, regaining strength by the fierceness of his passion, supported him; and he struggled onward toward the northern slope of the mountain.

" You must not go down till it is light; it is as much as your life is worth."

" I am going to Bangor, sir; and go I will! "

" I tell you there are fifteen hundred feet of slippery screes below you."

" As steep as a house-roof, and with every tile on it loose. You will roll from top to bottom before you have gone a hundred yards."

" What care I? Let me go, I say! Curse you, sir! Do you mean to use force? "

" I do," said Wynd, quietly, as he took him round arms and body, and set him down on the rock like a child.

" You have assaulted me, sir! The law shall avenge this insult, if there be law in England! "

" I know nothing about law: but I suppose it will justify me in saving any man's life who is rushing to certain death."

" Look here, sir! " said Naylor. " Go down, if you will, when it grows light: but from this place you do not stir yet. Whatever you may think of our conduct to-night, you will thank us for it to-morrow morning, when you see where you are."

The unhappy man stamped with rage. The red glare of the lanthorn showed him his two powerful warders, standing right and left. He felt that there was no escape from them, but in darkness; and suddenly he dashed at the lanthorn, and tried to tear it out of Wynd's hands.

"Steady, sir!" said Wynd, springing back, and parrying his outstretched hand. "If you wish us to consider you in your senses, you will be quiet."

"And if you don't choose to appear sane," said Naylor, "you must not be surprised if we treat you as men are treated who — you understand me."

Elsley was silent awhile; his rage, finding itself impotent, subsided into dark cunning. "Really, gentlemen," he said at length, "I believe you are right; I have been very foolish, and you very kind; but you would excuse my absurdities if you knew their provocation."

"My dear sir," said Naylor, "we are bound to believe that you have good cause enough for what you are doing. We have no wish to interfere impertinently. Only wait till daylight, and wrap yourself in one of our plaids, as the only possible method of carrying out your own intentions; for dead men can't go to Bangor, whithersoever else they may go."

"You really are too kind: but I believe I must accept your offer, under penalty of being called mad;" and Elsley laughed a hollow laugh; for he was by no means sure that he was not mad. He took the proffered wrapper, lay down, and seemed to sleep.

Wynd and Naylor, congratulating themselves on his better mind, lay down also beneath the other plaid, intending to watch him. But worn out with fatigue, they were both fast asleep ere ten minutes had passed.

Elsley had determined to keep himself awake at all risks; and he paid a bitter penalty for so doing;

for now that the fury had passed away, his brain began to work freely again, and inflicted torture so exquisite, that he looked back with regret at the unreasoning madness of last night, as a less fearful hell than that of thought; of deliberate, acute recollections, suspicions, trains of argument, which he tried to thrust from him, and yet could not. Who has not known in the still, sleepless hours of night, how dark thoughts will possess the mind with terrors, which seem logical, irrefragable, inevitable?

So it was then with the wretched Elsley; within his mind a whole train of devil's advocates seemed arguing, with triumphant subtlety, the certainty of Lucia's treason; and justifying to him his rage, his hatred, his flight, his desertion of his own children — if indeed (so far had the devil led him astray) they were his own. At last he could bear it no longer. He would escape to Bangor, and then to London, cross to France, to Italy, and there bury himself amid the forests of the Apennines, or the sunny glens of Calabria. And for a moment the vision of a poet's life in that glorious land brightened his dark imagination. Yes! He would escape thither, and be at peace; and if the world heard of him again, it should be in such a thunder-voice as those with which Shelley and Byron, from their southern seclusion, had shaken the ungrateful motherland which cast them out. He would escape; and now was the time to do it! For the rain had long since ceased; the dawn was approaching fast; the cloud was thinning from black to pearly gray. Now was his time — were it not for those two men! To be kept, guarded, stopped by them, or by any man! Shameful!

intolerable! He had fled hither to be free, and
even here he found himself a prisoner. True, they
had promised to let him go if he waited till daylight; but perhaps they were deceiving him, as he
was deceiving them — why not? They thought
him mad. It was a ruse, a stratagem to keep him
quiet awhile, and then bring him back — "restore
him to his afflicted friends." His friends, truly!
He would be too cunning for them yet. And even
if they meant to let him go, would he accept liberty
from them, or any man? No; he was free. He
had a right to go; and go he would, that moment!

He raised himself cautiously. The lanthorn had
burned to the socket; and he could not see the
men, though they were not four yards off; but by
their regular and heavy breathing he could tell that
they both slept soundly. He slipped from under the
plaid, drew off his shoes for fear of noise among
the rocks, and rose. What if he did make a noise?
What if they woke, chased him, brought him back
by force? Curse the thought! And gliding close
to them, he listened again to their heavy breathing.

How could he prevent their following him?

A horrible, nameless temptation came over him.
Every vein in his body throbbed fire; his brain
seemed to swell to bursting; and ere he was aware,
he found himself feeling about in the darkness for a
loose stone.

He could not find one. Thank God that he
could not find one! But after that dreadful
thought had once crossed his mind, he must flee
from that place ere the brand of Cain be on his
brow.

With a cunning and activity utterly new to him,
he glided away like a snake; downward over crags

and boulders, he knew not how long or how far;
all he knew was, that he was going down, down,
down, into a dim abyss. There was just light
enough to discern the upper surface of a rock
within arm's length; beyond that all was blank.
He seemed to be hours descending; to be going
down miles after miles; and still he reached no
level spot. The mountain-side was too steep for
him to stand upright, except at moments. It
seemed one uniform quarry of smooth broken slate,
slipping down for ever beneath his feet. Whither?
He grew giddy, and more giddy; and a horrible
fantastic notion seized him, that he had lost his
way; that somehow the precipice had no bottom,
no end at all; that he was going down some infinite
abyss, into the very depths of the earth, and the
molten roots of the mountains, never to reascend.
He stopped, trembling, only to slide down again;
terrified, he tried to struggle upward, but the shale
gave way beneath his feet, and go he must.

What was that noise above his head? A falling
stone? Were his enemies in pursuit? Down to
the depth of hell rather than that they should take
him! He drove his heels into the slippery shale,
and rushed forward blindly, springing, slipping,
falling, rolling, till he stopped breathless on a jutting
slab.

And lo! below him, through the thin pearly veil
of cloud, a dim world of dark cliffs, blue lakes, gray
mountains with their dark heads wrapped in cloud,
and the straight vale of Nant Francon, magnified in
mist, till it seemed to stretch for hundreds of
leagues towards the rosy northeast dawning and
the shining sea.

With a wild shout he hurried onward. In five

minutes he was clear of the cloud. He reached the foot of that enormous slope, and hurried over rocky ways, till he stopped at the top of a precipice, full six hundred feet above the lonely tarn of Idwal.

Never mind. He knew where he was now; he knew that there was a passage somewhere, for he had once seen one from below. He found it, and almost ran along the boggy shore of Idwal, looking back every now and then at the black wall of the Twll du, in dread lest he should see two moving specks in hot pursuit.

And now he had gained the shore of Ogwen, and the broad coach-road; and down it he strode, running at times, past the roaring cataract, past the enormous cliffs of the Carnedds, past Tin-y-maes, where nothing was stirring but a barking dog; on through the sleeping streets of Bethesda, past the black stairs of the Penrhyn quarry. The huge clicking ant-heap was silent now, save for the roar of Ogwen, as he swirled and bubbled down, rich coffee-brown from last night's rain.

On, past rich woods, past trim cottages, gardens gay with flowers; past rhododendron shrubberies, broad fields of golden stubble, sweet clover, and gray swedes, with Ogwen making music far below. The sun is up at last, and Colonel Pennant's grim slate castle, towering above black woods, glitters metallic in its rays, like Chaucer's house of fame. He stops, to look back once. Far up the vale, eight miles away, beneath a roof of cloud, the pass of Nant Francon gapes high in air between the great jaws of the Carnedd and the Glyder, its cliffs marked with the upright white line of the waterfall. He is clear of the mountains; clear of that cursed place, and all its cursed thoughts! On, past

Llandegai and all its rose-clad cottages; past yellow quarrymen walking out to their work, who stare as they pass at his haggard face, drenched clothes, and streaming hair. He does not see them. One fixed thought is in his mind, and that is, the railway station at Bangor.

He is striding through Bangor streets now, beside the summer sea, from which fresh scents of shore-weed greet him. He had rather smell the smoke and gas of the Strand.

The station is shut. He looks at the bill outside. There is no train for full two hours; and he throws himself, worn-out with fatigue, upon the doorstep.

Now a new terror seizes him. Has he money enough to reach London? Has he his purse at all? Too dreadful to find himself stopped short, on the very brink of deliverance! A cold perspiration breaks from his forehead, as he feels in every pocket. Yes, his purse is there; but he turns sick as he opens it, and dare hardly look. Hurrah! Five pounds, six — eight! That will take him as far as Paris. He can walk, beg the rest of the way, if need be.

What will he do now? Wander over the town, and gaze vacantly on one little object and another about the house fronts. One thing he will not look at; and that is the bright summer sea, all golden in the sun rays, flecked with gay white sails. From all which is bright, and calm, and cheerful, his soul shrinks as from an impertinence; he longs for the lurid gas-light of London, and the roar of the Strand, and the everlasting stream of faces, among whom he may wander free, sure that no one will recognize him, the disgraced, the desperate.

The weary hours roll on. Too tired to stand

longer, he sits down on the shafts of a cart, and tries not to think. It is not difficult. Body and mind are alike worn out, and his brain seems filled with uniform dull mist.

A shop-door open in front of him; a boy comes out. He sees bottles inside, and shelves, the look of which he knows too well.

The bottle-boy, whistling, begins to take the shutters down. How often, in Whitbury of old, had Elsley done the same! Half amused, he watched the lad, and wondered how he spent his evenings, and what works he read, and whether he ever thought of writing poetry.

And as he watched, all his past life rose up before him, ever since he served out medicines fifteen years ago — his wild aspirations, heavy labors, struggles, plans, brief triumphs, long disappointments; and here was what it had all come to — a failure — a miserable, shameful failure! Not that he thought of it with repentance, with a single wish that he had done otherwise; but only with disappointed rage. "Yes!" he said bitterly to himself —

> " ' We poets in our youth begin in gladness,
>   But after come despondency and madness.'

This is the way of the world with all who have nobler feelings in them than will fit into its cold rules. Curse the world! what on earth had I to do with mixing myself up in it, and marrying a fine lady? Fool that I was! I might have known from the first that she could not understand me; that she would go back to her own! Let her go! I will forget her, and the world, and everything — and I know how!"

And, springing up, he walked across to the druggist's shop.

Years before, Elsley had tried opium, and found, unhappily for him, that it fed his fancy without inflicting those tortures of indigestion which keep many, happily for them, from its magic snare. He had tried it more than once of late; but Lucia had had a hint of the fact from Thurnall: and in just terror had exacted from him a solemn promise never to touch opium again. Elsley was a man of honor, and the promise had been kept. But now: "I promised her, and therefore I will break my promise! She has broken hers, and I am free!"

And he went in and bought his opium. He took a little on the spot, to allay the cravings of hunger. He reserved a full dose for the railway carriage. It would bridge over the weary gulf of time which lay between him and town.

He took his second-class place at last; not without stares and whispers from those round at the wild figure which was starting for London without bag or baggage. But as the clerks agreed, "If he was running away from his creditors, it was a shame to stop him. If he was running from the police, they would have the more sport the longer the run. At least it was no business of theirs."

There was one thing more to do, and he did it. He wrote to Campbell a short note.

"If, as I suppose, you expect from me 'the satisfaction of a gentleman,' you will find me at . . . Adelphi. I am not escaping from you, but from the whole world. If, by shooting me, you can quicken my escape, you will do me the first and last favor which I am likely to ask for from you."

He posted his letter, settled himself in a corner

of the carriage, and took his second dose of opium. From that moment he recollected little more. A confused whirl of hedges and woods, rattling stations, screaming and flashing trains, great red towns, white chalk cuttings; while the everlasting roar and rattle of the carriages shaped themselves in his brain into a hundred snatches of old tunes, all full of a strange merriment, as if mocking at his misery, striving to keep him awake and conscious of who and what he was. He closed his eyes and shut out the hateful, garish world; but that sound he could not shut out. Too tired to sleep, too tired even to think, he could do nothing but submit to the ridiculous torment; watching in spite of himself every note, as one jig-tune after another was fiddled by all the imps close to his ear, mile after mile, and county after county, for all that weary day, which seemed full seven years long.

At Euston Square the porter called him several times ere he could rouse him. He could hear nothing for awhile but that same imps' melody, even though it had stopped. At last he got out, staring round him, shook himself awake by one strong effort, and hurried away, not knowing whither he went.

Wrapt up in self, he wandered on till dark, slept on a doorstep, and awoke, not knowing at first where he was. Gradually all the horror came back to him, and with the horror the craving for opium wherewith to forget it.

He looked round to see his whereabouts. Surely this must be Golden Square? A sudden thought struck him. He went to a chemist's shop, bought a fresh supply of his poison, and, taking only enough to allay the cravings of his stomach, hurried tottering in the direction of Drury Lane.

CHAPTER XXII

FOND, YET NOT FOOLISH

NEXT morning only Claude and Campbell made their appearance at breakfast.

Frank came in; found that Valentia was not down: and, too excited to eat, went out to walk till she should appear. Neither did Lord Scoutbush come. Where was he?

Ignorant of the whole matter, he had started at four o'clock to fish in the Traeth Mawr; half for fishing's sake, half (as he confessed) to gain time for his puzzled brains before those explanations with Frank Headley, of which he stood in mortal fear.

Mellot and Campbell sat down together to breakfast; but in silence. Claude saw that something had gone very wrong; Campbell ate nothing, and looked nervously out of the window every now and then.

At last Bowie entered with the letters and a message. There were two gentlemen from Pen-y-gwryd must speak with Mr. Mellot immediately.

He went out and found Wynd and Naylor. What they told him we know already. He returned instantly, and met Campbell leaving the room.

"I have news of Vavasour," whispered he. "I have a letter from him. Bowie, order me a car instantly for Bangor. I am off to London, Claude.

You and Bowie will take care of my things, and send them after me."

"Major Cawmill has only to command," said Bowie, and vanished down the stairs.

"Now, Claude, quick; read that, and counsel me. I ought to ask Scoutbush's opinion; but the poor dear fellow is out, you see."

Claude read the note written at Bangor.

"Fight him I will not! I detest the notion: a soldier should never fig⊦t a duel. His life is the Queen's, and not his own. And yet, if the honor of the family has been compromised by my folly, I must pay the penalty, if Scoutbush thinks it proper."

So said Campbell, who, in the over-sensitiveness of his conscience, had actually worked himself round during the past night into this new fancy, as a chivalrous act of utter self-abasement. The proud self-possession of the man was gone, and nothing but self-distrust and shame remained.

"In the name of all wit and wisdom, what is the meaning of all this?"

"You do not know, then, what passed last night?"

"I? I can only guess that Vavasour has had one of his rages."

"Then you must know," said Campbell, with an effort: "for you must explain all to Scoutbush when he returns; and I know no one more fit for the office." And he briefly told him the story.

Mellot was much affected. "The wretched ape! Campbell, your first thought was the true one: you must not fight that cur. After all, it's a farce: you won't fire at him, and he can't hit you — so leave ill alone. Beside, for Scoutbush's sake, her sake, every one's sake, the thing must be hushed up. If the fellow chooses to duck under into the London mire, let him lie there, and forget him!"

"No, Claude; his pardon I must beg, ere I go out to the war: or I shall die with a sin upon my soul."

"My dear, noble creature! if you must go, I go with you. I must see fair play between you and that madman; and give him a piece of my mind, too, while I am about it. He is in my power, or if not quite that, I know one in whose power he is! and to reason he shall be brought."

"No; you must stay here. I cannot trust Scoutbush's head, and these poor dear souls will have no one to look to but you. I can trust you with them, I know. Me you will perhaps never see again."

"You can trust me!" said the affectionate little painter, the tears starting to his eyes, as he wrung Campbell's hand.

"Mind one thing! If that Vavasour shows his teeth, there is a spell will turn him to stone. Use it!"

"Heaven forbid! Let him show his teeth. It is I who am in the wrong. Why should I make him more my enemy than he is?"

"Be it so. Only, if the worst comes to the worst, call him not Elsley Vavasour, but plain John Briggs — and see what follows."

Valentia entered.

"The post has come in! O dear Major Campbell, is there a letter?"

He put the note into her hand in silence. She read it, and darted back to Lucia's room.

"Thank God that she did not see that I was going! One more pang on earth spared!" said Campbell to himself.

Valentia hurried to Lucia's door. She was holding it ajar and looking out with pale face, and wild hungry eyes. "A letter? Don't be silent, or I shall go mad! Tell me the worst! Is he alive?"

"Yes."

She gasped, and staggered against the door-post.

"Where? Why does he not come back to me?" asked she, in a confused, abstracted way.

It was best to tell the truth, and have it over.

"He has gone to London, Lucia. He will think over it all there, and be sorry for it, and then all will be well again."

But Lucia did not hear the end of that sentence. Murmuring to herself, "To London! To London!" she hurried back into the room.

"Clara! Clara! have the children had their breakfast?"

"Yes, ma'am!" says Clara, appearing from the inner room.

"Then help me to pack up, quick! Your master is gone to London on business; and we are to follow him immediately."

And she began bustling about the room.

"My dearest Lucia, you are not fit to travel now!"

"I shall die if I stay here; die if I do nothing! I must find him!" whispered she. "Don't speak loud, or Clara will hear. I can find him, and nobody can but me! Why don't you help me to pack, Valentia?"

"My dearest! but what will Scoutbush say when he comes home, and finds you gone?"

"What right has he to interfere? I am Elsley's wife, am I not? and may follow my husband if I like;" and she went on desperately collecting, not her own things, but Elsley's.

Valentia watched her with tear-brimming eyes; collecting all his papers, counting over his clothes, murmuring to herself that he would want this and that in London. Her sanity seemed failing her, under the fixed idea that she had only to see him, and set all right with a word.

"I will go and get you some breakfast," said she at last.

"I want none. I am too busy to eat. Why don't you help me?"

Valentia had not the heart to help, believing, as she did, that Lucia's journey would be as bootless as it would be dangerous to her health.

"I will bring you some breakfast, and you must try; then I will help to pack:" and utterly bewildered she went out; and the thought uppermost in her mind was, "Oh, that I could find Frank Headley!"

Happy was it for Frank's love, paradoxical as it may seem, that it had conquered just at that moment of terrible distress. Valentia's acceptance of him had been hasty, founded rather on sentiment and admiration than on deep affection; and her feeling might have faltered, waned, died away in self-distrust of its own reality, if giddy amusement, if mere easy happiness, had followed it. But now the fire of affliction was branding in the thought of him upon her softened heart.

Living at the utmost strain of her character, Campbell gone, her brother useless, and Lucia and the children depending utterly on her, there was but one to whom she could look for comfort while she needed it most utterly; and happy for her and for her lover that she could go to him.

"Poor Lucia! thank God that I have some one who will never treat me so! who will lift me up and shield me, instead of crushing me!—dear creature! Oh that I may find him!" And her heart went out after Frank with a gush of tenderness which she had never felt before.

"Is this, then, love?" she asked herself; and she found time to slip into her own room for a moment and arrange her dishevelled hair, ere she entered the breakfast-room.

Frank was there, luckily alone, pacing nervously up and down. He hurried up to her, caught both her hands in his, and gazed into her wan and haggard face with the intensest tenderness and anxiety.

Valentia's eyes looked into the depths of his, passive and confiding, till they failed before the keenness of his gaze, and swam in glittering mist.

"Ah!" thought she; "sorrow is a light price to pay for the feeling of being so loved by such a man!"

"You are tired—ill? What a night you must have had! Mellot has told me all."

"O my poor sister!" and wildly she poured out to Frank her wrath against Elsley, her inability to comfort Lucia, and all the misery and confusion of the past night.

"This is a sad dawning for the day of my triumph!" thought Frank, who longed to pour out his heart to her on a thousand very different matters: but he was content; it was enough for him that she could tell him all, and confide in him;

a truer sign of affection than any selfish love-making; and he asked, and answered, with such tenderness and thoughtfulness for poor Lucia, with such a deep comprehension of Elsley's character, pitying while he blamed, that he won his reward at last.

"Oh! it would be intolerable, if I had not through it all the thought ——" and blushing crimson, her head drooped on her bosom. She seemed ready to drop with exhaustion.

"Sit down, sit down, or you will fall!" said Frank, leading her to a chair; and as he led her, he whispered with fluttering heart, new to its own happiness, and longing to make assurance sure: "What thought?"

She was silent still; but he felt her hand tremble in his.

"The thought of me?"

She looked up in his face; how beautiful! And in another moment, neither knew how, she was clasped to his bosom.

He covered her face, her hair with kisses: she did not move; from that moment she felt that he was her husband.

"Oh, guide me! counsel me! pray for me!" sobbed she. "I am all alone, and my poor sister, she is going mad, I think, and I have no one to trust but you; and you — you will leave me to go to those dreadful wars; and then, what will become of me? Oh, stay! only a few days!" and holding him convulsively, she answered his kisses with her own.

Frank stood as in a dream, while the room reeled round and vanished; and he was alone for a moment upon earth with her and his great love.

"Tell me," said he at last, trying to awaken himself to action. "Tell me! Is she really going to seek him?"

"Yes, selfish and forgetful that I am! You must help me! she will go to London, nothing can stop her; and it will kill her!"

"It may drive her mad to keep her here."

"It will! and that drives me mad also. What can I choose?"

"Follow where God leads. It is she, after all, who must reclaim him. Leave her in God's hands, and go with her to London."

"But my brother?"

"Mellot or I will see him. Let it be me. Mellot shall go with you to London."

"Oh that you were going!"

"Oh that I were! I will follow, though. Do you think that I can be long away from you? . . . But I must tell your brother. I had a very different matter on which to speak to him this morning," said he, with a sad smile: "but better as it is. He shall find me, I hope, reasonable and trustworthy in this matter; perhaps enough so to have my Valentia committed to me. Precious jewel! I must learn to be a man now, at least; now that I have you to care for."

"And yet you go and leave me?"

"Valentia! Because God has given us to each other, shall our thank-offering be to shrink cowardly from His work?"

He spoke more sternly than he intended, to awe into obedience rather himself than her; for he felt, poor fellow, his courage failing fast, while he held that treasure in his arms.

She shuddered in silence.

"Forgive me!" he cried; "I was too harsh, Valentia!"

"No!" she cried, looking up at him with a glorious smile. "Scold me! Be harsh to me! It is so delicious now to be reproved by you." And as she spoke she felt as if she would rather endure torture from that man's hand than bliss from any other. How many strange words of Lucia's that new feeling explained to her; words at which she had once grown angry, as doting weaknesses, unjust and degrading to self-respect. Poor Lucia! She might be able to comfort her now, for she had learnt to sympathize with her by experience the very opposite to hers. Yet there must have been a time when Lucia clung to Elsley as she to Frank. How horrible to have her eyes opened thus! To be torn and flung away from the bosom where she longed to rest! It could never happen to her. Of course her Frank was true, though all the world was false: but poor Lucia! She must go to her. This was mere selfishness at such a moment.

"You will find Scoutbush, then?"

"This moment. I will order the car now, if you will only eat. You must!"

And he rang the bell, and then made her sit down and eat, almost feeding her with his own hand. That, too, was a new experience; and one so strangely pleasant, that when Bowie entered, and stared solemnly at the pair, she only looked up smiling, though blushing a little.

"Get a car instantly," said she.

"For Mrs. Vavasour, my lady? She has ordered hers already."

"No; for Mr. Headley. He is going to find

my lord. Frank, pour me out a cup of tea for Lucia."

Bowie vanished, mystified. "It's no concern of mine; but better tak' up wi' a godly meenister than a godless pawet," said the worthy warrior to himself as he marched downstairs.

"You see that I am asserting our rights already before all the world," said she, looking up.

"I see you are not ashamed of me."

"Ashamed of you?"

"And now I must go to Lucia."

"And to London."

Valentia began to cry like any baby; but rose and carried away the tea in her hand. "Must I go? and before you come back, too?"

"Is she determined to start instantly?"

"I cannot stop her. You see she has ordered the car."

"Then go, my darling! My own! My Valentia! Oh, a thousand things to ask you, and no time to ask them in! I can write?" said Frank, with an inquiring smile.

"Write? Yes; every day — twice a day. I shall live upon those letters. Good-bye!" And out she went, while Frank sat himself down at the table, and laid his head upon his hands, stupefied with delight, till Bowie entered.

"The car, sir."

"Which? Who?" asked Frank, looking up as from a dream.

"The car, sir."

Frank rose, and walked downstairs abstractedly. Bowie kept close to his side.

"Ye'll pardon me, sir," said he, in a low voice; "but I see how it is — the more blessing for you.

Ye 'll be pleased, I trust, to take more care of this jewel than others have of that one: or —— "

"Or you 'll shoot me yourself, Bowie?" said Frank, half amused, half awed, too, by the stern tone of the guardsman. "I 'll give you leave to do it if I deserve it."

"It 's no my duty, either as a soldier or as a valet. And, indeed, I 've that opeenion of you, sir, that I don't think it 'll need to be any one else's duty either."

And so did Mr. Bowie signify his approbation of the new family romance, and went off to assist Mrs. Clara in getting the trunks downstairs.

Clara was in high dudgeon. She had not yet completed her flirtation with Mr. Bowie, and felt it hard to have her one amusement in life snatched out of her hard-worked hands.

"I 'm sure I don't know why we 're moving. I don't believe it 's business. Some of his tantrums, I dare say. I heard her walking up and down the room all last night, I 'll swear. Neither she nor Miss Valentia has been to bed. He 'll kill her at last, the brute!"

"It 's no concern of either of us, that. Have you got another trunk to bring down?"

"No concern? Just like your hard-heartedness, Mr. Bowie. And as soon as I 'm gone, of course you will be flirting with these impudent Welsh-women, in their horrid hats."

"May be, yes; may be, no. But flirting 's no marrying, Mrs. Clara."

"True for you, sir! Men were deceivers ever," quoth Clara, and flounced upstairs; while Bowie looked after her with a grim smile, and caught her, when she came down again, long enough to give her a great kiss; the only language which he used in wooing, and that but rarely.

"Dinna fash, lassie. Mind your lady and the poor bairns, like a godly handmaiden, and I'll buy the ring when the sawmon fishing's over, and we'll just be married ere I start for the Crimee."

"The sawmon!" cried Clara. "I'll see you turned into a mermaid first, and married to a sawmon!"

"And ye won't do anything o' the kind," said Bowie to himself, and shouldered a valise.

In ten minutes the ladies were packed into the carriage, and away, under Mellot's care. Frank watched Valentia looking back, and smiling through her tears, as they rolled through the village; and then got into his car, and rattled down the southern road to Pont Aberglaslyn, his hand still tingling with the last pressure of Valentia's.

CHAPTER XXIII

THE BROAD STONE OF HONOR

BUT where has Stangrave been all this while?
Where any given bachelor has been, for
any given month, is difficult to say, and no man's
business but his own. But where he happened to
be on a certain afternoon in the first week of
October, on which he had just heard the news of
Alma, was — upon the hills between Ems and
Coblentz. Walking over a high tableland of
stubbles, which would be grass in England; and
yet with all its tillage is perhaps not worth more
than English grass would be, thanks to that small-
farm system much be-praised by some who know
not wheat from turnips. Then along a road, which
might be a Devon one, cut in the hillside, through
authentic " Devonian " slate, where the deep choco-
late soil is lodged on the top of the upright strata,
and a thick coat of moss and wood sedge clusters
about the oak-scrub roots, round which the delicate
and rare oak-fern mingles its fronds with great
blue campanulas; while the " white admirals "
and silver-washed " fritillaries " flit round every
bramble bed, and the great " purple emperors "
come down to drink in the road puddles, and sit
fearless, flashing off their velvet wings a blue as of
that empyrean which is " dark by excess of light."

Down again through cultivated lands, corn and
clover, flax and beet, and all the various crops

with which the industrious German yeoman ekes out his little patch of soil. Past the thrifty husbandman himself, as he guides the two milch-kine in his tiny plough, and stops at the furrow's end, to greet you with the hearty German smile and bow; while the little fair-haired maiden, walking beneath the shade of standard cherries, walnuts, and pears, all gray with fruit, fills the cows' mouths with chicory, and wild carnations, and pink saint-foin, and many a fragrant weed which richer England wastes.

Down once more into a glen; but such a glen as neither England nor America has ever seen; or, please God, ever will see, glorious as it is. Stangrave, who knew all Europe well, had walked the path before; but he stopped then, as he had done the first time, in awe. On the right, slope up the bare slate downs, up to the foot of cliffs: but only half of those cliffs God has made. Above the gray slate ledges rise cliffs of man's handiwork, pierced with a hundred square black embrasures; and above them the long barrack-ranges of a soldiers' town; which a foeman stormed once, when it was young: but what foeman will ever storm it again? What conqueror's foot will ever tread again upon the "broad stone of honor," and call Ehrenbreitstein his?

On the left the clover and the corn range on, beneath the orchard boughs, up to yon knoll of chestnut and acacia, tall poplar, feathered larch: but what is that stonework which gleams gray beneath their stems? A summer-house for some great duke, looking out over the glorious Rhine vale, and up the long vineyards of the bright Moselle, from whence he may bid his people eat, drink, and take their ease, for they have much goods laid up for many years?

Bank over bank of earth and stone, cleft by deep embrasures, from which the great guns grin across the rich gardens, studded with standard fruit-trees, which clothe the glacis to its topmost edge. And there, below him, lie the vineyards: every rock-ledge and narrow path of soil tossing its golden tendrils to the sun, gray with ripening clusters, rich with noble wine; but what is that wall which winds among them, up and down, creeping and sneaking over every ledge and knoll of vantage ground, pierced with eyelet-holes, backed by strange stairs and galleries of stone; till it rises close before him, to meet the low round tower full in his path, from whose deep casemates, as from dark scowling eye-holes, the ugly cannon-eyes stare up the glen?

Stangrave knows them all — as far as any man can know. The wards of the key which locks apart the nations; the yet maiden Troy of Europe; the greatest fortress of the world.

He walks down, turns into the vineyards, and lies down beneath the mellow shade of vines. He has no sketch-book — article forbidden; his pass-port is in his pocket; and he speaks all tongues of German men. So, fearless of gendarmes and soldiers, he lies down, in the blazing German afternoon, upon the shaly soil; and watches the bright-eyed lizards hunt flies along the roasting walls, and the great locusts buzz and pitch and leap; green locusts with red wings, and gray locusts with blue wings; he notes the species, for he is tired and lazy, and has so many thoughts within his head that he is glad to toss them all away, and give up his soul, if possible, to locusts and lizards, vines and shade.

And far below him fleets the mighty Rhine, rich with the memories of two thousand stormy years; and on its further bank the gray-walled Coblentz town, and the long arches of the Moselle bridge, and the rich flats of Kaiser Franz, and the long poplar-crested uplands, which look so gay, and are so stern; for everywhere between the poplar-stems the saw-toothed outline of the western forts cuts the blue sky.

And far beyond it all sleeps, high in air, the Eifel with its hundred crater peaks; blue mound behind blue mound, melting into white haze. Stangrave has walked upon those hills, and stood upon the crater-lip of the great Moselkopf, and dreamed beside the Laacher See, beneath the ancient abbey walls; and his thoughts flit across the Moselle flats towards his ancient haunts, as he asks himself — How long has that old Eifel lain in such soft sleep? How long ere it awake again?

It may awake, geologists confess — why not? and blacken all the skies with smoke of Tophet, pouring its streams of boiling mud once more to dam the Rhine, whelming the works of men in flood, and ash, and fire. Why not? The old earth seems so solid at first sight: but look a little nearer, and this is the stuff of which she is made! The wreck of past earthquakes, the leavings of old floods, the washings of cold cinder heaps — which are smouldering still below.

Stangrave knew that well enough. He had climbed Vesuvius, Etna, Popocatepetl. He had felt many an earthquake shock; and knew how far to trust the everlasting hills. And was old David right, he thought that day, when he held the earthquake and the volcano as the truest symbols of the history of human kind, and of the dealings of their Maker with them?   All the magnificent Plutonic imagery of the Hebrew poets, had it no meaning for men now?   Did the Lord still uncover the foundations of the world, spiritual as well as physical, with the breath of His displeasure?   Was the solfa-tara of Tophet still ordained for tyrants?   And did the Lord still arise out of His place to shake terribly the earth?   Or had the moral world grown as sleepy as the physical one had seemed to have done?   Would anything awful, unexpected, tragical, ever burst forth again from the heart of earth, or from the heart of man?

Surprising question!   What can ever happen henceforth, save infinite railroads and crystal palaces, peace and plenty, cockaigne and dilettanteism, to the end of time?   Is it not full sixty whole years since the first French revolution, and six whole years since the revolution of all Europe?   Bah!—change is a thing of the past, and tragedy a myth of our forefathers; war a bad habit of old barbarians, eradicated by the spread of an enlightened philanthropy.   Men know now how to govern the world far too well to need any divine visitations, much less divine punishments; and Stangrave was a Utopian dreamer, only to be excused by the fact that he had in his pocket the news that three great nations were gone forth to tear each other as of yore.

Nevertheless, looking round upon those grim earth-mounds and embrasures, he could not but give the men who put them there credit for supposing that they might be wanted.   Ah! but that might be only one of the direful necessities of the decaying civilization of the old world.   What a contrast to the unarmed and peaceful prosperity of his own country! Thank Heaven, New England needed no fortresses, military roads, or standing armies! True, but why that flush of contemptuous pity for the poor old world, which could only hold its own by such expensive and ugly methods?

He asked himself that very question, a moment after, angrily; for he was out of humor with himself, with his country, and indeed with the universe in general. And across his mind flashed a memorable conversation at Constantinople long since, during which he had made some such unwise remark to Thurnall, and received from him a sharp answer, which parted them for years.

It was natural enough that that conversation should come back to him just then; for, in his jealousy, he was thinking of Tom Thurnall often enough every day; and in spite of his enmity, he could not help suspecting more and more that Thurnall had had some right on his side of the quarrel.

He had been twitting Thurnall with the miserable condition of the laborers in the south of England, and extolling his own country at the expense of ours. Tom, unable to deny the fact, had waxed all the more wroth at having it pressed on him; and at last had burst forth:

"Well, and what right have you to crow over us on that score? I suppose, if you could hire a man in America for eighteen-pence a day, instead of a dollar and a half, you would do it? You Americans are not accustomed to give more for a thing than it's worth in the market, are you?"

"But," Stangrave had answered, "the glory of America is, that you cannot get the man for less than the dollar and a half; that he is too well fed, too prosperous, too well educated, to be made a slave of."

"And therefore makes slaves of the niggers instead? I'll tell you what, I'm sick of that shallow fallacy — the glory of America! Do you mean, by America, the country or the people? You boast, all of you, of your country, as if you had made it yourselves; and quite forget that God made America, and America has made you.'

"Made us, sir?" quoth Stangrave fiercely enough.

"Made you!" replied Thurnall, exaggerating his half truth from anger. "To what is your comfort, your high feeding, your very education, owing, but to your having a thin population, a virgin soil, and unlimited means of emigration? What credit to you if you need no poor laws, when you pack off your children, as fast as they grow up, to clear more ground westward? What credit to your yeomen that they have read more books than our clods have, while they can earn more in four hours than our poor fellows in twelve? It all depends on the mere physical fact of your being in a new country, and we in an old one: and as for moral superiority, I sha'n't believe in that while I see the whole of the Northern States so utterly given up to the 'almighty dollar,' that they leave the honor of their country to be made ducks and drakes of by a few Southern slave-holders. Moral superiority? We hold in England that an honest man is a match for three rogues. If the same law holds good in the United States, I leave you to settle whether Northerners or Southerners are the honester men."

Whereupon (and no shame to Stangrave) there

was a heavy quarrel, and the two men had not met
since.

But now, those words of Thurnall's, backed by far
bitterer ones of Marie's, were fretting Stangrave's
heart. What if they were true? They were not
the whole truth. There was beside, and above them
all, a nobleness in the American's heart, which
could, if he chose, and when it chose, give the lie
to that bitter taunt: but had it done so already?

At least, he himself had not. . . . If Thurnall
and Marie were unjust to his nation, they had not
been unjust to him. He, at least, had been
making, all his life, mere outward blessings causes
of self-congratulation, and not of humility. He had
been priding himself on wealth, ease, luxury, culti-
vation, without a thought that these were God's
gifts, and that God would require an account of
them. If Thurnall were right, was he himself too
truly the typical American? And bitterly enough
he accused at once himself and his people.

" Noble ? Marie is right! We boast of our
nobleness: better to take the only opportunity of
showing it which we have had since we have
become a nation! Heaped with every blessing
which God could give; beyond the reach of
sorrow, a check, even an interference; shut out
from all the world in God's new Eden, that we
might freely eat of all the trees of the garden, and
grow and spread, and enjoy ourselves like the
birds of heaven — God only laid on us one duty,
one command, to right one simple, confessed, conscious wrong. . . .

" And what have we done? — what have even I
done? We have steadily, deliberately, cringed at
the feet of the wrong-doer, even while we boasted

our superiority to him at every point, and at last,
for the sake of our own selfish ease, helped him to
forge new chains for his victims, and received as
our only reward fresh insults. White slaves! We,
perhaps, and not the English peasant, are the white
slaves? At least, if the Irishman emigrates to
England, or the Englishman to Canada, he is not
hunted out with blood-hounds, and delivered back
to his landlord to be scourged and chained. He is
not practically out of the pale of law, unrepre-
sented, forbidden even the use of books; and even
if he were, there is an excuse for the old country;
for she was founded on no political principles, but
discovered what she knows step by step — a sort of
political Topsy, as Claude Mellot calls her, who has
'kinder growed,' doing from hand to mouth what
seemed best. But that we, who profess to start as
an ideal nation, on fixed ideas of justice, freedom,
and equality — that we should have been stultify-
ing ever since every great principle of which we so
loudly boast! ——

. . . .

"The old Jew used to say of his nation, 'It is
God that hath made us, and not we ourselves.'
We say, 'It is we that have made ourselves, while
God ——' Ah, yes; I recollect. God's work is
to save a soul here and a soul there, and to leave
America to be saved by the Americans who made
it. We must have a broader and deeper creed than
that if we are to work out our destiny. The battle
against Middle Age slavery was fought by the old
Catholic Church, which held the Jewish notion, and
looked upon the Deity as the actual King of
Christendom, and every man in it as God's own
child. I see now! No wonder that the battle in

America has as yet been fought by the Quakers, who believe that there is a divine light and voice in every man; while the Calvinist preachers, with their isolating and individualizing creed, have looked on with folded hands, content to save a negro's soul here and there, whatsoever might become of the bodies and the national future of the whole negro race. No wonder, while such men have the teaching of the people, that it is necessary still in the nineteenth century, in a Protestant country, amid sane human beings, for such a man as Mr. Sumner to rebut, in sober earnest, the argument that the negro was the descendant of Canaan, doomed to eternal slavery by Noah's curse!"

.   .   .   .

He would rouse himself. He would act, speak, write, as many a noble fellow-countryman was doing. He had avoided them of old as bores and fanatics who would needs wake him from his luxurious dreams. He had even hated them, simply because they were more righteous than he. He would be a new man henceforth.

He strode down the hill through the cannon-guarded vineyards, among the busy groups of peasants.

"Yes, Marie was right. Life is meant for work, and not for ease; to labor in danger and in dread, to do a little good ere the night comes, when no man can work; instead of trying to realize for oneself a Paradise; not even Bunyan's shepherd-paradise, much less Fourier's casino-paradise; and perhaps least of all, because most selfish and isolated of all, my own heart-paradise — the apotheosis of loafing, as Claude calls it. Ah, Tennyson's Palace of Art is a true word — too true, too true!

"Art? What if the most necessary of human art, next to the art of agriculture, be, after all, the art of war? It has been so in all ages. What if I have been befooled — what if all the Anglo-Saxon world has been befooled by forty years of peace? We have forgotten that the history of the world has been as yet written in blood; that the history of the human race is the story of its heroes and its martyrs — the slayers and the slain. Is it not becoming such once more in Europe now? And what divine exemption can we claim from the law? What right have we to suppose that it will be aught else, as long as there are wrongs unredressed on earth; as long as anger and ambition, cupidity and wounded pride, canker the hearts of men? What if the wise man's attitude, and the wise nation's attitude, is that of the Jews rebuilding their ruined walls — the tool in one hand, and the sword in the other; for the wild Arabs are close outside, and the time is short, and the storm has only lulled awhile in mercy, that wise men may prepare for the next thunder-burst? It is an ugly fact: but I have thrust it away too long, and I must accept it now and henceforth. This, and not luxurious Broadway; this, and not the comfortable New England village, is the normal type of human life: and this is the model city! Armed industry, which tills the corn and vine among the cannons' mouths; which never forgets their need, though it may mask and beautify their terror; but knows that as long as cruelty and wrong exist on earth, man's destiny is to dare and suffer, and, if it must be so, to die. . . .

"Yes, I will face my work; my danger, if need be. I will find Marie. I will tell her that I accept her quest; not for her sake, but for its own. Only I will demand the right to work at it as I think best, patiently, moderately, wisely if I can; for a fanatic I cannot be, even for her sake. She may hate these slaveholders — she may have her reasons — but I cannot. I cannot deal with them as *feras natura*. I cannot deny that they are no worse men than I; that I should have done what they are doing, have said what they are saying, had I been bred up, as they have been, with irresponsible power over the souls and bodies of human beings. God! I shudder at the fancy! The brute that I might have been — that I should have been!

"Yes; one thing at least I have learnt, in all my experiments on poor humanity — never to see a man do a wrong thing, without feeling that I could do the same in his place. I used to pride myself on that once, fool that I was, and call it comprehensiveness. I used to make it an excuse for sitting by, and seeing the devil have it all his own way, and call that toleration. I will see now whether I cannot turn the said knowledge to a better account, as common sense, patience, and charity; and yet do work of which neither I nor my country need be ashamed."

He walked down, and on to the bridge of boats. They opened in the center; as he reached it a steamer was passing. He lounged on the rail as the boat passed through, looking carelessly at the groups of tourists.

Two ladies were standing on the steamer, close to him, looking up at Ehrenbreitstein. Was it? Yes, it was Sabina, and Marie by her!

But ah, how changed! The cheeks were pale and hollow; dark rings — he could see them but

too plainly as the face was lifted up toward the
light — were round those great eyes, bright no
longer. Her face was listless, careworn; looking
all the more sad and impassive by the side of
Sabina's, as she pointed smiling and sparkling, up
to the fortress; and seemed trying to interest
Marie in it, but in vain.

He called out. He waved his hand wildly, to
the amusement of the officers and peasants who
waited by his side; and who, looking first at his
excited face, and then at the two beautiful women,
were not long in making up their minds about him;
and had their private jests accordingly.

They did not see him, but turned away to look
at Coblenz; and the steamer swept by.

Stangrave stamped with rage — upon a Prussian
officer's thin boot.

" Ten thousand pardons ! "

" You are excused, dear sir, you are excused,"
says the good-natured German, with a wicked
smile, which raises a blush on Stangrave's cheek.
"Your eyes were dazzled; why not ? it is not
often that one sees two such suns together in the
same sky. But calm yourself, the boat stops at
Coblenz."

Stangrave could not well call the man of war to
account for his impertinence; he had had his toes
half crushed, and had a right to indemnify himself
as he thought fit. And with a hundred more
apologies, Stangrave prepared to dart across the
bridge as soon as it was closed.

Alas ! after the steamer, as the fates would have
it, came lumbering down one of those monster tim-
ber rafts ; and it was a full half hour before Stangrave
could get across, having suffered all the while the

torments of Tantalus, as he watched the boat sweep round to the pier and discharge its freight, to be scattered whither he knew not.   At last he got across, and went in chase to the nearest hotel; but they were not there; thence to the next, and the next, till he had hunted half the hotels in the town; but hunted all in vain.

He is rushing wildly back again, to try if he can obtain any clue at the steamboat pier, through the narrow, dirty street at the back of the Rhine Cavalier, when he is stopped short by a mighty German embrace, and a German kiss on either cheek, as the kiss of a housemaid's broom; while a jolly voice shouts in English:

"Ah, my dear, dear friend! and you would pass me! Whither the hangman so fast are you running in the mud?"

"My dear Salomon! But let me go, I beseech you; I am in search ——"

"In search?" cries the jolly Jew banker, "for the philosopher's stone? You had all that man could want a week since, except that. Search no more, but come home with me; and we will have a night as of the gods on Olympus!"

"My dearest fellow, I am looking for two ladies!"

"Two? ah, rogue! shall not one suffice?"

"Don't, my dearest fellow! I am looking for two English ladies."

"Potz! You shall find two hundred in the hotels, ugly and fair; but the two fairest are gone this two hours."

"When? which?" cries Stangrave, suspecting at once.

"Sabina Mellot, and a Sultana.   I thought her

of The Nation, and would have offered my hand on the spot; but Madame Mellot says she is a Gentile."

"Gone? And you have seen them? Where?"

"To Bertrich. They had luncheon with my mother, and then started by private post."

"I must follow."

"*Ach lieber !* But it will be dark in an hour."

"What matter ?"

"But you shall find them to-morrow, just as well as to-day. They stay at Bertrich for a fortnight more. They have been there now a month, and only left it last week for a pleasure tour, across to the Ahrthal, and so back by Andernach."

"Why did they leave Coblenz, then, in such hot haste ?"

"Ah, the ladies never give reasons. There were letters waiting for them at our house; and no sooner read, but they leaped up, and would forth. Come home now, and go by the steamer to-morrow morning."

"Impossible! most hospitable of Israelites."

"To go to-night — for see the clouds! Not a postilion will dare to leave Coblenz, under that quick-coming *allgemein und ungeheuer henker-hund-und-teufel's-gewitter.*"

Stangrave looked up, growling; and gave in. A Rhine-storm was rolling up rapidly.

"They will be caught in it."

"No. They are far beyond its path by now; while you shall endure the whole visitation; and if you try to proceed, pass the night in a flea-pestered post-house, or in a ditch of water."

So Stangrave went home with Herr Salomon, and heard from him, amid clouds of Latakia, of

wars and rumors of wars, distress of nations, and
perplexity, seen by the light, not of the gospel,
but of the stock-exchange; while the storm fell
without in lightning, hail, rain, of right Rhenish
potency.

CHAPTER XXIV

THE THIRTIETH OF SEPTEMBER

WE must go back a week or so, to England, and to the last day of September. The world is shooting partridges, and asking nervously, when it comes home, what news from the Crimea? The flesh who serves it is bathing at Margate. The devil is keeping up his usual correspondence with both. Eaton Square is a desolate wilderness, where dusty sparrows alone disturb the dreams of frowzy charwomen, who, like Anchorites amid the tombs of the Thebaid, fulfil the contemplative life each in her subterranean cell. Beneath St. Peter's spire the cabman sleeps within his cab, the horse without; the waterman, seated on his empty bucket, contemplates the untrodden pavement between his feet, and is at rest. The blue butcher's boy trots by, with empty cart, five miles an hour, instead of full fifteen, and stops to chat with the red postman, who, his occupation gone, smokes with the green gatekeeper, and reviles the Czar. Along the whole north pavement of the square only one figure moves, and that is Major Campbell.

His face is haggard and anxious; he walks with a quick, excited step; earnest enough, whoever else is not. For in front of Lord Scoutbush's house the road is laid with straw. There is sickness there, anxiety, bitter tears. Lucia has not found her husband, but she has lost her child.

Trembling, Campbell raises the muffled knocker, and Bowie appears. "What news to-day?" he whispers.

"As well as can be expected, sir, and as quiet as a lamb now, they say. But it has been a bad time, and a bad man is he that caused it."

"A bad time, and a bad man. How is Miss St. Just?"

"Just gone to lie down, sir. Mrs. Clara is on the stairs, if you'd like to see her."

"No; tell Miss St. Just that I have no news yet." And the major turns wearily away.

Clara, who has seen him from above, hurries down after him into the street, and coaxes him to come in. "I am sure you have had no breakfast, sir; and you look so ill and worn. And Miss St. Just will be so vexed not to see you. She will get up the moment she hears you are here."

"No, my good Miss Clara," says Campbell, looking down with a weary smile, "I should only make gloom more gloomy. Bowie, tell his lordship that I shall be at the afternoon train to-morrow, let what will happen."

"Ay, ay, sir. We're a' ready to march. The major looks very ill, Miss Clara. I wish he'd have taken your counsel. And I wish ye'd take mine, and marry me ere I march, just to try what it's like."

"I must mind my mistress, Mr. Bowie," says Clara.

"And how should I interfere with that, as I've said twenty times, when I'm safe in the Crimea? I'll get the license this day, say what ye will; and then ye would not have the heart to let me spend two pounds twelve and sixpence for nothing."

Whether the last most Caledonian argument conquered or not, Mr. Bowie got the license, was married before breakfast the next morning, and started for the Crimea at four o'clock in the afternoon; most astonished, as he confided in the train to Sergeant MacArthur, " to see a lassie that never gave him a kind word in her life, and had not been married but barely six hours, greet and greet at his going, till she vanished away into hystericals. They 're a very unfathomable species, sergeant, are they women: and if they were taken out o' man, they took the best part o' Adam wi' them, and left us to shift with the worse."

But to return to Campbell. The last week has altered him frightfully. He is no longer the stern, self-possessed warrior which he was; he no longer even walks upright; his cheek is pale, his eye dull; his whole countenance sunken together. And now that the excitement of anxiety is past, he draws his feet along the pavement slowly, his hands clasped behind him, his eyes fixed on the ground, as if the life was gone from out of him, and existence was a heavy weight.

" She is safe, at least, then! One burden off my mind. And yet had it not been better if that pure spirit had returned to Him who gave it, instead of waking again to fresh misery? I must find that man! Why, I have been saying so to myself for seven days past, and yet no ray of light. Can the coward have given me a wrong address? Yet why give me an address at all if he meant to hide from me? Why, I have been saying that, too, to myself every day for the last week! Over and over again the same round of possibilities and suspicions. However, I must be quiet now, if I am a man. I can hear nothing before the detective comes at two. How to pass the weary, weary time? For I am past thinking — almost past praying — though not quite, thank God!"

He paces up still noisy Piccadilly, and then up silent Bond Street; pauses to look at some strange fish on Groves's counter — anything to while away the time; then he plods on toward the top of the street, and turns into Mr. Pillischer's shop, and upstairs to the microscopic club-room. There, at least, he can forget himself for an hour.

He looks round the neat pleasant little place, with its cases of curiosities, and its exquisite photographs, and bright brass instruments; its glass vases stocked with delicate water-plants and animalcules, with the sunlight gleaming through the green and purple seaweed fronds, while the air is fresh and fragrant with the seaweed scent; a quiet, cool little hermitage of science amid that great, noisy, luxurious west-end world. At least, it brings back to him the thought of the summer sea, and Aberalva, and his shore-studies: but he cannot think of that any more. It is past; and may God forgive him!

At one of the microscopes on the slab opposite him stands a sturdy bearded man, his back toward the major; while the wise little German, hopeless of customers, is leaning over him in his shirt sleeves.

"But I never have seen its like; it had just like a painter's easel in its stomach yesterday!"

"Why, it's an Echinus Larva; a sucking sea-urchin! Hang it, if I had known you had n't seen one, I 'd have brought up half a dozen of them!"

" May I look, sir? " asked the major; " I, too, never have seen an Echinus Larva."

The bearded man looks up.

" Major Campbell ! "

" Mr. Thurnall ! I thought I could not be mistaken in the voice."

" This is too pleasant, sir, to renew our watery loves together here," said Tom: but a second look at the major's face showed him that he was in no jesting mood. " How is the party at Beddgelert? I fancied you with them still."

"They are all in London, at Lord Scoutbush's house, in Eaton Square."

" In London, at this dull time? I trust nothing unpleasant has brought them here."

" Mrs. Vavasour is very ill. We had thoughts of sending for you, as the family physician was out of town: but she was out of danger, thank God, in a few hours. Now let me ask in turn after you. I hope no unpleasant business brings you up three hundred miles from your practice? "

" Nothing, I assure you. Only I have given up my Aberalva practice. I am going to the East."

" Like the rest of the world."

" Not exactly. You go as a dignified soldier of her Majesty's; I as an undignified Abel Drugger, to dose Bashi-Bazouks."

" Impossible! and with such an opening as you had there! You must excuse me; but my opinion of your prudence must not be so rudely shaken."

" Why do you ask the question which Balzac's old Tourangeois judge asks, whenever a culprit is brought before him, — ' Who is she? ' "

" Taking for granted that there was a woman at

the bottom of every mishap? I understand you,"
said the major, with a sad smile. "Now let you
and I walk a little together, and look at the
Echinoid another day — or when I return from
Sevastopol —— "

Tom went out with him. A new ray of hope
had crossed the major's mind. His meeting with
Thurnall might be providential; for he recollected
now, for the first time, Mellot's parting hint.

"You know Elsley Vavasour well?"

"No man better."

"Did you think that there was any tendency to
madness in him?"

"No more than in any other selfish, vain, irri-
table man, with a strong imagination left to run
riot."

"Humph! you seem to have divined his character. May I ask if you knew him before you met
him at Aberalva?"

Tom looked up sharply in the major's face.

"You would ask, what cause I have for inquiring? I will tell you presently. Meanwhile I may
say, that Mellot told me frankly that you had
some power over him; and mentioned, mysteriously, a name — John Briggs, I think — which it
appears that he once assumed."

"If Mellot thought fit to tell you anything, I
may frankly tell you all. John Briggs is his real
name. I have known him from childhood." And
then Tom poured into the ears of the surprised
and somewhat disgusted major all he had to tell.

"You have kept your secret mercifully, and
used it wisely, sir; and I and others shall be always
your debtors for it. Now I dare tell you in turn,
in strictest confidence of course —— "

"I am far too poor to afford the luxury of babbling."

And the major told him what we all know.

"I expected as much," said he, drily. "Now, I suppose that you wish me to exert myself in finding the man?"

"I do."

"Were Mrs. Vavasour only concerned, I should say — Not I! Better that she should never set eyes on him again."

"Better, indeed!" said he, bitterly: "but it is I who must see him, if but for five minutes. I must!"

"Major Campbell's wish is a command. Where have you searched for him?"

"At his address, at his publisher's, at the houses of various literary friends of his, and yet no trace."

"Has he gone to the Continent?"

"Heaven knows! I have inquired at every passport office for news of any one answering his description; indeed, I have two detectives, I may tell you, at this moment, watching every possible place. There is but one hope, if he be alive. Can he have gone home to his native town?"

"Never! Anywhere but there."

"Is there any old friend of the lower class with whom he may have taken lodgings?"

Tom pondered.

"There was a fellow, a noisy blackguard, whom Briggs was asking after this very summer — a fellow who went off from Whitbury with some players. I know Briggs used to go to the theatre with him as a boy — what was his name? He tried acting, but did not succeed; and then became a scene-shifter, or something of the kind, at the Adelphi. He has some complaint, I forget what, which made him an out-patient at St. Mumpsimus's, some months every year. I know that he was there this summer, for I wrote to ask, at Briggs's request, and Briggs sent him a sovereign through me."

"But what makes you fancy that he can have taken shelter with such a man, and one who knows his secret?"

"It is but a chance: but he may have done it from the mere feeling of loneliness — just to hold by some one whom he knows in this great wilderness; especially a man in whose eyes he will be a great man, and to whom he has done a kindness; still, it is the merest chance."

"We will take it, nevertheless, forlorn hope though it be."

They took a cab to the hospital, and, with some trouble, got the man's name and address, and drove in search of him. They had some difficulty in finding his abode, for it was up an alley at the back of Drury Lane, in the top of one of those foul old houses which hold a family in every room; but, by dint of knocking at one door and the other, and bearing meekly much reviling consequent thereon, they arrived, "*per modum tollendi*," at a door which must be the right one, as all the rest were wrong.

"Does John Barker live here?" asks Thurnall, putting his head in cautiously for fear of drunken Irishmen, who might be seized with the national impulse to "slate" him.

"What's that to you?" answers a shrill voice from among soapsuds and steaming rags.

"Here is a gentleman who wants to speak to him."

"So do a many as won't have that pleasure, and would be little the better for it if they had. Get along with you, I knows your lay."

"We really want to speak to him, and to pay him, if he will —— "

"Go along! I'm up to the something-to-your-advantage dodge, and to the mustachio dodge too. Do you fancy I don't know a bailiff, because he's dress'd like a swell?"

"But, my good woman!" said Tom, laughing.

"You put your crocodile foot in here, and I'll hit the hot water over the both of you!" and she caught up the pan of soapsuds.

"My dear soul! I am a doctor belonging to the hospital which your husband goes to; and have known him since he was a boy, down in Berkshire."

"You?" and she looked keenly at him.

"My name is Thurnall. I was a medical man once in Whitbury, where your husband was born."

"You?" said she again, in a softened tone. "I knows that name well enough."

"You do? What was your name, then?" said Tom, who recognized the woman's Berkshire accent beneath its coat of cockneyism.

"Never you mind: I'm no credit to it, so I'll let it be. But come in, for the old county's sake. Can't offer you a chair, he's pawned 'em all. Pleasant old place it was down there, when I was a young girl; they say it's growed a grand place now, wi' a railroad. I think many times I'd like to go down and die there." She spoke in a rough, sullen, careless tone, as if life-weary.

"My good woman," said Major Campbell, a little impatiently, "can you find your husband for us?"

"Why, then?" asked she, sharply, her suspicion seeming to return.

"If he will answer a few questions, I will give him five shillings. If he can find out for me what I want, I will give him five pounds."

"Should n't I do as well? If you gi' it he, it 's little out of it I shall see, but he coming home tipsy when it 's spent. Ah, dear! it was a sad day for me when I first fell in with they play-goers!"

"Why should she not do it as well?" said Thurnall. "Mrs. Barker, do you know anything of a person named Briggs — John Briggs, the apothecary's son, at Whitbury?"

She laughed a harsh bitter laugh.

"Know he? yes, and too much reason. That was where it all begun, along of that play-going of he's and my master's."

"Have you seen him lately?" asked Campbell, eagerly.

"I seen un? I 'd hit this water over the fellow, and all his play-acting merryandrews, if ever he sot a foot here!"

"But have you heard of him?"

"Ees——" said she, carelessly; "he 's round here now, I heard my master say, about the 'Delphy with my master: a drinking, I suppose. No good, I 'll warrant."

"My good woman," said Campbell, panting for breath, "bring me face to face with that man, and I 'll put a five-pound note in your hand there and then."

"Five pounds is a sight to me; but it's a sight more than the sight of he's worth," said she, suspiciously again.

"That's the gentleman's concern," said Tom. "The money's yours. I suppose you know the worth of it by now?"

"Ees, none better. But I don't want he to get hold of it; he's made away with enough already;" and she began to think

"Curiously impassive people, we Wessex worthies, when we are a little ground down with trouble. You must give her time and she will do our work. She wants the money, but she is long past being excited at the prospect of it."

"What's that you're whispering?" asked she, sharply.

Campbell stamped with impatience.

"You don't trust us yet, eh? — then, there!" and he took five sovereigns from his pocket, and tossed them on the table. "There's your money! I trust you to do the work, as you've been paid beforehand."

She caught up the gold, rang every piece on the table to see if it was sound; and then:

"Sally, you go down with these gentlemen to the Jonson's Head, and if he ben't there, go to the Fighting Cocks; and if he ben't there, go to the Duke of Wellington; and tell he there's two gentlemen has heard of his poetry, and wants to hear un excite. And then you give he a glass of liquor, and praise up his nonsense, and he'll tell you all he knows, and a sight more. Gi' un plenty to drink. It'll be a saving and a charity, for if he don't get it out of you, he will out of me."

And she returned doggedly to her washing.

"Can't I do anything for you?" asked Tom, whose heart always yearned over a Berkshire soul. "I have plenty of friends down at Whitbury still."

"More than I have. No, sir," said she, sadly, and with the first touch of sweetness they had yet heard in her voice. "I've cured my own bacon, and I must eat it. There's none down there minds me, but them that would be ashamed of me. And I couldn't go without he, and they wouldn't take he in; so I must just bide." And she went on washing.

"God help her!" said Campbell, as he went downstairs.

"Misery breeds that temper, and only misery, in our people. I can show you as thorough gentlemen and ladies, people round Whitbury, living on ten shillings a week, as you will show me in Belgravia living on five thousand a year."

"I don't doubt it," said Campbell. . . . "So 'she couldn't go without he,' drunken dog as he is! Thus it is with them all the world over."

"So much the worse for them," said Tom, cynically, "and for the men too. They make fools of us first with our over-fondness of them; and then they let us make fools of ourselves with their over-fondness of us."

"I fancy sometimes that they were all meant to be the mates of angels, and stooped to men as a *pis aller;* reversing the old story of the sons of heaven and the daughters of men."

"And accounting for the present degeneracy. When the sons of heaven married the daughters of men, their offspring were giants and men of renown.   Now the sons of men marry the daughters of heaven, and the offspring is Wiggle, Waggle, Windbag, and Redtape. '

They visited one pub ic-house after another, till the girl found for them the man they wanted, a shabby, sodden-visaged fellow, with a would-be jaunty air of conscious srewdness and vanity, who stood before the bar, hi . thumbs in his armholes, and laying down the law to a group of coster-boys, for want of a better aud ence.

The girl, after sundry plucks at his coat-tail, stopped him in the midst of his oration, and explained her errand somewhat fearfully.

Mr. Barker bent down his head on one side, to signify that he was absorbed in attention to her news; and then drawing himself up once more, lifted his greasy hat high in air, bowed to the very floor, and broke forth—

> " Most potent, grave, and reverend signiors:
> A man of war, and eke a man of peace —
> That is, if you come peaceful; and if not,
> Have we not Hiren here ? "

And the fellow put himself into a fresh attitude.

"We come in peace, my good sir," said Tom; " first to listen to your talented effusions, and next for a little private conversation on a subject on which ——" but Mr. Barker interrupted —

> "To listen, and to drink?   The muse is dry,
> And Pegasus doth thirst for Hippocrene,
> And fain would paint — imbibe the vulgar call —
> Or hot or cold, or long or short — Attendant!"

The bar girl, who knew his humor, came forward —

"Glasses all round —these noble knights will pay —
　Of hottest hot, and stiffest stiff.　Thou mark'st me?
　Now to your quest!"

And he faced round with a third attitude.

"Do you know, Mr. Briggs?" asked the straight-forward major.

He rolled his eyes to every quarter of the seventh sphere, clapped his hand upon his heart, and assumed an expression of angelic gratitude —

"My benefactor!　Were the world a waste,
　A thistle-waste, ass-nibbled, goldfinch-pecked,
　And all the men and women merely asses,
　I still could lay this hand upon this heart
　And cry, 'Not yet alone!　I know a man —
　A man Jove-fronted, and Hyperion-curled —
　A gushing, flushing, blushing human heart!' '

"As sure as you live, sir," said Tom, "if you won't talk honest prose, I won't pay for the brandy-and-water."

"Base is the slave who pays, and baser prose —
　Hang uninspired patter!　'T is in verse
　That angels praise, and fiends in Limbo curse."

"And asses bray, I think," said Tom, in despair. "Do you know where Mr. Briggs is now?"

"And why the devil do you want to know?
　For that 's a verse, sir, although somewhat slow"

The two men laughed in spite of themselves.

"Better tell the fellow the plain truth," said Campbell to Thurnall.

"Come out with us, and I will tell you."　And Campbell threw down the money, and led him off, after he had gulped down his own brandy, and half Tom's beside.

"What? leave the nepenthe untasted?"

They took him out, and he tucked his arms through theirs, and strutted down Drury Lane.

"The fact is, sir — I speak to you, of course, in confidence, as one gentleman to another ——"

Mr. Barker replied by a lofty and gracious bow.

"That his family are exceedingly distressed at his absence, and his wife, who, as you may know, is a lady of high family, dangerously ill; and he cannot be aware of the fact. This gentleman is the medical man of her family, and I — I am an intimate friend. We should esteem it, therefore, the very greatest service if you would give us any information which ——"

> "Weep no more, gentle shepherds, weep no more;
> For Lycidas your sorrow is not dead,
> Sunk though he be upon a garret floor,
> With fumes of Morpheus' crown about his head."

"Fumes of Morpheus' crown?" asked Thurnall.

> "That crimson flower which crowns the sleepy god,
> And sweeps the soul aloft, though flesh may nod."

"He has taken to opium!" said Thurnall to the bewildered major. "What I should have expected."

"God help him! we must save him out of that last lowest deep!" cried Campbell. "Where is he, sir?"

> "A vow! a vow! I have a vow in heaven!
> Why guide the hounds toward the trembling hare?
> Our Adonais hath drunk poison; Oh!
> What deaf and viperous murderer could crown
> Life's early cup with such a draught of woe?"

"As I live, sir," cried Campbell, losing his self-possession in disgust at the fool; "you may rhyme your own nonsense as long as you will, but you sha'n't quote the Adonais about that fellow in my presence."

Mr. Barker shook himself fiercely free of Campbell's arm, and faced round at him in a fighting attitude. Campbell stood eyeing him sternly, but at his wit's end.

"Mr. Barker," said Tom, blandly, "will you have another glass of brandy-and-water, or shall I call a policeman ?"

"Sir," sputtered he, speaking prose at last, "this gentleman has insulted me! He has called my poetry nonsense, and my friend a fellow. And blood shall not wipe out — what liquor may!"

The hint was sufficient: but ere he had drained another glass, Mr. Barker was decidedly incapable of managing his affairs, much less theirs; and became withal exceedingly quarrelsome, returning angrily to the grievance of Briggs having been called a fellow; in spite of all their entreaties, he talked himself into a passion, and at last, to Campbell's extreme disgust, rushed out of the bar into the street.

"This is too vexatious! To have kept half an hour's company with such an animal, and then to have him escape me after all! A just punishment on me for pandering to his drunkenness."

Tom made no answer, but went quietly to the door, and peeped out.

"Pay for his liquor, major, and follow. Keep a few yards behind me; there will be less chance of his recognizing us than if he saw us both together."

"Why, where do you think he's going ?"

"Not home, I can see. Ten to one that he

will go raging off straight to Briggs, to put him on his guard against us. Just like a drunkard's cunning it would be. There, he has turned up that side street. Now follow me quick. Oh that he may only keep his legs!"

They gained the bottom of that street before he had turned out of it; and so through another, and another, till they ran him to earth in one of the courts out of St. Martin's Lane.

Into a doorway he went, and up a stair. Tom stood listening at the bottom, till he heard the fellow knock at a door far above, and call out in a drunken tone. Then he beckoned to Campbell, and both, careless of what might follow, ran up-stairs, and pushing him aside, entered the room without ceremony.

Their chances of being on the right scent were small enough, considering that, though every one was out of town, there were a million and a half of people in London at that moment; and, unfortunately, at least fifty thousand who would have considered Mr. John Barker a desirable visitor; but somehow, in the excitement of the chase, both had forgotten the chances against them, and the probability that they would have to retire down-stairs again, apologizing humbly to some wrathful Joseph Buggins, whose convivialities they might have interrupted. But no; Tom's cunning had, as usual, played him true; and as they entered the door, they beheld none other than the lost Elsley Vavasour, *alias* John Briggs.

Major Campbell advanced bowing, hat in hand, with a courteous apology on his lips.

It was a low lean-to garret; there was a deal table and an old chair in it, but no bed. The windows were broken; the paper hanging down in strips. Elsley was standing before the empty fire-place, his hand in his bosom, as if he had been startled by the scuffle outside. He had not shaved for some days.

So much Tom could note; but no more. He saw the glance of recognition pass over Elsley's face, and that an ugly one. He saw him draw something from his bosom, and spring like a cat almost upon the table. A flash — a crack. He had fired a pistol full in Campbell's face.

Tom was startled, not at the thing, but that such a man should have done it. He had seen souls, and too many, flit out of the world by that same tiny crack, in Californian taverns, Arabian deserts, Australian gullies. He knew all about that: but he liked Campbell; and he breathed more freely the next moment, when he saw him standing still erect, a quiet smile on his face, and felt the plaster dropping from the wall upon his own head. The bullet had gone over the major.

All was right.

"He is not man enough for a second shot," thought Tom, quietly, "while the major's eye is on him."

"I beg your pardon, Mr. Vavasour," he heard the major say, in a gentle, unmoved voice, "for this intrusion. I assure you that there is no cause for any anger on your part; and I am come to entreat you to forget and forgive any conduct of mine which may have caused you to mistake either me or a lady whom I am unworthy to mention."

"I am glad the beggar fired at him," thought

Tom. "One spice of danger, and he's himself again, and will overawe the poor cur by mere civility. I was afraid of some abject Methodist parson humility, which would give the other party a handle."

Elsley heard him with a stupefied look, like that of a trapped wild beast, in which rage, shame, suspicion, and fear, were mingled with the vacant glare of the opium-eater's eye. Then his eye drooped beneath Campbell's steady gentle gaze, and he looked uneasily round the room, still like a trapped wild beast, as if for a hole to escape by; then up again, but sidelong, at Major Campbell.

"I assure you, sir, on the word of a Christian and a soldier, that you are laboring under an entire misapprehension. For God's sake and Mrs. Vavasour's come back, sir, to those who will receive you with nothing but affection! Your wife has been all but dead; she thinks of no one but you, asks for no one but you! In God's name, sir, what are you doing here, while a wife who adores you is dying from your — I do not wish to be rude, sir, but let me say at least — neglect?"

Elsley looked at him still askance, puzzled, inquiring. Suddenly his great beautiful eyes opened to preternatural wideness, as if trying to grasp a new thought. He started, shifted his feet to and fro, his arms straight down by his sides, his fingers clutching after something. Then he looked up hurriedly again at Campbell; and Thurnall looked at him also; and his face was as the face of an angel.

"Miserable ass!" thought Tom; "if he don't see innocence in that man's countenance, he would n't see it in his own child's."

Elsley suddenly turned his back to them, and thrust his hand into his bosom. Now was Tom's turn.

In a moment he had vaulted over the table, and seized Elsley's wrist ere he could draw the second pistol.

"No, my dear Jack," whispered he, quietly, "once is enough in a day!"

"Not for him, Tom, for myself!" moaned Elsley.

"For neither, dear lad! Let bygones be bygones, and do you be a new man, and go home to Mrs. Vavasour."

"Never, never, never, never, never, never!" shrieked Elsley, like a baby, every word increasing in intensity, till the whole house rang; and then threw himself into the crazy chair, and dashed his head between his hands upon the table.

"This is a case for me, Major Campbell. I think you had better go now."

"You will not leave him?"

"No, sir. It is a very curious psychological study, and he is a Whitbury man."

Campbell knew quite enough of the would-be cynical doctor, to understand what all that meant. He came up to Elsley.

"Mr. Vavasour, I am going to the war, from which I expect never to return. If you believe me, give me your hand before I go."

Elsley, without lifting his head, beat on the table with his hand.

"I wish to die at peace with you and all the world. I am innocent in word, in thought. I shall not insult another person by saying that she is so. If you believe me, give me your hand."

Elsley stretched his hand, his head still buried. Campbell took it, and went silently downstairs.

"Is he gone?" moaned he, after a while.

"Yes."

"Does she — does she care for him?"

"Good heavens! How did you ever dream such an absurdity?"

Elsley only beat upon the table.

"She has been ill?"

"Is ill. She has lost her child."

"Which?" shrieked Elsley.

"A boy whom she should have had."

Elsley only beat on the table; then:

"Give me the bottle, Tom!"

"What bottle?"

"The laudanum; — there, in the cupboard."

"I shall do no such thing. You are poisoning yourself."

"Let me, then! I must, I tell you! I can live on nothing else. I shall go mad if I do not have it. I should have been mad by now. Nothing else keeps off these fits; — I feel one coming now. Curse you! give me the bottle?"

"What fits?"

"How do I know? Agony and torture — ever since I got wet on that mountain."

Tom knew enough to guess his meaning, and felt Elsley's pulse and forehead.

"I tell you it turns every bone to red-hot iron!" almost screamed he.

"Neuralgia; rheumatic, I suppose," said Tom to himself. "Well, this is not the thing to cure you; but you shall have it to keep you quiet." And he measured him out a small dose.

" More, I tell you, more! " said Elsley, lifting up his head, and looking at it.

" Not more while you are with me."

" With you! Who the devil sent you here ? "

" John Briggs, John Briggs, if I did not mean you good, should I be here now? Now do, like a reasonable man, tell me what you intend to do."

" What is that to you, or any man ? " said Elsley, writhing with neuralgia.

" No concern of mine, of course: but your poor wife — you must see her."

" I can't, I won't! — that is, not yet! I tell you I cannot face the thought of her, much less the sight of her, and her family — that Valentia! I 'd rather the earth should open and swallow me! Don't talk to me, I say! "

And hiding his face in his hands, he writhed with pain, while Thurnall stood still patiently watching him, as a pointer dog does a partridge. He had found his game, and did not intend to lose it.

" I am better now; quite well! " said he, as the laudanum began to work. " Yes! I 'll go — that will be it — go to . . . at once. He 'll give me an order for a magazine article; I 'll earn ten pounds, and then off to Italy."

" If you want ten pounds, my good fellow, you can have them without racking your brains over an article."

Elsley looked up proudly.

" I do not borrow, sir! "

" Well — I 'll give you five for those pistols. They are of no use to you, and I shall want a spare brace for the East."

" Ah! I forgot them. I spent my last money on them," said he, with a shudder; " but I won't

sell them to you at a fancy price — no dealings
between gentleman and gentleman. I'll go to a
shop, and get for them what they are worth."

"Very good.   I'll go with you, if you like.
I fancy I may get you a better price for them than
you would yourself: being rather a knowing one
about the pretty little barkers."   And Tom took
his arm, and walked him quietly down into the
street.

"If you ever go up those kennel-stairs again,
friend," said he to himself, "my name's not Tom
Thurnall."

They walked to a gunsmith's shop in the Strand,
where Tom had often dealt, and sold the pistols
for some three pounds.

"Now then, let's go into 333, and get a mutton
chop."

"No."

Elsley was too shy; he was "not fit to be seen."

"Come to my rooms, then, in the Adelphi, and
have a wash and a shave. It will make you as
fresh as a lark again, and then we'll send out for
the eatables, and have a quiet chat."

Elsley did not say no.   Thurnall took the thing
as a matter of course, and he was too weak and
tired to argue with him.   Beside, there was a sort
of relief in the company of a man who, though he
knew all, chatted on to him cheerily and quietly,
as if nothing had happened; who at least treated
him as a sane man.   From any one else he would
have shrunk, lest they should find him out: but a
companion, who knew the worst, at least saved
him suspicion and dread.   His weakness, now that
the collapse after passion had come on, clung to
any human friend.   The very sound of Tom's clear

sturdy voice seemed pleasant to him, after long
solitude and silence. At least it kept off the fiends
of memory.

Tom, anxious to keep Elsley's mind employed
on some subject which should not be painful,
began chatting about the war and its prospects.
Elsley soon caught the cue, and talked with wild
energy and pathos, opium-fed, of the coming
struggle between despotism and liberty, the arising
of Poland and Hungary, and all the grand dreams
which then haunted minds like his.

"By Jove!" said Tom, "you are yourself again
now. Why don't you put all that into a book?"

"I may, perhaps," said Elsley, proudly.

"And if it comes to that, why not come to the
war, and see it for yourself? A new country —
one of the finest in the world. New scenery, new
actors, — why, Constantinople itself is a poem!
Yes, there is another 'Revolt of Islam' to be
written yet. Why don't you become our war poet?
Come and see the fighting; for there 'll be plenty
of it, let them say what they will. The old bear is
not going to drop his dead donkey without a snap
and a hug. Come along, and tell people what it's
all really like. There will be a dozen Cockneys
writing battle songs, I 'll warrant, who never saw a
man shot in their lives, not even a hare. Come
and give us the real genuine grit of it, — for if you
can't, who can?"

"It is a grand thought! The true war poets, after
all, have been warriors themselves. Körner and
Alcæus fought as well as sang, and sang because
they fought. Old Homer, too, — who can believe
that he had not hewn his way through the very battles which he describes, and seen every wound, every

shape of agony?   A noble thought, to go out with that army against the northern Anarch, singing in the van of battle, as Taillefer sang the song of Roland before William's knights, and to die like him, the proto-marty of the crusade, with the melody yet upon one's lips!"

And his face blazed up with excitement.

"What a handsome fellow he is, after all, if there were but more of him!" said Tom to himself.   "I wonder if h·'d fight, though, when the singing-fever was off him."

He took Elsley upstairs into his bedroom, got him washed and shaved, and sent out the woman of the house for mutton chops and stout, and began himself setting out the luncheon table, while Elsley in the room within chanted to himself snatches of poetry.

"The notion has taken; he's composing a war song already, I believe."

It actually was so: but Elsley's brain was weak and wandering; and he was soon silent; and motionless so long, that Tom opened the door and looked in anxiously.

He was sitting on a chair, his hands fallen on his lap, the tears running down his face.

"Well?" asked Tom, smilingly, not noticing the tears; "how goes on the opera?   I heard through the door the orchestra tuning for the prelude."

Elsley looked up in his face with a puzzled piteous expression.

"Do you know, Thurnall, I fancy at moments that my mind is not what it was.   Fancies flit from me as quickly as they come.   I had twenty verses five minutes ago and now I cannot recollect one."

"No wonder," thought Tom to himself. "My dear fellow, recollect all that you have suffered with this neuralgia. Believe me, all you want is animal strength. Chops and porter will bring all the verses back, or better ones instead of them."

He tried to make Elsley eat; and Elsley tried himself: but failed. The moment the meat touched his lips he loathed it, and only courtesy prevented his leaving the room to escape the smell. The laudanum had done its work upon his digestion. He tried the porter, and drank a little: then, suddenly stopping, he pulled out a phial, dropped a heavy dose of his poison into the porter, and tossed it off.

"Sold, am I?" said Tom to himself. "He must have hidden the bottle as he came out of the room with me. Oh, the cunning of those opium-eaters! However, it will keep him quiet just now, and to Eaton Square I must go."

"You had better be quiet now, my dear fellow, after your dose; talking will only excite you. Settle yourself on my bed, and I'll be back in an hour."

So he put Elsley on his bed, carefully removing razors and pistols (for he had still his fears of an outburst of passion), then locked him in, ran down into the Strand, threw himself into a cab for Eaton Square, and asked for Valentia.

Campbell had been there already: so Tom took care to tell nothing which he had not told, expecting, and rightly, that he would not mention Elsley's having fired at him. Lucia was still all but senseless, too weak even to ask for Elsley; to attempt any meeting between her and her husband would be madness.

"What will you do with the unhappy man, Mr. Thurnall?"

"Keep him under my eye, day and night, till he is either rational again, or ——"

"Do you think that he may? Oh, my poor sister!"

"I think that he may yet end very sadly, madam. There is no use concealing the truth from you. All that I can promise is, that I will treat him as my own brother."

Valentia held out her fair hand to the young doctor. He stooped and lifted the tips of her fingers to his lips.

"I am not worthy of such an honor, madam. I shall study to deserve it." And he bowed himself out, the same sturdy, self-confident Tom, doing right, he hardly knew why, save that it was all in the way of business.

And now arose the puzzle, what to do with Elsley? He had set his heart on going down to Whitbury the next day. He had been in England nearly six months, and had not yet seen his father; his heart yearned, too, after the old place, and Mark Armsworth, and many an old friend, whom he might never see again. "However, that fellow I must see to, come what will: business first and pleasure afterwards. If I make him all right — if I even get him out of the world decently, I get the Scoutbush interest on my side — though I believe I have it already. Still, it's as well to lay people under as heavy an obligation as possible. I wish Miss Valentia had asked me whether Elsley wanted any money: it's expensive keeping him myself. However, poor thing, she has other matters to think of; and, I dare say, never knew the pleasures of an empty purse. Here we are! Three-and-sixpence — eh, cabman? I suppose you think I was born Saturday night? There's three shillings. Now, don't chaff me, my excellent friend, or you will find you have met your match, and a leetle more!"

And Tom hurried into his rooms, and found Elsley still sleeping.

He set to work, packing and arranging, for with him every moment found its business; and presently heard his patient call faintly from the next room.

"Thurnall!" said he; "I have been a long journey. I have been to Whitbury once more, and followed my father about his garden, and sat upon my mother's knee. And she taught me one text, and no more. Over and over again she said it, as she looked down at me with still sad eyes, the same text which she spoke the day I left her for London. I never saw her again. 'By this, my son, be admonished; of making of books there is no end; and much study is a weariness of the flesh. Let us hear the conclusion of the whole matter. Fear God, and keep His commandments; for this is the whole duty of man.' . . . Yes, I will go down to Whitbury, and be a little child once more. I will take poor lodgings, and crawl out day by day, down the old lanes, along the old river-banks, where I fed my soul with fair and mad dreams, and reconsider it all from the beginning; — and then die. No one need know me; and if they do, they need not be ashamed of me, I trust — ashamed that a poet has risen up among them, to speak words which have been heard across the globe. At least, they need never know my shame

— never know that I have broken the heart of an angel, who gave herself to me, body and soul — attempted the life of a man whose shoes I am not worthy to unloose — never know that I have killed my own child! — that a blacker brand than Cain's is on my brow! — Never know — Oh, my God, what care I? Let them know all, as long as I can have done with shams and affectations, dreams, and vain ambitions, and be just my own self once more for one day, and then die!"

And he burst into convulsive weeping.

"No, Tom, do not comfort me! I ought to die, and I shall die. I cannot face her again; let her forget me, and find a husband who will — and be a father to the children whom I neglected! Oh, my darlings, my darlings! If I could but see you once again: but no! you too would ask me where I had been so long. You too would ask me — your innocent faces at least would — why I had killed your little brother! — Let me weep it out, Thurnall; let me face it all! This very misery is a comfort, for it will kill me all the sooner."

"If you really mean to go to Whitbury, my poor dear fellow," said Tom at last, "I will start with you to-morrow morning. For I too must go; I must see my father."

"You will really?" asked Elsley, who began to cling to him like a child.

"I will indeed. Believe me, you are right; you will find friends there, and admirers too. I know one."

"You do?" asked he, looking up.

"Mary Armsworth, the banker's daughter."

"What! That purse-proud, vulgar man?"

"Don't be afraid of him. A truer and more delicate heart don't beat. No one has more cause to say so than I. He will receive you with open arms, and need be told no more than is necessary; while, as his friend, you may defy gossip, and do just what you like."

Tom slipped out that afternoon, paid Elsley's pittance of rent at his old lodgings; bought him a few necessary articles, and lent him, without saying anything, a few more. Elsley sat all day as one in a dream, moaning to himself at intervals, and following Tom vacantly with his eyes, as he moved about the room. Excitement, misery, and opium, were fast wearing out body and mind, and Tom put him to bed that evening, as he would have put a child.

Tom walked out into the Strand to smoke in the fresh air, and think, in spite of himself, of that fair saint from whom he was so perversely flying. Gay girls slithered past him, looked round at him, but in vain; those two great sad eyes hung in his fancy, and he could see nothing else. Ah — if she had but given him back his money — why, what a fool he would have made of himself! Better as it was. He was meant to be a vagabond and an adventurer to the last; and perhaps to find at last the luck which had flitted away before him.

He passed one of the theatre doors; there was a group outside, more noisy and more earnest than such groups are wont to be; and ere he could pass through them, a shout from within rattled the doors with its mighty pulse, and seemed to shake the very walls. Another; and another! — What was it? Fire?

No. It was the news of Alma.

And the group surged to and fro outside, and talked, and questioned, and rejoiced; and smart

gents forgot their vulgar pleasures, and looked for
a moment as if they too could have fought — had
fought — at Alma; and sinful girls forgot their
shame, and looked more beautiful than they had
done for many a day, as, beneath the flaring gas-
light, their faces glowed for a while with noble
enthusiasm and woman's sacred pity, while they
questioned Tom, taking him for an officer, as to
whether he thought there were many killed.

"I am no officer: but I have been in many a
battle, and I know the Russians well, and have
seen how they fight; and there is many a brave
man killed, and many a one more will be."

"Oh, does it hurt them much?" asked one poor
thing.

"Not often," quoth Tom.

"Thank God, thank God!" and she turned suddenly away, and with the impulsive nature of her
class, burst into violent sobbing and weeping.

Poor thing! perhaps among the men who fought
and fell that day was he to whom she owed the
curse of her young life; and after him her lonely
heart went forth once more, faithful even in the
lowest pit.

"You are strange creatures, women, women!"
thought Tom: "but I knew that many a year ago.
Now then — the game is growing fast and furious,
it seems. Oh, that I may find myself soon in the
thickest of it!"

So said Tom Thurnall; and so said Major Campbell, too, that night, as he prepared everything to
start next morning to Southampton. "The better
the day, the better the deed," quoth he. "When
a man is travelling to a better world, he need not
be afraid of starting on a Sunday."

CHAPTER XXV

THE BANKER AND HIS DAUGHTER

TOM and Elsley are safe at Whitbury at last; and Tom, ere he has seen his father, has packed Elsley safe away in lodgings with an old dame whom he can trust. Then he asks his way to his father's new abode; a small old-fashioned house, with low bay windows jutting out upon the narrow pavement.

Tom stops, and looks in the window. His father is sitting close to it, in his arm-chair, his hands upon his knees, his face lifted to the sunlight, with chin slightly outstretched, and his pale eyes feeling for the light. The expression would have been painful, but for its perfect sweetness and resignation. His countenance is not, perhaps, a strong one; but its delicacy and calm, and the high forehead, and the long white locks, are most venerable. With a blind man's exquisite sense, he feels Tom's shadow fall on him, and starts, and calls him by name; for he has been expecting him, and thinking of nothing else all the morning, and takes for granted that it must be he.

In another moment Tom is at his father's side. What need to describe the sacred joy of those first few minutes, even if it were possible? But unrestrained tenderness between man and man, rare as it is, and, as it were, unaccustomed to itself, has no passionate fluency, no metaphor or poetry, such as man pours out to woman, and woman again to man. All its language lies in the tones, the looks, the little half-concealed gestures, hints which pass themselves off modestly in jest; and such was Tom's first interview with his father; till the old Isaac, having felt Tom's head and hands again and again, to be sure whether it were his very son or no, made him sit down by him, holding him still fast, and began:

"Now tell me, tell me, while Jane gets you something to eat. No Jane, you must n't talk to Master Tom yet, to bo her about how much he's grown; — nonsense, I must have him all to myself, Jane. Go and get him some dinner. Now, Tom," as if he was afraid of losing a moment, " you have been a dear boy to write to me every week; but there are so many questions which only word of mouth will answer, and I have stored up dozens of them! I want to know what a coral reef really looks like, and if you saw any trepangs upon them? And what sort of strata is the gold really in? And you saw one of those giant rays; I want a whole hour's talk about the fellow. And — what an old babbler I am! talking to you when you should be talking to me. Now begin. Let us have the trepangs first. Are they real Holothurians or not?"

And Tom began, and told for a full half-hour, interrupted then by some little comment of the old man's, which proved how prodigious was the memory within, imprisoned and forced to feed upon itself.

" You seem to know more about Australia than I do, father," said Tom at last.

" No, child; but Mary Armsworth, God bless her! comes down here almost every evening to read your letters to me; and she has been reading to me a book of Mrs. Lee's Adventures in Australia, which reads like a novel; delicious book — to me at least. Why, there is her step outside, I do believe, and her father's with her!"

The lighter woman's step was inaudible to Tom; but the heavy, deliberate waddle of the banker was not. He opened the house-door, and then the parlor-door, without knocking; but when he saw the visitor, he stopped on the threshold with out-stretched arms.

"Hillo, ho! who have we here? Our prodigal son returned, with his pockets full of nuggets from the diggings. Oh, mum's the word, is it?" as Tom laid his finger on his lips. "Come here, then, and let's have a look at you!" And he catches both Tom's hands in his, and almost shakes them off. "I knew you were coming, old boy! Mary told me — she's in all the old man's secrets. Come along, Mary, and see your old playfellow. She has got a little fruit for the old gentleman. Mary, where are you? always colloguing with Jane."

Mary comes in: a little dumpty body, with a yellow face, and a red nose, the smile of an angel, and a heart full of many little secrets of other people's — and of one great one of her own, which is no business of any man's — and with fifty thousand pounds as her portion, for she is an only child. But no man will touch that fifty thousand; for "no one would marry me for myself," says Mary; "and no one shall marry me for my money."

So she greets Tom shyly and humbly, without looking in his face, yet very cordially; and then slips away to deposit on the table a noble pine-apple.

"A little bit of fruit from her greenhouse," says

the old man, in a disparaging tone: "and, oh Jane, bring me a saucer. Here's a sprat I just capered out of Hemmelford mill-pit; perhaps the doctor would like it fried for supper, if it's big enough not to fall through the gridiron."

Jane, who knows Mark Armsworth's humor, brings in the largest dish in the house, and Mark pulls out of his basket a great three-pound trout.

"Aha! my young rover; old Mark's right hand hasn't forgot its cunning, eh? And this is the month for them; fish all quiet now. When fools go a-shooting, wise men go a-fishing! Eh? Come here, and look me over. How do I wear, eh? As like a Muscovy duck as ever, you young rogue? Do you recollect asking me, at the Club dinner, why I was like a Muscovy duck? Because I was a fat thing in green velveteen, with a bald red head, that was always waddling about the river bank. Ah, those were days! We'll have some more of them. Come up to-night and try the old '21 bin."

"I must have him myself to-night; indeed I must, Mark," says the doctor.

"All to yourself, you selfish old rogue?"

"Why — no ——"

"We'll come down, then, Mary and I, and bring the '21 with us, and hear all his cock-and-bull stories. Full of travellers' lies as ever, eh? Well, I'll come and smoke my pipe with you. Always the same old Mark, my lad," nudging Tom with his elbow; "one fellow comes and borrows my money, and goes out and calls me a stingy old hunks because I won't let him cheat me; another comes, and eats my pines, and drinks my port, goes home, and calls me a purse-proud upstart, because he can't match 'em. Never mind; old

Mark's old Mark, sound in the heart, and sound in the liver, just the same as thirty years ago, and will be till he takes his last *quietus est* —

"'And drops into his grassy nest.'

Bye, bye, doctor! Come, Mary!"

And out he toddled, with silent little Mary at his heels.

"Old Mark wears well, body and soul," said Tom.

" He is a noble, generous fellow, and as delicate-hearted as a woman withal, in spite of his conceit and roughness. Fifty and odd years now, Tom, have we been brothers, and I never found him change. And brothers we shall be, I trust, a few years more, till I see you back again from the East, comfortably settled. And then——"

"Don't talk of that, sir, please!" said Tom, quite quickly and sharply. " How ill poor Mary looks!"

"So they say, poor child; and one hears it in her voice. Ah, Tom, that girl is an angel; she has been to me daughter, doctor, clergyman, eyes, and library; and would have been nurse, too, if it had not been for making old Jane jealous. But she is ill. Some love-affair, I suppose——"

" How quaint it is, that the father has kept all the animal vigor to himself, and transmitted none to the daughter."

" He has not kept the soul to himself, Tom, or the eyes either. She will bring me in wild flowers, and talk to me about them, till I fancy I can see them as well as ever. Ah, well! It is a sweet world still, Tom, and there are sweet souls in it. A sweet world: I was too fond of looking at it

once, I suppose, so God took away my sight, that
I might learn to look at Him." And the old man
lay back in his chair, and covered his face with
his handkerchief, and was quite still awhile. And
Tom watched him, and ·hought that he would give
all his cunning and power to be like that old man.

Then Jane came in, ard laid the cloth — a coarse
one enough — and Tom picked a cold mutton bone
with a steel fork, and d ank his pint of beer from
the public-house, and li ;hted his father's pipe and
then his own, and vowe l that he had never dined
so well in his life, and began his traveller's stories
again.

And in the evening Mark came in, with a bottle
of the '21 in his coat-tail pocket; and the three
sat and chatted, while Mary brought out her
work, and stitched, listening silently, till it was
time to lead the old man upstairs.

Tom put his father to bed, and then made a
hesitating request :

"There is a poor sick man whom I brought
down with me, sir, if you could spare me half an
hour. It really is a professional case; he is
under my charge, I may say."

"What is it, boy?"

"Well, laudanum and a broken heart."

"Exercise and ammonia for the first. For the
second, God's grace and the grave; and those
latter medicines you can't exhibit, my dear boy.
Well, as it is professional duty, I suppose you
must: but don't exceed the hour; I shall lie
awake till you return, and then you must talk me
to sleep."

So Tom went out and homeward with Mark
and Mary, for their roads lay together; and as

he went, he thought good to tell them somewhat of
the history of John Briggs, *alias* Elsley Vavasour.

"Poor fool!" said Mark, who listened in silence
to the end. "Why did n't he mind his bottles,
and just do what Heaven sent him to do? Is he
in want of the rhino, Tom?"

"He had not five shillings left after he had
paid his fare; and he refuses to ask his wife for a
farthing."

"Quite right — very proper spirit." And Mark
walked on in silence a few minutes.

"I say, Tom, a fool and his money are soon
parted. There's a five-pound note for him, you
begging, insinuating dog, and be hanged to you
both! I shall die in the workhouse at this rate."

"Oh, father, you will never miss ——"

"Who told you I thought I should, pray?
Don't you go giving another five pounds out
of your pocket-money behind my back, ma'am.
I know your tricks of old. Tom, I'll come and
see the poor beggar to-morrow with you, and
call him Mr. Vavasour — Lord Vavasour, if he
likes — if you 'll warrant me against laughing in
his face." And the old man did laugh, till he
stopped and held his sides again.

"Oh, father, father, don't be so cruel. Remember how wretched the poor man is."

"I can't think of anything but old Bolus's boy
turned poet. Why did you tell me, Tom, you
bad fellow? It's too much for a man at my time
of life, and after his dinner too."

And with that he opened the little gate by the
side of the grand one, and turned to ask Tom:

"Won't come in, boy, and have one more
cigar?"

"I promised my father to be back as quickly as possible."

"Good lad — that's the plan to go on --

" 'You 'll be church warden before all 's over,
And so arrive at wealth and fame.'

Instead of writing po-o o-etry! Do you recollect that morning, and the black draught? Oh dear, my side!"

And Tom heard him keckling to himself up the garden walk to his house; went off to see that Elsley was safe; and hen home, and slept like a top; no wonder, for he would have done so the night before his execution.

And what was little Mary doing all the while?

She had gone up to the room, after telling her father, with a kiss, not to forget to say his prayers. And then she fed her canary bird, and made up the Persian cat's bed; and then sat long at the open window, gazing out over the shadow-dappled lawn, away to the poplars sleeping in the moonlight, and the shining silent stream, and the shining silent stars, till she seemed to become as one of them, and a quiet heaven within her eyes took counsel with the quiet heaven above. And then she drew in suddenly, as if stung by some random thought, and shut the window. A picture hung over her mantelpiece — a portrait of her mother, who had been a country beauty in her time. She glanced at it, and then at the looking-glass. Would she have given her fifty thousand pounds to have exchanged her face for such a face as that?

She caught up her little Thomas à Kempis, marked through and through with lines and references, and sat and read steadfastly for an hour and more. That was her school, as it has been the school of many a noble soul. And, for some cause or other, that stinging thought returned no more; and she knelt and prayed like a little child; and like a little child slept sweetly all the night, and was away before breakfast the next morning, after feeding the canary and the cat, to old women who worshipped her as their ministering angel, and said, looking after her, "That dear Miss Mary, pity she is so plain! Such a match as she might have made! But she'll be handsome enough when she is a blessed angel in heaven."

Ah, true sisters of mercy, whom the world sneers at as "old maids," if you pour out on cats and dogs and parrots a little of the love which is yearning to spend itself on children of your own flesh and blood! As long as such as you walk this lower world, one needs no Butler's "Analogy" to prove to us that there is another world, where such as you will have a fuller and a fairer (I dare not say a juster) portion.

.   .   .   .

Next morning Mark started with Tom to call on Elsley, chatting and puffing all the way.

"I'll butter him, trust me. Nothing comforts a poor beggar like a bit of praise when he's down; and all fellows that take to writing are as greedy after it as trout after the drake, even if they only scribble in county newspapers. I've watched them when I've been electioneering, my boy!"

"Only," said Tom, "don't be angry with him if he is proud and peevish. The poor fellow is all but mad with misery."

"Poh! quarrel with him? whom did I ever

quarrel with?   If he barks, I'll stop his mouth
with a good dinner.   I suppose he's gentleman
enough to invite?"

"As much a gentleman as you and I; not of the
very first water, of course.   Still, he eats like other
people, and don't break many glasses during a
sitting.   Think! he couldn't have been a very
great cad to marry a nobleman's daughter!"

"Why, no.   Speaks well for him, that, considering his breeding.   He must be a very clever fellow
to have caught the trick of the thing so soon."

"And so he is, a very clever fellow; too clever
by half; and a very fine-hearted fellow, too, in
spite of his conceit and his temper.   But that don't
prevent his being an awful fool!"

"You speak like a book, Tom!" said old Mark,
clapping him on the back.   "Look at me! no one
can say I was ever troubled with genius: but I can
show my money, pay my way, eat my dinner, kill
my trout, hunt my hounds, help a lame dog over a
stile" (which was Mark's phrase for doing a generous thing), "and thank God for all; and who
wants more, I should like to know?   But here we
are — you go up first!"

They found Elsley crouched up over the empty
grate, his head in his hands, and a few scraps of
paper by him, on which he had been trying to
scribble.   He did not look up as they came in, but
gave a sort of impatient half-turn, as if angry at
being disturbed.   Tom was about to announce the
banker; but he announced himself.

"Come to do myself the honor of calling on
you, Mr. Vavasour.   I am sorry to see you so
poorly; I hope our Whitbury air will set all
right."

"You mistake me, sir; my name is Briggs!" said Elsley, without turning his head; but a moment after he looked up angrily.

"Mr. Armsworth? I beg your pardon, sir; but what brings you here? Are you come, sir, to use the rich successful man's right, and lecture me in my misery?"

"'Pon my word, sir, you must have forgotten old Mark Armsworth, indeed, if you fancy him capable of any such dirt. No, sir, I came to pay my respects to you, sir, hoping that you'd come up and take a family dinner. I could do no less," ran on the banker, seeing that Elsley was preparing a peevish answer, "considering the honor that, I hear, you have been to your native town. A very distinguished person, our friend Tom tells me; and we ought to be proud of you, and behave to you as you deserve, for I am sure we don't send too many clever fellows out of Whitbury."

"Would that you had never sent me!" said Elsley, in his bitter way.

"Ah, sir, that's matter of opinion! You would never have been heard of down here, never have had justice done you, I mean; for heard of, you have been. There's my daughter has read your poems again and again — always quoting them; and very pretty they sound too. Poetry is not in my line, of course; still, it's a credit to a man to do anything well, if he has the gift; and she tells me that you have it, and plenty of it. And though she's no fine lady, thank Heaven, I'll back her for good sense against any woman. Come up, sir, and judge for yourself if I don't speak the truth; she will be delighted to meet you, and bade me say so."

By this time good Mark had talked himself out of breath; and Elsley, flushing up, as of old, at a little praise, began to stammer an excuse. "His nerves were so weak, and his spirits so broken with late troubles."

"My dear sir, that's the very reason I want you to come. A bottle of port will cure the nerves, and a pleasant chat the spirits. Nothing like forgetting all for a little time; and then to it again with a fresh lease of strength, and beat it at last like a man."

"Too late, my dear sir; I must pay the penalty of my own folly," said Elsley, really won by the man's cordiality.

"Never too late, sir, while there's life left in us. And," he went on in a gentler tone, "if we all were to pay for our own follies, or lie down and die when we saw them coming full cry at our heels, where would any one of us be by now? I have been a fool in my time, young gentleman, more than once or twice; and that too when I was old enough to be your father; and down I went, and deserved what I got: but my rule always was — Fight fair; fall soft; know when you've got enough; and don't cry out when you've got it: but just go home; train again; and say — better luck next fight." And so old Mark's sermon ended (as most of them did) in somewhat Socratic allegory, savoring rather of the market than of the study; but Elsley understood him, and looked up with a smile.

"You too are somewhat of poet in your way, I see, sir!"

"I never thought to live to hear that, sir. I can't doubt now that you are cleverer than your neighbors, for you have found out something which they never did. But you will come? — for that's my business."

Elsley looked inquiringly at Tom; he had learnt now to consult his eye, and lean on him like a child. Tom looked a stout yes, and Elsley said languidly:

"You have given me so much new and good advice in a few minutes, sir, that I must really do myself the pleasure of coming and hearing more."

"Well done, our side!" cried old Mark. "Dinner at half-past five. No London late hours here, sir. Miss Armsworth will be out of her mind when she hears you're coming."

And off he went.

"Do you think he'll come up to the scratch, Tom?"

"I am very much afraid his courage will fail him. I will see him again, and bring him up with me: but now, my dear Mr. Armsworth, do remember one thing; that if you go on with him at your usual rate of hospitality, the man will as surely be drunk, as his nerves and brain are all but ruined; and if he is so, he will most probably destroy himself to-morrow morning."

"Destroy himself?"

"He will. The shame of making a fool of himself just now before you will be more than he could bear. So be stingy for once. He will not wish for it unless you press him; but if he talks (and he will talk after the first half-hour), he will forget himself, and half a bottle will make him mad; and then I won't answer for the consequences."

"Good gracious! why, these poets want as tender handling as a bag of gunpowder over the fire."

"You speak like a book there in your turn." And Tom went home to his father.

He returned in due time. A new difficulty had arisen. Elsley, under the excitement of expectation, had gone out and deigned to buy laudanum — so will an unhealthy craving degrade a man! — of old Bolus himself, who luckily did not recognize him. He had taken his fullest dose, and was now unable to go anywhere or do anything. Tom did not disturb him: but went away, sorely perplexed, and very much minded to tell a white lie to Armsworth, in whose eyes this would be an offence — not unpardonable, for nothing with him was unpardonable, save lying or cruelty — but very grievous. If a man had drunk too much wine in his house, he would have simply kept his eye on him afterwards, as a fool who did not know when he had his "quotum," but laudanum drinking — involving, too, the breaking of an engagement, which, well managed, might have been of immense use to Elsley — was a very different matter. So Tom knew not what to say or do; and not knowing, determined to wait on Providence, smartened himself as best he could, went up to the great house, and found Miss Mary.

"I'll tell her. She will manage it somehow, if she is a woman; much more if she is an angel, as my father says."

Mary looked very much shocked and grieved; answered hardly a word; but said at last, "Come in while I go and see my father." He came into the smart drawing-room, which he could see was seldom used; for Mary lived in her own room, her father in his counting-house, or in his "den." In ten minutes she came down. Tom thought she had been crying.

"I have settled it. Poor unhappy man! We will talk of something more pleasant. Tell me about your shipwreck, and that place — Aberalva, is it not? What a pretty name!"

Tom told her, wondering then, and wondering long afterwards, how she had "settled it" with her father. She chatted on artlessly enough, till the old man came in, and to dinner, in capital humor, without saying one word of Elsley.

"How has the old lion been tamed?" thought Tom. "The two greatest affronts you could offer him in old times were, to break an engagement, and to despise his good cheer." He did not know what the quiet oil on the waters of such a spirit as Mary's can effect.

The evening passed pleasantly enough till nine, in chatting over old times, and listening to the history of every extraordinary trout and fox which had been killed within twenty miles, when the footboy entered with a scared face.

"Please, sir, is Mr. Vavasour here?"

"Here? Who wants him?"

"Mrs. Brown, sir, in Hemmelford Street. Says he lodges with her, and has been to seek for him at Dr. Thurnall's."

"I think you had better go, Mr. Thurnall," said Mary, quietly.

"Indeed you had, boy. Bother poets, and the day they first began to breed in Whitbury! Such an evening spoilt! Have a cup of coffee? No? then a glass of sherry?"

Out went Tom. Mrs. Brown had been up, and seen him seemingly sleeping; then had heard him run downstairs hurriedly. He passed her in the passage, looking very wild. "Seemed, sir, just like my nevy's wife's brother, Will Ford, before he made away with hes'self."

Tom goes off post haste, revolving many things in a crafty heart. Then he steers for Bolus's shop. Bolus is at "The Angler's Arms;" but his assistant is in.

"Did a gentleman call here just now, in a long cloak, with a felt wide-awake?"

"Yes."   And the assistant looks confused enough for Tom to rejoin:

"And you sold him laudanum?"

"Why — ah——"

"And you had sold him laudanum already this afternoon, you young rascal! How dare you, twice in six hours? I'll hold you responsible for the man's life!"

"You dare call me a rascal?" blusters the youth, terror-stricken, at finding how much Tom knows.

"I am a member of the College of Surgeons," says Tom, recovering his coolness, "and have just been dining with Mr. Armsworth. I suppose you know him?"

The assistant shook in his shoes at the name of that terrible justice of the peace and of the war also; and meekly and contritely he replied:

"Oh, sir, what shall I do?"

"You're in a very neat scrape; you could not have feathered your nest better," says Tom, quietly filling his pipe, and thinking. "As you behave now, I will get you out of it, or leave you to — you know what, as well as I. Get your hat."

He went out, and the youth followed trembling, while Tom formed his plans in his mind.

"The wild beast goes home to his lair to die,

and so may he; for I fear it's life and death now. I'll try the house where he was born. Somewhere in Water Lane it is, I know."

And toward Water Lane he hurried. It was a low-lying offshoot of the town, leading along the water-meadows, with a straggling row of houses on each side, the perennial haunts of fever and ague. Before them, on each side of the road, and fringed with pollard willows and tall poplars, ran a tiny branch of the Whit, to feed some mill below; and spread out, meanwhile, into ponds and mires full of offal and duckweed and rank floating grass. A thick mist hung knee-deep over them, and over the gardens right and left; and as Tom came down on the lane from the main street above, he could see the mist spreading across the water-meadows and reflecting the moon-beams like a lake; and as he walked into it, he felt as if he were walking down a well. And he hurried down the lane, looking out anxiously ahead for the long cloak.

At last he came to a better sort of house. That might be it. He would take the chance. There was a man of the middle class, and two or three women, standing at the gate. He went up:

" Pray, sir, did a medical man named Briggs ever live here! "

" What do you want to know for? "

" Why " — Tom thought matters were too serious for delicacy — " I am looking for a gentleman, and thought he might have come here."

" And so he did, if you mean one in a queer hat and a cloak."

" How long since? "

" Why, he came up our garden an hour or more ago; walked right into the parlor without with your leave, or by your leave, and stared at us all round like one out of his mind; and so away, as soon as ever I asked him what he was at —— "

"Which way?"

"To the river, I expect: I ran out, and saw him go down the lane, b it I was not going far by night alone with any suc 1 strange customers."

"Lend me a lanthorn, then, for Heaven's sake!"

The lanthorn is lent, a id Tom starts again down the lane.

Now to search. At he end of the lane is a cross road parallel to the river. A broad still ditch lies beyond it, with a little bridge across, where one gets minnows for bait; then a broad water-meadow; then silver Whit.

The bridge-gate is open. Tom hurries across the road to it. The lanthorn shows him fresh foot-marks going into the meadow. Forward!

Up and down in that meadow for an hour or more did Tom and the trembling youth beat like a brace of pointer dogs, stumbling into gripes, and over sleeping cows; and more than once stopping short just in time, as they were walking into some broad and deep feeder.

Almost in despair, and after having searched down the river bank for full two hundred yards, Tom was on the point of returning, when his eye rested on a part of the stream where the mist lay higher than usual, and let the reflection of the moonlight off the water reach his eye; and in the moonlight ripples, close to the farther bank of the river — what was that black lump?

Tom knew the spot well; the river there is very broad, and very shallow, flowing round low islands of gravel and turf. It was very low just now too, as it generally is in October; there could not be four inches of water where the black lump lay, but on the side nearest him the water was full knee-deep.

The thing, whatever it was, was forty yards from him; and it was a cold night for wading. It might be a hassock of rushes; a tuft of the great water-dock; a dead dog; one of the "hangs" with which the club-water was studded, torn up and stranded: but yet, to Tom, it had not a canny look.

"As usual! Here am I getting wet, dirty, and miserable, about matters which are not the slightest concern of mine! I believe I shall end by getting hanged or shot in somebody else's place, with this confounded spirit of meddling. Yah! how cold the water is!"

For in he went, the grumbling honest dog; stepped across to the black lump; and lifted it up hastily enough — for it was Elsley Vavasour.

Drowned?

No. But wet through, and senseless from mingled cold and laudanum.

Whether he had meant to drown himself, and lighting on the shallow, had stumbled on till he fell exhausted, or whether he had merely blundered into the stream, careless whither he went, Tom knew not, and never knew; for Elsley himself could not recollect.

Tom took him in his arms, carried him ashore and up through the water-meadow; borrowed a blanket and a wheelbarrow at the nearest cottage; wrapped him up; and made the offending surgeon's assistant wheel him to his lodgings.

He sat with him there an hour; and then entered Mark's house again with his usual composed face, to find Mark and Mary sitting up in great anxiety.

"Mr. Armsworth, does the telegraph work at this time of night?"

"I'll make it, if it is wanted. But what's the matter?"

"You will indeed?"

"Gad, I'll go myself and kick up the station-master. What's the matter?"

"That if poor Mrs. Vavasour wishes to see her husband alive, she must be here in four-and-twenty hours. I'll tell you all presently ——"

"Mary, my coat and comforter!" cries Mark, jumping up.

"And, Mary, a pen and ink to write the message," says Tom.

"Oh! cannot I be of any use?" says Mary.

"No, you angel."

"You must not call me an angel, Mr. Thurnall. After all, what can I do which you have not done already?"

Tom started. Grace had once used to him the very same words. By the by, what was it in the two women which made them so like? Certainly, neither face nor fortune. Something in the tones of their voices.

"Ah! if Grace had Mary's fortune, or Mary Grace's face!" thought Tom, as he hurried back to Elsley, and Mark rushed down to the station.

Elsley was conscious when he returned, and only too conscious. All night he screamed in agonies of rheumatic fever; by the next afternoon he was failing fast; his heart was affected; and Tom knew that he might die any hour.

The evening train brings two ladies, Valentia and Lucia. At the risk of her life, the poor faithful wife has come.

A gentleman's carriage is waiting for them, though they have ordered none; and as they go through the station-room, a plain little well-dressed body comes humbly up to them:

"Is either of these ladies Mrs. Vavasour?"

"Yes! I! — I! — is he alive?" gasps Lucia.

"Alive, and better! and expecting you ——"

"Better? — expecting me?" almost shrieks she, as Valentia and Mary (for it is she) help her to the carriage. Mary puts them in, and turns away.

"Are you not coming too?" asks Valentia, who is puzzled.

"No, thank you, madam; I am going to take a walk. John, you know where to drive these ladies."

Little Mary does not think it necessary to say that she, with her father's carriage, has been down to two other afternoon trains, upon the chance of finding them.

But why is not Frank Headley with them, when he is needed most? And why are Valentia's eyes more red with weeping than even her sister's sorrow need have made them?

Because Frank Headley is rolling away in a French railway on his road to Marseilles, and to what Heaven shall find for him to do.

Yes, he is gone Eastward Ho among the many; will he come Westward Ho again among the few?

They are at the door of Elsley's lodgings now. Tom Thurnall meets them there, and bows them upstairs silently. Lucia is so weak that she has to cling to the banister a moment; and then, with a

strong shudder, the spirit conquers the flesh, and
she hurries up before them both.

It is a small low room — Valentia had expected
that: but she had expected, too, confusion and
wretchedness: for a note from Major Campbell,
ere he started, had told her of the condition in
which Elsley had been found. Instead, she finds
neatness — even gaiety; fresh damask linen, comfortable furniture, a vase of hothouse flowers, while
the air is full of cool perfumes. No one is likely
to tell her that Mary has furnished all at Tom's
hint — "We must smarten up the place, for the
poor wife's sake. It will take something off the
shock; and I want to avoid shocks for her."

So Tom had worked with his own hands that
morning; arranging the room as carefully as any
woman, with that true doctor's forethought and
consideration, which often issues in the loftiest,
because the most unconscious, benevolence.

He paused at the door.

"Will you go in?" whispered he to Valentia, in
a tone which meant — "you had better not."

"Not yet — I daresay he is too weak."

Lucia darted in, and Tom shut the door behind
her, and waited at the stair-head. "Better,"
thought he, "to let the two poor creatures settle
their own concerns. It must end soon, in any
case."

Lucia rushed to the bedside, drew back the
curtains:

"Tom!" moaned Elsley.

"Not Tom! — Lucia!"

"Lucia? — Lucia St. Just!" answered he, in a
low abstracted voice, as if trying to recollect.

"Lucia Vavasour! — your Lucia!"

Elsley slowly raised himself upon his elbow, and looked into her face with a sad inquiring gaze.

"Elsley — darling Elsley! — don't you know me?"

"Yes, very well indeed; better than you know me. I am not Vavasour at all. My name is Briggs — John Briggs, the apothecary's son, come home to Whitbury to die."

She did not hear, or did not care for those last words.

"Elsley! I am your wife! — your own wife! — who never loved any one but you — never, never, never!"

"Yes, my wife at least! — Curse them, that they cannot deny!" said he, in the same abstracted voice.

"Oh God! is he mad?" thought she. "Elsley, speak to me! — I am your Lucia — your love ——"

And she tore off her bonnet, and threw herself beside him on the bed and clasped him in her arms, murmuring : "Your wife! who never loved any one but you!"

Slowly his frozen heart and frozen brain melted beneath the warmth of her great love: but he did not speak: only he passed his weak arm round her neck; and she felt that his cheek was wet with tears, while she murmured on, like a cooing dove, the same sweet words again :

"Call me your love once more, and I shall know that all is past."

"Then call me no more Elsley, love!" whispered he. "Call me John Briggs, and let us have done with shams for ever."

"No; you are my Elsley — my Vavasour! and I am your wife once more!" and the poor thing fondled his head as it lay upon the pillow. "My own Elsley, to whom I gave myself, body and soul; for whom I would die now — oh, such a death! any death!"

"How could I doubt you? — fool that I was!"

"No, it was all my fault. It was all my odious temper! But we will be happy now, will we not?"

Elsley smiled sadly, and began babbling — Yes, they would take a farm, and he would plough, and sow, and be of some use before he died. "But promise me one thing " cried he, with sudden strength.

"What?"

"That you will go home and burn all the poetry — all the manuscripts, and never let the children write a verse — a verse — when I am dead?" And his head sank back, and his jaw dropped.

"He is dead!" cried the poor impulsive creature, with a shriek which brought in Tom and Valentia.

"He is not dead, madam; but you must be very gentle with him, if we are to —— "

Tom saw that there was little hope.

"I will do anything — only save him! — save him! Mr. Thurnall, till I have atoned for all."

"You have little enough to atone for, madam," said Tom, as he busied himself about the sufferer. He saw that all would soon be over, and would have had Mrs. Vavasour withdraw; but she was so really good a nurse as long as she could control herself, that he could hardly spare her.

So they sat together by the sick bedside, as the short hours passed into the long, and the long hours into the short again, and the October dawn began to shine through the shutterless window.

A weary eventless night it was, a night as of many years, as worse and worse grew the weak frame; and Tom looked alternately at the heaving chest, and shortening breath, and rattling throat, and then at the pale still face of the lady.

"Better she should sit by," thought he, "and watch him till she is tired out. It will come on her the more gently, after all. He will die at sunrise, as so many die."

At last he began gently feeling for Elsley's pulse. Her eye caught his movement, and she half sprang up; but at a gesture from him she sank quietly on her knees, holding her husband's hand in her own.

Elsley turned toward her once, ere the film of death had fallen, and looked her full in the face, with his beautiful eyes full of love. Then the eyes paled and faded; but still they sought for her painfully long after she had buried her head in the coverlet, unable to bear the sight.

And so vanished away Elsley Vavasour, poet and genius, into his own place.

"Let us pray," said a deep voice from behind the curtain: it was Mark Armsworth's. He had come over with the first dawn, to bring the ladies food; had slipped upstairs to ask what news, found the door open, and entered in time to see the last gasp.

Lucia kept her head still buried; and Tom, for the first time for many a year, knelt, as the old banker commended to God the soul of our dear brother just departing this life. Then Mark glided quietly downstairs, and Valentia, rising, tried to lead Mrs. Vavasour away.

But then broke out in all its wild passion the Irish temperament. Let us pass it over; why try to earn a little credit by depicting the agony and the weakness of a sister?

At last Thurnall got her downstairs. Mark was there still, having sent off for his carriage. He quietly put her arm through his, led her off, worn out and unresisting, drove her home, delivered her and Valentia into Mary's keeping, and then asked Tom to stay and sit with him.

"I hope I've no very bad conscience, boy; but Mary's busy with the poor young thing, mere child she is, too, to go through such a night; and, somehow, I don't like to be left alone after such a sight as that!"

.   .   .   .

"Tom!" said Mark, as they sat smoking in silence, after breakfast, in the study. "Tom!"

"Yes, sir!"

"That was an awful death-bed, Tom!"

Tom was silent.

"I don't mean that he died hard, as we say; but so young, Tom. And I suppose poets' souls are worth something, like other people's — perhaps more. I can't understand 'em: but my Mary seems to, and people, like her, who think a poet the finest thing in the world. I laugh at it all when I am jolly, and call it sentiment and cant: but I believe that they are nearer heaven than I am: though I think they don't quite know where heaven is, nor where" (with a wicked wink, in spite of the sadness of his tone) — "where they themselves are either."

"I'll tell you, sir. I have seen men enough die — we doctors are hardened to it: but I have seen unprofessional deaths — men we didn't kill ourselves; I have seen men drowned, shot, hanged, run over, and worse deaths than that, sir, too; —

and, somehow, I never felt any death like that man's. Granted, he began by trying to set the world right, when he had n't yet set himself right; but was n't it some credit to see that the world was wrong?"

"I don't know that. The world's a very good world."

"To you and me; but there are men who have higher notions than I of what this world ought to be; and, for aught I know, they are right. That Aberalva curate, Headley, had; and so had Briggs, in his own way. I thought him once only a poor discontented devil, who quarrelled with his bread and butter because he had n't teeth to eat it with; but there was more in the fellow, coxcomb as he was. 'T is n't often that I let that croaking old bogy, Madam-might-have-been, trouble me; but I cannot help thinking that if, fifteen years ago, I had listened to his vaporings more, and bullied him about them less, he might have been here still."

"You would n't have been, then. Well for you that you did n't catch his fever."

"And write verses too? Don't make me laugh, sir, on such a day as this; I always comfort myself with — 'It 's no business of mine:' but, somehow, I can't do so just now." And Tom sat silent, more softened than he had been for years.

"Let 's talk of something else," said Mark at last. "You had the cholera very bad down there, I hear?"

"Oh, sharp, but short," said Tom, who disliked any subject which brought Grace to his mind.

"Any on my lord's estate with the queer name?"

"Not a case. We stopped the devil out there, thanks to his lordship."

"So did we here. We were very near in for it, though, I fancy. At least, I chose to fancy so — thought it a good opportunity to clean Whitbury once for all."

"It's just like you. Well?"

"Well, I offered the Town Council to drain the whole town at my own expense, if they'd let me have the sewage. And that only made things worse; for as soon as the beggars found out the sewage was worth anything, they were down on me, as if I wanted to do then — I, Mark Armsworth! — and would sooner let half the town rot with an epidemic, than have reason to fancy I'd made any money out of them. So a pretty fight I had, for half-a-dozen meetings, till I called in my lord; and, sir, he came down by the next express, like a trump, all the way from town, and gave them such a piece of his mind — was going to have the Board of Health down, and turn on the Government tap, commissioners and all, and cost 'em hundreds: till the fellows shook in their shoes; — and so I conquered, and here we are, as clean as a nut, — and a fig for the cholera! — except down in Water Lane, which I don't know what to do with; for if tradesmen will run up houses on spec in a water-meadow, who can stop them? There ought to be a law for it, say I; but I say a good many things in the twelve months that nobody minds. But, my dear boy, if one man in a town has pluck and money, he may do it. It'll cost him a few: I've had to pay the main part myself, after all: but I suppose God will make it up to a man somehow. That's old Mark's faith, at least. Now I want to talk to you about yourself. My lord comes into town to-day, and you must see him."

" Why, then? He can't help me with the Bashi-Bazouks, can he?"

" Bashi-fiddles! I say, Tom, the more I think over it, the more it won't do. It's throwing yourself away. They say that Turkish contingent is getting on terribly ill."

" More need of me to make them well."

" Hang it — I mean — has n't justice done it, and so on. The papers are full of it."

" Well," quoth Tom, " and why should it?"

" Why, man alive, if England spends all this money on the men, she ought to do her duty by them."

" I don't see that. As Pecksniff says, ' If England expects every man to do his duty, she 's very sanguine, and will be much disappointed.' They don't intend to do their duty by her, any more than I do; so why should she do her duty by them?"

" Don't intend to do your duty?"

" I 'm going out because England's money is necessary to me; and England hires me because my skill is necessary to her. I did n't think of duty when I settled to go, and why should she? I 'll get all out of her I can in the way of pay and practice, and she may get all she can out of me in the way of work. As for being ill-used, I never expect to be anything else in this life. I 'm sure I don't care; and I 'm sure she don't; so live and let live; talk plain truth, and leave Bunkum for right honorables who keep their places thereby. Give me another weed."

" Queer old philosopher you are; but go you sha'n't! "

" Go I will, sir; don't stop me. I 've my reasons, and they 're good ones enough."

The conversation was interrupted by the servant;—Lord Minchampstead was waiting at Mr. Armsworth's office.

"Early bird, his lordship, and gets the worm accordingly," says Mark, as he hurries off to attend on his ideal hero. "You come over to the shop in half-an-hour, mind."

"But why?"

"Confound you, sir! you talk of having your reasons: I have mine!"

Mark looked quite cross; so Tom gave way, and went in due time to the bank.

Standing with his back to the fire in Mark's inner room, he saw the old cotton prince.

"And a prince he looks like," quoth Tom to himself, as he waited in the bank outside, and looked through the glass screen. "How well the old man wears! I wonder how many fresh thousands he has made since I saw him last, seven years ago."

And a very noble person Lord Minchampstead did look; one to whom hats went off almost without their owners' will; tall and portly, with a soldier-like air of dignity and command, which was relieved by the good-nature of the countenance. Yet it was a good-nature which would stand no trifling. The jaw was deep and broad, though finely shaped; the mouth firm set; the nose slightly aquiline; the brow of great depth and height, though narrow; — altogether a Julius Cæsar's type of head; that of a man born to rule self, and therefore to rule all he met.

Tom looked over his dress, not forgetting, like a true Englishman, to mark what sort of boots he wore. They were boots not quite fashionable, but carefully cleaned on trees; trousers strapped tightly over them, which had adopted the military stripe, but retained the slit at the ankle which was in vogue forty years ago; frock coat with a velvet collar, buttoned up, but not too far; high and tight blue cravat below an immense shirt collar; a certain care and richness of dress throughout, but soberly behind the fashion: while the hat was a very shabby and broken one, and the whip still more shabby and broken; all which indicated to Tom that his lordship let his tailor and his valet dress him; and though not unaware that it behoved him to set out his person as it deserved, was far too fine a gentleman to trouble himself about looking fine.

Mark looks round, sees Tom, and calls him in.

"Mr. Thurnall, I am glad to meet you, sir. You did me good service at Pentremochyn, and did it cheaply. I was agreeably surprised, I confess, at receiving a bill for four pounds seven shillings and sixpence, where I expected one of twenty or thirty."

"I charged according to what my time was really worth there, my lord. I heartily wish it had been worth more."

"No doubt," says my lord, in the blandest, and the dryest tone.

Some men would have, under a sense of Tom's merits, sent him a cheque off-hand for five-and-twenty pounds; but that is not Lord Minchampstead's way of doing business. He had paid simply the sum asked: but he had set Tom down in his memory as a man whom he could trust to do good work, and to do it cheaply; and now:

"You are going to join the Turkish contingent?"

"I am."

"You know that part of the world well, I believe?"

"Intimately."

"And the languages spoken there?"

"By no means all. Russian and Tartar well; Turkish tolerably; with a smattering of two or three Circassian dialects."

"Humph! A fair list. Any Persian?"

"Only a few words."

"Humph! If you can learn one language, I presume you can learn another. Now, Mr. Thurnall, I have no doubt that you will do your duty in the Turkish contingent."

Tom bowed.

"But I must ask you if your resolution to join it is fixed?"

"I only join it because I can get no other employment at the seat of war."

"Humph! You wish to go, then, in any case, to the seat of war?"

"Certainly."

"No doubt you have sufficient reasons. . . . Armsworth, this puts the question in a new light."

Tom looked round at Mark, and, behold, his face bore a ludicrous mixture of anger and disappointment and perplexity. He seemed to be trying to make signals to Tom, and to be afraid of doing so openly before the great man.

"He is as wilful and as foolish as a girl, my lord; and I've told him so."

"Everybody knows his own business best, Armsworth; Mr. Thurnall, have you any fancy for the post of Queen's messenger?"

"I should esteem myself only too happy as one."

"They are not to be obtained now as easily as they were fifty years ago; and are given, as you may know, to a far higher class of men than they were formerly. But I shall do my best to obtain you one, when an opportunity offers."

Tom was beginning his profusest thanks: for was not his fortune made? but Lord Minchampstead stopped him with an uplifted finger.

"And, meanwhile, there are foreign employments of which neither those who bestow them, nor those who accept them, are expected to talk much; but for which you, if I am rightly informed, would be especially fitted."

Tom bowed; and his face spoke a hundred assents.

"Very well; if you will come over to Minchampstead to-morrow, I will give you letters to friends of mine in town. I trust that they may give you a better opportunity than the Bashi-Bazouks will, of displaying that courage, address, and self-command which, I understand, you possess in so uncommon a degree. Good morning!" And forth the great man went.

Most opposite were the actions of the two whom he had left behind him.

Tom dances about the room, hurrahing in a whisper:

"My fortune's made? The secret service! Oh, what bliss! The thing I've always longed for!"

Mark dashes himself desperately back in his chair, and shoots his angry legs straight out, almost tripping up Tom.

"You abominable ass! You have done it with a vengeance! Why, he has been pumping me about you this month! One word from you to say you 'd have stayed, and he was going to make you agent for all his Cornish property."

"Don't he wish he may get it? Catch a fish climbing trees! Catch me staying at home when I can serve my Queen and my country, and find a sphere for the full development of my talents! Oh, won't I be as wise as a serpent? Won't I be complimented by . . . himself as his best lurcher, worth any ten needy Joles, greedy Armenians, traitors, renegades, rag tag and bob-tail! I 'll shave my head to-morrow, and buy me an assortment of wigs of every hue!"

Take care, Tom Thurnall. After pride comes a fall; and he who digs a pit may fall into it himself. Has this morning's death-bed given you no lesson that it is as well not to cast ourselves down from where God has put us, for whatsoever seemingly fine ends of ours, lest, doing so, we tempt God once too often?

Your father quoted that text to John Briggs, here, many years ago. Might he not quote it now to you? True, not one word of murmuring, not even of regret, or fear, has passed his good old lips about your self-willed plan. He has such utter confidence in you, such utter carelessness about himself, such utter faith in God, that he can let you go without a sigh. But will you make his courage an excuse for your own rashness? Again, beware; after pride may come a fall.

.   .   .   .

On the fourth day Elsley was buried. Mark and Tom were the only mourners; Lucia and Valentia stayed at Mark's house, to return next day under Tom's care to Eaton Square.

The two mourners walked back sadly from the

churchyard. "I shall put a stone over him, Tom. He ought to rest quietly now; for he had little rest enough in this life. . . ."

"Now I want to talk to you about something; when I've taken off my hatband, that is; for it would be hardly lucky to mention such matters with a hatband on."

Tom looked up, wondering.

"Tell me about his wife, meanwhile. What made him marry her? Was she a pretty woman?"

"Pretty enough, I believe, before she married: but I hardly think he married her for her face."

"Of course not!" said the old man with emphasis: "of course not! Whatever faults he had, he'd be too sensible for that. Don't you marry for a face, Tom! I did n't."

Tom opened his eyes at this last assertion; but humbly expressed his intention of not falling into that snare.

"Ah? you don't believe me: well, she was a beautiful woman, — I'd like to see her fellow now in the county! — and I won't deny I was proud of her. But she had ten thousand pounds, Tom. And as for her looks, why, if you'll believe me, after we'd been married three months, I did n't know whether she had any looks or not. What are you smiling at, you young rogue?"

"Report did say that one look of Mrs. Armsworth's, to the last, would do more to manage Mr. Armsworth than the opinions of the whole bench of bishops."

"Report's a liar, and you're a puppy! You don't know yet whether it was a pleasant look, or a cross one, lad. But still — well, she was an angel, and kept old Mark straighter than he's

ever been since; not that he's so very bad, now.
Though I sometimes think Mary's better even than
her mother. That girl's a good girl, Tom."

"Report agrees with you in that, at least."

"Fool if it did n't. And as for looks — I can
speak to you as to my own son — Why, handsome
is that handsome does."

"And that handsome has; for you must honestly
put that into the account. '

"You think so? So do I! Well, then, Tom,"
—and here Mark was seized with a tendency to
St. Vitus's dance, and began overhauling every
button on his coat, twitching up his black gloves,
till (as undertakers' gloves are generally meant to
do) they burst in half a dozen places; taking off
his hat, wiping his head fiercely, and putting the
hat on again behind before; till at last he snatched
his arm from Tom's, and gripping him by the
shoulder, recommenced:

"You think so, eh? Well, I must say it, so I'd
better have it out now, hatband or none! What
do you think of the man who married my daughter,
face and all?"

"I should think," quoth Tom, wondering who
the happy man could be, "that he would be so
lucky in possessing such a heart, that he would be
a fool to care about the face."

"Then be as good as your word, and take her
yourself. I've watched you this last week, and
you'll make her a good husband. There, I have
spoken; let me hear no more about it."

And Mark half pushed Tom from him, and puffed
on by his side, highly excited.

If Mark had knocked the young doctor down,
he would have been far less astonished and far less

puzzled too. "Well," thought he, "I fancied nothing could throw my steady old engine off the rails; but I am off them now, with a vengeance." What to say he knew not; at last:

"It is just like your generosity, sir; you have been a brother to my father; and now——"

"And now I'll be a father to you! Old Mark does nothing by halves."

"But, sir, however lucky I should be in possessing Miss Armsworth's heart, what reason have I to suppose that I do so? I never spoke a word to her. I need n't say that she never did to me — which——"

"Of course she did n't, and of course you did n't. Should like to have seen you making love to my daughter, indeed! No, sir; it's my will and pleasure. I've settled it, and done it shall be! I shall go home and tell Mary, and she 'll obey me — I should like to see her do anything else! Hoity, toity, fathers must be masters, sir! even in these fly-away new times, when young ones choose their own husbands, and their own politics, and their own hounds, and their own religion too, and be hanged to them!"

What did this unaccustomed bit of bluster mean? for unaccustomed it was; and Tom knew well that Mary Armsworth had her own way, and managed her father as completely as he managed Whitbury.

"Humph! It is impossible; and yet it must be. This explains his being so anxious that Lord Minchampstead should approve of me. I have found favor in the poor dear thing's eyes, I suppose: and the good old fellow knows it, and won't betray her, and so shams tyrant. Just like him!" But——

that Mary Armsworth should care for him! Vain fellow that he was to fancy it! And yet, when he began to put things together, little silences, little looks, little nothings, which all together might make something. He would not slander her to himself by supposing that her attentions to his father were paid for his sake: but he could not forget that it was she, always, who read his letters aloud to the old man: or that she had taken home and copied out the story of his shipwreck. Beside, it was the only method of explaining Mark's conduct, save on the supposition that he had suddenly been " changed by the fairies " in his old age, instead of in the cradle, as usual.

It was a terrible temptation; and to no man more than to Thomas Thurnall. He was no boy, to hanker after mere animal beauty: he had no delicate visions or lofty aspirations; and he knew (no man better) the plain English of fifty thousand pounds, and Mark Armsworth's daughter — a good house, a good consulting practice (for he would take his M.D. of course), a good station in the county, a good clarence with a good pair of horses, good plate, a good dinner with good company thereat; and, over and above all, his father to live with him; and with Mary, whom he loved as a daughter, in luxury and peace to his life's end. — Why, it was all that he had ever dreamed of, three times more than he ever hoped to gain! — Not to mention (for how oddly little dreams of selfish pleasure slip in at such moments!) that he would buy such a Ross's microscope! and keep such a horse for a sly by-day with the Whitford Priors! Oh, to see once again a fox break from Coldharbour gorse!

And then rose up before his imagination those drooping steadfast eyes; and Grace Harvey, the suspected, the despised, seemed to look through and through his inmost soul, as through a home which belonged of right to her, and where no other woman must dwell, or could dwell; for she was there; and he knew it; and knew that, even if he never married till his dying day, he should sell his soul by marrying any one but her. " And why should I not sell my soul?" asked he, almost fiercely. " I sell my talents, my time, my strength; I 'd sell my life to-morrow, and go to be shot for a shilling a day, if it would make the old man comfortable for life; and why not my soul too? Don't that belong to me as much as any other part of me? Why am I to be condemned to sacrifice my prospects in life to a girl of whose honesty I am not even sure? What is this intolerable fascination? Witch! I almost believe in mesmerism now! — Again, I say, why should I not sell my soul, as I 'd sell my coat, if the bargain 's but a good one?"

And if he did, who would ever know? — Not even Grace herself. The secret was his, and no one else's. Or if they did know, what matter? Dozens of men sell their souls every year, and thrive thereon: tradesmen, lawyers, squires, popular preachers, great noblemen, kings and princes. He would be in good company, at all events: and while so many live in glass houses, who dare throw stones?

But then, curiously enough, there came over him a vague dread of possible evil, such as he had never felt before. He had been trying for years to raise himself above the power of fortune; and

he had succeeded ill enough: but he had never
lost heart. Robbed, shipwrecked, lost in deserts,
cheated at cards, shot in revolutions, begging his
bread, he had always been the same unconquerable light-hearted Tom, whose motto was, " Fall
light, and don't whimper: better luck next round."
But now, what if he played his last court-card, and
Fortune, out of her close-hidden hand, laid down a
trump thereon with quiet sneering smile? And
she would! He knew, somehow, that he should
not thrive. His children would die of the measles,
his horses break their knees, his plate be stolen,
his house catch fire, and Mark Armsworth die
insolvent. What a fool he was, to fancy such
nonsense! Here he had been slaving all his life
to keep his father: and now he could keep him;
why, he would be justified, right, a good son, in
doing the thing. How hard, how unjust of those
upper Powers in which he believed so vaguely, to
forbid his doing it!

And how did he know that they forbid him? That
is too deep a question to be analyzed here: but
this thing is noteworthy, that there came next over
Tom's mind a stranger feeling still — a fancy that
if he did this thing, and sold his soul, he could not
answer for himself thenceforth on the score of
merest respectability; could not answer for himself not to drink, gamble, squander his money,
neglect his father, prove unfaithful to his wife; that
the innate capacity for blackguardism, which was
as strong in him as in any man, might, and probably would, run utterly riot thenceforth. He felt
as if he should cast away his last anchor, and drift
helplessly down into utter shame and ruin. It
may have been very fanciful: but so he felt; and

felt it so strongly too, that in less time than I have taken to write this he had turned to Mark Armsworth:

"Sir, you are what I have always found you. Do you wish me to be what you have always found me?"

"I'd be sorry to see you anything else, boy."

"Then, sir, I can't do this. In honor, I can't."

"Are you married already?" thundered Mark.

"Not quite as bad as that;" and in spite of his agitation Tom laughed, but hysterically, at the notion. "But fool I am; for I am in love with another woman. I am, sir," went he on hurriedly. "Boy that I am! and she don't even know it: but if you be the man I take you for, you may be angry with me, but you'll understand me. Anything but be a rogue to you and to Mary, and to my own self too. Fool I'll be, but rogue I won't!"

Mark strode on in silence, frightfully red in the face for full five minutes. Then he turned sharply on Tom, and catching him by the shoulder, thrust him from him.

"There — go! and don't let me see or hear of you; — that is, till I tell you! Go along, I say! Hum-hum!" (in a tone half of wrath, and half of triumph) "his father's child! If you will ruin yourself, I can't help it."

"Nor I, sir," said Tom, in a really piteous tone, bemoaning the day he ever saw Aberalva, as he watched Mark stride into his own gate. "If I had but had common luck! If I had but brought my £1500 safe home here, and never seen Grace, and married this girl out of hand! Common luck is all I ask, and I never get it!"

And Tom went home sulkier than a bear: but

he did not let his father find out his trouble. It
was his last evening with the old man. To-morrow
he must go to London, and then — to scramble
and twist about the world again till he died?
"Well, why not? A man must die somehow: but
it's hard on the poor old father," said Tom.

As Tom was packing his scanty carpet-bag next
morning, there was a knock at the door. He
looked out, and saw Armsworth's clerk. What
could that mean? Had the old man determined
to avenge the slight, and to do so on his father, by
claiming some old debt? There might be many
between him and the doctor. And Tom's heart
beat fast as Jane put a letter into his hand.

"No answer, sir, the clerk says."

Tom opened it, and turned over the contents
more than once ere he could believe his own eyes.

It was neither more nor less than a cheque on
Mark's London banker for just five hundred
pounds.

A half sheet was wrapped round it, on which
were written these words: —

"To Thomas Thurnall, Esq., for behaving like a gentleman. The cheque will be duly honored at Messrs.
Smith, Brown, and Jones, Lombard Street. No acknowl-
edgement is to be sent. Don't tell your father.

"MARK ARMSWORTH."

"Queer old world it is!" said Tom, when the
first burst of childish delight was over. "And
jolly old flirt, Dame Fortune, after all! If I had
written this in a book now, who'd have believed
it?"

"Father," said he, as he kissed the old man
farewell, "I've a little money come in. I'll send

you fifty from London in a day or two, and lodge a hundred and fifty more with Smith and Co. So you'll be quite in clover while I am poisoning the Turkeys, or at some better work."

The old man thanked God for his good son, and only hoped that he was not straitening himself to buy luxuries for a useless old fellow.

Another sacred kiss on that white head, and Tom was away for London, with a fuller purse, and a more self-contented heart too, than he had known for many a year.

And Elsley was left behind, under the gray church spire, sleeping with his fathers, and vexing his soul with poetry no more. Mark has covered him now with a fair Portland slab. He took Claude Mellot to it this winter before church time, and stood over it long with a puzzled look, as if dimly discovering that there were more things in heaven and earth than were dreamed of in his philosophy.

"Wonderful fellow he was, after all! Mary shall read us out some of his verses to-night. But, I say, why should people be born clever, only to make them all the more miserable?"

"Perhaps they learn the more, papa, by their sorrows," said quiet little Mary; "and so they are the gainers after all."

And none of them having any better answer to give, they all three went into the church, to see if one could be found there.

And so Tom Thurnall, too, went Eastward Ho, to take, like all the rest, what God might send.

TOO LATE

A ND how was poor Grace Harvey prospering
the while? While comfortable folks were
praising her, at their leisure, as a heroine, Grace
Harvey was learning, so she opined, by fearful les-
sons, how much of the unheroic element was still left
in her. The first lesson had come just a week after
the yacht sailed for Port Madoc, when the cholera
had all but subsided; and it came in this wise.
Before breakfast one morning she had to go up to
Heale's shop for some cordial. Her mother had
passed, so she said, a sleepless night, and come
downstairs nervous and without appetite, oppressed
with melancholy, both in the spiritual and the
physical sense of the word. It was not often so
with her now. She had escaped the cholera. The
remoteness of her house; her care never to enter
the town; the purity of the water, which trickled
always fresh from the cliff close by; and last, but
not least, the scrupulous cleanliness which (to do
her justice) she had always observed, and in which
she had trained up Grace — all these had kept her
safe.

But Grace could see that her dread of the
cholera was intense. She even tried at first to
prevent Grace from entering an infected house;
but that proposal was answered by a look of horror

which shamed her into silence, and she contented herself with all but tabooing Grace; making her change her clothes whenever she came in; refusing to sit with her, almost to eat with her. But, over and above all this, she had grown moody, peevish, subject to violent bursts of crying, fit of superstitious depression; spent, sometimes, whole days in reading experimental books, arguing with the preachers, gadding to and fro to every sermon, Arminian or Calvinist; and at last even to church — walking in dry places, poor soul; seeking rest, and finding none.

All this betokened some malady of the mind, rather than of the body; but what that malady was, Grace dare not even try to guess. Perhaps it was one of the fits of religious melancholy so common in the West country — like her own, in fact: perhaps it was all "nerves." Her mother was growing old, and had a great deal of business to worry her; and so Grace thrust away the horrible suspicion by little self-deceptions.

She went into the shop. Tom was busy upon his knees behind the counter. She made her request.

"Ah, Miss Harvey!" and he sprang up. "It will be a pleasure to serve you once more in one's life. I am just going."

"Going where?"

"To Turkey. I find this place too pleasant and too poor. Not work enough, and certainly not pay enough. So I have got an appointment as surgeon in the Turkish contingent, and shall be off in an hour."

"To Turkey! to the war?"

"Yes. It's a long time since I have seen any

fighting. I am quite out of practice in gunshot wounds. There is the medicine. Good-bye! You will shake hands once, for the sake of our late cholera work together?"

Grace held out her hand mechanically across the counter, and he took it. But she did not look into his face. Only she said, half to herself:

"Well, better so. I have no doubt you will be very useful among them '

"Confound the icicle!" thought Tom. "I really believe that she wants to get rid of me." And he would have withdrawn his hand in a pet: but she held it still.

Quaint it was; those two strong natures, each loving the other better than anything else on earth, and yet parted by the thinnest pane of ice, which a single look would have melted. She longing to follow that man over the wide world, slave for him, die for him; he longing for the least excuse for making a fool of himself, and crying, "Take me, as I take you, without a penny, for better, for worse!" If their eyes had but met! But they did not meet; and the pane of ice kept them asunder as surely as a wall of iron.

Was it that Tom was piqued at her seeming coldness; or did he expect, before he made any advances, that she should show that she wished at least for his respect, by saying something to clear up the ugly question which lay between them? Or was he, as I suspect, so ready to melt, and make a fool of himself, that he must needs harden his own heart by help of the devil himself? And yet there are excuses for him. It would have been a sore trial to any man's temper to quit Aberalva in the belief that he left fifteen hundred pounds

behind him.   Be that as it may, he said carelessly,
after a moment's pause:

"Well, farewell!   And, by the by, about that
little money matter.   The month of which you
spoke once was up yesterday.   I suppose I am
not worthy yet; so I shall be humble, and wait
patiently.   Don't hurry yourself, I beg of you, on
my account."

She snatched her hand from his without a word,
and rushed out of the shop.

He returned to his packing, whistling away as
shrill as any blackbird.

Little did he think that Grace's heart was bursting, as she hurried down the street, covering her
face in her veil, as if every one would espy her
dark secret in her countenance.

But she did not go home to hysterics and vain
tears.   An awful purpose had arisen in her mind,
under the pressure of that great agony.   Heavens,
how she loved that man!   To be suspected by
him was torture.   But she could bear that.   It was
her cross; she could carry it, lie down on it, and
endure: but wrong him she could not — would
not!   It was sinful enough while he was there;
but doubly, unbearably sinful, when he was going
to a foreign country, when he would need every
farthing he had.   So not for her own sake, but for
his, she spoke to her mother when she went home,
and found her sitting over her Bible in the little
parlor, vainly trying to find a text which suited her
distemper.

"Mother, you have the Bible before you
there."

"Yes, child!   Why?   What?" asked she, looking up uneasily.

Grace fixed her eyes on the ground. She could not look her mother in the face.

"Do you ever read the thirty-second Psalm, mother?"

"Which? Why not, child?"

"Let us read it together then, now."

And Grace, taking up her own Bible, sat quietly down and read, as none in that parish save she could read : —

"Blessed is he whose ransgression is forgiven, and whose sin is covered.

"Blessed is the man unto whom the Lord imputeth not iniquity, and in whose spirit there is no guile.

"When I kept silence, my bones waxed old, through my groaning all the day long.

"For day and night Thy hand was heavy upon me: my moisture is turned to the drought of summer.

"I acknowledge my sin unto Thee, and mine iniquity have I not hid.

"I said, I will confess my transgressions unto the Lord ; and Thou forgavest the iniquity of my sin."

Grace stopped, choked with tears which the pathos of her own voice had called up. She looked at her mother. There were no tears in her eyes: only a dull thwart look of terror and suspicion. The shaft, however bravely and cunningly sped, had missed its mark.

Poor Grace! Her usual eloquence utterly failed her, as most things do in which one is wont to trust, before the pressure of a real and horrible evil. She had no heart to make fine sentences, to preach a brilliant sermon of commonplaces. What could she say that her mother had not known long before she was born? And throwing herself on her knees at her mother's feet, she grasped both her hands and looked into her face imploringly: "Mother! mother! mother!" was all that she could say: but their tone meant more than all words. Reproof, counsel, comfort, utter tenderness, and under-current of clear deep trust, bubbling up from beneath all passing suspicions, however dark and foul, were in it: but they were vain.

Base terror, the parent of baser suspicion, had hardened that woman's heart for the while; and all she answered was:

"Get up! What is this foolery?"

"I will not! I will not rise till you have told me."

"What?"

"Whether," — and she forced the words slowly out in a low whisper, — "whether you know — anything of — of — Mr. Thurnall's money — his belt?"

"Is the girl mad? Belt? Money? Do you take me for a thief, wench?"

"No! no! no! Only say you — you know nothing of it!"

"Psha! girl! Go to your school:" and the old woman tried to rise.

"Only say that! only let me know that it is a dream — a hideous dream which the devil put into my wicked, wicked heart — and let me know that I am the basest, meanest of daughters for harboring such a thought a moment! It will be comfort, bliss, to what I endure! Only say that, and I will crawl to your feet, and beg for your forgiveness, — ask you to beat me, like a child, as I shall deserve! Drive me out, if you will, and let me die, as I shall deserve! Only say the word, and take this fire from before my eyes, which burns day and night, — till my brain is dried up with misery and shame! Mother, mother, speak "

But then burst out the horrible suspicion, which falsehood, suspecting all others of being false as itself, had engendered in that mother's heart.

"Yes, viper! I see your plan! Do you think I do not know that you are in love with that fellow?"

Grace started as if she had been shot, and covered her face with her hands

"Yes! and want me to betray myself — to tell a lie about myself, that you may curry favor with him — a penniless, unbelieving —— "

"Mother!" almost shrieked Grace, "I can bear no more! Say that it is a lie, and then kill me if you will!"

"It is a lie, from beginning to end! What else should it be?" And the woman, in the hurry of her passion, confirmed the equivocation with an oath; and then ran on, as if to turn her own thoughts, as well as Grace's, into commonplaces about "a poor old mother, who cares for nothing but you; who has worked her fingers to the bone for years to leave you a little money when she is gone! I wish I were gone! I wish I were out of this wretched ungrateful world, I do! To have my own child turn against me in my old age!"

Grace lifted her hands from her face, and looked steadfastly at her mother. And behold, she knew not how or why, she felt that her mother had forsworn herself. A strong shudder passed through her; she rose and was leaving the room in silence.

"Where are you going, hussy? Stop!" screamed

her mother between her teeth, her rage and cruelty rising, as it will with weak natures, in the very act of triumph, — "to your young man?"

"To pray," said Grace, quietly; and locking herself into the empty schoolroom, gave vent to all her feelings, but not in tears.

How she upbraided herself! She had not used her strength; she had not told her mother all her heart. And yet how could she tell her heart? How face her mother with such vague suspicions, hardly supported by a single fact? How argue it out against her like a lawyer, and convict her to her face? What daughter could do that, who had human love and reverence left in her? No! to touch her inward witness, as the Quakers well and truly term it, was the only method: and it had failed. "God help me!" was her only cry: but the help did not come yet; there came over her instead a feeling of utter loneliness. Willis dead; Thurnall gone; her mother estranged; and, like a child lost upon a great moor, she looked round all heaven and earth, and there was none to counsel, none to guide — perhaps not even God. For would He help her as long as she lived in sin? And was she not living in sin, deadly sin, as long as she knew what she was sure she knew, and left the wrong unrighted?

It is sometimes true, the popular saying, that sunshine comes after storm. Sometimes true, or who could live? but not always: not even often. Equally true is the popular antithet, that misfortunes never come single; that in most human lives there are periods of trouble, blow following blow, wave following wave, from opposite and unexpected quarters, with no natural or logical sequence, till all God's billows have gone over the soul.

How paltry and helpless, in such dark times, are all theories of mere self-education; all proud attempts, like that of Goethe's Wilhelm Meister, to hang self-poised in the center of the abyss, and there organize for oneself a character by means of circumstances! Easy enough and graceful enough does that dream look, while all the circumstances themselves — all which stands around — are easy and graceful, obliging and commonplace, like the sphere of petty experiences with which Goethe surrounds his insipid hero. Easy enough it seems for a man to educate himself without God, as long as he lies comfortably on a sofa, with a cup of coffee and a review: but what if that "demonic element of the universe," which Goethe confessed, and yet in his luxuriousness tried to ignore, because he could not explain — what if that broke forth over the graceful and prosperous student, as it may any moment? What if something, or some person, or many things, or many persons, one after the other (questions which he must get answered then, or die), took him up and dashed him down, again, and again, and again, till he was ready to cry, "I reckoned till morning that like a lion he will break all my bones; from morning till evening he will make an end of me?" What if he thus found himself hurled perforce amid the real universal experiences of humanity; and made free, in spite of himself, by doubt and fear and horror of great darkness, of the brotherhood of woe, common alike to the simplest peasant-woman, and to every great soul, perhaps, who has left his impress and sign-manual upon the hearts of after generations? Jew, Heathen, or Christian; men of the most opposite creeds and aims; whether it be Moses or Socrates, Isaiah or Epictetus, Augustine or Mohammed, Dante or Bernard, Shakspeare or Bacon, or Goethe's self, no doubt, though in his tremendous pride he would not confess it even to himself, — each and all of them have this one fact in common — that once in their lives, at least, they have gone down into the bottomless pit and "*stato all' inferno*" — as the children used truly to say of Dante; and there, out of the utter darkness, have asked the question of all questions — "Is there a God? And if there be, what is He doing with me?"

What refuge, then, in self-education; when a man feels himself powerless in the gripe of some unseen and inevitable power, and knows not whether it be chance, or necessity, or a devouring fiend? To wrap himself sternly in himself, and cry, "I will endure, though all the universe be against me;" — how fine it sounds! But who has done it? Could a man do it perfectly but for one moment, — could he absolutely and utterly for one moment isolate himself, and accept his own isolation as a fact, he were then and there a madman or a suicide. As it is, his nature, happily too weak for that desperate self-assertion, falls back recklessly on some form, more or less graceful according to the temperament, of the ancient panacea, "Let us eat and drink, for to-morrow we die." Why should a man educate self, when he knows not whither he goes, what will befall him to-night? No. There is but one escape, one chink through which we may see light, one rock on which our feet may find standing-place, even in

the abyss: and that is the belief, intuitive, inspired,
due neither to reasoning nor to study, that the billows are God's billows; and that though we go
down to hell, He is there also; — the belief that
not we, but He, is educating us; that these seemingly fantastic and incoherent miseries, storm following earthquake, and earthquake fire, as if the
caprice of all the demons were let loose against us,
have in His mind a spiritual coherence, an organic
unity and purpose (though we see it not); that
sorrows do not come singly, only because He is
making short work with our spirits; and because
the more effect He sees produced by one blow, the
more swiftly He follows it up by another; till, in
one great and varied crisis, seemingly long to us,
but short enough compared with immortality, our
spirits may be —

> " Heated hot with burning fears,
> And bathed in baths of hissing tears,
> And battered with the strokes of doom,
> To shape and use."

And thus, perhaps, it was with poor Grace
Harvey. At least, happily for her, she began
after a while to think that it was so. Only after
a while, though. There was at first a phase of re-
pining, of doubt, almost of indignation against high
heaven. Who shall judge her? What blame if
the crucified one writhe when the first nail is
driven? What blame if the stoutest turn sick
and giddy at the first home-thrust of that sword
which pierces the joints and marrow, and lays bare
to self the secrets of the heart? God gives poor souls
time to recover their breaths, ere he strikes again;
and if He be not angry, why should we condemn?

Poor Grace! Her sorrows had been thickening fast during the last few months. She was schoolmistress again, true; but where were her children? Those of them whom she loved best, were swept away by the cholera; and could she face the remnant, each in mourning for a parent or a brother? That alone was grief enough for her; and yet that was the lightest of all her griefs. She loved Tom Thurnall — how much, she dared not tell herself; she longed to "save him." She had thought, and not untruly, during the past cholera weeks, that he was softened, opened to new impressions: but he had avoided her more than ever — perhaps suspected her again more than ever — and now he was gone, gone for ever. That, too, was grief enough alone. But darkest and deepest of all, darker and deeper than the past shame of being suspected by him she loved, was the shame of suspecting her own mother — of believing herself, as she did, privy to that shameful theft, and yet unable to make restitution. There was the horror of all horrors, the close prison which seemed to stifle her whole soul. The only chink through which a breath of air seemed to come, and keep her heart alive, was the hope that somehow, somewhere, she might find that belt, and restore it without her mother's knowledge.

But more — the first of September was come and gone; the bill for five-and-twenty pounds was due, and was not met. Grace, choking down her honest pride, went off to the grocer, and, with tears which he could not resist, persuaded him to renew the bill for one month more; and now that month was all but past, and yet there was no money. Eight or ten people who owed Mrs. Harvey money had died of the cholera. Some, of course, had left no effects; and all hope of their working out their debts was gone. Some had left money behind them: but it was still in the lawyer's hands, some of it at sea, some on mortgage, some in houses which must be sold; till their affairs were wound up — (a sadly slow affair when a country attorney has a poor man's unprofitable business to transact) — nothing could come in to Mrs. Harvey. To and fro she went with knitted brow and heavy heart; and brought home again only promises, as she had done a hundred times before. One day she went up to Mrs. Heale. Old Heale owed her thirteen pounds and more: but that was not the least reason for paying. His cholera patients had not paid him; and whether Heale had the money by him or not, he was not going to pay his debts till other people paid theirs. Mrs. Harvey stormed; Mrs. Heale gave her as good as she brought; and Mrs. Harvey threatened to County Court her husband; whereon Mrs. Heale, *en revanche*, dragged out the books, and displayed to the poor widow's horror-struck eyes an account for medicine and attendance, on her and Grace, which nearly swallowed up the debt. Poor Grace was overwhelmed when her mother came home and upbraided her, in her despair, with being a burden. Was she not a burden? Must she not be one henceforth? No, she would take in needle-work, labor in the fields, heave ballast among the coarse pauper-girls on the quay-pool, anything rather: but how to meet the present difficulty?

"We must sell our furniture, mother!"

"For a quarter of what it's worth? Never, girl! No! The Lord will provide," said she, between her clenched teeth, with a sort of hysteric chuckle. "The Lord will provide!"

"I believe it; I believe it," said poor Grace; "but faith is weak, and the day is very dark, mother."

"Dark, ay? And may be darker yet; but the Lord will provide. He prepares a table in the wilderness for His saints that the world don't think of."

"Oh, mother! and do you think there is any door of hope?"

"Go to bed, girl; go to bed, and leave me to see to that. Find my spectacles. Wherever have you laid them to, now? I'll look over the books awhile."

"Do let me go over them for you."

"No, you sha'n't! I suppose you'll be wanting to make out your poor old mother's been cheating somebody. Why not, if I'm a thief, miss, eh?"

"Oh, mother! mother! don't say that again."

And Grace glided out meekly to her own chamber, which was on the ground-floor adjoining the parlor, and there spent more than one hour in prayer, from which no present comfort seemed to come; yet who shall say that it was all unanswered?

At last her mother came upstairs, and put her head in angrily: "Why be n't you in bed, girl? sitting up this way?"

"I was praying, mother," says Grace, looking up as she knelt.

"Praying! What's the use of praying? and who'll hear you if you pray? What you want's a husband, to keep you out of the workhouse;

and you won't get that by kneeling here. Get to bed, I say, or I'll pull you up!"

Grace obeyed uncomplaining, but utterly shocked; though she was not unacquainted with those frightful fits of morose unbelief, even of fierce blasphemy, to which the excitable West-country mind is liable, after having been over-strained by superstitious self-inspection, and by the desperate attempt to prove itself right and safe from frames and feelings, while fact and conscience proclaim it wrong.

The West-country people are apt to attribute these paroxysms to the possession of a devil; and so did Grace that night.

Trembling with terror and loving pity, she lay down, and began to pray afresh for that poor wild mother.

At last the fear crossed her that her mother might make away with herself. But a few years before, another class-leader in Aberalva had attempted to do so, and had all but succeeded. The thought was intolerable. She must go to her; face reproaches, blows, anything. She rose from her bed, and went to the door. It was fastened on the outside.

A cold perspiration stood on her forehead. She opened her lips to shriek to her mother; but checked herself when she heard her stirring gently in the outer room. Her pulses throbbed too loudly at first for her to hear distinctly: but she felt that it was no moment for giving way to emotion; by a strong effort of will, she conquered herself; and then, with that preternatural acuteness of sense which some women possess, she could hear everything her mother was doing.

She heard her put on her shawl, her bonnet; she heard her open the front door gently. It was now long past midnight. Whither could she be going at that hour?

She heard her go gently to the left, past the window; and yet her footfall was all but inaudible. No rain had fallen, and her shoes ought to have sounded on the hard earth. She must have taken them off. There, she was stopping, just by the school-door. Now she moved again. She must have stopped to put on her shoes; for now Grace could hear her steps distinctly, down the earth bank, and over the rattling shingle of the beach. Where was she going? Grace must follow!

The door was fast; but in a moment she had removed the table, opened the shutter and the window.

"Thank God that I stayed here on the ground-floor, instead of going back to my own room when Major Campbell left. It is a providence! The Lord has not forsaken me yet!" said the sweet saint, as, catching up her shawl, she wrapped it round her, and slipping through the window, crouched under the shadow of the house, and looked for her mother.

She was hurrying over the rocks, a hundred yards off. Whither? To drown herself in the sea? No; she held on along the mid-beach, right across the cove, toward Arthur's Nose. But why? Grace must know.

She felt, she knew not why, that this strange journey, that wild "The Lord will provide," had to do with the subject of her suspicion. Perhaps this was the crisis; perhaps all will be cleared up to-night, for joy or for utter shame.

The tide was low; the beach was bright in the

western moonlight: only along the cliff foot lay a strip of shadow a quarter of a mile long, till the Nose, like a great black wall, buried the corner of the cove in darkness.

Along that strip of shadow she ran, crouching; now stumbling over a boulder, now crushing her bare feet between the sharp pebbles, as, heedless where she stepped, she kept her eye fixed on her mother. As if fascinated, she could see nothing else in heaven or earth but that dark figure, hurrying along with a dogged determination, and then stopping a moment to look round, as if in fear of a pursuer. And then Grace lay down on the cold stones, and pressed herself into the very earth; and the moment her mother turned to go forward, sprang up and followed.

And then a true woman's thought flashed across her, and shaped itself into a prayer. For herself she never thought: but if the coastguardsman above should see her mother, stop her, question her? God grant that he might be on the other side of the point! And she hurried on again.

Near the Nose the rocks ran high and jagged; her mother held on to them, passed through a narrow chasm, and disappeared.

Grace now, not fifty yards from her, darted out of the shadow into the moonlight, and ran breathlessly toward the spot where she had seen her mother last. Like Andersen's little sea-maiden she went, every step on sharp knives, across the rough beds of barnacles; but she felt no pain, in the greatness of her terror and her love.

She crouched between the rocks a moment; heard her mother slipping and splashing among the pools; and glided after her like a ghost—a guardian angel rather—till she saw her emerge again for a moment into the moonlight, upon a strip of beach beneath the Nose.

It was a weird and lonely spot; and a dangerous spot withal. For only at low spring-tide could it be reached from the land, and then the flood rose far up the cliff, covering all the shingle, and filling the mouth of a dark cavern. Had her mother gone to that cavern? It was impossible to see, so utterly was the cliff shrouded in shadow.

Shivering with cold and excitement, Grace crouched down, and gazed into the gloom, till her eyes swam, and a hundred fantastic figures, and sparks of fire, seemed to dance between her and the rock. Sparks of fire!—yes; but that last one was no fancy. An actual flash; the crackle and sputter of a match! What could it mean? Another match was lighted; and a moment after, the glare of a lanthorn showed her her mother entering beneath the polished arch of rock which glared lurid overhead, like the gateway of the pit of fire.

The light vanished into the windings of the cave. And then Grace, hardly knowing what she did, rushed up the beach, and crouched down once more at the cave's mouth. There she sat, she knew not how long, listening, listening, like a hunted hare; her whole faculties concentrated in the one sense of hearing; her eyes wandering vacantly over the black saws of rock, and glistening oar-weed beds, and bright phosphoric sea. Thank Heaven, there was not a ripple to break the silence. Ah, what was that sound within? She pressed her ear against the rock, to hear more surely. A rumbling as of stones rolled down.

And then — was it a fancy, or were her powers of hearing, intensified by excitement, actually equal to discern the chink of coin? Who knows? but in another moment she had glided in, silently, swiftly, holding her very breath; and saw her mother kneeling on the ground, the lanthorn by her side, and in her hand the long-lost belt.

She did not speak, she did not move. She always knew, in her heart of hearts, that so it was: but when the sin took bodily shape, and was there before her very eyes, it was too dreadful to speak of, to act upon yet. And amid the most torturing horror and disgust of that great sin, rose up in her the divinest love for the sinner; she felt — strange paradox — that she had never loved her mother as she did at that moment. "Oh, that it had been I who had done it, and not she!" And her mother's sin was to her her own sin, her mother's shame her shame, till all sense of her mother's guilt vanished in the light of her divine love. "Oh, that I could take her up tenderly, tell her that all is forgiven and forgotten by man and God! — serve her as I have never served her yet! — nurse her to sleep on my bosom, and then go forth and bear her punishment, even if need be on the gallows-tree!" And there she stood, in a silent agony of tender pity, drinking her portion of the cup of Him who bore the sins of all the world.

Silently she stood; and silently she turned to go, to go home and pray for guidance in that dark labyrinth of confused duties. Her mother heard the rustle; looked up; and sprang to her feet with a scream, dropping gold pieces on the ground.

Her first impulse was wild terror. She was discovered; by whom, she knew not. She clasped her evil treasure to her bosom, and thrusting Grace against the rock, fled wildly out.

"Mother! mother!" shrieked Grace, rushing after her. The shawl fell from her shoulders. Her mother looked back, and saw the white figure.

"God's angel! God's angel, come to destroy me! as he came to Balaam!" and in the madness of her guilty fancy she saw in Grace's hand the fiery sword which was to smite her.

Another step, looking backward still, and she had tripped over a stone. She fell, and striking the back of her head against the rock, lay senseless.

Tenderly Grace lifted her up: went for water to a pool near by; bathed her face, calling on her by every term of endearment. Slowly the old woman recovered her consciousness, but showed it only in moans. Her head was cut and bleeding. Grace bound it up, and then taking that fatal belt, bound it next to her own heart, never to be moved from thence till she should put it into the hands of him to whom it belonged.

And then she lifted up her mother.

"Come home, darling mother;" and she tried to make her stand and walk.

The old woman only moaned, and waved her away impatiently. Grace put her on her feet; but she fell again. The lower limbs seemed all but paralyzed.

Slowly that sweet saint lifted her, and laid her on her own back; and slowly she bore her homeward, with aching knees and bleeding feet; while before her eyes hung the picture of Him who bore

His cross up Calvary, till a solemn joy and pride in that sacred burden seemed to intertwine itself with her deep misery. And fainting every moment with pain and weakness, she still went on, as if by supernatural strength; and murmured:

"Thou didst bear more for me, and shall not I bear even this for Thee?"

Surely, if blest spirits can weep and smile over the woes and heroisms of us mortal men, faces brighter than the stars looked down on that fair girl that night, and in loving sympathy called her, too, blest.

At last it was over. Undiscovered she reached home, laid her mother on the bed, and tended her till morning: but long ere morning dawned stupor had changed into delirium, and Grace's ears were all on fire with words — which those who have ever heard will have no heart to write.

And now, by one of those strange vagaries, in which epidemics so often indulge, appeared other symptoms; and by day-dawn cholera itself.

Heale, though recovering, was still too weak to be of use; but, happily, the medical man sent down by the Board of Health was still in the town.

Grace sent for him; but he shook his head after the first look. The wretched woman's ravings at once explained the case, and made it, in his eyes, all but hopeless.

The sudden shock to body and mind, the sudden prostration of strength, had brought out the disease which she had dreaded so intensely, and against which she had taken so many precautions, and which yet lay, all the while, lurking unfelt in her system.

A hideous eight-and-forty hours followed. The preachers and class-leaders came to pray over the dying woman: but she screamed to Grace to send them away. She had just sense enough left to dread that she might betray her own shame. Would she have the new clergyman then? No; she would have no one; — no one could help her! Let her only die in peace!

And Grace closed the door upon all but the doctor, who treated the wild sufferer's wild words as the mere fancies of delirium; and then Grace watched and prayed, till she found herself alone with the dead.

She wrote a letter to Thurnall:

"Sir, — I have found your belt, and all the money, I believe and trust, which it contained. If you will be so kind as to tell me where and how I shall send it to you, you will take a heavy burden off the mind of

"Your obedient humble servant,

who trusts that you will forgive her having been unable to fulfil her promise."

She addressed the letter to Whitbury; for thither Tom had ordered his letters to be sent; but she received no answer.

The day after Mrs. Harvey was buried, the sale of all her effects was announced in Aberalva.

Grace received the proceeds, went round to all the creditors, and paid them all which was due. She had a few pounds left. What to do with that she knew full well.

She showed no sign of sorrow: but she spoke rarely to any one. A dead dull weight seemed to hang over her. To preachers, class-leaders, gossips, who upbraided her for not letting them see her

mother, she replied by silence. People thought
her becoming idiotic.

The day after the last creditor was paid she
packed up her little box: hired a cart to take her
to the nearest coach; and vanished from Aberalva,
without bidding farewell to a human being, even to
her school-children.

. . . .

Vavasour had been buried more than a week.
Mark and Mary were sitting in the dining-room,
Mark at his port and Mary at her work, when the
footboy entered.

"Sir, there's a young woman wants to speak
with you."

"Show her in, if she looks respectable," said
Mark, who had slippers on, his feet on the fender,
and was, therefore, loth to move.

"Oh, quite respectable, sir, as ever I see;" and
the lad ushered in a figure, dressed and veiled in
deep black.

"Well, ma'am, sit down, pray; and what can I
do for you?"

"Can you tell me, sir," answered a voice of extraordinary sweetness and gentleness, very firm and
composed withal, "if Mr. Thomas Thurnall is in
Whitbury?"

"Thurnall? He has sailed for the East a week
ago. May I ask your business with him? Can I
help you in it?"

The black damsel paused so long, that both
Mary and her father felt uneasy, and a cloud passed
over Mark's brow.

"Can the boy have been playing tricks?" said
he to himself.

"Then, sir, as I hear that you have influence, can

you get me a situation as one of the nurses who are
going out thither, so I hear?"

"Get you a situation? Yes, of course, if you
are competent."

"Thank you, sir. Perhaps, if you could be so
very kind as to tell me to whom I am to apply in
town; for I shall go thither to-night."

"My goodness!" cried Mark. "Old Mark
don't do things in this off-hand, cold-blooded way.
Let us know who you are, my dear, and about Mr.
Thurnall. Have you anything against him?"

She was silent.

"Mary, just step into the next room."

"If you please, sir," said the same gentle voice,
"I had sooner that the lady should stay. I
have nothing against Mr. Thurnall, God knows.
He has rather something against me."

Another pause.

Mary rose, and went up to her and took her hand.

"Do tell us who you are, and if we can do anything for you."

And she looked winningly up into her face.

The stranger drew a long breath and lifted her
veil. Mary and Mark both started at the beauty
of the countenance which she revealed — but in a
different way. Mark gave a grunt of approbation:
Mary turned pale as death.

"I suppose that it is but right and reasonable
that I should tell you, at least give proof of my
being an honest person. For my capabilities as a
nurse — I believe you know Mrs. Vavasour? I
heard that she has been staying here."

"Of course. Do you know her?"

A sad smile passed over her face.

"Yes, well enough, at least for her to speak for

me. I should have asked her or Miss St. Just to help me to a nurse's place: but I did not like to trouble them in their distress. How is the poor lady now, sir?"

"I know who she is!" cried Mary, by a sudden inspiration. "Is not your name Harvey? Are you not the schoolmistress who saved Mr. Thurnall's life? who behaved so nobly in the cholera? Yes! I knew you were! Come and sit down, and tell me all! I have so longed to know you! Dear creature, I have felt as if you were my own sister. He — Mr. Thurnall — wrote often about all your heroism."

Grace seemed to choke down somewhat: and then answered steadfastly:

"I did not come here, my dear lady, to hear such kind words, but to do an errand to Mr. Thurnall. You have heard, perhaps, that when he was wrecked last spring, he lost some money. Yes? Then, it was stolen. Stolen!" she repeated with a great gasp: "never mind by whom. Not by me."

"You need not tell us that, my dear," interrupted Mark.

"God kept it. And I have it; here!" and she pressed her hands tight over her bosom. "And here I must keep it till I give it into his hands, if I follow him round the world!" And as she spoke her eyes shone in the lamplight, with an unearthly brilliance which made Mary shudder.

Mark Armsworth poured a libation to the goddess of Puzzledom, in the shape of a glass of port, which first choked him, and then descended over his clean shirt-front. But after he had coughed himself black in the face, he began:

"My good girl, if you are Grace Harvey, you 're welcome to my roof, and an honor to it, say I: but as for taking all that money with you across the seas, and such a pretty helpless young thing as you are, God help you, it must n't be, and sha'n't be, and that 's flat."

"But I must go to him!" said she, in so naïve half-wild a fashion, that Mary, comprehending all, looked imploringly at her father, and putting her arm round Grace, forced her into a seat.

"I must go, sir, and tell him — tell him myself. No one knows what I know about it."

Mark shook his head.

"Could I not write to him? He knows me as well as he knows his own father."

Grace shook her head, and pressed her hand upon her heart, where Tom's belt lay.

"Do you think, madam, that after having had the dream of this belt, the shape of this belt, and of the money which is in it, branded into my brain for months — years it seems like — by God's fire of shame and suspicion; — and seen him poor, miserable, fretful, unbelieving, for the want of it — O God! I can't tell even your sweet face all. — Do you think that now I have it in my hands, I can part with it, or rest till it is in his? No, not though I walked barefoot after him to the ends of the earth."

"Let his father have the money, then, and do you take him the belt as a token, if you must ——"

"That 's it, Mary!" shouted Mark Armsworth, "you always come in with the right hint, girl!" and the two, combining their forces, at last talked poor Grace over. But upon going out herself she was bent. To ask his forgiveness in her mother's

name, was her one fixed idea. He might die, and
not know all, not have forgiven all, and go she must.

"But it is a thousand to one against your seeing
him. We, even, don't know exactly where he is
gone."

Grace shuddered a moment; and then recovered
her calmness.

"I did not expect this: but be it so. I shall
meet him if God wills; and if not, I can still work
— work."

"I think, Mary, you'd better take the young
woman upstairs, and make her sleep here to-night,"
said Mark, glad of an excuse to get rid of them;
which, when he had done, he pulled his chair round
in front of the fire, put a foot on each hob, and
began rubbing his eyes vigorously.

"Dear me! Dear me! What a lot of good
people there are in this old world, to be sure! Ten
times better than me, at least — make one ashamed
of oneself: — and if one is n't even good enough
for this world, how 's one to be good enough for
heaven?"

And Mary carried Grace upstairs, and into
her own bedroom. "A bed should be made up
there for her. It would do her good just to have
anything so pretty sleeping in the same room."
And then she got Grace supper, and tried to make
her talk: but she was distrait, reserved; for a new
and sudden dread had seized her at the sight of
that fine house, fine plate, fine friends. These were
his acquaintances, then : no wonder that he would
not look on such as her. And as she cast her
eye round the really luxurious chamber, and (after
falteringly asking Mary whether she had any
brothers and sisters) guessed that she must be the

heiress of all that wealth, she settled in her heart that Tom was to marry Mary; and the intimate tone in which Mary spoke of him to her, and her innumerable inquiries about him, made her more certain that it was a settled thing. Handsome she was not, certainly; but so sweet and good; and that her own beauty (if she was aware that she possessed any) could have any weight with Tom, she would have considered as an insult to his sense; so she made up her mind slowly, but steadily, that thus it was to be; and every fresh proof of Mary's sweetness and goodness was a fresh pang to her, for it showed the more how probable it was that Tom loved her.

Therefore she answered all Mary's questions carefully and honestly, as to a person who had a right to ask; and at last went to her bed, and, worn out in body and mind, was asleep in a moment. She had not remarked the sigh which escaped Mary, as she glanced at that beautiful head, and the long black tresses which streamed down for a moment over the white shoulders ere they were knotted back for the night, and then at her own poor countenance in the glass opposite.

．　．　．　．　．　．　．

It was long past midnight when Grace woke, she knew not how, and looking up, saw a light in the room, and Mary sitting still over a book, her head resting on her hands. She lay quiet and thought she heard a sob. She was sure she heard tears drop on the paper. She stirred, and Mary was at her side in a moment.

"Did you want anything?"

"Only to — to remind you, ma'am, it is not wise to sit up so late."

"Only that?" said Mary, laughing. "I do that every night, alone with God; and I do not think He will be the farther off for your being here!"

"One thing I had to ask," said Grace. "It would lessen my labor so, if you could give me any hint of where he might be."

"We know, as we told you, as little as you. His letters are to be sent to Constantinople. Some from Aberalva are gone thither already."

"And mine among them!" thought Grace. "It is God's will! . . . Madam, if it would not seem forward on my part — if you could tell him the truth, and what I have for him, and where I am, in case he might wish — wish to see me — when you were writing."

"Of course I will, or my father will," said Mary, who did not like to confess either to herself or to Grace that it was very improbable that she would ever write again to Tom Thurnall.

And so the two sweet maidens, so near that moment to an explanation, which might have cleared up all, went on each in her ignorance; for so it was to be.

The next morning Grace came down to breakfast, modest, cheerful, charming. Mark made her breakfast with them; gave her endless letters of recommendation; wanted to take her to see old Doctor Thurnall, which she declined, and then sent her to the station in his own carriage, paid her fare first-class to town, and somehow or other contrived, with Mary's help, that she should find in her bag two ten-pound notes, which she had never seen before. After which he went out to his counting-house, only remarking to Mary:

"Very extraordinary young woman, and very

handsome, too. Will make some man a jewel of a wife, if she don't go mad, or die of the hospital fever."

To which Mary fully assented. Little she guessed, and little did her father, that it was for Grace's sake that Tom had refused her hand.

A few days more, and Grace Harvey also had gone Eastward Ho.

CHAPTER XXVII

A RECENT EXPLOSION IN AN ANCIENT CRATER

IT is, perhaps, a pity for the human race in general that some enterprising company cannot buy up the Moselle (not the wine, but the river), cut it into five-mile lengths, and distribute them over Europe, wherever there is a demand for lovely scenery. For lovely is its proper epithet; it is not grand, not exciting — so much the better; it is scenery to live and die in; scenery to settle in, and study a single landscape, till you know every rock, and walnut-tree, and vine-leaf by heart: not merely to run through in one hasty steam-trip, as you now do, in a long burning day, which makes you not " drunk" — but weary — " with excess of beauty." Besides, there are two or three points so superior to the rest, that having seen them, one cares to see nothing more. That paradise of emerald, purple, and azure, which opens behind Treis; and that strange heap of old-world houses at Berncastle, which have scrambled up to the top of a rock to stare at the steamer, and have never been able to get down again — between them, and after them, one feels like a child who, after a great mouthful of pine-apple jam, is condemned to have poured down its throat an everlasting stream of treacle.

So thought Stangrave on board the steamer, as he smoked his way up the shallows, and wondered which turn of the river would bring him to his destination. When would it all be over? And he never leaped on shore more joyfully than he did at Alf that afternoon, to jump into a carriage, and trundle up the gorge of the Issbach some six lonely weary miles, till he turned at last into the wooded caldron of the Romer-kessel, and saw the little chapel crowning the central knoll, with the white high-roofed houses of Bertrich nestling at its foot.

He drives up to the handsome old Kurhaus, nestling close beneath heather-clad rocks, upon its lawn shaded with huge horse-chestnuts, and set round with dahlias, and geraniums, and delicate tinted German stocks, which fill the air with fragrance; a place made only for young lovers — certainly not for those black-petticoated worthies, each with that sham of a sham, the modern tonsure, pared down to a poor florin's breadth among their bushy, well-oiled curls, who sit at little tables, passing the lazy day "*à muguetter les bourgeoises*" of Sarrebruck and Treves, and sipping the fragrant Josephshofer — perhaps at the good bourgeois' expense.

Past them Stangrave slips angrily; for that "development of humanity" can find no favor in his eyes; being not human at all, but professedly superhuman, and therefore, practically, sometimes inhuman. He hurries into the public room; seizes on the visitor's book.

The names are there, in their own handwriting: but where are they?

Waiters are seized and questioned. The English ladies came back last night, and are gone this afternoon.

" Where are they gone? "

Nobody recollects: not even the man from whom they hired the carriage. But they are not gone far. Their servants and their luggage are still here. Perhaps the Herr Ober-Badmeister, Lieutenant D——, will know. "Oh, it will not trouble him. An English gentleman? *Der Herr* Lieutenant will be only too happy;" and in ten minutes *der Herr* Lieutenant appears, really only too happy; and Stangrave finds himself at once in the company of a soldier and a gentleman. Had their acquaintance been a longer one, he would have recognized likewise the man of taste and of piety.

"I can well appreciate, sir," says he, in return to Stangrave's anxious inquiries, " your impatience to rejoin your lovely country-women, who have been for the last three weeks the wonder and admiration of our little paradise; and whose four days' absence was regarded, believe me, as a public calamity."

" I can well believe it; but they are not country-women of mine. The one lady is an English-woman; the other — I believe — an Italian."

" And *der Herr?* "

" An American."

" Ah! A still greater pleasure, sir. I trust that you will carry back across the Atlantic a good report of a spot all but unknown, I fear, to your compatriots. You will meet one, I think, on the return of the ladies."

" A compatriot? "

" Yes. A gentleman who arrived here this morning, and who seemed, from his conversation with them, to belong to your noble fatherland.

He went out driving with them this afternoon, whither I unfortunately know not. Ah! good Saint Nicholas!—For though I am a Lutheran, I must invoke him now—Look out yonder!"

Stangrave looked, and joined in the general laugh of lieutenant, waiters, priests, and bourgeoises.

For under the chestnuts strutted, like him in "Struwelpeter," as though he were a very king of Ashantee, Sabina's black boy, who had taken to himself a scarlet umbrella and a great cigar; while after him came, also like them in "Struwelpeter," Caspar, bretzel in hand, and Ludwig with his hoop, and all the naughty boys of Bertrich town, hooting and singing in chorus, after the fashion of German children.

The resemblance to the well-known scene in the German child's book was perfect, and as the children shouted—

> "Ein kohlpechrabenschwarzer Mohr,
> Die Sonne schien ihm ins gehirn,
> Da nahm er seinen Sonnenschirm"—

more than one grown person joined therein.

Stangrave longed to catch hold of the boy, and extract from him all news; but the blackamoor was not quite in respectable company enough at that moment; and Stangrave had to wait till he strutted proudly up to the door, and entered the hall with a bland smile, evidently having taken the hooting as a homage to his personal appearance.

"Ah? Mas' Stangrave? glad see you, sir! Quite a party of us now, 'mong dese 'barian heathen foreigners. Mas' Thurnall he come dis mornin'; gone up pickin' bush wid de ladies. He! he! Not seen him dis tree year afore."

"Thurnall!" Stangrave's heart sunk within him. His first impulse was to order a carriage, and return whence he came; but it would look so odd, and, moreover, be so foolish, that he made up his mind to stay and face the worst. So he swallowed a hasty dinner, and then wandered up the narrow valley, with all his suspicions of Thurnall and Marie seething more fiercely than ever in his heart.

Some half mile up, a path led out of the main road to a wooden bridge across the stream. He followed it, careless whither he went; and in five minutes found himself in the quaintest little woodland cavern he ever had seen.

It was simply a great block of black lava, crowned with brushwood, and supported on walls and pillars of Dutch cheeses, or what should have been Dutch cheeses by all laws of shape and color, had not his fingers proved to them that they were stone. How they got there, and what they were, puzzled him; for he was no geologist; and finding a bench inside, he sat down and speculated thereon.

There was more than one doorway to the "Cheese Cellar." It stood beneath a jutting knoll, and the path ran right through: so that, as he sat, he could see up a narrow gorge to his left, roofed in with trees; and down into the main valley on his right, where the Issbach glittered clear and smooth beneath red-berried mountain ash and yellow leaves.

There he sat, and tried to forget Marie in the tinkling of the streams, and the sighing of the autumn leaves, and the cooing of the sleepy doves, while the ice-bird, as the Germans call the water-ousel, sat on a rock in the river below, and warbled his low sweet song, and then flitted up the grassy reach to perch and sing again on the next rock above.

And, whether it was that he did forget Marie awhile; or whether he were tired, as he well might have been; or whether he had too rapidly consumed his bottle of red Walporzheimer, forgetful that it alone of German wines combines the delicacy of the Rhine sun with the potency of its Burgundian vinestock, transplanted to the Ahr by Charlemagne; — whether it were any of these causes, or whether it were not, Stangrave fell fast asleep in the Käsekeller, and slept till it was dark, at the risk of catching a great cold.

How long he slept, he knew not: but what wakened him he knew full well. Voices of people approaching; and voices which he recognized in a moment.

Sabina? Yes; and Marie too, laughing merrily; and among their shriller tones the voice of Thurnall. He had not heard it for years; but, considering the circumstances under which he had last heard it, there was no fear of his forgetting it again.

They came down the side glen; and before he could rise, they had turned the sharp corner of the rock, and were in the Käsekeller, close to him, almost touching him. He felt the awkwardness of his position. To keep still was, perhaps, to overhear, and that too much. To discover himself was to produce a scene; and he could not trust his temper that the scene would not be an ugly one, and such as women must not witness.

He was relieved to find that they did not stop.

They were laughing about the gloom; about being out so late.

"How jealous some one whom I know would be," said Sabina, "if he found you and Tom together in this darksome den!"

"I don't care," said Tom; "I have made up my mind to shoot hin out of hand, and marry Marie myself. Sha'n't I now, my —— " and they passed on; and down t) their carriage, which had been waiting for them in the road below.

What Marie's answer was, or by what name Thurnall was about to address her, Stangrave did not hear: but he had heard quite enough.

He rose quietly after a while, and followed them.

He was a dupe, an ass! The dupe of those bad women, and of his ancient enemy! It was maddening! Yet, how could Sabina be in fault? She had not known Marie till he himself had introduced her; and he could not believe her capable of such baseness. The crime must lie between the other two. Yet —

However that might be mattered little to him now. He would return, order his carriage once more, and depart, shaking off the dust of his feet against them! "Pah! There were other women in the world; and women, too, who would not demand of him to become a hero."

He reached the Kurhaus, and went in; but not into the public room, for fear of meeting people whom he had no heart to face.

He was in the passage, in the act of settling his account with the waiter, when Thurnall came hastily out, and ran against him.

Stangrave stood by the passage lamp, so that he saw Tom's face at once.

Tom drew back; begged a thousand pardons; and saw Stangrave's face in turn.

The two men looked at each other for a few seconds. Stangrave longed to say, "You intend to shoot me? Then try at once;" but he was ashamed, of course, to make use of words which he had so accidentally overheard.

Tom looked carefully at Stangrave, to divine his temper from his countenance. It was quite angry enough to give Tom excuse for saying to himself:

"The fellow is mad at being caught at last. Very well."

"I think, sir," said he, quietly enough, "that you and I had better walk outside for a few minutes. Allow me to retract the apology I just made, till we have had some very explicit conversation on other matters."

"Curse his impudence!" thought Stangrave. "Does he actually mean to bully me into marrying her?" and he replied haughtily enough:

"I am aware of no matters on which I am inclined to be explicit with Mr. Thurnall, or on which Mr. Thurnall has a right to be explicit with me."

"I am, then," quoth Tom, his suspicion increasing in turn. "Do you wish, sir, to have a scene before this waiter and the whole house, or will you be so kind as to walk outside with me?"

"I must decline, sir; not being in the habit of holding intercourses with an actress's bully."

Tom did not knock him down: but replied smilingly enough:

"I am far too much in earnest in this matter, sir, to be stopped by any coarse expressions. Waiter, you may go. Now will you fight me to-morrow morning, or will you not?"

"I may fight a gentleman: but not you."

"Well, I shall not call you a coward, because I know that you are none; and I shall not make a row here, for a gentleman's reasons, which you, calling yourself a gentleman, seem to have forgotten. But this I will do I will follow you till you do fight me, if I have to throw up my own prospects in life for it. I will proclaim you, wherever we meet, for what you are — a mean and base intriguer; I will insult you in Kursaals, and cane you on public places; I will be Frankenstein's man to you day and night, til I have avenged the wrongs of this poor girl, the dust of whose feet you are not worthy to kiss off."

Stangrave was surprised at his tone. It was certainly not that of a conscious villain: but he only replied sneeringly:

"And pray what may give Mr. Thurnall the right to consider himself the destined avenger of this frail beauty's wrongs?"

"I will tell you that after we have fought; and somewhat more. Meanwhile, that expression, 'frail beauty,' is a fresh offence for which I should certainly cane you, if she were not in the house."

"Well," drawled Stangrave, feigning an ostentatious yawn, "I believe the wise method of ridding oneself of impertinents is to grant their requests. Have you pistols? I have none."

"I have both duellers and revolvers at your service."

"Ah? I think we'll try the revolvers then," said Stangrave, savage from despair, and disbelief in all human goodness. "After what has passed, five or six shots apiece will be hardly *outré*."

"Hardly, I think," said Tom. "Will you name your second?"

"I know no one. I have not been here two hours; but I suppose they do not matter much."

"Humph! it is as well to have witnesses in case of accident. There are a couple of roistering Burschen in the public room, who, I think, would enjoy the office. Both have scars on their faces, so they will be *au fait* at the thing. Shall I have the honor of sending one of them to you?"

"As you will, sir; my number is 34." And the two fools turned on their respective heels, and walked off.

.   .   .   .

At sunrise next morning Tom and his second are standing on the Falkenhohe, at the edge of the vast circular pit, blasted out by some explosion which has torn the slate into mere dust and shivers, now covered with a thin coat of turf.

"*Schöne aussicht!*" says the Bursch, waving his hand round, in a tone which is benevolently meant to withdraw Tom's mind from painful considerations.

"Very pretty prospect indeed. You 're sure you understand that revolver thoroughly?"

The Bursch mutters to himself something about English nonchalance, and assures Thurnall that he is competently acquainted with the weapon; as indeed he ought to be; for having never seen one before, he has been talking and thinking of nothing else since they left Bertrich.

And why does not Tom care to look at the prospect? Certainly not because he is afraid. He slept as soundly as ever last night; and knows not what fear means. But somehow, the glorious view reminds him of another glorious view, which he saw last summer walking by Grace Harvey's side from Tolchard's farm. And that subject he will sternly put away. He is not sure but what it might unman even him.

The likeness certainly exists; for the rock, being the same in both places has taken the same general form; and the wanderer in Rhine-Prussia and Nassau might often fancy himself in Devon or Cornwall. True, here there is no sea: and there no Moselkopf raises its huge crater-cone far above the uplands, all golden in the level sun. But that brown Taunus far away, or that brown Hundsruck opposite, with its deep-wooded gorges barred with level gleams of light across black gulfs of shade, might well be Dartmoor, or Carcarrow moor itself, high over Aberalva town, which he will see no more. True, in Cornwall there would be no slag-cliffs of the Falkenley beneath his feet, as black and blasted at this day as when yon orchard meadow was the mouth of hell, and the southwest wind dashed the great flame against the cinder-cliff behind, and forged it into walls of time-defying glass. But that might well be Alva stream, that Issbach in its green gulf far below, winding along toward the green gulf of the Moselle — he will look at it no more, lest he see Grace herself come to him across the down, to chide him, with sacred horror, for the dark deed which he has come to do.

And yet he does not wish to kill Stangrave. He would like to "wing him." He must punish him for his conduct to Marie; punish him for last night's insult. It is a necessity, but a disagreeable one; he would be sorry to go to the war with that

man's blood upon his hand.   He is sorry that he
is out of practice.

"A year ago I could have counted on hitting
him where I liked.   I trust I shall not blunder
against his vitals now.   However, if I do, he has
himself to blame!"

The thought that Stangrave may kill him never
crosses his mind.   Of course, out of six shots, fired
at all distances from forty paces to fifteen, one may
hit him: but as for being killed! . . .

Tom's heart is hardened; melted again and
again this summer for a moment, only to freeze
again.   He all but believes that he bears a charmed
life.   All the miraculous escapes of his past years,
instead of making him believe in a living, guiding,
protecting Father, have become to that proud hard
heart the excuse for a deliberate, though unconscious, atheism.   His fall is surely near.

At last Stangrave and his second appear.
Stangrave is haggard, not from fear, but from
misery, and rage, and self-condemnation.   This
is the end of all his fine resolves!   Pah! what use
in them?   What use in being a martyr in this
world?   All men are liars, and all women too!

Tom and Stangrave stand a little apart from each
other, while one of the seconds paced the distance.
He steps out away from them, across the crater
floor, carrying Tom's revolver in his hand, till he
reaches the required point, and turns.

He turns: but not to come back.   Without a
gesture or an exclamation which could explain his
proceedings, he faces about once more, and rushes
up the slope as hard as legs and wind permitted.

Tom is confounded with astonishment: either
the Bursch is seized with terror at the whole busi-

ness, or he covets the much-admired revolver; in either case he is making off with it before the owner's eyes.

"Stop! Hillo! Stop, thief! He's got my pistol!" and away goes Thurnall in chase after the Bursch, who, never looking behind, never sees that he is followed: while Stangrave and the second Bursch look on with wide eyes.

Now the Bursch is a "gymnast," and a capital runner; and so is Tom likewise; and brilliant is the race upon the Falkenhohe. But the victory, after a while, becomes altogether a question of wind; for it was all up hill. The crater, being one of "explosion," and not of elevation, as the geologists would say, does not slope downward again, save on one side, from its outer lip; and Tom and the Bursch were breasting a fair hill, after they had emerged from the "kessel" below.

Now the Bursch had had too much Thronerhofberger the night before; and possibly, as Burschen will in their vacations, the night before that also; whereby his diaphragm surrendered at discretion, while his heels were yet unconquered; and he suddenly felt a strong gripe, and a stronger kick, which rolled him over on the turf.

The hapless youth, who fancied himself alone upon the mountain tops, roared mere incoherences; and Tom, too angry to listen, and too hurried to punish, tore the revolver out of his grasp; whereon one barrel exploded:

"I have done it now!"

No: the ball had luckily buried itself in the ground.

Tom turned, to rush down hill again, and meet the impatient Stangrave.

Crack — whing — g — g!

" A bullet ! "

Yes! And, prodigy on prodigy, up the hill towards him charged, as he would upon a whole army, a Prussian gendarme, with bayonet fixed.

Tom sat down upon the mountain-side, and burst into inextinguishable laughter, while the gendarme came charging up, right toward his very nose.

But up to his nose he charged not; for his wind was short, and the noise of his roaring went before him. Moreover, he knew that Tom had a revolver, and was a " mad Englishman."

Now he was not afraid of Tom, or of a whole army: but he was a man of drills and of orders, of rules and of precedents, as a Prussian gendarme ought to be; and for the modes of attacking infantry, cavalry, and artillery, man, woman, and child, thief and poacher, stray pig, or even stray wolf, he had drill and orders sufficient: but for attacking a Colt's revolver, none.

Moreover, for arresting all manner of riotous Burschen, drunken boors, French red republicans, Mazzini-hatted Italian refugees, suspect Polish incendiaries, or other *feras naturæ*, he had precedent and regulation: but for arresting a mad Englishman, none. He held fully the opinion of his superiors, that there was no saying what an Englishman might not, could not, and would not do. He was a sphinx, a chimera, a lunatic broke loose, who took unintelligible delight in getting wet, and dirty, and tired, and starved, and all but killed; and called the same " taking exercise : " — who would see everything that nobody ever cared to see, and who knew mysteriously everything about everywhere; whose deeds were like his opinions, utterly subversive of all constituted order in heaven and earth; being, probably, the inhabitant of another planet; possibly the man in the moon himself, who had been turned out, having made his native satellite too hot to hold him. All that was to be done with him was to inquire whether his passport was correct, and then (with a due regard to self-preservation) to endure his vagaries in pitying wonder.

So the gendarme paused panting; and not daring to approach, walked slowly and solemnly round Tom, keeping the point of his bayonet carefully towards him, and roaring at intervals:

"You have murdered the young man!"

"But I have not!" said Tom. "Look and see."

"But I saw him fall!"

"But he has got up again, and run away."

"So! Then where is your passport?"

That one other fact, cognizable by the mind of a Prussian gendarme, remained as an anchor for his brains under the new and trying circumstances, and he used it. "Here!" quoth Tom, pulling it out.

The gendarme stepped cautiously forward.

"Don't be frightened. I'll stick it on your bayonet-point;" and suiting the action to the word, Tom caught the bayonet-point, put the passport on it, and pulled out his cigar-case.

"Mad Englishman!" murmured the gendarme. "So! The passport is correct. But *der Herr* must consider himself under arrest. *Der Herr* will give up his death-instrument."

"By all means," says Tom: and gives up the revolver.

The gendarme takes it very cautiously; medi-tates awhile how to carry it; sticks the point of his bayonet into its muzzle, and lifts it aloft.

"*Schon! Das kriegt!* Has *der Herr* any more death-instruments?"

"Dozens!" says Tom, and begins fumbling in his pockets; from whence he pulls a case of surgical instruments, another of mathematical ones, another of lancets, and a knife with innumerable blades, saws, and pickers, every one of which he opens carefully, and then spreads the whole fearful array upon the grass before him.

The gendarme scratches his head over those two plain proofs of some tremendous conspiracy.

"So! Man must have a dozen hands! He is surely Palmerston himself; or at least Hecker, or Mazzini!" murmurs he, as he meditates how to stow them all.

He thinks now that the revolver may be safe elsewhere; and that the knife will do best on the bayonet-point. So he unships the revolver.

Bang goes barrel number two, and the ball goes into the turf between his feet.

"You will shoot yourself soon, at that rate," says Tom.

"So! *Der Herr* speaks German like a native," says the gendarme, growing complimentary in his perplexity. "Perhaps *der Herr* would be so good as to carry his death-instruments himself and attend on the Herr Polizeirath, who is waiting to see him."

"By all means!" And Tom picks up his tackle, while the prudent gendarme reloads; and Tom marches down the hill, the gendarme following, with his bayonet disagreeably near the small of Tom's back.

"Don't stumble! Look out for the stones, or you 'll have that skewer through me!"

"So! *Der Herr* speaks German like a native," says the gendarme, civilly. "It is certainly *der* Palmerston," thinks he, "his manners are so polite."

Once at the crater edge, and able to see into the pit, the mystery is, in part at least, explained: for there stand not only Stangrave and Bursch number two, but a second gendarme, two elderly gentlemen, two ladies, and a black boy.

One is Lieutenant D——, by his white moustache. He is lecturing the Bursch, who looks sufficiently foolish. The other is a portly and awful-looking personage in uniform, evidently the Polizeirath of those parts, armed with the just terrors of the law; but Justice has, if not her eyes bandaged, at least her hands tied; for on his arm hangs Sabina, smiling, chatting, entreating. The Polizeirath smiles, bows, ogles, evidently a willing captive. Venus had disarmed Rhadamanthus, as she has Mars so often; and the sword of justice must rust in its scabbard.

Some distance behind them is Stangrave, talking in a low voice, earnestly, passionately — to whom but to Marie?

And lastly, opposite each other, and like two dogs who are uncertain whether to make friends or fight, are a gendarme and Sabina's black boy: the gendarme, with shouldered musket, is trying to look as stiff and cross as possible, being scandalized by his superior officer's defection from the path of duty; and still more by the irreverence of the black boy, who is dancing, grinning, snapping his fingers, in delight at having discovered and prevented the coming tragedy.

Tom descends, bowing courteously, apologizes for having been absent when the highly distinguished gentleman arrived; and turning to the Bursch, begs him to transmit to his friend who has run away his apologies for the absurd mistake which led him to, etc., etc.

The Polizeirath looks at him with much the same blank astonishment as the gendarme had done; and at last ends by lifting up his hands, and bursting into an enormous German laugh; and no one on earth can laugh as a German can, so genially and lovingly, and with such intense self-enjoyment.

"Oh, you English! you English! You are all mad, I think! Nothing can shame you, and nothing can frighten you! *Potz!* I believe when your Guards at Alma walked into that battery, the other day, every one of them was whistling your Jim Crow, even after he was shot dead!" And the jolly Polizeirath laughed at his own joke, till the mountain rang. "But you must leave the country, sir; indeed you must. We cannot permit such conduct here — I am very sorry."

"I entreat you not to apologize, sir. In any case, I was going to Alf by eight o'clock, to meet the steamer for Treves. I am on my way to the war in the East *via* Marseilles. If you would, therefore, be so kind as to allow the gendarme to return me that second revolver, which also belongs to me ——"

"Give him his pistol!" shouted the magistrate, "*Potz!* Let us be rid of him at any cost, and live in peace, like honest Germans. Ah, poor Queen Victoria! What a lot! To have the government of five-and-twenty million such!"

"Not five-and-twenty millions," says Sabina. "That would include the ladies; and we are not mad too, surely, your Excellency?"

The Polizeirath likes to be called your Excellency, of course, or any other mighty title which does or does not belong to him; and that Sabina knows full well.

"Ah, my dear madam, how do I know that? The English ladies do every day here what no other dames would da e or dream — what then must you be at home? . *Ich!* your poor husbands!"

"Mr. Thurnall!" calls Marie, from behind. "Mr. Thurnall!"

Tom comes with a quaint, dogged smile on his face.

"You see him, Mr. Stangrave! You see the man who risked for me liberty, life — who rescued me from slavery, shame, suicide — who was to me a brother, a father, for years! — without whose disinterested heroism you would never have set eyes on the face which you pretend to love. And you repay him by suspicion — insult. Apologize to him, sir! Ask his pardon now, here, utterly, humbly: or never speak to Marie Lavington again!"

Tom looked first at her, and then at Stangrave. Marie was convulsed with excitement; her thin cheeks were crimson, her eyes flashed very flame. Stangrave was pale — calm outwardly, but evidently not within. He was looking on the ground, in thought so intense that he hardly seemed to hear Marie. Poor fellow! he had heard enough in the last ten minutes to bewilder any brain.

At last he seemed to have strung himself for an effort, and spoke, without looking up.

" Mr. Thurnall ! "

" Sir ? "

" I have done you a great wrong ! "

"We will say no more about it, sir. It was a mistake, and I do not wish to complicate the question. My true ground of quarrel with you is your conduct to Miss Lavington. She seems to have told you her true name, so I shall call her by it."

"What I have done, I have undone !" said Stangrave, looking up. "If I have wronged her, I have offered to right her; if I have left her, I have sought her again; and if I left her when I knew nothing, now that I know all, I ask her here, before you, to become my wife !"

Tom looked inquiringly at Marie.

"Yes; I have told him all — all ! " and she hid her face in her hands.

"Well," said Tom, "Mr. Stangrave is a very enviable person; and the match, in a worldly point of view, is a most fortunate one for Miss Lavington; and that stupid rascal gendarme has broken my revolver."

"But I have not accepted him," cried Marie; "and I will not, unless you give me leave."

Tom saw Stangrave's brow lower, and pardonably enough, at this.

"My dear Miss Lavington, as I have never been able to settle my own love affairs satisfactorily to myself, I do not feel at all competent to settle other people's. Good-bye. I shall be late for the steamer." And, bowing to Stangrave and Marie, he turned to go.

"Sabina! stop him!" cried she; "he is going, without even a kind word ! "

"Sabina," whispered Tom as he passed her, — "a bad business — selfish coxcomb; when her beauty goes, won't stand her temper and her flightiness: but I know you and Claude will take care of the poor thing, if anything happens to me."

"You're wrong — prejudiced — indeed!"

"Tut, tut, tut! Good-bye, you sweet little sunbeam. Good morning, gentlemen!"

And Tom hurried up the slope and out of sight, while Marie burst into an agony of weeping.

"Gone, without a kind word!"

Stangrave bit his lip, not in anger, but in manly self-reproach.

"It is my fault, Marie! my fault! He knew me too well of old, and had too much reason to despise me! But he shall have reason no longer. He will come back, and find me worthy of you; and all will be forgotten. Again I say it, I accept your quest, for life and death. So help me God above, as I will not fail or falter, till I have won justice for you and for your race, Marie!"

He conquered: how could he but conquer; for he was man, and she was woman; and he looked more noble in her eyes, while he was confessing his past weakness, than he had ever done in his proud assertion of strength.

But she spoke no word in answer. She let him take her hand, pass her arm through his, and lead her away, as one who had a right.

They walked down the hill behind the rest of the party, blest, but silent and pensive; he with the weight of the future, she with that of the past.

"It is very wonderful," she said at last. "Wonderful . . . that you can care for me. . . . Oh, if I

had known how noble you were, I should have told
you all at once."

"Perhaps I should have been as ignoble as
ever," said Stangrave, "if that young English
viscount had not put me on my mettle by his
own nobleness."

"No! no! Do not belie yourself. You know
what he does not — what I would have died
sooner than tell him."

Stangrave drew the arm closer through his, and
clasped the hand. Marie did not withdraw it.

"Wonderful, wonderful love!" she said, quite
humbly. Her theatric passionateness had passed —

> "Nothing was left of her,
> Now, but pure womanly."

"That you can love me — me, the slave; me,
the scourged; the scarred — Oh, Stangrave! it is
not much — not much really; — only a little mark
or two . . ."

"I will prize them," he answered, smiling through
tears, "more than all your loveliness. I will see in
them God's commandment to me, written not on
tables of stone, but on fair, pure, noble flesh. My
Marie! You shall have cause even to rejoice in
them!"

"I glory in them now; for, without them, I
never should have known all your worth."

.   .   .   .

The next day Stangrave, Marie, and Sabina were
hurrying home to England! while Tom Thurnall
was hurrying to Marseilles, to vanish Eastward Ho.

He has escaped once more; but his heart is
hardened still. What will his fall be like?

CHAPTER XXVIII

LAST CHRISTMAS EVE

AND now two years and more are past and gone; and all whose lot it was have come Westward Ho once more, sadder and wiser men to their lives' end; save one or two, that is, from whom not even Solomon's pestle and mortar discipline would pound out the innate folly.

Frank has come home stouter and browner, as well as heartier and wiser, than he went forth. He is Valentia's husband now, and rector, not curate, of Aberalva town; and Valentia makes him a noble rector's wife.

She, too, has had her sad experiences — of more than absent love; for when the news of Inkerman arrived, she was sitting by Lucia's death-bed; and when the ghastly list came home, and with it the news of Scoutbush "severely wounded by a musket-ball," she had just taken her last look of the fair face, and seen in fancy the fair spirit greeting in the eternal world the soul of him whom she loved unto the death. She had hurried out to Scutari, to nurse her brother; had seen there many a sight — she best knows what she saw. She sent Scoutbush back to the Crimea, to try his chance once more; and then came home to be a mother to those three orphan children, from whom she vowed never to part. So the children went with Frank and her to Aberalva, and Valentia had learnt half a mother's duties ere she had a baby of her own.

And thus to her, as to all hearts, has the war brought a discipline from heaven.

Frank shrank at first from returning to Aberalva, when Scoutbush offered him the living on old St. Just's death. But Valentia all but commanded him; so he went: and behold, his return was a triumph.

All was understood now, all forgiven, all forgotten, save his conduct in the cholera, by the loving, honest, brave West-country hearts; and when the new-married pair were rung into the town, amid arches and garlands, flags and bonfires, the first man to welcome Frank into his rectory was old Tardrew.

Not a word of repentance or apology ever passed the old bulldog's lips. He was an Englishman, and kept his opinions to himself. But he had had his lesson like the rest, two years ago, in his young daughter's death; and Frank had thenceforth no faster friend than old Tardrew.

Frank is still as High Church as ever; and likes all pomp and circumstance of worship. Some few whims he has given up, certainly, for fear of giving offence; but he might indulge them once more, if he wished, without a quarrel. For now that the people understand him, he does just what he likes. His congregation is the best in the archdeaconry; one meeting-house is dead, and the other dying. His choir is admirable; for Valentia has had the art of drawing to her all the musical talent of the tuneful West-country folk; and all that he needs, he thinks, to make his parish perfect, is to see Grace Harvey schoolmistress once more.

What can have worked the change? It is difficult to say, unless t be that Frank has found out, from cholera and hospital experiences, that his parishioners are b ings of like passions with himself; and found out, too, that his business is to leave the gospel of damnation to those whose hapless lot it is to earn their bread by pandering to popular superstition; and to employ his independent position, as a free rector, in telling his people the gospel of salvation — that they have a Father in heaven.

Little Scoutbush comes down often to Aberalva now, and oftener to his Irish estates. He is going to marry the Manchester lady after all, and to settle down; and try to be a good landlord; and use for the benefit of his tenants the sharp experience of human hearts, human sorrows, and human duty, which he gained in the Crimea two years ago.

And Major Campbell?

Look on Cathcart's Hill. A stone is there, which is the only earthly token of that great experience of all experiences which Campbell gained two years ago.

A little silk bag was found, hung round his neck, and lying next his heart. He seemed to have expected his death; for he had put a label on it:

"To be sent to Viscount Scoutbush for Miss St. Just."

Scoutbush sent it home to Valentia, who opened it, blind with tears.

It was a note, written seven years before; but not by her; by Lucia ere her marriage. A simple invitation to dinner in Eaton Square, written for

Lady Knockdown, but with a postscript from Lucia herself: "Do come, and I will promise not to tease you as I did last night."

That was, perhaps, the only kind or familiar word which he had ever had from his idol; and he had treasured it to the last. Women can love, as this book sets forth: but now and then men can love too, if they be men, as Major Campbell was.

And Trebooze of Trebooze?

Even Trebooze got his new lesson two years ago. Terrified into sobriety, he went into the militia, and soon took delight therein. He worked, for the first time in his life, early and late, at a work which was suited for him. He soon learnt not to swear and rage, for his men would not stand it; and not to get drunk, for his messmates would not stand it. He got into better society and better health than he ever had had before. With new self-discipline has come new self-respect; and he tells his wife frankly, that if he keeps straight henceforth, he has to thank for it his six months at Aldershot.

And Mary?

When you meet Mary in heaven, you can ask her there.

But Frank's desire, that Grace should become his schoolmistress once more, is not fulfilled.

How she worked at Scutari and at Balaklava, there is no need to tell. Why mark her out from the rest, when all did more than nobly? The lesson which she needed was not that which hospitals could teach; she had learnt that already. It was a deeper and more dreadful lesson still. She had set her heart on finding Tom; on righting him, on righting herself. She had to learn to be content not to find him; not to right him, not to right herself.

And she learnt it. Tearless, uncomplaining, she "trusted in God, and made no haste." She did her work, and read her Bible; and read too, again and again, at stolen moments of rest, a book which some one lent her, and which was to her as the finding of an unknown sister — Longfellow's "Evangeline." She was Evangeline; seeking as she sought, perhaps to find as she found — No! merciful God! Not so ' yet better so than not at all. And often and often, when a new freight of agony was landed, she looked round from bed to bed, if his face, too, might be there. And once, at Balaklava, she knew she saw him: but not on a sick-bed.

Standing beneath the window, chatting merrily with a group of officers — It was he! Could she mistake that figure, though the face was turned away?

Her head swam, her pulses beat like church bells, her eyes were ready to burst from their sockets. But — she was assisting at an operation. It was God's will, and she must endure.

When the operation was over, she darted wildly down the stairs without a word.

He was gone.

Without a word she came back to her work, and possessed her soul in patience.

Inquiries, indeed, she made, as she had a right to do; but no one knew the name. She questioned, and caused to be questioned, men from Varna, from Sevastopol, from Kertch, from the Circassian coast; English, French, and Sardinian, Pole and Turk. No one had ever heard the name.

She even found at last, and questioned, one of the officers who had formed that group beneath the window.

"Oh! that man? He was a Pole, Michaelowyzcki, or some such name. At least, so he said; but he suspected the man to be really a Russian spy."

Grace knew that it was Tom: but she went back to her work again, and in due time went home to England.

Home, but not to Aberalva. She presented herself one day at Mark Armsworth's house in Whitbury, and humbly begged him to obtain her a place as servant to old Dr. Thurnall. What her purpose was therein she did not explain; perhaps she hardly knew herself.

Jane, the old servant who had clung to the doctor through his reverses, was growing old and feeble, and was all the more jealous of an intruder: but Grace disarmed her.

"I do not want to interfere; I will be under your orders. I will be kitchen-maid — maid-of-all-work. I want no wages. I have brought home a little money with me; enough to last me for the little while I shall be here."

And, by the help of Mark and Mary, she took up her abode in the old man's house; and ere a month was past she was to him as a daughter.

Perhaps she had told him all. At least, there was some deep and pure confidence between them; and yet one which, so perfect was Grace's humility, did not make old Jane jealous. Grace cooked, swept, washed, went to and fro as Jane bade her; submitted to all her grumblings and tossings; and then came at the old man's bidding to read to him every evening, her hand in his; her voice cheerful, her face full of quiet light. But her hair was becoming streaked with gray. Her face, howsoever gentle, was sharpened, as if with continual pain. No wonder; for she had worn that belt next her heart for now two years and more, till it had almost eaten into the heart above which it lay. It gave her perpetual pain: and yet that pain was a perpetual joy — a perpetual remembrance of him, and of that walk with h m from Tolchard's farm.

Mary loved her — wanted to treat her as an equal — to call her sister: but Grace drew back lovingly, but humbly, from all advances; for she had divined Mary's secret with the quick eye of woman; she saw how Mary grew daily paler, thinner, sadder, and knew for whom she mourned. Be it so; Mary had a right to him, and she had none.

. . . .

And where was Tom Thurnall all the while?
No man could tell.

Mark inquired; Lord Minchampstead inquired; great personages who had need of him at home and abroad inquired; but all in vain.

A few knew, and told Lord Minchampstead, who told Mark, in confidence, that he had been heard of last in the Circassian mountains, about Christmas, 1854; but since then all was blank. He had vanished into the infinite unknown.

Mark swore that he would come home some day; but two full years were past, and Tom came not.

The old man never seemed to regret him; never mentioned his name after a while.

"Mark," he said once, "remember David. Why weep for the child? I shall go to him, but he will not come to me."

None knew, meanwhile, why the old man needed

not to talk of Tom to his friends and neighbors;
it was because he and Grace never talked of anything else.

   .   .   .   .   .   .

So they had lived, and so they had waited, till
that week before last Christmas Day, when Mellot
and Stangrave made their appearance in Whitbury,
and became Mark Armsworth's guests.

The week slipped on. Stangrave hunted on
alternate days; and on the others went with Claude,
who photographed (when there was sun to do it
with) Stangrave End, and Whitford Priory, interiors
and exteriors; not forgetting the Stangrave monu-
ments in Whitbury Church; and sat, too, for many
a pleasant hour with the good doctor, who took to
him at once, as all men did. It seemed to give fresh
life to the old man to listen to Tom's dearest friend.
To him, as to Grace, he could talk openly about
the lost son, and live upon the memory of his
prowess and his virtues; and ere the week was out,
the doctor, and Grace too, had heard a hundred
gallant feats, to tell all which would add another
volume to this book.

And Grace stood silently by the old man's chair,
and drank all in without a smile, without a sigh,
but not without full many a prayer.

   .   .   .   .   .   .

It is the blessed Christmas Eve; the light is failing fast; when down the High Street comes the
mighty Roman-nosed rat-tail which carries Mark's
portly bulk, and by him Stangrave, on a right
good horse.

They shog on side by side — not home, but to
the doctor's house. For every hunting evening
Mark's groom meets him at the doctor's door to lead

the horses home, while he, before he will take his bath and dress, brings to his blind friend the gossip of the field, and details to him every joke, fence, find, kill, hap, and mishap of the last six hours.

The old man, meanwhile, is sitting quietly, with Claude by him, talking — as Claude can talk. They are not speaking of Tom just now: but the eloquent artist's conversation suits well enough the temper of the good old man, yearning after fresh knowledge, even on the brink of the grave: but too feeble now, in body and in mind, to do more than listen. Claude is telling him about the late Photographic Exhibition; and the old man listens with a triumphant smile to wonders which he will never behold with mortal eyes. At last:

"This is very pleasant — to feel surer and surer, day by day, that one is not needed; that science moves forward swift and sure, under a higher guidance than one's own; that the sacred torch-race never can stand still; that He has taken the lamp out of old and failing hands, only to put it into young and brave ones, who will not falter till they reach the goal."

Then he lies back again, with closed eyes, waiting for more facts from Claude.

"How beautiful!" says Claude. — "I must compliment you, sir — to see the childlike heart thus still beating fresh beneath the honors of the gray head, without envy, without vanity, without ambition, welcoming every new discovery, rejoicing to see the young outstripping them."

"And what credit, sir, to us? Our knowledge did not belong to us, but to Him who made us, and the universe; and our sons' belonged to Him like-wise. If they be wiser than their teachers, it is only because they, like their teachers, have made His testimonies their study. When we rejoice in the progress of science, we rejoice not in ourselves, not in our children, but in God our Instructor."

And all the while, hidden in the gloom behind, stands Grace, her arms folded over her bosom, watching every movement of the old man; and listening, too, to every word. She can understand but little of it: but she loves to hear it, for it reminds her of Tom Thurnall. Above all she loves to hear about the microscope, a mystery inseparable in her thoughts from him who first showed her its wonders.

At last the old man speaks again :

" Ah ! How delighted my boy will be when he returns, to find that so much has been done during his absence."

Claude is silent awhile, startled.

" You are surprised to hear me speak so confidently? Well, I can only speak as I feel. I have had, for some days past, a presentiment — you will think me, doubtless, weak for yielding to it. I am not superstitious."

" Not so," said Claude, "but I cannot deny that such things as presentiments may be possible. However miraculous they may seem, are they so very much more so than the daily fact of memory? I can as little guess why we can remember the past as why we may not, at times, be able to foresee the future."

" True. You speak, if not like a physician, yet like a metaphysician ; so you will not laugh at me, and compel the weak old man and his fancy to take refuge with a girl — who is not weak. Grace, darling, you think still that he is coming?"

She came forward and leaned over him.

"Yes," she half whispered. "He is coming soon to us: or else we are soon going to him. It may mean that, sir. Perhaps it is better that it should."

"It matters little, child, if he be near, as near he is. I tell you, Mr. Mellot, this conviction has become so intense during the last week, that — that I believe I should not be thrown off my balance if he entered at this moment . . . I feel him so near me, sir, that — that I could swear, did not I know how the weak brain imitates expected sounds, that I heard his footstep outside now."

"I heard horses' footsteps," says Claude. "Ah, there comes Stangrave and our host."

"I heard them: but I heard my boy's likewise," said the old man, quietly.

The next minute he seemed to have forgotten the fancy, as the two hunters entered, and Mark began open-mouthed as usual:

"Well, Ned! In good company, eh? That's right. Mortal cold I am! We shall have a white Christmas, I expect. Snow's coming."

"What sport?" asked the doctor, blandly.

"Oh! Nothing new. Bothered about Sidric-stone till one. Got away at last with an old fox, and over the downs into the vale. I think Mr. Stangrave liked it?"

"Mr. Stangrave likes the vale better than the vale likes him. I have fallen into two brooks following, Claude; to the delight of all the desperate Englishmen."

"Oh! You rode straight enough, sir! You must pay for your fun in the vale: — but then you have your fun. But there were a good many falls the last ten minutes: ground heavy, and pace awful; old Rat-tail had enough to do to hold his own. Saw one fellow ride bang into a pollard-willow, when there was an open gate close to him — cut his cheek open, and lay; but some one said it was only Smith of Ewebury, so I rode on."

" I hope you English showed more pity to your wounded friends in the Crimea," quoth Stangrave, laughing, "I wanted to stop and pick him up: but Mr. Armsworth would not hear of it."

" Oh, sir, if it had been a stranger like you, half the field would have been round you in a minute: but Smith don't count — he breaks his neck on purpose three days a week. By the by, doctor, got a good story of him for you. Suspected his keepers last month. Slips out of bed at two in the morning; into his own covers, and blazes away for an hour. Nobody comes. Home to bed, and tries the same thing next night. Not a soul comes near him. Next morning has up keepers, watchers, beaters, the whole posse; and 'Now, you rascals! I've been poaching my own covers two nights running, and you've been all drunk in bed. There are your wages to the last penny; and vanish! I'll be my own keeper henceforth; and never let me see your faces again!'"

The old doctor laughed cheerily. "Well: but did you kill your fox?"

" All right: but it was a burster — just what I always tell Mr. Stangrave. Afternoon runs are good runs; pretty sure of an empty fox and a good scent after one o'clock."

" Exactly," answered a fresh voice from behind; "and fox-hunting is an epitome of human life. You chop or lose your first two or three: but keep up your pluck, and you'll run into one before sundown;—and I seem to have run into a whole earthful!"

All looked round; for all knew that voice.

Yes! There he was, in bodily flesh and blood; thin, sallow, bearded to the eyes, dressed in ragged sailor's clothes: but Tom himself.

Grace uttered a long, low, soft, half-laughing cry, full of the delicious agony of sudden relief; a cry as of a mother when her child is born; and then slipped from the room past the unheeding Tom, who had no eyes but for his father. Straight up to the old man he went, took both his hands, and spoke in the old cheerful voice:

"Well, my dear old daddy! So you seem to have expected me; and gathered, I suppose, all my friends to bid me welcome. I'm afraid I have made you very anxious: but it was not my fault; and I knew you would be certain I should come at last, eh?"

"My son! my son! Let me feel whether thou be my very son Esau or not!" murmured the old man, finding half-playful expression in the words of Scripture, for feelings beyond his failing powers.

Tom knelt down: and the old man passed his hands in silence over and over the forehead, and face, and beard; while all stood silent.

Mark Armsworth burst out blubbering like a great boy:

"I said so! I always said so! The devil could not kill him, and God wouldn't!"

"You won't go away again, dear boy? I'm getting old — and — and forgetful; and I don't think I could bear it again, you see."

Tom saw that the old man's powers were failing.

"Never again, as long as I live, daddy!" said he, and then, looking round, — "I think that we are too many for my father. I will come and shake hands with you all presently."

"No, no," said the doctor. "You forget that I cannot see you, and so must only listen to you. It will be a delight to hear your voice and theirs; — they all love you."

A few moments of breathless congratulation followed, during which Mark had seized Tom by both his shoulders, and held him admiringly at arm's length.

"Look at him, Mr. Mellot! Mr. Stangrave! Look at him! As they said of Liberty Wilkes, you might rob him, strip him, and hit him over London Bridge: and you find him the next day in the same place, with a laced coat, a sword by his side, and money in his pocket! But how did you come in without our knowing?"

"I waited outside, afraid of what I might hear — for how could I tell?" said he, lowering his voice; "but when I saw you go in, I knew all was right, and followed you; and when I heard my father laugh, I knew that he could bear a little surprise. But, Stangrave, did you say? Ah! this is too delightful, old fellow! How's Marie and the children?"

Stangrave, who was very uncertain as to how Tom would receive him, had been about to make his *amende honorable* in a fashion graceful, magnificent, and, as he expressed it afterwards laughingly to Thurnall himself, "altogether highfalutin':" but whatsoever chivalrous and courtly words had arranged themselves upon the tip of his tongue, were so utterly upset by Tom's matter-of-fact *bon-*

homie, and by the cool way in which he took for granted the fact of his marriage, that he burst out laughing, and caught both Tom's hands in his:

"It is delightful; and all it needs to make it perfect is to have Marie and the children here."

"How many?" asked Tom.

"Two."

"Is she as beautiful as ever?"

"More so, I think."

"I dare say you're right; you ought to know best, certainly."

"You shall judge for yourself. She is in London at this moment."

"Tom!" says his father, who has been sitting quietly, his face covered in his handkerchief, listening to all, while holy tears of gratitude steal down his face.

"Sir!"

"You have not spoken to Grace yet!"

"Grace?" cries Tom, in a very different tone from that in which he had yet spoken.

"Grace Harvey, my boy. She was in the room when you came in."

"Grace? Grace? What is she doing here?"

"Nursing him, like an angel as she is!" said Mark.

"She is my daughter now, Tom; and has been these twelve months past."

Tom was silent, as one astonished.

"If she is not, she will be soon," said he, quietly, between his clenched teeth. "Gentlemen, if you'll excuse me for five minutes, and see to my father:"—and he walked straight out of the room, closing the door behind him—to find Grace waiting in the passage.

She was trembling from head to foot, stepping to and fro, her hands and face all but convulsed; her left hand over her bosom, clutching at her dress, which seemed to have been just disarranged; her right drawn back, holding something; her lips parted, struggling to speak; her great eyes opened to preternatural wideness, fixed on him with an intensity of eagerness; — was she mad?

At last words bubbled forth: "There! there! There it is! — the belt! — your belt! Take it! take it, I say!"

He stood silent and wondering; she thrust it into his hand.

"Take it! I have carried it for you — worn it next my heart, till it has all but eaten into my heart. — To Varna, and you were not there! — Scutari, Balaklava, and you were not there! — I found it, only a week after! — I told you I should! and you were gone! — Cruel, not to wait! And Mr. Armsworth has the money — every farthing — and the gold: — he has had it these two years! — I would give you the belt myself; and now I have done it, and the snake is unclasped from my heart at last, at last, at last!"

Her arms dropped by her side, and she burst into an agony of tears.

Tom caught her in his arms: but she put him back, and looked up in his face again.

"Promise me!" she said, in a low clear voice; "promise me this one thing only, as you are a gentleman; as you have a man's pity, a man's gratitude, in you ——"

"Anything!"

"Promise me that you will never ask, or seek to know, who had that belt."

"I promise: but, Grace!———"

"Then my work is over," said she, in a calm collected voice. "Amen. So lettest thou thy servant depart in peace. Good-bye, Mr. Thurnall. I must go and pack up my few things now. You will forgive and forget '"

"Grace!" cried Tom; "stay!" and he girdled her in a grasp of iron "You and I never part more in this life, perhaps not in all lives to come!"

"Me? I?—let me go! I am not worthy of you!"

"I have heard that once already;—the only folly which ever came out of those sweet lips. No! Grace. I love you, as man can love but once; and you shall not refuse me! You will not have the heart, Grace! You will not dare, Grace! For you have begun the work; and you must finish it."

"Work? What work?"

"I don't know," said Tom. "How should I? I want you to tell me that."

She looked up in his face, puzzled. His old self-confident look seemed strangely past away.

"I will tell *you*," he said, "because I love you. I don't like to show it to them; but I've been frightened, Grace, for the first time in my life."

She paused for an explanation; but she did not struggle to escape from him.

"Frightened; beat; run to earth myself, though I talked so bravely of running others to earth just now. Grace, I've been in prison!"

"In prison? In a Russian prison? Oh, Mr. Thurnall!"

"Aye, Grace, I'd tried everything but that; and

I could not stand it. Death was a joke to that. Not to be able to get out!—To rage up and down for hours like a wild beast;—long to fly at one's jailer and tear his heart out;—beat one's head against the wall in the hope of knocking one's brains out; anything to get rid of that horrid notion, night and day over one—I can't get out!"

Grace had never seen him so excited.

"But you are safe now," said she, soothingly. "Oh, those horrid Russians!"

"But it was not Russians!—If it had been, I could have borne it.—That was all in my bargain;—the fair chance of war, but to be shut up by a mistake!—at the very outset, too—by a boorish villain of a khan, on a drunken suspicion;—a fellow whom I was trying to serve, and who could n't, or would n't, or dare n't understand me—Oh, Grace, I was caught in my own trap! I went out full blown with self-conceit. Never was any one so cunning as I was to be!—Such a game as I was going to play, and make my fortune by it!—And this brute to stop me short—to make a fool of me—to keep me there eighteen months threatening to cut my head off once a quarter, and would n't understand me, let me talk with the tongue of the old serpent!"

"He did not stop you: God stopped you!"

"You're right, Grace; I saw that at last! I found out that I had been trying for years which was the stronger, God or I; I found out I had been trying whether I could not do well enough without Him: and there I found that I could not, Grace;—could not! I felt like a child who had marched off from home, fancying it can find its way, and is lost at once. I felt like a lost child in Australia once, for one moment but not as I felt in that prison; for I had not heard you, Grace, then. I did not know that I had a Father in heaven, who had been looking after me, when I fancied that I was looking after myself; — I don't half believe it now — If I did, I should not have lost my nerve as I have done! — Grace, I dare hardly stir about now, lest some harm should come to me. I fancy at every turn, what if that chimney fell? what if that horse kicked out? — and, Grace, you, and you only, can cure me of my new cowardice. I said in that prison, and all the way home, — If I can but find her! — let me but see her — ask her — let her teach me; and I shall be sure! Let her teach me, and I shall be brave again! Teach me, Grace! and forgive me!"

Grace was looking at him with her great soft eyes opening slowly, like a startled hind's, as if the wonder and delight were too great to be taken in at once. The last words unlocked her lips.

"Forgive you? What? Do you forgive me?"

"You? It is I am the brute; ever to have suspected you. My conscience told me all along I was a brute! And you — have you not proved it to me in this last minute, Grace? — proved to me that I am not worthy to kiss the dust from off your feet?"

Grace lay silent in his arms: but her eyes were fixed upon him; her hands were folded on her bosom; her lips moved as if in prayer.

He put back her long tresses tenderly, and looked into her deep glorious eyes.

"There! I have told you all. Will you forgive my baseness; and take me, and teach me, about this Father in heaven, through poverty and wealth, for better, for worse, as my wife — my wife?"

She leapt up at him suddenly as if waking from a dream, and wreathed her arms about his neck.

"Oh, Mr. Thurnall! my dear, brave, wise, wonderful Mr. Thurnall! come home again! — home to God! — and home to me! I am not worthy! Too much happiness, too much, too much: — but you will forgive, will you not, — and forget — forget?"

And so the old heart passed away from Thomas Thurnall: and instead of it grew up a heart like his father's; even the heart of a little child.

THE END